A NOVEL BOOKSTORE

Laurence Cossé

A NOVEL BOOKSTORE

Translated from the French
by Alison Anderson

Europa
editions

Europa Editions
214 West 29th Street
New York, N.Y. 10001
www.europaeditions.com
info@europaeditions.com

Translation by Alison Anderson
Original title: *Au bon roman*
Translation copyright © 2010 by Europa Editions

This work has been published thanks to the support from the
French Ministry of Culture – Centre National du Livre
Ouvrage publié avec le concours du
Ministère franc̦ais chargé de la Culture – Centre National du Livre

Library of Congress Cataloging in Publication Data is available
ISBN 978-1-60945-578-1

Cossé, Laurence
A Novel Bookstore

Book design by Emanuele Ragnisco
www.mekkanografici.com

Cover photo: edmondlafoto / Pixabay

Prepress by Grafica Punto Print – Rome

Printed in the USA

A NOVEL BOOKSTORE

Writers who belong to a press organization, a literary-prize jury, an academy, or any other cultural institution could not be quoted in this novel. Many of them would have been, naturally, if they had not occupied said positions of power.

PART ONE

1.

One could hardly say that Paul Néon's disappearance caused a stir in the canton of Biot, where he had apparently settled for good, nor in Les Crêts, the scrawny village where he inhabited the very last house.

Paul collapsed on a thick bed of rotting leaves below the forestry road, along which he must have been staggering for some time already (ten days later, young Jules Reveriaz would find his scarf at the edge of the path, fifty feet from the place where he had fallen). Two or three dead branches cracked beneath his weight. When silence returned, there was a brief moment of vibration. The black leaves, as they were compressed, gave off a rustling sound like the one that water spiders alone can hear when, for example, a cat at the edge of a pond, after peering into the darkness for a few minutes, immobile, his neck outstretched, lies down upon the moss. It was ten o'clock at night. A blurred crescent moon gave off just enough light to be able to make out the path in the dark.

Paul must have let go of his bottle only after his muscles had relaxed, once he had completely lost consciousness and his fingers loosened. It was Suzon who, six days later, found the square-bottomed bottle, empty, a yard from the imprint left by the tall, heavy fifty year old's body. Suzon had been looking for precisely that sort of clue, and would have given a great deal not to find it. Did Paul pass out the moment he fell, that night of a pale moon, or did he lie there on the ground with his eyes open; did he call out, or say anything, or was he already unable to move even his lips? No one knew the answer, certainly not in Les Crêts. Only later was it confirmed that there had been at least two witnesses—and to call them "witness" is putting it lightly.

Paul had planned to read the next morning—or, at least, what was left of the morning by the time he normally got started—the two versions of *Mina de Vanghel,* in order. But who could know that? Van reconstructed Paul's days only after the fact. Paul had already read *Mina de Vanghel,* he remembered it well. Stendhal was one of those authors whose entire oeuvre he thought he knew. It was only that autumn, however, when he opened once again the second volume of an old edition of *Romans et nouvelles,* that he discovered *Le Rose et le Vert,* and that he realized that this beginning to a novel, even though it was dated seven years later than *Mina,* was like an introduction to it, and was also unfinished. And on his agenda for that morning of November 8 was his intention to read first *Le Rose et le Vert,* and then to reread *Mina de Vanghel.*

"Agenda," for want of a better word. Paul Néon had no more of an agenda than he had a schedule, no more of a routine than a healthy diet. Let no one make me say what I have not written, for I did not add: the lucky man.

Perhaps that afternoon, on the ground floor of his chalet—if you could call it that—the phone rang for a particularly long time. And then maybe it rang again, an hour or two later, and met with equal silence? But who could have heard either of those calls?

From time to time a young woman had been seen going up to the chalet. It was often the same young woman, always at the wheel of a cheap little car, often a cherry-colored Twingo, sometimes a black Fiat, more rarely a gray-blue Nissan.

The Twingo, often? Let's not exaggerate. Once or twice every trimester, the proprietor of L'Alpette would have guessed. Madame Huon at L'Etoile des Alpes would have cor-rected him: once a month, every month, and always on a Saturday. Madame Antonioz would have confirmed this: the red car on Saturdays, the other ones during the week. Can you imagine?

In my opinion, they were his students, was Madame Huon's hypothesis. You mean female students, said Madame Antonioz, formerly librarian at the high school in Albertville, now retired and resident in Les Crêts. She was almost certain that Monsieur Néon was a professor at the university in Chambéry. Well, she added, during the week that is.

Because the little woman who came on Saturday, if indeed she came on Saturday, must have been at work during the week. And if she was at work during the week, well then she couldn't be a student.

The only thing, in fact, that anyone was certain about in Les Crêts, as far as Néon was concerned, was that every Wednesday, no matter the weather or the state of the roads, he'd get his jalopy out of the shed behind his chalet and leave Les Crêts at around ten in the morning, to return only after nightfall.

That's the way they are, those university professors, said Madame Huon, they work one day a week. One day! echoed Madame Antonioz. You need at least two hours to get to Chambéry. If you take off an hour for lunch, that leaves half a day.

You might conclude from what precedes that the village had its eye on Néon. And yet no one in Les Crêts—neither the proprietor of the seedy café nor these good ladies—had noticed that on the morning of Wednesday, November 9, Paul Néon did not take his car from the shed, he did not head toward the valley, and he had not slept in his bed on the night from Tuesday to Wednesday—nor the previous night, in fact. You can't really say that people were all that curious. In depopulated Alpine villages, just as in the suburbs of Paris, nowadays it's every man for himself. Local indiscretion, and the social control which is the other side of the same coin, may seem hard to bear. The fact remains that in the old days when a fellow didn't get up in the morning, it would be common knowledge by noon in the ten nearest houses, and if he were a bachelor, with graying temples, not inclined to conversation, an awkward customer originally from God knows where, there'd be a neighbor who'd go knock on his door to say something like, You all right, M'sieur Néon? Hey in there! Are you all right in there?

Nothing remotely like that happened on Wednesday, November 9. No one had noticed that Paul had failed to fulfill his sole obligation. The weather had predicted showers. As a result the air was warm; there wouldn't be any snow just yet. No matter what they said, there wouldn't be any rain either, opined Alfred from L'Alpette while considering the sky. Dreary, nothing more. He delighted in comparing the forecast from the *Dauphiné* to the reality before his eyes. Weather reports, said he to Old Mr. Parmentier (who kept to himself the fact that he knew by heart the words that were about to follow), don't err when it comes to what will happen, but they're always off the mark when it comes to the here and now. If they say it's going to rain, well it will rain, but when? This afternoon, tonight? Tomorrow? Day after, maybe? That's no more reliable than old folks used to be, when they'd consult their joints. I'd reckon it's even less so.

2.

Anne-Marie Montbrun's accident was another story altogether. And she was the mother of four children. And generally had two or three more at home. She often had to traipse all over Vauvert after supper because one of them—one of her own kids—was missing. She'd go to give everyone a kiss at bedtime and there would only be three of her four.

A fantastic girl. She looked twenty-five in her tight little jeans and her size 6 Paraboots. Ninety pounds, she weighed, if that, and enough energy to knock you over. Bringing up her kids virtually on her own, with a husband who was a petroleum prospector and spent at most one week a month at home in Vauvert; she was supreme mistress of her domain, her house in the woods, always willing to help out, she'd take her old Renault Espace to go and get a butane bottle for Monsieur Menthaleau, or ferry Madame Ageron to the supermarket, because the old lady couldn't see anymore but wasn't about to admit it.

Never in a bad mood, Anne-Marie Montbrun was always on time, so punctual that you could set your clock by her trips in the car, four times a day when school was in session, at eight, half past noon, two, and half past four: four roundtrips between Vauvert and Longpré in her old rattletrap, one trip empty, one trip full of kids that she would pick up or drop off here and there, depending on which way she was headed.

So it was a sad day—that Tuesday, November 15—when her car left the road in the wide bend at the top of the hill at Les Galardons; two hundred yards from home, she went hurtling down the slope, and the only reason the car came to a halt before the pond was the good graces of a poplar growing along the bank. Thank God—so to speak—she was alone in her Renault. She was deadheading back to school, just before half past four. There was no reason for her to have gone off the road. It was a gray day, that's true, and there was a bit of fog lingering on the hills. But Anne-Marie was very sure of herself, she was familiar with all the local roads, and she tended to drive fast. Once or twice she'd been told off by the boys in blue. But they never took it any further. She was a skilled driver, and there wasn't a family for miles around who would have hesitated to trust her with their kids.

There were no witnesses. There must not be more than ten vehicles a day using the road that leads from the Montbrun house to Les Galardons, and of the ten, eight of them would be trucks from the Rémy Bonnier vineyards on their way to the bottling plant at Saint-Lair. According to the investigation, instead of coming out of the bend, Anne-Marie left the road, for no reason, in the middle of the curve and skidded nose first down the slope as if she really had lost her head, going faster and faster until she finally came to a stop against the poplar tree.

Because she was always so punctual, they were able to establish a time frame for the accident, and she must have spent at most a quarter of an hour unconscious in her beat-up old car. One of the Rémy Bonnier drivers spotted her as he drove up the hill, and he sounded the alarm.

At the school, they hadn't had time to get worried yet. The Montbrun kids were taken for an after-school snack to the principal's house, above the school, along with Anthony Fabre and Diane Ottaviani, who normally went home with them. While they were eating their bread and butter in silence—not because they were distressed by any premonitions, but because they were intimidated by the principal—Anne-Marie was removed from her car and transported, inanimate, to the nearest hospital.

It took some time to reach Monsieur Montbrun, who was in a helicopter at the time of the accident, somewhere between Port Arthur and Lagos, but the Fabre family agreed to look after Montbrun children. Arthur Montbrun, from the vantage point of his nine years, nevertheless understood that his mom must be in bad shape, and they had to lie to him quite firmly to get him to go to bed.

3.

At half past eight on Tuesday, November 22, Maïté got a shock. Wearing his thick sweater and slippers, Armel went to get the mail in the letter box by the gate, came back in the house, removed *Ouest-France* from its plastic envelope, and opened it as he sat down on the sofa by the fireplace. Maïté could not get over it. In the seventeen years they had been living together, every day at half past eight, whether it was raining a little, a lot, or torrentially, Armel had put on his raincoat, opened the door, and, from the threshold, turned to say, See you later, Maï.

On that November 22, Armel folded the paper at nine o'clock and only then did he put on his raincoat and his boots—it was raining fairly hard, that Tuesday—and open the door and say, See you later, darling. Maïté wondered why he had changed his schedule, and why he had offered up that very conventional "darling," but she wasn't worried. Or at least that's how she put it when she told the story. When someone that anal suddenly throws a wrench into one of their own obsessions, there is a reason for it, that is what she had learned in seventeen years as Armel's companion. And the very next morning, November 23, and the morning after that, the twenty-fourth, her hypothesis was confirmed. If Armel no longer put on his raincoat at half past eight exactly but at nine, and if instead of reading *Ouest-France* between nine-thirty and ten when he got back from his walk he read it before his walk between eight-thirty and nine, he knew what he was doing, figured Maïté.

But when, on November 25, at nine-fifteen, she said, Are you still here?, because she was walking through the living room getting ready to go out herself to do the shopping, and he replied in a nonchalant way that sounded utterly fake to her that he wouldn't be going out that day, even though it was almost dry out and, for as long as she had known Armel, she had always heard him insist that he could not get to work in the morning until he'd had his dose of fresh air, she asked him what on earth could have incited him to abandon such a strong conviction, such a steady practice. And he seemed upset, she would say when she told the story. He had given her an evasive reply. Tired, he said, hoarsely. She looked at him. He looked at her. He's furious, thought Maïté.

She'd got it completely wrong, and would find out soon enough. In fact, he was afraid, she explained. For the first time in his life, he was experiencing fear.

4.

Néon reappeared forty hours later, at a time when, ordinarily, he would not be in Les Crêts at all. After lunch, on Wednesday, November 9, a zombie was seen emerging from the forest, at the end of the village, then he dragged himself to L'Alpette. The use of the passive voice here, "was seen," should not be seen as referring to a collective, which very frequently replaces the collective "we," (as in "five hundred were known to have departed"), but in a personal sense, less usual and more elegant ("the rascal was struck with a cane and his crown was readjusted"). The personage behind the passive voice was, to be exact, a single individual, a young woman, who at that hour was very weary—but infinitely less weary than the zombie—the young Mademoiselle Benarbi, commonly known in Les Crêts as "the plum," who was using the time while all three children were having their naps and it wasn't raining to hang out her laundry. There was not a more timid soul in the entire village or even the entire canton than Aisha Benarbi. Deep inside, Aisha was desperate when, on the day after her wedding, her young husband ordered her to give up wearing the veil forever. I am a modern husband, he said. There would be no discussing the matter.

However, when from over the top of her laundry line she saw the ghost zigzagging along the road in the direction of the seedy café, then stop next to the sawn-off tree-trunk bench next to the entrance, and lean first this way, then that, then go into a sort of whirl and nearly miss the bench before finally collapsing onto it, Aisha left her basket of wet sheets right there where she stood, rolled up the collar of her turtleneck in order to hide her chin, at least, pulled together her best French and went over to the ghost to ask, Are you okay?

No, he wasn't okay. Néon didn't say as much. It was self-evident. His teeth were chattering. He was the color of plaster beneath his reddish two-day beard. His hair was wet and sticking to his skull, and his clothes were covered in dirt. Aisha touched his wrist. He was burning with fever.

"That fever," Dr. Clair would say at a later point in time (he was from Réunion, and he had his office in Moureix), "that's what saved him. It's not cold just yet, but still."

Néon was carried home (the passive voices belonged this time to Alfred Deneriaz from the café, who had heard Aisha pounding on his shutter, and Marcellin Prot, his father-in-law, and Stevie Perrault, the lumberjack). The door to Néon's chalet was found unlocked and inside a huge mess was discovered (passive voice, this time: Alfred's wife, Elisa, young Aisha, Madame Huon, whose grocery was right next to the café-restaurant, and Madame Antonioz, who had seen the group go by her window and had come along). The doctor was sent for (by Madame Huon), and he arrived within the half-hour. Half an hour: a godsend for the ladies, truth be told, giving them the time to go all around the house on the pretext of finding clothes for him and making coffee; the older women, that is, because little Benarbi, after a quick glance around the bachelor pad, all the same, had gone back to work (he may be modern, her husband, but he was still Moroccan). Marcellin remained by the bed where they had laid Néon—the other men had also returned to work—and heard him muttering deliriously, two or three times, the word Mina, and then, quite distinctly, Mina green and pink. He was puzzled. But when he spoke to Madame Huon of his surprise, she immediately understood that Paul Néon was referring to one of his visitors and the color of her eye shadow or her lingerie.

Dr. Clair diagnosed pneumonia. Does the gentleman live alone? he asked, worried. He didn't like the idea of leaving him unattended. But was it really necessary to send him to the hospital . . .

No one knew whether Néon had any family or close friends (since nowadays, it's different). No one knew who to contact. No one mentioned the intermittent young women, although everyone had them in mind. The doctor opted for home care, which would mean, he explained, morning and evening visits by the nurse from Villard, Vera Polonowska. As for the doctor himself, he would come back that very evening, and every day thereafter.

Marcellin offered to spend the night in an armchair at the patient's bedside, when the man himself was heard to bellow, "Can't you fucking leave me in peace?" (In this case, "you" meant more than just you who are present in this room, more than the medical body, more than the women: "you" meant more or less all of humankind.)

Clair explained to Néon that he was not allowed to leave him without supervision. The deontological-judicial argument must not have sufficed because the neighbors, who had retreated to the back of the room, now heard the doctor say menacingly, In that case, I'll have you hospitalized. That argument seemed to do the trick and the doctor, while he was organizing the silent retreat of the municipal choir, notified them in a low voice of the outcome of his negotiations. Néon would accept the presence of health professionals, no one else.

Vera Polonowska was a beautiful, haughty blonde. On leaving Néon's house on the following Saturday at ten o'clock, she found herself face to face with a green-eyed brunette whose expression changed suddenly on seeing her.

"He had a good night," said Vera.

"Delighted to hear it," said the brunette, furious. One can hardly be more tactful.

"You are unaware that Mr. Néon is sick. I'm the nurse who comes by to check on him in the morning and evening. Are you a close relation?"

"I'm afraid I cannot answer either yes or no to that question. I've been wondering, myself, for the last year and a half, and believe me, I'd like nothing better than to know where I stand. What's the matter with Paul?"

"I see," said Vera, putting off her reply. "You are neither his wife, nor his little sister, nor someone from the village."

"None of that," confirmed the little brunette. "I played a supporting role in a play he directed two years ago in Vizille."

"If I suggested it, would you mind staying with Monsieur Néon?" interrupted Vera, who was seeing things more and more clearly.

"I dream of it," said the brunette. "I've never spent more than two or three hours in a row with him. And never at night: he says he can only sleep alone."

"Don't get ideas. He's not in the greatest of shape."

"What's wrong with him?"

"Pneumonia, and probably something else."

"Is it serious?"

"It could be. The attending physician is supposed to come some time during the morning. Here's his card. And here's mine."

"Thanks. My name is Suzon Petitbeurre."

Suzon stayed with Paul until lunchtime on Sunday. A day, a night, and a morning in succession: this had never happened.

But there was nothing particularly pleasurable about those thirty hours. Paul was unwell, mute, in a foul mood. "As soon as I'm back on my feet, I'm moving," was all he muttered, on Saturday evening, without any additional commentary.

On Sunday, when Dr. Clair returned to see him at the end of the morning, he figured out what his patient was suffering from, in addition to pneumonia. Néon had turned yellow. The doctor made him jump, palpating his abdomen.

He motioned to Suzon that he wanted to speak to her outside the bedroom.

"Does your friend have a fondness for alcohol?" he asked her, straight to the point.

"For alcohol and for women, but as far as I know, he has a marked preference for alcohol," said Suzon, not without a certain bitterness.

"Excuse me a minute," said Clair, taking a phone from his pocket. "I can't leave him here."

Suzon stopped him, placing her hand on his arm.

"There are too many things I don't get. I feel like I'm the only one here who doesn't know what's wrong with him. What happened? I went to buy some cheese yesterday and they asked me for news. Everyone in the village seems to know. This is not like Paul."

The doctor told her what they had told him—Néon coming out of the forest at siesta time, staggering along the road, trying in vain to get back up to his house, and collapsing outside L'Alpette—soaking, frozen, burning with fever.

"Soaking?" insisted Suzon.

"Soaking wet and covered in dirt," said Clair. "Like someone who's spent the night out, so the village women said. I mean: outdoors in nature."

"Yes," said Suzon. "Like someone who can't find their way home on leaving the bar at night."

Paul had fallen asleep. The doctor dialed a number. He uttered a series of strange words; Suzon got the impression he was speaking Greek.

"Maybe Lyon, then?" she heard him repeat, in French, finally. "Lyon would be better?"

He put his phone back in his pocket.

"He has to be hospitalized," he said. "This sort of thing can suddenly flare up out of control. There's a large hematology unit in the Hospices de Lyon, the Emergency Services are going to check whether they have room."

His phone rang. Clair made two more phone calls—to the ambulance, and to his wife.

"The ambulance is coming," he told Suzon. "It will take a quarter of an hour. I'll wait with you. I'm not sure Monsieur Néon will be very willing to leave with them."

He was silent for ten seconds then continued, in a less professional tone: "Did I hear you right, did you say cheese there, earlier? I have to confess, I'm dying of hunger."

It was half past twelve. Suzon and Parfait Clair attacked the beaufort on a small corner of the kitchen table that they'd managed to clear. Hundreds of bottles, empty and full, filled a rack at the back of the room, but neither one of them felt like drinking any wine. Clair, looking at Suzon, decided that "plump" was one of the most pleasant adjectives he could think of.

"Tell me," he asked, "what does Monsieur Néon do for a living?"

"At present, not too much of anything anymore, if I've been correctly informed," said Suzon. "You'll have grasped that I'm not terribly well-informed where Paul is concerned. He's a very cultured man. He has a certain notoriety among people like himself, under another name, not Néon. Something similar, though. Well, yes, fairly different: Néant. He prefers it. I've always seen him introduce himself as Néant. But what he lives on—total mystery. When I met him, two and a half years ago, he was directing a little theatre troupe, in Vizille. He did everything—staging, production, lights, retranslating Shakespeare, writing vitriolic articles for a limited audience. And already people wondered what he lived on.

"We mounted *Coriolanus*, and it was a flop. I think Paul had obtained a grant and he lost it after the disaster. After that, as far as I know, he started a film club in Val-d'Isère, financed mostly by the town hall. Screenings were held in the village hall. It wasn't a bad idea, with the crowds you get up there between early December and the end of April. But holidaymakers prefer to see the third-rate blockbuster of the month in a well-heated multiplex. More pleasant for a good nap after a day of skiing, said Paul.

"Already at that point he wasn't exactly the playful sort. He became an out-and-out misanthrope. He crossed theatre and cinema off his list, and came to settle in this hole. To the best of my knowledge, he doesn't have any income. What I don't know is how he can pay his rent for this place and pay the milkman too."

She pointed with her chin to the bottle rack. There was another short silence.

"It's not bad, this chalet," said Clair.

"You don't mean that!" choked Suzon.

The ambulance arrived and put an end to this new chapter of their discussion.

Paul raged, but it lasted little more than the space of one breath—which produced a strange rattling sound.

"I didn't give you my authorization," he croaked.

"I didn't ask for it," said Parfait Clair, simply, firmly, and decisively.

Paul could not stand on his own feet, which made things easier.

"Do I have to go with him to Lyon?" asked Suzon, when the stretcher went through the door. "To be honest, I didn't even expect to be in Les Crêts today, I've got the week's bookkeeping to do."

"Don't worry," said Clair. "I know the ambulance driver, Alain N'Guyen, very well. He can be trusted. I'll write it all out very clearly—the hospital, the unit, the name of the physician on duty this afternoon. There won't be any problems. Monsieur Néon is in no condition to protest, as you can see. It's not tonight that he'll start thrashing around. In my opinion, he won't be on his feet again for ten or fifteen days. I'll call Lyon at the end of the day to make sure everything's under control. And I'll stay in touch, of course. Are you an accountant?"

"No," said Suzon, "an electrician."

"Electrician?" echoed Clair.

"You know what an electrician looks like."

"Yes, but I've never seen one as pleasant to look at."

"What a chauvinist remark!" grumbled Suzon.

"Have you been an electrician for long?" asked Clair.

"Nearly ten years. I studied to be a semiologist. A semasiologist, to be exact. But semasiology, to make a living . . . It's like semiology in general: no jobs, just temp positions paid the minimum wage. I won't bore you with the various stages of my conversion. It was nothing more than a return to family tradition. My father is in the trade. At age nine, all on my own, I did the wiring in my grandmother's garage. It hasn't been too hard to build up a clientele, so long as I'm careful to advertise as S. Petitbeurre, never Suzon."

Once the ambulance and the doctor had left, Suzon went back into the chalet to get her bag and her parka. She turned down the heat, finished the cheese along the way, and, her mouth full, locked the front door twice over. On the threshold she hesitated for a few seconds, motionless, the keys in her hand. Then she walked down to L'Alpette. The café-restaurant was open. She told Elisa, who already knew but acted as if she didn't, that Paul had just been taken to the hospital, and she anticipated her question by specifying the hospital in Lyon, without going so far as to give the name of the unit.

To forestall any inquiries that Suzon knew would cause her pain, she added, "His pneumonia has gotten worse." And she handed the keys to Elisa.

She went back to the chalet, started up her Twingo, then headed down toward the valley. Once she was safely beyond the reach of curious gazes, below the village, she stopped the car, changed her moccasins for some boots, and walked hurriedly into the forest. She knew the path, there was only one. She walked for two hundred yards, went right by the sodden scarf of the man who filled her thoughts, and never even saw it. A few yards further on, at the bottom of the path, she saw the square-bottomed bottle shining in a beam of light and, next to it, the imprint of a human form that she assumed must be Paul's. There was an odor of cool earth and mushrooms, of outings for retired folk, of tales for children; the air was soft, and yet Suzon was shivering. In an almost conjugal gesture of modesty, holding onto the low branches as she passed, she went to pick up the bottle, noticed that it was empty, and read on the label, "White planter's rum Imperial 40%." She turned around with the object in her hand, then hid it beneath her parka as she left the forest and hurried to her car.

5

By the morning of the sixteenth, the day after the accident, they were able to tell Arthur Montbrun the truth, since the news was reassuring. His mother had two shattered ribs, her sternum was in pieces, and they had had to operate, because of a pneumothorax. But there would not be any after-effects. In two weeks she'd be home again. As for his father, he'd be flying in that very evening, to Nantes, and the four Montbrun children would have spent only one night away from home.

What remained inexplicable was why Anne-Marie had gone off the road. The gendarmes spent the two hours immediately after the accident in the bend at Les Galardons and were unable to determine what might have forced the driver off the road.

The asphalt was dry. There were no skid marks or any other helpful clues, pools of oil or cowpats or even any quality droppings from one of those exceptional thoroughbreds that were the glory of the canton.

"Could there have been a wild boar crossing the road?" ventured police cadet Nicos Hariri, a dark-haired young man who looked so much like Nicolas Sarkozy that everyone got his first name wrong and called him Nicolas.

"And why not a seven-year-old stag, while you're at it?" said Colonel de Billepint irritably, for he'd been about to talk about big game the very moment his subordinate did.

The head of the surgery unit where Anne-Marie had been admitted made Billepint wait three days before allowing him to question the accident victim. In her loose white nightgown with its lace collar, her curls spread in a halo across the pillow, the young woman resembled a broken doll. Her husband was by her side. He got to his feet when the police officer arrived. Anne-Marie held him back by the hand: "No, stay. I'm not going to be telling the colonel anything other than what I've been telling you for the last two days."

The cadet whose name wasn't Nicolas had not been far off the mark, Billepint had to admit. It was not a wild boar crossing that had caused Anne-Marie's accident; it was a car, stopped perpendicular to her oncoming vehicle. "An empty car," said Anne-Marie. "No driver, no passenger, no one standing by it. As I was hurtling down the slope that was what I saw, the only thing in my head: I had seen a phantom car. You may think I'm crazy, but it frightened the hell out of me."

A big saloon car, navy blue or black, said Anne-Marie. A rather old model, probably, something like a Peugeot from fifteen or twenty years ago. But she didn't want to go any further with the description. Things like that happen in a split second. She was sure of nothing, except that there wasn't a soul around, either in the car or near it.

While he was walking Billepint back to the elevator, Montbrun confided, "I'm not sure my wife has all her wits about her just yet. An empty car, right across the bend—it's not very plausible. Particularly if the car disappeared immediately and no one saw it at all."

6.

It was a rare thing for Armel to be in a bad mood. Maïté almost asked him, "Hey, what's the matter with you, anyway?" But she decided not to be put off by his gloomy air, and to go out as she'd planned, to get a few things for lunch.

"What would you like for lunch?" she asked him from the threshold, trying to keep her voice cheerful, hoping it might ease the tension.

"Don't give a damn one way or the other," replied Armel.

Maïté was more surprised than hurt. Armel was never vulgar, or only on paper when he had to be, and to a carefully measured degree. Besides, he immediately took back his words.

"Forgive me. Get what you want."

"Mussels?" suggested Maïté.

"Yes, that's a fine idea, mussels," said Armel, automatically. "That's fine, absolutely fine."

That was not like him, either, to repeat himself, mused Maïté as she was waiting her turn at the fishmonger's. Armel had often said to her, "There is nothing more difficult to master than repetition. If you do it badly, it's clumsy, stupid. When it's well done, it's a little echo, like waves, poetry itself."

"Say that again?" he was shouting, at that very moment, to someone on the telephone.

He was afraid that if Maïté thought he was unwell he might not go out. The idea of eating mussels made him nauseous, but he would have gone along with anything she suggested just to get her out the door.

She had hesitated, then out she went. He saw her open and close the gate, her hair whipped by the wind, and he waited for a minute, fearful she might have forgotten her wallet, or her keys, and come back.

She didn't come back. Armel dialed Ivan's number, praying like a kid to some deity, he wasn't too sure who—just let him be at home, so I can get hold of him.

"Hello?" said Van.

"Ivan Georg?" said Armel, just to be sure.

"Speaking."

"It's Ballon. Ballon d'Alsace."

"No need to explain, I recognized you right away. But you do sound strange."

"Forgive me, something really bizarre has been happening to me. Listen, Ivan, I might get interrupted at any second, so I'll be brief. I've received threats. I've been hesitating to call you for the last twenty-four hours. I didn't fall asleep until three in the morning last night. And the only reason I managed to fall asleep then was because, beyond the point of feeling any shame, I decided to call you."

"What's going on?"

"Let me tell you. I've always been in the habit of going for a walk in the morning before I start work. Regular as clockwork. For years—ever since I moved to Ploulec'h—winter and summer alike I go out at eight-thirty in the morning and walk for exactly one hour so that I'll be back home at nine-thirty. Then I read the paper. Then I sit down at my desk. What's the date today?"

"The twenty-fifth."

"Friday the twenty-fifth, right."

Armel was silent, the time it took for him to count six fingers.

"Exactly six days ago, last Saturday, I ran across two men on the path, and they seemed to be waiting for me. I forgot to mention that for years now I take the same walk every day. In Ploulec'h you don't have much choice. To the west you've got the town, the port, and bipeds. But to the east you're on your own, right away. A little customs path starts a hundred yards from my place and in twenty minutes you're at the top of the cliff. It's steep, but it's worth the climb. The view is extraordinary. I've never tired of it. In any kind of weather, the sea—well, you know what the sea is like, never the same twice in a row. There's always wind up there, and it lightens my spirit. In short, it gets me going for the entire day.

"Now I'm tempted to say, it *used* to get me going. I'm not sure I'll ever set foot up on the cliff again.

"Last Saturday, as I was saying, I get to the top . . . must have been around nine o'clock. I never see a soul up there in the morning. But that day, in the drizzle, I see two men. Immobile. Watching me as I draw nearer them.

"I think nothing of it . . . the path is narrow, where they were stationed, and there's a steep drop right near there. But it's also the place where you get the best view. The landscape belongs to everyone, after all. I go closer. I can see that the men are staring at me, and they don't look exactly friendly. That's their business. I go up to them, I say, Good morning, like everyone around here. No answer. I continue on my way and think, those two joes aren't locals.

"I must not have been as calm as I may sound now because to go home again, instead of just turning around and taking the same customs path home again, the way I usually do, I went inland, through the pine forest, five hundred yards from the coast. It's nice, too. I go that way from time to time.

"The next day, Sunday, I wouldn't go so far as to say I'd forgotten, but I wasn't worried. It wasn't raining that day. I set off on my usual walk, and what do I see? The two guys, at that critical spot on the path, like the day before. I figure, Okay, let's chat a bit. I get closer, fifteen feet away, I say hello. Not a word. Murder in their eyes. When I get up to them I stop. And I ask, You visiting around here? When I think back on it, I might as well have said something like, Fine weather we're having! They don't say a word, don't budge, keep staring at me insistently. I figure that's their problem and I walk by them, on the inland side, twenty inches away. I've had better memories.

"So I go home through the woods, once again. The rest of the day, Sunday, oh, there's no use hiding the fact: I went back over the scene in my mind more than once. Are you there?"

"I'm listening, Ballon. Go on."

"On Monday, I get to the top of the cliff, and there are the two watchdogs. I don't feel too good. My legs are like jelly. I figure: this time, no point trying to be nice. No nice little smiles. Keep your mouth shut. But just as I'm getting near them, they move over on the inland side of the path, which obliges me to go by them cliff-side. So I go by, quick as I can, Van. I have an urgent need to sit down. I force myself to go on until I'm out of sight and then I collapse on the ground. I confess that once I was in the woods, I lay on my back, flat out, for five whole minutes.

"On Tuesday, I decided to stop trying to act the tough guy. Change of routine. I got started half an hour later. And this time, to my relief, the two brutes weren't on the cliff. I spent the day in a state of euphoria.

"Wednesday, day before yesterday, I stuck to my new timetable. I saw no one. Everything was fine. I figured, go on, end of the alert.

"But yesterday, here we go again, the two guys were there, waiting for me. A fine little drizzle was falling. I gave up. Ten yards from them, I panicked, and turned back. I have to be honest: I got out of there as fast as I could, walking very quickly. But not quickly enough to avoid hearing a voice shouting, 'It's like being in a bad crime novel, huh, Le Gall? With vulgar characters, and a stupid plot. Poor Le Gall, who likes *good* literature. So, this isn't a *good* novel, huh?' You hear them, Van, they were insisting on the word good. 'Not a *good* novel at all . . .'"

"Incredible," said Van.

"Isn't it?"

"Even more incredible than you think."

"In what way?"

"What you've just told me, this very particular threat, someone told me three days ago they'd heard exactly the same thing. Ballon, we have to meet."

"Wait a minute. Who told you, the same threat?"

"Can't you guess? A member of the committee, of course. Threatened in exactly the same terms as you, word for word. Ballon, when can we meet and where?"

7

L e Gall suggested the next day. "In Rennes, at the TGV station. It's halfway between my cliffs and your bookstore. At least time-wise."

Ivan was a bit annoyed that it was a Saturday. Saturday was his busiest day, and he could not afford to neglect business, however much his natural inclination was to give a damn.

"And Sunday?" said Le Gall.

Sunday was fine with Van. He preferred the afternoon.

"I save Sunday mornings for . . . let's say slowness."

"A nice word," said Armel.

If he took the TGV at around two, Van could be in Rennes by teatime, and back in Paris for dinner. "When you leave the train," said Le Gall, "take the escalator up to the second floor. When you get off the escalator, you'll see a café called Le Parisien. They put it there just for you. Go no further. Let's meet there."

Le Gall himself preferred to go by car. Every time he drove more than a hundred kilometers, he got an idea for a novel. And he always said that if he had carried on and driven for two thousand kilometers, by the time he arrived the novel would be finished.

He took the back roads in his venerable Renault, through astonishingly empty farmland, very green for the month of November. He left the car under the station, in the huge parking lot that still smelled of paint and fresh cement, and he was the first to arrive for the meeting. His watch said 4:02 when he sat down in Le Parisien. He thought, this Sunday, that he had found the ideal place to sit, at a corner table near the entrance, against the glass.

He ordered a liter of good cider and two mugs from a red-head of indeterminate age and indeterminate bad love affairs, or so he gathered from her expression. He had to wait twenty minutes before Van was to join him, so he opened the first volume of *Papiers collés* by Perros. He had carefully chosen a book of short pieces that would not require his sustained attention. He needn't have bothered: here in Le Parisien it was no better than last night on his own sofa—he could not read more than three lines. What was worse, in reality he could read eight or ten lines, but at this stage he noticed that he was not listening to what his eyes were reading. His mind was elsewhere. Like last night, like a hundred times on the road on his way here, he heard the hoarse voice bellowing, Le Gall likes *good* novels, and he felt breathless, and was glad he was sitting down.

He was reading "Paintings think, language works" for the third time, and finishing his first mug of cider, when he saw Ivan come off the escalator, immediately find Le Parisien, and unwrap his scarf with one hand before coming in. Van had once confided that he was nearing fifty, but he still looked like a sleepless student, with his scruffy clothes, his nearsighted way of walking, and his disheveled curls.

Armel got up out of his corner to greet him. He had him sit down opposite him at the table.

"I am dismayed," said Ivan. "I didn't think I'd be putting you in any danger. Up to now they've only gone after Francesca and me. That's normal. But I was certain you weren't at risk."

Armel wrinkled his nose.

"To tell the truth, all that really happened to me was that for the first time in my life I was scared to death."

He looked at his watch.

"We're going to fight back. What train are you looking at, to go back?"

Van had a good hour and a half ahead of him. He was the one who spoke the most. The previous night, it had been his turn not to sleep a wink.

"I'll tell you why," he said, lowering his voice. "Things came to a head after you called. But I'll begin with what I hinted at over the phone. The threatening words they shouted at you on the cliff: Brother Brandy also heard them on November 7, the evening of November 7.

"There are many of us," he whispered to Le Gall, bringing his head closer to his across the table, "who think that Brother is the greatest prose writer alive today in France."

"I think I see where you're headed," said Armel.

"Keep your hypothesis for yourself, please. No names. Not here. Brother lives out in the boonies, in the mountains. I got a call from him ten days ago. He asked me to come and see him at the hospital, in Lyon."

Armel suddenly looked up.

"He'll pull through," said Van.

He was being treated for cirrhosis that had been latent up to then, but now had suddenly broken out. Brother Brandy had been evasive with the doctors, only talking about a well-watered evening. That can be enough, reckoned the professors. But to Van, Brother had revealed that he had been alone in the forest, unconscious, from the evening of November 7 to the middle of the day of November 9—in other words one night, a day, another night, and half a day.

"Let me backtrack a little bit," said Van. "Brother was going through a bad patch. He's something of a genius, you'd agree with me if you knew who it was, but he's a man who goes through very long periods of sterility, where nothing happens. It drives him crazy. He's told me as much. There are not many of us who are aware of this. At times like that, he finds consolation, or maybe it's distraction, in alcohol, in the most tragic sense of the word distraction."

"*Dis-trahere*," said Armel. "He's asking the alcohol to drag him out of himself."

"Ah, I see you're a Latinist," smiled Van. "These last few months, Brother has been seeking oblivion in alcohol, and a bit of hope in Stendhal. Everyone knows he wrote *La Chartreuse de Parme* in fifty-two days, just before Christmas, 1838. But what a lot of people don't know is that Stendhal was fifty-five years old at the time, and he hadn't done any good work in nearly ten years. The pseudonym that Brother Brandy chose is the one Stendhal gave an English boyhood companion, Édouard Edwards. And it's perfectly possible that it was also a brotherly term each of them used to designate alcohol.

"Between 1830 and the end of 1838, Stendhal began a lot of projects but couldn't finish anything. *Le Rouge et le Noir* was published in 1830, when Stendhal was forty-seven. After that, he made no headway.

"He started *Mina de Vanghel* and stopped after fifty pages. He was appointed consul in Italy. He moped. He wrote constantly and stalled just as much. He tried to tell his life story, he wrote down his memories. He plotted several novels. He got fairly far along with *Lucien Leuwen*. But he would get disgusted with all of the books he started, one after the other.

"In 1836, he got leave. He came back to Paris. He was happy to be back there, he wrote articles and short stories, and thought up dozens of projects. In 1837 he returned to the character of Mina, and started the novel over with a long introduction that would be published after his death under the title *Le Rose et le Vert*. It is like the beginning of the book for which *Mina de Vanghel* was a rough draft. Stendhal wrote a hundred and seventy-two pages and, yet again, he stopped. We know from his notes that for this novel he planned two volumes of four hundred and fifty pages each.

"In 1838 he published *Mémoires d'un touriste*, and several short stories in journals—*Vittoria Accramboni, Les Cenci, La Duchesse de Palliano*. He began *L'abbesse de Castro*. At the beginning of September he got the idea for *La Chartreuse*. He set to work on November 4. By December 26 he'd finished.

"Impotence, doubt, the obsessive fear that he might never write anything good again—that is what Brother has been experiencing for years," said Van. "I don't have the details about the manuscripts he has started and then abandoned. What he did tell me was that he could no longer do without Stendhal. He has read and reread the novels, the biography, the letters, the personal texts. All of this because he has been waiting for the day when some sort of *Charterhouse* would take hold of him, and he'd grasp the project and run with it.

"Brother has never written in any other way than in a trance. Between trances, he waits. The longer it lasts, the worse he feels. This year he didn't leave his village. He only saw the people who went up to see him and, according to what he told me, only women would come. He was not always kind to them."

There was only one activity that still occupied him. Van had found this out during their conversation in Lyon three days earlier. Brother went down to Chambéry once a week. He merely drove through the town, and he stopped in the outskirts. On Wednesdays he was in charge of what ATD Fourth World calls a street library. This man of genius, the greatest prose writer of his generation, was known only by his first name in this wilderness without culture. He would lay out a blanket at the foot of an apartment block, on a bare patch of ground or, if it was raining, in the entrance to a building, and the children would come. He had a suitcase full of books with him. The children who knew how to read would help themselves. To the others, Brother would read aloud.

"That doesn't sound anything like the earlier description

you gave of him," observed Le Gall. "The awkward customer, the misanthrope."

"Don't you sometimes have the feeling that most people, deep inside, have another self that doesn't resemble them?" said Van. "And it can go either way—someone much less agreeable, or much nicer altogether."

Be that as it may, six days out of seven Brother went around in circles in a village he hated, rarely had visits, and discouraged even the best-intentioned. He ate badly. In the evening, disgusted with himself but equally famished, he often went for supper in a seedy café by the roadside.

He got on well with Alfred, the proprietor, who refused to put fondue on the menu even though all the tourists asked for it; he said, It's only good for Swiss cows. So he served salt pork, and blanquette, and home made blood pudding. Brother sat down to dinner there two nights out of three. By the third night he couldn't even take Alfred anymore.

"It was in that café," said Ivan, "that on November 7, after dinner, probably quite late, a stranger came up to him.

"He hadn't had a lot to eat, but plenty to drink. The stranger came and sat at his table, bringing from his own table the bottle he hadn't finished. He introduced himself as a documentary filmmaker, scouting for locations. Brother couldn't remember what sort. He remembers a fairly friendly man, who drank heavily, refilling the glasses without counting and when the wine was gone, he moved on to pear brandy, then gentian and plum.

"It was a dark night, and the proprietor was slowly nodding off at the bar.

"Brother got up," said Van, "and said goodbye. The man got up, too. They both went out and walked a ways together. Then a second stranger arrived, and suggested they take a walk in the forest. Brother didn't feel like it. They didn't leave him a choice. They pulled out a very convincing argument, hard and metallic, and stuck it up against his ribs. He was in no state to fight back. He said something about a path in the darkness, and these two heavies making him walk, practically carrying him, and branches scratching his face. And then one of the guys said to him, Drink this. He remembers how terrified he was, how he had to obey, the alcohol burning his stomach. And a rough voice saying, Isn't that *good?* Not *good* enough for you? It's not like a *good* novel, is it? But this is a pretty good scene, don't you think, maybe a bit noir, obviously . . . Wouldn't it make a *good* opening for a novel?"

"Oh, no," said Armel.

"When Brother regained consciousness," continued Ivan, "he was shaking with fever. He doesn't know how he found the strength to drag himself back to the village. But he does know what was driving him—and he's not proud of it. He was dead scared his two aggressors would come back."

"Can you be cured of cirrhosis?" asked Armel.

"Yes and no. There's no real treatment. The only thing you can do, if you really want to live, is to never drink another drop of alcohol."

"And does Brother want to live?"

"I get the impression he does. He'll go through the mill, though. He'll have a hard time going straight on the wagon. But that's not what worries him the most. The worst of it now, for him, is the prospect of going back to the village. He told me he let them take him to the hospital because that was the easiest way for him to be protected. The day he gets out, he doesn't know where he'll go."

"I'd gladly look after him in Brittany. But I'm not sure it's a good idea, given the people who hang out on the cliff. If I listened to my own advice, I'd get out of town for a few weeks, too."

"I'd be surprised if anyone tried to get you in your own house," said Van.

And yet something in his tone of voice indicated that in fact he did not exclude the possibility. He noticed it himself as he was speaking. Le Gall, on the other side of the little table, suddenly seemed old and fragile. What Van recalled from their first and only encounter was a block of impassivity, as if he were carved in granite. This time he evoked a substance more like clay—massive, dull brown, not so very compact, and covered in cracks.

He owed him the truth.

"You're going to think I'm exaggerating," he continued. "The chain of events doesn't stop with you. Another member of the committee has been given a rough time, Strait-laced. You called me on Friday morning. And the next day, yesterday, Saturday, at the end of the day it was her turn."

"Strait-laced is a woman?"

"Quite an extraordinary one. She has only written three books, but—"

Armel didn't let Ivan finish.

"When will you stop evaluating writers on the basis of how much they've produced? You can write a very small amount and still be a significant author. If Pierre Michon had never written anything other than *Small Lives,* if he'd stopped with that first book, he'd already have an entire oeuvre."

"I like the fact you say that, particularly as you've published so much."

"What happened to this woman?"

"She also called me from the hospital, somewhere out *en province.* She had a car accident, and she's sure it was caused deliberately. It doesn't help that she's on the road a lot, every day. She told me all this yesterday. She's got a flock of kids who are the apple of her eye and she drives them around at regular hours. She lives in the country."

"Was it serious?"

"It could have been. She had a very close call. Her seat belt saved her. She's got several fractures and, since the accident, constant headaches. Armel, if you only knew her! She's a lovely woman, the English rose type. Blonde, diaphanous skin. I'd better stop there . . ."

"Rest assured, I don't have a clue who it could be."

"And as a matter of fact, no one has ever seen her photo, I'll tell you why."

"Well, the accident? What happened?"

Ivan summed up the incident in a few sentences. He insisted on the most disturbing element. The accident seemed to have been caused deliberately.

"A trap," said Armel slowly.

"No doubt about it. Ten minutes later, when the ambulance arrived, the road was deserted. Strait-laced had the hardest time getting them to accept her version of what happened. All things considered, she's not angry. She has absolutely no desire to be on the front page of all the local papers. The less they talk about her, the better she'll feel."

If she had called Ivan, it was in order to tell him something that she could tell no one else. Armel was the second person to find out. On the day of the accident, five minutes before she got into her car, Strait-laced had been called to the phone. A man's voice, chanting: *Good, good*, the *good* novel . . . oh, the *good, good* novel! Because they're not all *good*, novels. There's *good*, and then there's *good* . . . Each time, the man had accentuated the word "good." After that, he had hung up.

"At the time," said Van, "Strait-laced wasn't worried, because she thought it was me. There was something cocky about the tone, and she figured I wanted to convey some good news, in code.

"But she was surprised all the same. From the start, I'd respected the rules of the game: I didn't call, on principle. She only called if she had to. And never once had she or I uttered the words Good Novel."

"You gave me the same instructions," said Armel.

This was neither a nod of approval nor an observation intended to change the subject. It sounded exactly like, We're in a fine fix, and Ivan must have understood as much because he was silent for a few moments.

"I haven't told you the worst of it," he continued. "The cruelest. They've readjusted their aim. The worst of it for Strait-laced is not the accident but the fact she was identified by the brutes who went after her. Let me explain. This woman may not write very much, but she writes very particular things. Let's say, fairly violent things. Violent isn't exactly the right word, but it's not entirely inappropriate either. If I tell you more, you'll recognize her. And she can only write because she uses a pen name that even those who are close to her do not know. Her publisher has never met her. She has a post office box. We have no photographs of her. No one in real life knows that she's a writer, let alone what she writes, apart from the man who inspires her books and for whom they are intended. It is essential for her to have an absolutely secret existence in an invisible world, where her inspiration can take root and blossom.

"How do I know all this? Because she told us, Francesca and me, the one time we met her. And why did she tell us, when she is so eager to hide her life away? So that before agreeing to join us, she could be sure we would commit to silence and protect her secrecy. When we met her to ask her if she would be part of the committee (something which was only possible through the intermediary of her publisher), neither Francesca nor I knew anything about her other than her talent and her pen name. We knew nothing about her true identity. That day, she set out the conditions for her participation on the committee. She was very enthusiastic about the project, but she made us promise not to try and find out her real name. And on the telephone, last night, she lifted the veil on the type of life she leads, but not on her true identity."

Armel was nibbling at the tip of his thumb.

"I've just thought of something," he said. "Do those bastards who pushed her off the road really know who they were going after? Do they know everything about her? You can't be sure. Strait-laced was probably attacked for being a member of the Good Novel committee, like Brother Brandy, like me. Let's suppose for the sake of the argument that her real name is Mrs. Englishrose. The brutes managed to identify Mrs. Englishrose as Strait-laced. But do they know that Mrs. Englishrose writes under a pen name? And what she writes? Maybe not."

Van was slowly nodding his head.

"It would reassure Strait-laced to hear that hypothesis. I'll talk it over with Francesca."

He let his gaze wander above Armel's head. Le Parisien, a Breton café, he reminded himself. He had forgotten he was in Rennes.

Armel brought him back to the fundamental issue: "How could they have got their hands on us, all three of us, despite all the precautions we took?"

"In principle it's impossible. The list of committee members has never been written down. You all have a pseudonym. No one knows who the other members are. You have all communicated only with me, from a cell phone. We've always called each other by our pseudonyms. Even if they were able to hack my computer, they couldn't have found you. Someone gave them your names, but who? Francesca is above suspicion. And Anis doesn't know you."

"Francesca, that goes without saying. Who is Anis?" asked Armel.

"The woman I adore," said Van.

Armel noticed the formula, and he was the one who repeated it later on. He found it precise and vague at the same time— but no more so, he said, than the most common of such formulas, "the girl of my dreams" or "the love of my life."

"She works at the bookstore," said Van. "Of course she

knows there is a secret committee. Everybody knows, anyway, it's public knowledge. But she has no idea who the committee is made up of."

Ivan stopped and thought. It was as if he were talking to himself.

"I might have said a word about this or that member, but I am sure I never did so using real names. Anis, no . . . not her."

He changed his tone.

"We'll find out where the leak came from. That's not the most urgent thing. What's absolutely essential now is to put a stop to the series of disasters. We must protect the others. Tomorrow morning, I'm going to tell the police everything. I'd be very surprised if Francesca doesn't go along with it. Never mind if the makeup of the committee gets out. We can't do nothing. There are eight of you on the committee. I don't want a fourth attack."

"Eight?" asked Armel. "I thought there were only four or five of us."

"If there were only four or five of you, there'd be a risk you might have rather similar tastes. With a greater number of committee members, we were sure of having a greater diversity in our choices. And having eight consultants right from the beginning allowed us to start with plenty of titles."

8

When night fell, that same Sunday, Anne-Marie found herself alone again. Visits stopped after seven o'clock. There was not a sound. A nurse's aide had come to remove her dinner tray, a West Indian woman with a deep voice. Then the night nurse went by to make sure her patient didn't need anything. She placed two fingers on Anne-Marie's forehead. Anne-Marie had immediately recognized her perfume, Ô by Lancôme, a dream.

"Shall I close your jalousies?" suggested the nurse, using an old-fashioned word for some very contemporary plastic blinds.

"Not right away," requested Anne-Marie.

It had been a lovely day, one of those autumn days when the blue of the sky seems smoky, and the brown earth is bluish. Anne-Marie wanted to watch as daylight faded and night gradually came on. She loved this moment of twilight turning.

Checking for the hundredth time that her sensors were still intact had become an obsession. It was more or less the only weapon she had against the terrors of the night. Her heart heavy, she thought of how she had enjoyed solitude, under normal circumstances—before.

Night was coming, and with it, inseparable, the two fears that had been haunting her since the accident.

The first stemmed from the very nature of the aggression she had suffered.

That they had targeted her while she was in her car was a torment beyond measure. For it was in her car that she did her writing. No one knew this, but it was the only place she wrote—so she would confess to Francesca at a later point, or Van, I can't remember which. Until the time of her accident, she had told no one. It was her business. But afterwards, it seemed to her that it was important for the investigation. It was proof of the stupefying degree of information that the brutes had in their possession. (As if they had consulted each other—which could not be the case—Paul, Anne-Marie, and Armel, all three, referred to them to Van—or to Francesca—as "brutes." And Ivan thought it was the best term to use, and both he and Francesca called their enemy by that name.)

Anne-Marie explained that she had not had much time to write in the twelve years she'd been married. To be more precise—because time was not the only issue, space was also a considerable factor—the attention she had to devote to the children she loved, and her home, in the broadest sense of the word, and everything that is commonly included under the vast heading of *life*—meals, homework, garden, vacation, sorrows, fevers, relations with loved ones, friends passing through, lifelong friendships—all these thoughts and obligations required her undivided attention when she was at home. The moment she was alone in the car, everything changed. She had discovered this through experience: the moment she climbed in behind the wheel, provided she was alone, and did not have any children to pick up at the other end of the ride, she broke off with *life*, with its obligations, its ties. Ideas came to her. She had an urgent desire to write. Nothing else mattered but that desire. Anne-Marie parked her car wherever she could—anywhere at all, off to the side, on the shoulder, beneath a tree, at the edge of a cornfield. She'd made it a habit. The moment she switched off the engine, all she had to do was jot down the words, words that asked for nothing more.

And she had made it her method. She was not allowed to be even a minute late as she drove the children to and fro. Anne-Marie met her deadlines with perfect punctuality. But in the intervals, her time was her own. If there was a passage she had to locate in a book, or a spice that was missing for the evening cake, off she would go in her car, on the least little pretext. Because she knew she'd find everything she needed, as if the sound of the engine brought it all to the surface: sentences—images, ideas—were knocking on her brain to be let in. She would hunt for a place where she could pull over and not be seen. It hardly mattered whether it was a street in town or at the crossing of the horse trails in the woods: there she would write, with her spiral notebook on her lap, for a quarter of an hour. Then off she'd go again. For several years that was how she'd been filling two or three pages a day.

No one knew her secret. How had the brutes managed to find out? Anne-Marie always chose isolated spots. What sort of surveillance had they devised in order to find out the only place where she could write?

And there was something else that was worrying her. If they knew that she sat in her car to write, it meant they knew she was a writer, and they knew what she wrote, and under what name, and that she had a life other than the one she led on the surface. And the clandestine, secret nature of her undertaking was the very wellspring of her inspiration.

Anne-Marie had only ever written for one person and one alone. She only wrote about him. She liked to think that, in fact, she was writing *to* him. It came about as simply as could be, necessitated no discipline, no effort. Inspiration and an awareness of joy were the two sides of a same excitement that came in waves, imperiously. And she wanted nothing more than to surrender to that excitement, to find shelter, at last, in her customary asylum.

But if her secret had been discovered, all would be lost.

Anne-Marie didn't know how to explain it—can you explain what it is that compels you to write?—but she was sure of one thing: she would write no more.

Her throat was tight, she said, on that Sunday evening in late November, in her little hospital room that was as dark, now, as the night outside her window.

9.

I haven't read much, in comparison to Van or Francesca, but I had read three books by Le Gall. The other members of the committee may have been cult writers with small devoted followings—with the exception of Ida Messmer, and even then . . . —but Le Gall was a popular, successful novelist.

The year they opened The Good Novel, he had published over thirty books, a fairly astonishing amount when you think that he only started writing after the age of forty.

Before that, he'd been a Latin teacher for a while, and then for a few years he'd worked for the marine weather service—the one that professionals and true yachtsmen use, and you know who they are because they never use the words "yachting" or "yachtsmen." Then he'd worked as a proofreader for some small-circulation local rags that had nothing in common with one another than their anarchist-libertarian line. And Armel Le Gall chose all these activities for a single, secret, decisive reason: the possibility they offered for him to remain in his little corner of Brittany.

A local story about a shipwreck, an impossible love, and a sunken city had provided the background for his first novel. He couldn't have told you where he'd heard the story (he protested if you said he was the author behind that local story, though it was the truth, or else "author" doesn't mean a thing). The book had been an instant success.

Armel had continued in the same mold, not because it was easy or because he enjoyed his success but because he could not imagine writing anything other than old-fashioned stories, where the sea was always the main character, stories with such a wealth of images that are etched as powerfully on the reader's memory as films shot in natural locations. His readership continued to expand. His books were sold by his readers: no sooner did you finish one than you bought five or six copies to give as gifts to all your friends.

Armel didn't change his way of life. It was as if his success did not exist. It gave him no sense of assurance, and he refused all interviews, radio and television programs, and any other invitations to talk about himself. He was convinced that his impressive print runs stemmed from the fact that he was a writer *for mediocrity*, in the Latin sense of "middle height," in other words, a banal writer. And on a regular basis he would make out a generous check to Maritime Rescue or Handicap International—he called the operation his "annual oil dumping"—in order to rid himself of the extremely consistent revenues from his work, the way he would have reimbursed any sum he'd been given by mistake.

And yet there was nothing particularly surprising about his success. Armel was a wonderful storyteller. And that was precisely why Van had wanted him to be on the committee. They couldn't have stylists alone in the group, even stylists as powerful as Paul or as refined as Sarah Gestelents. In addition, Armel's novels conveyed an infectious love of life, and they were the only ones that did, among all the novels written by the committee members, along with Ida Messmer's rather unusual books.

Scribblers don't always resemble their works. Le Gall, whose work emanated so much joy, was a shy, awkward man, so sparing with words that at times he seemed a regular grouch. This old fur seal had found a companion rather late in life. A more apt description, actually, would be that she was a kindred spirit, because she was more often giving him the slip than keeping him company. He was already very well-known, and Maïté had been working as a photographer for years when she had been sent to Ploulec'h by a weekly magazine.

"Taking any photographs of me is out of the question," Armel had insisted, as he only understood who she was when he opened the door and saw all her equipment.

Maïté had retorted, annoyed, "Already you refuse to give interviews."

"It's all the same," Armel explained with his habitual loquacity. "But I can offer you a cup of tea, we can go for a walk on the cliff, or talk about photography—I rather like photography when it isn't using me for target practice."

Maïté had accepted all three of his propositions—the tea, the walk, and the discussion, and after that she had stayed on, according to her definition of the words "stay on." She was the same age as Le Gall, had only just turned fifty at the time, and other than her total inability to spend more than a week in the same place, she shared his tastes, particularly for autonomy, silence, big dogs, black rocks, and the spectacle of rain on the sea.

She made no changes where her professional life was concerned. She continued to take photos, as a freelance photographer, the way she always had, most often at her own initiative.

Nor was she very talkative. She did not tell lies. She had not known Armel for even three months and already she had pinned above her writing table a paper on which she had written, in her big, angular handwriting, "Armel Le Gall is the only person who has yet to be persuaded of his talent." Armel had not remarked on the paper, but seventeen years later, it was still there, faded, crinkled, but quite legible.

When you saw them together, you would say that they looked alike, in a way, perhaps because their faces were brown and wrinkled, and their eyes very fair beneath their rumpled gray hair. You might take them for brother and sister. But only to a slight degree, for far from being indifferent toward each other, the way old cousins can be by virtue of looking alike, these two were intrigued by one another and were always so happy in each other's company that they hardly noticed anyone else.

Part Two

10.

Ivan Georg had already seen policemen. He'd even seen them fairly close up. But never on his own initiative. They had always been the ones to take the first step.

And on that morning where, for the first time in his life, he had resolved to go and speak to a policeman, he didn't quite know how to go about it. He wondered which subdivision of which specialized brigade he was supposed to contact in order to tell them a story like the one that was on his mind.

He had woken up very early in the morning and hadn't managed to get back to sleep. At six o'clock he got up and headed out into the dark under a fine, icy rain, to go to the Odéon.

The bookstore would not open for another few hours, and he went straight up to his desk on the second floor. The big room seemed impossibly comfortable to him that morning, with its paneled walls, its white roughcast, and the sisal rug that covered the entire floor. Francesca had arranged it as she saw fit—I've always thought that it looked like her—perfect taste, monastic rigor, nothing conformist about it at all. Van had quickly left his mark upon it, in the piles of books waiting to be examined that sprung up here and there like baroque columns.

The office was impeccably soundproofed, so he could make his phone call safely sheltered from indiscreet ears. However, one hour, four coffees, and three *beedies* later, he still hadn't made the call.

He switched on his computer, went onto the Internet, called up Google, and typed "novel police." One million, one hundred and eighty thousand results in one second, all to do with crime novels, policemen in novels, the police as seen in detective fiction, police slang in noir novels, and police films.

Van typed "police publishing" and saw the first page of twenty-nine million six hundred thousand entries on instances where police had been involved in publishing (J.K. Rowling seemed to be a popular hit) and on the publishing (fairly specialized) of police publications, both technical and fantastical.

He got it. He typed "police," took a quick glance at what came up, then typed "criminal investigation." The first site, at the top of the first page, belonged to the Ministry of the Interior. Van scrolled through it rapidly. He skipped over "history of the criminal investigation department," "organization," "structure," "key figures," "results,"—although this last page might have been of some interest—and finally stopped at "struggle against organized crime."

This serious criminality was in turn subdivided into sixteen categories, and Ivan went through them all. "Procuring," "traffic in stolen vehicles," "terrorism," "narcotics," "money laundering": nowhere was there any mention of bookstores or novels. There was one section on "traffic in cultural goods." Van had a look. It was about the theft and sale of fine art alone—to which category books do not belong.

"Sensitive substances": Van hesitated. He got the impression that he himself was made solely of such matter, as was everything he loved in life—literature, poetry, snow, Anis, sweet peas, Sicilian granitas. Here, however, sensitive substances were solely being considered for their use, implying the traffic therein, perforce associated with that of arms and explosives.

The "struggle against counterfeit money and goods": what better definition was there for the Good Novel bookstore's very existence? But Van knew that for the Ministry of the

Interior that struggle was the literal, not figurative, one—which, for Van, meant suffering, action, life.

He thought he was getting close when he came to "damage to individuals and property." This particular division of the Criminal Investigation Department comprised some very specialized units (such as the "unit responsible for child victims of sexual abuse, and against the dissemination of child pornography," or the "unit responsible for dismantling agencies producing false administrative documents", and finally a "unit for general matters covering all sorts of offenses"). Van took note of the generous title of this unit and its unlimited mandate, by definition. At the very least, his problems must come under the heading "all sorts of offenses," and for a moment he imagined it as some sort of back yard overflowing with dirty tricks and shaggy-dog stories. He decided he would call these general practitioners of the criminal investigation department for help.

He also read that the jurisdiction of the officers of the criminal investigation department was "not limited to the remit of a single tribunal" but "extended to the entire national territory." This seemed just as well. He then learned that the criminal investigation department employed seven thousand eight hundred civil servants including, for the regional branch of Paris alone, two thousand three hundred and fifty-nine "policemen and administrative agents," eighty-four police detective superintendents, and one thousand one hundred and forty-two officers.

Van printed out two pages of summary where there was a very legible organizational chart of the department and a list of their employees, and studied them carefully, pressing his lips.

There were so many people, it was too much for him. What he needed from the diagram and the list, far too abstract for him, was one person of confidence, one alone, who would listen to his story without raising an eyebrow or smiling or starting a criminal investigation straight off the bat, at this stage, but who would go for one of those secret preliminary investigations which, Van had just discovered, could be conducted "for an unlimited amount of time."

He was prepared to believe that the detective superintendent placed in charge of the "unit of general matters" could be that ideal interface. But something told him that if he called and asked for that gentleman alone, they wouldn't connect him just like that. Something told him that he would have to start off by going to see the basic policeman on duty at his local police station. And Van didn't feel comfortable with that. He sensed that if he went to the local police station they would give him a knowing smile, and raise their eyebrows mockingly; worse yet was the risk of indiscreet and well-organized connections to the gutter press.

It was eight twenty-five. Van dialed Francesca's number. She picked up on the first ring.

"Francesca?"

"Yes, Van?"

"Francesca, forgive me for calling you so early. I was afraid I would miss you later. Do you have some time this morning? I need to see you."

"More . . . problems?"

"Yes, problems, of a new kind. Don't worry. We'll deal with them. But I would like to see you."

"Are you calling from the office?"

"Yes."

"I'm coming."

"This is the best place to talk, without anyone hearing."

Talk without anyone hearing . . . while waiting for Francesca to come from her home on the rue de Condé, Van went to the window nearest his desk and let his gaze drift over the courtyard. He once again heard their conversation that morning from six months earlier when, in this same office, they had spoken as never before, nor since.

That brief conversation, which had changed the course of their friendship, revealing a secret door in what had seemed an impregnable wall separating their lives, had taken place in April, 2005. The bookstore had been in operation for six months. The attacks had been going on for several months by then. They had become dreadful. Francesca was holding up. She had not disappointed Van, on the contrary, and the reverse seemed as well, because one morning in April, while they were discussing what was to be done with the requests for information from abroad—Van remembered it very clearly, he could see Francesca as she was that day, in a sober dress of off-white wool—she had asked, "Van, do you understand that I no longer view you as an associate?"

She gave a little laugh: "Or rather, that I view you as an associate in the most . . ."

She did not finish her sentence. Van saw her lovely, anxious eyes, so light in her long face.

No, he hadn't understood a thing, and for a very good reason. They had been working together for over a year, and in all that time Francesca had let nothing show through of her change of attitude. On seeing her emotion, Van realized that while he had been informed of the major fractures in her life— very briefly, once, she had talked to him about her daughter, and two or three times she had mentioned her husband—she knew absolutely nothing about him and his affairs of the heart.

"You intimidate me," he said before she could go any further. "I am so . . . ordinary, compared to you. I have told you nothing about myself. These days, my mind is filled with a young woman who . . . how to describe it? I have trouble understanding her. It's not a simple story. Nor has there been"—he hesitated—"any resolution. I don't know how things are going to develop. But this friend has, in her way, been active in our adventure at The Good Novel. She has always believed in it, she didn't try to dissuade me from embarking on the project. On the contrary, even though it has put four hundred miles between us, she has supported me in the—"

Francesca interrupted him in turn. Van could still hear the note of contrition in her voice when she said, "Forgive me, I have nothing to ask you. Above all, don't get me wrong, I am expecting nothing from you."

She said again, "Forgive me."

"What for?" asked Van.

Francesca had already taken herself in hand.

"It's time for you to tell me a few things about yourself," she said without replying. "What is the young woman's name?"

"Anis."

"That's no ordinary name."

"In fact, her name is Anne-Isabelle. She thinks the double name is ridiculous. So she made up the nickname."

"Is she working?"

"She has several things going. She's doing a Master's in sociology, and she's working, here and there. It's not cheap to live in Paris. I get the impression she's doing odd jobs."

Van paused for a moment.

"I hardly know anything about how she spends her time."

"Ivan," said Francesca then, "two things would help me. First of all: the bookstore is keeping you busy ten hours a day, you have no time left to read. Would Anis agree to work at The Good Novel? Second thing: spare me any ridicule. Please. Don't talk to anybody about my . . . effusiveness."

"It's a promise," Van had said.

And he had kept his word. Only recently did I learn what they had said to each other that day, a conversation which further explained Francesca's melancholy.

11.

There was a knock at the door. Francesca came in.

She was wearing flowing garments this morning, in gray and sand-colored tones, a sort of long cardigan, floating slacks, but what you noticed, above all, today like any other day, no matter what she wore, was how tall and slim she was, her long neck, her regal bearing. Her face was bare beneath her short curls, combed back, and she wore no jewelry apart from the heavy ring she could not remove from her left hand, and she was smiling.

The saddest smile you could imagine. Van had known her for years—if you can say you know someone who comes in to buy books from you five or six times a year—and he had always seen her like this, with her half-regal, half-broken air. You could not say that she had become any less sad since their conversation in April. Since then, all the same, in Van's presence there was a simplicity about her that contained an element of serenity.

Van moved away from the window and went over to her.

"Tell me everything," she asked, straight off. "What is going on, now?"

"Francesca," said Van, standing opposite her in the middle of the big room, "since the beginning of November, there have been three attacks against three of the committee members. To be precise, on November 7, November 15, and then last week, some time between November 18 and 24. I didn't hear about the events right away. But now it's clear, I've spoken to all three of them, we're not talking about a coincidence."

He listed the facts and Francesca did not interrupt him. Neither of them had thought about sitting down. When Van finished, Francesca said decisively, "These are warnings. I don't want real bullets, Van. It's too much for us. Let's tell the police everything."

Van refrained from taking her hands.

"That's what I intended to do, so long as you agree."

"Have you talked about these attacks with Anis?"

"No. I don't want to frighten her."

"That was wise. The fewer we are who know about it, the fewer points that gives our enemies. And there won't be so many sleepless nights."

"Francesca!"

"Don't get me wrong, I'm not giving up! What you've just told me is horrible, but I can't see myself giving up on The Good Novel. But I could understand perfectly well if you want to distance yourself. I would approve of your decision."

"I hadn't even thought of it."

"Well, I'm asking you to think about it."

"And give up? Now? What would become of me?"

At times there was a spark of joy in her eyes, piercing her restraint, like a ray of sunlight through a gray sky.

"As for you and me, we've burned our bridges," she said, radiating gratitude. "That is our strength. Ivan, who should we see at the police to denounce attacks against literature?"

It was Van's turn to smile.

"I've just spent an hour wondering the same thing. I think we have to go to the criminal investigation department. But that's an army of eight thousand people."

"Well, we needn't aim for the supreme commander," said Francesca, probably because that had indeed been her initial impulse. "We'd be wasting our time. What we need is a clever, sensitive colonel—in crime novels, they exist."

Ivan went to his desk to fetch the two sheets he'd printed

out before Francesca arrived: the organizational chart, in color, and the numbered list of all the staff.

"Eighty-four detective inspectors and one thousand one hundred and forty two officers for the Paris region alone," he read. "Just in the subdivision of criminal affairs, there are seven central offices, three divisions and thirty or more units specialized in a variety of crimes and offences. The hard part was finding which one would be the right one for us."

Francesca went to sit at her desk. She leafed through her address book.

"I haven't kept in contact with the police," she said, her voice changed. "My dealings with them date from the worst time in my life."

"Don't talk about it."

"No. But I have a nephew who's a prefect—one of my husband's nephews—who was the boss over at the DST for a few years and who must have some friends in the police. He's a boy with a lot of heart. A bit of a bear, not very talkative, but basically as good as gold. It always surprised me. You always imagine that a prefect must be hard as nails. I can call him."

"So he'll point us in the right direction?"

"Yes. He knows The Good Novel. I talked to him about our problems the last time I saw him, at a wedding in June. At that time they were still problems you could talk about with a glass in your hand."

"The tricky thing will be to ask for his advice without giving too much away. We can't have the slightest leak. Just imagine if the other committee members found out through the papers."

Francesca nodded. She sat thoughtfully for half a minute or so with her hand on the receiver, immobile, then called the prefect, managed to soften up a secretary who was giving her a hard time, got her nephew on the line, and explained her request to him in a few sentences that were magnificently graceful and vague.

Her nephew-prefect must have begun asking her questions, because after that Van only heard things like: If you want, Yes, In a way.

"So you'll call me back?" asked Francesca.

She hung up.

Her nephew would look into it, find the right person, try to get his consent, and call them back, went her summary to Van.

12.

Ten minutes later it had been taken care of. It was 9:20. Before going out, Van took just a moment to call Anis to make sure she could fill in for him at the bookstore, when they opened, at ten o'clock.

With Francesca he walked to the Quai des Orfèvres, via the rue Danton and the Pont Saint-Michel. They were expected as soon as possible, in the crime division, by a certain Gonzague Heffner.

He was in his forties, balding, with black hair and a large forehead, a thin, muscular man who looked like a sports coach. As soon as he had made sure he was dealing with the right people, he told them with a touch of irony in his voice and affectation in his language that he was curious to find out the details of this urgent matter, for his friend Dolmen had told him nothing about it, other than that he would find it particularly interesting.

"Do you like novels?" asked Francesca.

"*Good* novels," said Heffner.

Van frowned. Francesca leaned forward: "I thought you knew nothing about us. Do you know us?"

"No. I would have remembered," said Heffner, with a somewhat mechanical gallantry.

"Why did you talk about good novels?"

"You asked me if novels are something I like. And I answered, it depends. Before I joined the police force, I spent two years preparing for art school, then a few years in the humanities at the

Sorbonne. My decision to go for a life of action after that was made in order to obey a moral injunction that very soon no longer seemed appropriate, a self-inflicted injunction, I might point out. I'm passionate about literature, and like anyone who's passionate, I suffer. I expect a great deal from novels. I've been disappointed so often that over the last ten years or so I haven't even dared to open a new book. I wait for time to do the sorting. I only read classics now. I've spent these last eighteen months reading Balzac, whom I underestimated, but Proust brought me back to him. But that's enough about me. Why are you asking me about novels?"

Francesca looked at her watch and asked, "Can you give us an hour or two? We need at least that."

Heffner batted his eyelids, and that seemed a sufficient form of consent to Francesca. So she began by outlining her method.

"The simplest would be if we list the events chronologically. In the beginning, you'll think it seems like a fairly quiet story about the birth of a bookstore. But very quickly, you'll see, the tone will change. There will be aggression, then attacks, more and more violence, leading to the events that have made us decide to come to the police: three crimes in one month."

Heffner did not budge at the word "crime." Francesca sought to catch Van's eye, as if to be sure she had his support.

"Don't be surprised if we take turns speaking," she continued, "we get along well. We have the same idea at the same time so often that if one of us finishes the sentence the other began, it's not an interruption."

"Let's get started," suggested Heffner, firmly.

"I met Ivan Georg in Méribel," said Francesca.

She had adopted a narrative tone.

Ivan spent his days in a tiny basement in the famous ski resort. And yet he was one of their personalities.

"Nothing worldly," Francesca said, "no fear of that. Ivan

didn't put on an act. He had no time for skiing. He worked seven days a week from mid-December to mid-April, and in July and August in the tiniest bookstore-stationer in the village."

"There are thousands of stores like that," said Ivan, "and it was much more of a stationery store than a bookstore, but the division of labor was exceptionally well defined. I took care of the books, and the boss, Mr. Bono, took care of the rest. In a way, it was a dream. I didn't have to do either bookkeeping or paperwork, only order the books and renew the stock. Bono took care of running the store, as well as the sale of newspapers and stationery, not to mention the sun creams, sealskin key rings, and photo development—this was in 2003, just before the onslaught of digital."

Ivan made minimum wage, but the contract delighted him: he was to relieve Bono of any responsibility for the books, and in exchange, he would reign supreme over the little basement that was entirely devoted to them.

"And the customers who went past the piles of daily papers, around the revolving stands of postcards, to the back of the store and down the stairs were people who came back regularly," he said.

"You have to realize that Van Georg was no ordinary bookseller," insisted Francesca.

Francesca was someone who had been reading since childhood, who had received the best advice, and was nearly insatiable, but on her very first visit she immediately understood what was special about this book freak in his cellar.

"Literature freak," Ivan corrected.

"Important nuance," emphasized Francesca.

Van had no trouble convincing people, because he was passionate. He was enthusiastic, because he read one masterpiece after another. And if he found so many, it was because he examined everything that came out, new books and reprints. He might only choose one book out of a hundred, but nevertheless he chose vast amounts. No bookseller read as much as he did: he worked six months a year, and the rest of the time he read. In the beginning he had looked for jobs to fill in the six months he was unemployed. But he found nothing in Méribel or in Courchevel, nor in the valley nearby. He would have had to go a long way, all the way to Grenoble or Lyon. Van had done the figures. He paid rent in Méribel twelve months a year. If he left the resort, he would have to pay a second rent, restaurant meals, and gas. It would be better not to leave the mountain during the slack months, and make do with his seasonal employee benefit.

In September, October, and November (the bookstore opened mid-December), when so many new books were published, Van was the only bookseller in France who could read everything that came out. While others, nursing their sciatica and ten-donitis, were stacking boxes full of the books they did not have time to read all the way to their bedrooms, Van sat reading, out on his balcony in the deck chair whenever possible, facing the peaks with his feet up level with his face, the way the ergono-mists recommended. He had become extraordinarily discern-ing. From the very first pages, he could spot a good book, and he would read all of it. As for the others, he would devote no more time to them than they deserved— three minutes for a journalist's pseudo-investigation inflating an article that had already come out, five for the blockbuster when it was obvious there would be not a single sentence worth copying, a quarter of an hour for the much-awaited novel—in both senses of the term—by an author who always rewrote the same opus, reluc-tant to risk their reputation.

Necessity knows no law. In light of the fact that Bono had left him very little space in the cellar, Van had to choose. And in light of the fact, moreover, that he had absolutely no inter-est in sales figures and consequently in the amount of books he sold, he decided to make a selection that would be as arbitrary as it was brilliant.

He had started work there at the end of 2001. The first winter season had sufficed for him to establish his doctrine. You might also say, to make himself sick. That first winter, he had a bit of everything on offer. And the more people asked him, Is this good? the bolder he became, going from a hesitant Mmmyeah to an openly disparaging, Not bad, then soon to a frank, Good? It is downright awful. Very quickly the idea of selling books that he himself would not advise people to read infuriated him.

By July, when the store opened again for the summer, Ivan had resolved the contradiction. All that remained in his little shop were those books which enchanted him. Van would open the boxfuls of books sent automatically every week by the major publishers, and as soon as he had unpacked them and had a look through, nine times out of ten he put everything back in the box and returned it. On the other hand, he did spend a prodigious amount of time ordering rare books from publishers who were hard to reach because they, too, were indifferent to sales, so much so that some of them kept their telephone number secret.

Van raised his right hand slightly: "Let me get back to the distinction between book and novel. You will soon understand why I insist upon it. The books that enchanted me, to use Francesca's expression: 99 percent of them were novels. I am crazy about literature, and the rest doesn't really interest me— philosophy, essays, science. I only read novels, or books that are not novels but that belong to literature: short stories, of course, but also other sorts of texts, not necessarily short, but testimonies, chronicles, diaries, texts that don't belong to any particular genre. I also read poetry, and essays when they are truly *written*. They are rare, but they do exist. Claude Lévi-Strauss and Michel Foucault are writers, to give just two examples. That is the type of book that you would find in my little hole."

"In your treasure cave," corrected Francesca.

Lovers? Or not? wondered Heffner. It was hard to imagine two more dissimilar beings than this lady of the manor and her Pierrot. But he had seen more astonishing things. In the category Whims of Great Ladies, he'd seen it all.

"Van respected his customers," continued Francesca. "He had learned how to make them listen to him. If he loved a book, he would sell several hundred copies."

If someone asked him for a book by Danielle Steel or, less drastically, Pierre Benoit, he would say politely, "I don't have everything. But you can find it at the main bookstore."

Because there was another bookstore in Méribel, a big one, where they sold only books, not newspapers, or trinkets, and the proprietor, unlike Van, was interested first and foremost in his sales, and he specialized in books that are made to be sold.

Things might have continued like that, to the delight of Van and at least a good third of his customers if, the second summer, Mr. Bono had not received some complaints from the representatives of the other two-thirds. Bono had noticed that, oddly enough, since he had hired a bookseller books were not selling as well in his store, to put things bluntly. Although nothing was selling well, said the papers again and again, and he had not really bothered to look into it. But his customers' complaints started him thinking.

Bono had not been down in his cellar for nearly two years, and now he made a surprise inspection, looked for his favorite authors, Tom Wolfe and Frédérique Dardenne, did not find a single one of their books, found instead, under the tables, the boxes full of publishers' books ready to be returned, figured out what Ivan was up to, and got mad as hell.

Bono was in his sixties, and sanguine by nature, and Van

was afraid that his wrath might be fatal. He did not particularly like the man, but he knew it was to him that he owed his unique situation as a simple salaried employee with extraordinary freedom of action in his department.

"And my department had become my passion," said Van, "my raison d'être. I had finally found my vocation, clear as day."

The following winter, Bono put the book selection back in order, and sent people to buy things like *Three Days Before Christmas*, or *That's a Kiss*, or *You Never Do What You Really Want*, and he kept a close eye on the restocking and saw the sales curve of his bookstore rise once again.

Readers who were dear to Van also noticed the change. In previous years, they might have spent hours in the cellar, on their feet, never seeing the time go by nor feeling their legs, and they would go back upstairs at closing time enthralled, radiant, a bit drunk, and there were more and more of them who, when they got back to Paris or Basel, would tell those around them, "I only ever buy my books in Méribel now, once a year; obviously I've had to change my suitcase (my car / my leisure time / my life)"; now those clients would say, in an afflicted, questioning tone, with an almost inaudible question mark: Things have changed, here? For Ivan the little phrase was like a password. He took anyone who uttered it to one side. He showed them discreetly to the little corner in the bookstore that was still valid: two shelves where, at his own risk, he had brought together the best of his selection: he called it the "honey shelf." Bliss guaranteed, provided they were trusting enough to buy any book on that shelf.

But despite it all, his heart was no longer in it. Bono looked in on him several times a day and, at the same time, he sent spies who were about as discreet as deep-sea divers on a ski slope. Van withdrew, and sat reading behind the cash register all day long.

13.

He would not have lasted long on the job if, that same winter, in December, one afternoon during a lull he had not noticed in the bookstore a young woman dressed for town—in fact, a conventional formula like that cannot really describe a style that was anything but—let's just say she was dressed unusually for Méribel—who stood there reading, more and more enthralled as she progressed, less and less concerned that someone might see her; the book was *Rapport aux bêtes*, a novel by Noëlle Revaz that Ivan thought very highly of. After an hour and a half, she reached the last page, closed the book, was clearly moved, and put it back in its place on the top quality shelf, and then she saw Ivan watching her, and blushed and said to him, holding his gaze, I don't have any money. It doesn't matter, Van reassured her hastily; at least it was still up to him to welcome whom he wanted in his basement. He pointed with his chin to the book she had just put back: Well? he asked. What do you think?

The young woman was still in shock. She had not read anything that powerful for a long time. The contents, the context, the characters, that primate of a mountain farmer and his nameless wife: she was not about to forget them. But the most remarkable thing, in her opinion, was the way the long monologue had been used, the phrasing, the author's creativity in founding a new language that had no equivalent, a language that was lopsided and clumsy yet totally appropriate for the brute who was speaking, who also had no equal.

"When you finish the book, you realize you've never read anything like it, and that this man could only ever speak that language," said the young woman, dazzled. Ivan came out in front of his counter.

"The author claims that he is totally imaginary."

"Do you know Noëlle Revaz? What is she like, that she can write so powerfully?"

"I don't know her personally, but I heard a long program about her on the radio. She's a Swiss woman in her thirties, a Latin teacher, and this was her first novel."

A customer was gesturing to Van that he had a question. The young woman seemed to become aware of the place and the time once again.

"Thank you for letting me read," she said softly.

"Come again whenever you want," suggested Van, moving aside.

"I don't know," said the young woman, her eyes suddenly elsewhere.

But in the meantime, she didn't move. She was neither tall nor short, pretty nor ugly, thin nor fat. The only adequate epithet to describe her would be exquisite, thought Van, as he was slowly handing change to the customer. That girl was exquisite. The free-spirited way she wore her clothes, wool slacks tucked into brown rubber boots, a gabardine jacket, a child's red knit scarf, with a poorly folded collapsible umbrella sticking out of her pocket.

Once the customer had left, she told Van that she was in Méribel for the day. She didn't know how to ski, unlike her fellow students who had brought her along, and whom she had to meet at nightfall by their car. She was studying sociology in Grenoble, had grown up in the country in Belgium, and she even went to the trouble to explain, when Van asked her her name, where the unusual first name, Anis, came from, that it was the abbreviation of a double name that she had always despised.

*

Three weeks later, that same winter, in mid-January, 2004, one morning when despite a thick fog there were not many customers, Van was sitting behind his cash register, immersed in *Les Bottes rouges* by Franz Bartelt, an author he had recently discovered and whose novels he had been devouring one after the other, when someone standing in front of him put three books on the counter. Van recognized the three novels by Cormac McCarthy that made up the *Border Trilogy*. He raised his head. A tall woman was waiting with her eyes on him for him to notice her presence.

She was not a stranger to Van. He had seen her several times in the bookstore. She could hardly go unnoticed, with her height, her beauty, and the veil of sadness that never left her. In his mind Van called her Sylvana Mangano, because she reminded him of the mother of young Tadzio in Visconti's *Death in Venice* (he thought the film fell short of the novella). He gave nicknames to all of his customers who kept their names to themselves. One woman who bought classics and wore unfashionable tortoise-shell glasses was Simone Weil; a teenager who seemed to have made a solemn vow never to smile was the young Werther; a rowdy, fat young woman who laughed a lot and always asked loudly for the season's most over-hyped book was Nana.

The beautiful tall lady was just the opposite. Van had noticed her infallible taste. She only bought novels that were out of the ordinary, rarely recent publications and if, exceptionally, she did buy something that had just come out, it was the only one of that year's batch that Van found worth reading.

Other times when she had come he had always had a little word to congratulate her. What a book, or, Brilliant—never more, because she didn't seem to want to talk. But this time, because she had taken from the shelf three novels by the same McCarthy, whom Ivan set above any living author on the planet, he returned her gaze and said, "You've just chosen the three finest novels in the store."

"I'm willing to believe that," she said with a smile.

She had just read his first two, *All the Pretty Horses* and *The Crossing,* and she was eager to read the third one and then share the trilogy with people around her. She blessed the sky that augured bad weather: by this evening she'd have finished *Cities of the Plain.* She knew she was about to spend an unforgettable day. That is how she remembered reading the first two volumes, the first during a train trip between Florence and Rome, only a week ago, and the second the very next day in Rome where to the exclusion of everything else she had only one thought on her mind: to find out who this author was and what else he had written.

Van was spellbound.

"You have just confirmed to me that one of the most fortunate purposes of literature is to bring like-minded people together and get them talking."

In a train that previous month of June, he told her, he had spent an hour talking with a young mother on the other side of the aisle, two rows ahead of him, whom he'd gone to congratulate for three reasons. First of all, she could not take her eyes off the book she was reading and she seemed to be completely indifferent to the fact that her eldest child, who must have been eight or nine, was sucking his thumb, and that the two others, with the regularity of robots, were silently pounding on each other. Secondly, the book that so absorbed her was *L'amante senza fissa dimora* by Fruttero and Lucentini, whom Van held in great esteem. Finally, her three children were also reading, avidly. And although the two younger ones were squabbling, it was because they were both lost in the same book and, every two pages, the little girl said impatiently to her little brother, Turn the page! to which her brother replied, annoyed but calm, Wait!

Van and the young mother had talked about F. & L., as they are known in Italy, and agreed that they were marvelous prose writers, far more deserving than their reputation in France would seem to indicate, particularly as no French author had succeeded the way they had in reaching millions of readers without making the slightest concession to literary demagogy—with the exception of Echenoz, perhaps.

"Have you read them in Italian?" asked the beautiful lady, who seemed to have forgotten to pay for her McCarthy novels.

"No. But you've given me an idea. That's a reason to learn Italian."

"Did you like *A che punto è la notte?*"

"Delightful. As a sociological treatise on modern Italy—very funny."

The novel Van preferred by the Italian duo, he said, was *La donna della domenica.* The lady looked happy just on hearing the title.

"'On that Wednesday in June when he was assassinated, the architect Lamberto Garrone looked at his watch more than once,'" she recited, from memory.

"The perfect opening line," said Van. "Yet God knows the last thing I like is a tantalizing hook. And do you remember the last line?"

"Not word for word. I just remember that there's this undercurrent throughout the entire book of the classical springboard question of two centuries of the European novel: will they, or will they not end up in each other's arms? And that you get the answer in the last few lines."

"Precisely. The last two or three pages consist of a dialogue between the book's lovely heroine and the likeable police chief whom she's been finding quite attractive over the last three hundred pages. The conversation is about the crime committed in chapter one. The police chief has the key to the mystery, in the end. You find out who the murderer is and why he did it. And the novel finishes like this, just these words about where the conversation took place: '—Poor old me, Santa Madonna! said Anna Carla with a laugh. —How late it is. She jumped lightly to her feet from the bed, and hurriedly began to dress.' The French translation is by Philippe Jaccottet, the poet, had you noticed?"

"And when I think there are people around me who complain they can't find anything good to read. What nonsense."

"It's a pity. Whereas every month you and I discover a masterpiece. The problem is that 90 percent of the novels published are 'books not worth bothering with,' as Paulhan used to call them. Critics should only write about the other kind, but they're lazy and frivolous."

"They don't really care about the truth. There are only two laws that apply: your clan and your network. In a word, they're corrupt."

"I didn't quite dare say as much. They heap praise on books that are nothing but fluff, and in the rush they overlook real jewels. By definition, confusion is beneficial to mediocrity."

"And booksellers have no time left to read, and they promote such rubbish! It's amazing, you should hear them. So I add, in bursts, in a monotonous tone of voice—A truffle, Read it right away, Absolute genius. They look at me and wonder if I'm making fun of them and then they see that I am."

She grew thoughtful.

"You know, I could see what was going on here, how you tried to resist, and the way they put an end to it. I asked your boss about it. He replied exactly what I would have wagered he'd say, that you were going to make his business go under. And he was probably right. All that got me thinking. I think that your intuition was right, but your mistake was to think that the ideal bookstore could be profitable in a place the size of Méribel. The perfect bookstore, the kind where you'd sell nothing but good novels, could only be viable in a big city with a strong cultural tradition, like London or Paris. I'm willing to bet that in a city of that size there are five or ten thousand people like us who are passionate about fiction and are tired of having to go to bookstores jam-packed with books to place their orders for masterpieces they never have in stock."

"I'd be willing to bet as much myself," said Van, moved.

"I know what you'd call such a bookstore," said the lady. "You'd call it The Good Novel. I have what it would take to start it up. All I need is the bookseller."

Van slowly got to his feet.

14

Heffner emerged from his professionally attentive silence.

"I can't believe you're talking about The Good Novel," he said in a voice that no longer held any professional tones of distance or authority. "I know you! I'm a member. You'll find my name in your files."

Francesca felt a wave of gratitude toward her nephew, the prefect with a good heart. And a fine intelligence, she thought, before continuing.

It was on that day in January, 2004, that she found out that there was someone else who thought Cormac McCarthy was the greatest author alive, and that the ensuing conversation decided her, without further ado, to undertake a project she had only dreamt about up to that point. Because she could tell from Ivan's expression that she had just found the perfect bookseller. She would be staying in Méribel for eight days.

Ivan and Francesca saw each other every day. They met at the Mont Vallon, one of the resort's biggest hotels. The first evening, once they had agreed to continue their plan of action the next day, Francesca saw Van sit up straight on his chair and look around for the waiter, and she told him, simply, that she had a running account at the hotel. Van allowed himself to be treated. He explained with an equal lack of self-consciousness that he had just enough money to live on, and even then only if he did his own cooking at home, at every meal.

Francesca was staying near the Belvédère in a chalet—a family chalet, she said, without going into details, so Van couldn't tell whether she was referring to its size or its origin. She was there alone during the week. That is, she explained, when Van offered to walk her home after their first working dinner and she pointed to the gleaming black car waiting outside against the background of snow and dark night, alone with the caretaker couple.

For a split second Ivan mused that he wouldn't have minded that job as caretaker. Too late: he'd just been hired to open The Good Novel as soon as possible. Francesca had signed a check for his first month of salary. They had agreed that Van would hand in his resignation to Mr. Bono the very next day. Francesca would take care of the issue of notice: she knew the arguments that were likely to make an employer back down. February, March, April, May, June, July, August: she counted on her fingers. Seven months: that ought to be enough for The Good Novel to be ready to open at the end of the summer, before the fall season's huge crop of books.

"Whether it's before or after the new fall books," Van pointed out, "shouldn't matter one way or the other for a bookstore like that."

"That's true," said Francesca. "You're right. But you know what they're like in France: in October and November, they have these sort of 'fiction weeks' where people are reminded that literature has a certain importance. It would be a pity not to be open by then."

On that first evening, they remade the world, bookstores, and publishing, and they talked about all the books they loved. They exchanged their telephone numbers. Francesca made Ivan spell his name. "*Georg,*" said Van. "It's German. My father pronounced it the German way, go figure. But if my mother knew why, she never told me. The pronunciation of my name, that's the happiest thing I inherited from my father. Georg, in two syllables, it sounds like Gay-org, like an organ in a good mood. A real lifeline."

They spent the second evening talking about the type of books they'd have on offer at The Good Novel. Francesca was opting for a very strict selection: novels, nothing but novels.

"The only way to break through the general confusion is to stand out thanks to the simplicity of our concept. The Good Novel sells good novels: that has to be clear."

Van found her approach somewhat rigid. If the criterion for selection was literary quality, he felt sure there were a number of narrative texts that were just as good as the finest novels.

"There are even some authors whose stories or memoirs are even better than their novels, I mean better from a literary standpoint, Jean Rolin, for example."

He also wanted to include poetry, short story collections, and perfectly crafted essays.

"There aren't that many."

Francesca stood firm. In addition to novels, she'd agree to short stories and narratives, but nothing else.

Van frowned: "So we won't have any books by Pierre Michon?"

"Oh come on," said Francesca, lifting her hands from the table, "we will try not to be too stupid! We will have all of Pierre Michon, all the time, that's obvious. *Vies minuscules* and *Maîtres et serviteurs*, just to mention those two, which are my favorites, you could categorize them as short stories, and the other ones, *Rimbaud, le fils* or *La Grande Beune*, as novellas. Or rather, we shouldn't say anything. We'll display them prominently, and that's it. There are books that you can't categorize under any genre."

But as for Lévi-Strauss and Foucault, she would not budge. No essays at The Good Novel. The store was about to become one of two or three thousand bookstores in a huge city. It was not the first one to specialize. After all, there were bookstores that sold only science fiction, or history, or German-language books, and nowhere were all books sold. If people were looking for essays, they would find them elsewhere.

"And what about recent publications?" asked Van. "Will they have a place at The Good Novel?"

"I don't see why we should exclude great books just because they're new. To be exact: in France maybe ten or twenty great novels are published each year."

"It's going to be a titanic job to find them in the onslaught of fall books. And you know as well as I do that the few books worth saving are rarely the ones that get headline coverage."

"Another tactic might be to ignore the whole new book parameter altogether. We could decide not to order books when they come out, to let other bookstores sell them while they're hot, and then we'll look at them afterwards, when they've cooled down and are still just as good."

"Do you know the proportion of new books in a general bookstore's sales figures?"

"A huge part, I imagine."

"New books account for nearly 80 percent of an ordinary, general bookstore's sales. Which is why publishers are so keen on sending out their titles automatically—it's an irresistible invention on their part, to send their forthcoming books, en masse, every week, and the booksellers needn't feel obliged to subscribe, but they do anyway because they're given easy payment methods and discounts and the right to return the unsold books."

"Van, The Good Novel will not be an ordinary bookstore. That's our challenge. Our customers won't be ordinary customers. The people we'll see at our store will be people who never buy a book because it just came out, unless they adore the author already, but for other reasons that have nothing to do with its pub date, because they couldn't care less about that. They'll be the people who go into a bookstore knowing what they want to buy, and they go straight to the bookseller and say, I'd like *Titus Alone,* by Mervyn Peake. People who won't be surprised if we tell them the book is not in stock—the opposite would have surprised them—and who'll order it without hesitating, because they don't mind if it comes three or eight days later. And that doesn't mean they won't buy two or three other books as well before they leave the shop, books they hadn't previously thought of buying."

Van grew thoughtful.

"It's a challenge, like you said."

"A wager. But you agree, if we want to open The Good Novel it's because we don't want to open a bookstore like all the others? And then, let's not complicate things. All we need is to think of it as a specialized bookstore for everything to be clear. In nautical or art bookstores, the new books must only make up a small proportion of sales."

On the third evening, they discussed how the novels would be chosen.

Van had been dreading this moment to some degree. It was the crux of the matter, and he saw only one solution. Luckily— but as the term is used here, the notion of luck contains not the faintest trace of random chance that it usually implies— Francesca had thought about it and she had the same idea as Van. There was only one way: selection could not be entrusted to a single person, or even two, that would have been too arbitrary. A committee of several writers would have to be put together, chosen writers each of whom would submit a list of their three hundred favorite novels, and the bookstore would retain not only the titles that everyone had chosen, but everyone's lists in its entirety, excluding any duplicates, obviously.

"Three hundred?" said Van.

Three hundred titles, at least, for each elector, insisted

Francesca, for reasons of methodology. If you asked each writer for fifty novels, you ran the risk of having, each time, the same fifty novels. In order to come up with other novels in addition to the indisputable masterpieces, you had to incite the committee members to suggest great unknown works: and they would only do that if they could propose more titles than the fifty obvious suggestions. The two hundred and fifty other titles were the ones that mattered, for they would make the difference between The Good Novel and all the other good bookstores that existed.

In other words, three hundred titles per committee member—two hundred and fifty, in fact. How many people should make up the committee? Six? Eight? Ten? Twelve? Dinner on the fourth evening began with this issue. A vital one. Would The Good Novel sell a thousand novels? Two thousand? Ten thousand? How many great novels existed in the French language—including translations? (For on that very evening it became clear, and therefore imperative, that the novels would be in French, and the bookstore in a French-speaking country.)

Van and Francesca hesitated for several hours. As they did not set themselves any limits, either in time or in space, and did not assign any more importance to the present day than to centuries gone by, which were incredibly rich, and no countries were excluded, no matter how tiny, even if they had only one great novel translated into French, it became clear that the selection was going to be considerable. There were thousands of great novels available in the French language.

"It all hinges on what we mean by great novel," said Francesca.

"That's what I was going to say," confirmed Van. "Let's leave aside the obvious choices for now, the two thousand or so blatant masterpieces. Where things start to get complicated is for the other great novels. I'd like to take a different approach. I think we have to ask ourselves where we're going to draw the line, and our electors will have to ask themselves the same thing on a case-by-case basis. Take, for example, Nancy Mitford's *Love in a Cold Climate.* Do we order it for the store or not?"

"No," said Francesca. "It's a fabulous book, I've read it several times, it made me laugh out loud, you learn more about England than if you stayed there for months. But we'll have better books. Precisely because we've inherited from the English a taste for understatement—and for that reason alone—we won't be calling our bookstore The Great Novel."

Ivan thought for a moment.

"How many great novels exist in French, do you think? Thousands, but how many? Let me formulate the question yet another way: we needn't be afraid of being arbitrary, for our choice of books will be. Let's be downright arbitrary. We'll settle on a number that seems a good place to start, and we'll take it from there."

"Three thousand?" suggested Francesca.

"A bit more. In my little cellar, if I filled it to bursting, I could get eighteen hundred books, roughly. I can picture at least double that at The Good Novel, just to start."

"Between three thousand five hundred and four thousand?"

"Exactly. That represents roughly the capacity of an old-fashioned bookstore—that is, the old-fashioned size of the bookstore, you see what I mean?"

"Perfectly. Let's start with that. And are we even sure of finding three thousand five hundred great novels?"

"If you multiply the total body of literature written in French and translated into French by the four and a half centuries since the invention of the printing press: yes, I think so."

Of course the stock would have to change and develop. Every year, their consultants on the committee would have to nominate twenty or twenty-five new titles. Every year, the faithful customers of The Good Novel would also find two hundred or so new titles. Did that mean that two hundred others would be withdrawn?

"No," said Francesca. "We'll expand. It would be fatal if our first selection were insufficient. We'll grow as much as we need to."

Those were the words that Van had been waiting for. Finally, for the first and last time he brought up the issue of financing.

"Don't worry about that," said Francesca. "Just get it into your head that the financing is being taken care of, no matter what."

"Even if we operate at a loss?"

"Whatever those losses might be, and to the end of my days," smiled Francesca. "I'm forty-seven years old."

But she understood that for Ivan such vague verbal reassurance might not really be enough for him to embark on such an adventure.

Van exclaimed in protest.

"I know," she said, as if he hadn't said anything, "I'll endow the bookstore with a sizeable capital; it will all be legal. And with full guarantees where you're concerned."

"Don't worry about that."

"Yes, I'm committing myself."

"If you only knew how much I trust you. And the kinds of risks I've taken in the past. With you I feel safe for the first time in my life. Besides, safety is a pretty paltry word to describe such a change of plan. I am certain you're going to help me reach my true self. Forgive me all the grand words."

"We may fail."

"I don't think so."

"I don't think so, either, but I'm asking you to bear in mind that failure is a possibility."

Ivan promised. It was late, and they parted.

On the fifth evening, no sooner had they sat down on either side of their usual table than Van pulled from his pocket two sheets of paper covered with figures, and put them down in front of him.

"We made a mistake yesterday. Nothing serious," he said. "A mistake in our calculations."

"About the lists?"

"Yes. If you recall, we started with the idea of a dozen or so people on the committee, and we would ask each of them for three hundred titles. From there we moved on to another problem, the total number of books we'd need at the start, and we came up with roughly three thousand five hundred to four thousand. But that doesn't work. I woke up during the night. I did some calculations in my head. I had the feeling we had gone too quickly with our figures. I finally got up and took a pencil and a sheet of paper."

He pointed to the two sheets on the table.

"It's very simple," he said. "The error is with the number of titles to be given each elector. Let's suppose the committee consists of eight members. We started with the idea that of the three hundred titles, our eight committee members might have fifty in common. Now that makes a total of fifty plus eight times two hundred and fifty, which makes two thousand five hundred books, and that's not enough.

"Another thing, even more important, that I realized during the night is that we did not take into account the titles that might not be mentioned eight times, but between two and seven times. At a rough estimate, at least half of the titles will be mentioned several times. The difficulty is knowing how many will be mentioned twice, how many three times, and so on up to eight. One thing is for sure, to reach a minimum of three thousand five hundred books in the bookstore, we have to ask each member for six hundred titles."

"Six hundred!"

"If half of each list is mentioned several times, that makes eight times three hundred that won't make two thousand four hundred titles in all but, let's say, one thousand two hundred. To those titles you have to add eight times the three hundred titles that were only mentioned once. Two thousand four hundred plus one thousand two hundred, that makes three thousand six hundred titles."

"What we don't know is the half of the lists made up of titles that will be quoted several times. Will they be mentioned twice? Three or four times? Or five, six, seven times? Or eight? How can we find out? Did you calculate the way they might be distributed?"

"I spent half an hour on it, in my pajamas, frozen, before I realized I wouldn't manage. It's not an easy calculation to make. I began by reasoning as if the books were equivalent in units: with interchangeable units, you can use probability theory. But I understood pretty quickly that I was getting off track, precisely because novels are not undifferentiated, not at all. On the contrary, they contain greatly differing values and levels of notoriety. I went back to bed once I decided to call Serge for help."

"Serge?"

"My friend Serge is a math graduate so passionate about the mountains that he finally decided to settle in Méribel. Well, it was actually more complicated than that. At the age of fifty, he was tired of high school and high school students. As for his wife, she was tired of him and she'd just left him for a Hellenist. He took early retirement and moved into a small apartment he had inherited from his father. In addition to mathematics and peaks, he's passionate about books. I met him at the bookstore.

"This morning, first thing, I called him. I didn't tell him anything about our project. I talked to him about a newspaper that had asked me to imagine the ideal bookstore. Here's the problem, I explained: you've got a selection committee of eight members, and you need to have four thousand titles in the store, and you know that some titles will be chosen several times, how many do you need from each committee member?

"He called me back an hour later. He put his finger on the problem. According to him, mathematics cannot provide the answer. If all the books were equal, it would be possible, he explained, confirming my suspicion. But not all books are equal. Montaigne's *Essais* should be mentioned eight times, but it is impossible to know in advance how often *Le Cousin Pons* or Marcus Aurelius's *Meditations* will be chosen. Once? Twice? Or more?"

"I see," said Francesca. "We are left with trial and error. We'll ask for our lists and then we'll do the math."

"One thing is for sure, three hundred titles is not enough if we have eight electors."

"And six hundred?"

"With six hundred suggestions per elector, we should come up with four thousand books."

Long afterwards, when Van related these discussions to me, they seemed technical and austere. Van assured me of the contrary. He had recalled extraordinary moments. Time flew by with the quickness of thought, their project was coming to light, and its credibility was at stake.

"That's an enormous amount, six hundred," said Francesca. "Who will go along with that?"

"It's not as much as all that, you'll see. I've been thinking about it since this morning. Of the six hundred titles, let's say that three hundred of them might be French. Does it seem impossible to you to make a list of the three hundred greatest French novels?"

"Well, difficult in any case. You have to have read a lot."

"By definition. The committee members won't be kids. We have to think of people who are known to have been avid readers from childhood. We'll find them."

Francesca nodded, silent.

"We may indeed get up to three hundred fairly quickly," she continued. "In my head I've been drawing up a list of all the French novelists of the twentieth century who should be represented, and it goes quickly. Proust, Colette, Cendrars, Segalen, Renard, Gide, Drieu, Céline, Aragon, Giono, Bernanos, Malraux, Mauriac, Gracq . . ."

"You're mentioning the most famous," said Van. "Don't forget Calet, Dietrich, Fargue, Jouhandeau, Reverzy, Bove, Vialatte . . . Over four centuries, we'll have no difficulty at all in finding a hundred and fifty or two hundred great French authors. And for many of those authors, you can't possibly limit yourself to just one work. I can't see any other way but to include all of Stendhal, all of Flaubert, ten by Balzac at least, ten by Zola . . ."

"And more recently, too, there is no end of choice," said Francesca. "I'm thinking of all the novels that have come out in French in the last twenty years and that I love, there are loads of them, including Modiano, Michon, Laurrent, Gailly, Echenoz, Oster, Bobin, the two Rolins, Grenier, Roubaud, Rio, Bianciotti, Benoziglio, Bergounioux, Deville, Laclevetine, Cholodenko, Visage, Rousseau, Raphaële Billetdoux, Sylvie Germain, Annie Ernaux, Régine Detambel, Nicole Caligaris, Maryline Desbiolles—" she took a breath—"Carrère, Millet, Chevillard, Holder, di Nota—"

"Listen," Van stopped her. "For tomorrow, we can make up our own lists. Let's try. Let's see how long it takes us, and if we get up to three hundred."

"Very well. Let's try. Now for foreign literature. Three hundred great foreign novels, that's not very much either, given the number of countries involved. Thirty Italian novels, thirty Spanish, thirty German, thirty Belgian and Dutch, thirty English, thirty American . . ."

"North American," corrected Van. "In fact, thirty is nothing for the countries you have just mentioned. Each of them ought to be represented by three hundred novels. But, as our bookstore will be French-speaking, let's keep that as our basis. Thirty Latin American novels, thirty Russian, thirty from Eastern Europe—Poland, Hungary, the Czech Republic, Slovakia, thirty from the South Slav countries and the Balkans—Serbia, Romania, Bulgaria . . ."

". . . Albania. Ismael Kadare's Albania."

"Greece, Turkey . . ."

"Thirty from China, and from Japan . . ."

". . . from Korea, Vietnam, Indonesia."

"Thirty from Iran, Iraq, and Syria."

"Thirty from Israel and Egypt, thirty from New Zealand and Australia . . ."

"Let's stop there," said Ivan. "We've gone way over our total. You see, six hundred titles seems like a huge amount, but if you take into account the literary heritage of the entire globe, it's nothing. I even wonder if, when we draw up this list, we won't find the ceiling of six hundred low. I'm not so sure that sticking to that figure will be so easy. The difficult thing may be to come up with only six hundred titles."

"Let's try," said Francesca again. "Will you have time between today and tomorrow?"

On the sixth evening, they showed up with their drafts. Neither one of them had finished the list, it was impossible in one day, but they no longer wondered whether it was possible. Van had found inspiration on his shelves in the basement, and in the huge booksellers' yearbook—he called it his Bible— where all the books in print were listed. Francesca had spent the day on the Internet, every author made her think of another, one name led to another.

They got back to the issue of the committee. What would be a good number of electors? Without talking about it any further, on the basis of a common intuition they agreed upon eight.

"We have to choose eight great novelists," said Francesca.

"Great prose writers."

"Who are hooked on novels, and won't be intimidated by the figure six hundred."

"Exactly. Setting the limit high will help to promote an excellent choice. The ones who play along will be best at it."

"We'll have to find people who have read everything."

"By definition."

"The hardest thing will be to find people whose tastes are not too similar. Who are not too much alike."

The electors mustn't influence each other, said Francesca. Van: The best would be if each of them goes off to work on their own. Francesca: And what if they didn't even know who the others were? Van: Keep it secret, of course. If the makeup of the committee is kept secret that would make it easier, it would guarantee the members' freedom of choice. Secrecy would avoid any pressure. Francesca: And our electors would be truly sincere. Without the secrecy, they would find it hard not to include books by friends on their list, or by people who are on the juries of literary prizes. Van: Yes, we must insist upon the fact that the books on sale at The Good Novel have been chosen by members of a selection committee whose identities have been kept secret. Francesca: But we can say that they are writers. Van: Nothing more. For example, we mustn't say how many of them there are.

And they began to suggest names.

"I can't imagine the committee without Paul Néant," began Francesca.

"That goes without saying," said Van. "Or without Ida Messmer."

"I was thinking of her. I despise pornography, but I know of no one who writes more beautiful erotica."

When they saw that the same authors were springing to mind, they each jotted down on a piece of paper the names of the twelve Francophile authors for whom they had the greatest respect. They compared their lists. Of the twenty-four nominated, they had eight in common. They decided to begin with the eight whom or both liked.

"What shall we do in case they refuse, to make sure they respect the secrecy?" wondered Francesca suddenly. "How can we approach a candidate and explain to him or her what we expect, that is, what the committee will be, then if they refuse, be sure they'll tell no one about the project?"

"That's not really the problem," said Van. "I'm thinking out loud. Each writer will be sounded out separately. Whether they refuse or accept they won't know who the committee members are. The only thing they might say if they refuse and then talk about it would be: I'm not on the committee. And we'll also ask those who agree to be on the committee to deny that they are if anyone asks them about it. No," pursued Van, "the problem would be if one of the electors played along for a while, and then withdrew. There, he would have to be silent as the tomb."

"That's not a problem either," said Francesca in turn. "Once the committee is put together, all it takes is to make sure that the members never meet one another, and never find out who the others are. If one of them leaves, he can say, I was a member, but we can deny it. How could he possibly prove his claim, anyway?"

That meant that any written correspondence between the protagonists must be confidential, and destroyed upon receipt.

No, they would do without anything in writing as much as possible. They would avoid the Internet—everyone knows that it's accessible to all and sundry. They would communicate by telephone, using code names.

"We could give each of the eight members a cell phone," said Francesca. "It could be used exclusively for communicating about The Good Novel."

Van was reticent.

"A cell phone would probably be the surest way, but the problem would be eight contracts drawn up at the same time by you or me. It would be better if each of them used their usual cell phone, that way our conversations about the bookstore would be buried among all the others."

"Would you like another coffee?" asked Francesca.

"My third? Sure, I need it."

Then they talked about location. Where did the bookstore stand the best chance of finding its audience, given the fact they would only be selling books in French? The answer was so obvious that, without daring to say as much, they forced themselves to mention Brussels, Lyon, Geneva.

"Perhaps the simplest would be Paris, after all," said Francesca after five minutes had gone by.

"But where in Paris?" asked Van. "Given the cost of commercial leases . . ."

Francesca was the co-owner, with some cousins, of a building on the rue Dupuytren, right by the Odéon.

"A fine seventeenth-century building," she said. "We could occupy the ground floor and the second-floor."

"You could hardly find better," agreed Van.

On the back of her draft list, Francesca made a sketch of the premises. The street, the entrance, the rear courtyard, with its magnolia tree; there was already a display window; the layout of the rooms on the second floor.

"And it's available?" asked Van.

A few years earlier, the cousins had requested that the building, undivided at that point, be shared out in lots. Francesca was the only one who had a marked preference for the commercial space on the ground floor and the adjoining apartment on the second floor. She had an idea in mind. There were several artists she admired and who she knew were having difficulty breaking through: a painter, a photographer, and two sculptors, and she wanted to give them the opportunity to exhibit at a gallery . . . She hesitated: "Something not expensive," she said. "You see what I mean?"

Ivan understood perfectly. Not expensive at all.

"I read something in the papers that I found enchanting," continued Francesca. "Oe, the great Japanese novelist, founded a literary prize where he is the only member of the jury. He is not at all convinced by the leading critics, and he wants to act as a counterweight and support unknown authors."

Francesca had begun to redecorate the gallery on the ground floor. The work was fairly far along when the project suddenly changed.

"I was talking to a friend about it, and she said to me, That's my dream. I moved her in there. I didn't have the choice, I'll explain why. She was a woman who had been on her own, for a long time, and she was bitter. She had just been diagnosed with cancer. When her lover at the time found out, he packed up and left: a married man, a very sporadic lover, but the only man in her life. She was a sociologist, an academic, she was dissatisfied with teaching and she said she'd gone astray because her real vocation was art. She had carte blanche on the rue Dupuytren to exhibit what she liked. I didn't always agree with her choices, I hope she didn't realize. But that wasn't the issue. She had no success whatsoever. And it wasn't enough to give my friend her smile back, either. She died last spring, feeling bitter toward me. I haven't had the heart to do anything with the space."

"And now?" asked Van. "Would you use it, the space?"

"It would be ridiculous not to."

They talked about the space: how to arrange it, the layout, neighborhood traffic. The easiest would be to group the novels by country and alphabetical order. Or chronological? wondered Van. All three, proposed Francesca. "For example: England, nineteenth century, and the author, alphabetically. Van, what do you think about armchairs, in bookstores? In Switzerland and Germany, you often see sofas among the shelves."

They got up from dinner feeling light-headed. The next day they shared with each other the fact they'd had an awful time getting to sleep, from all their excitement, and joy.

15

On the seventh evening, they spoke of neither novels nor authors, nor about anyone else, they talked about themselves and their past lives. It wasn't deliberate. They had just sat down when Ivan asked cheerfully, "Do you always wear light colors? I've seen you wearing beige, white, and pale green."

Francesca's eyes filled with tears. "I wore black for four years in a row," she said. "I stopped completely two years ago. I might as well tell you right away, I lost my only daughter six years ago. She was nineteen. She threw herself under a train, between Vanves and Chaville, near Paris. She had walked along the railroad line, during the night, all the way from the Montparnasse station. All they could show me, when they lifted up the sheet at the mortuary, was her feet. The rest of her body was unrecognizable. But I knew her little feet right away, her ballet slippers with crossed straps, they were made of lambskin, old rose, we had bought them together two days earlier. My husband didn't come."

"You don't need to say anything else," said Van.

"Yes, just a bit, once and for all. You have to know about this, because it is at the heart of what I am, my identity, my name, now. Her name was Violette. She was seventeen when the illness swooped down on her like a bird of prey. Until then, she had been an easy child, and she'd turned into a dream of a young woman. Out of nowhere one day she came back from school shouting absolute insanities. They diagnosed her immediately. She was given every possible treatment, she saw the most intelligent doctors. Nothing helped. She got worse and worse. I dropped everything to fight with her. I never left her. She was sadder and sadder. One evening, she went to bed early. So did I. I was exhausted. Her father wasn't there. He always came back very late, for as long as I can remember. She left the apartment, I didn't hear.

"Things had been difficult between my husband and me for a long time. He's a businessman, intelligent and cold. Violette's death did not bring us closer, on the contrary. I had not been enough for him for many years. He no longer hid it. He could not stand to be in my company. And then he has this sort of ethics of compensation, the pseudo-ethic of a great realistic workaholic who says that the harder life is, the more you are entitled to consolation."

Francesca wiped a tear from the tip of her nose with her index finger, looked straight at Van and said, "Just one more thing, to give a precise answer to your question. I spent years wearing black, until a dream that I had, two years ago. It was Violette, beautiful and calm, intact. It was the first time since her death that I had seen her alive in a dream. I had seen her hundreds of times . . . otherwise. She was asking me to stop wearing mourning. She spoke like a teenager: Stop it, now, with those mourning clothes. I stopped the next day."

Van reached across the table and took Francesca's right hand between both of his and kissed it gently. They sat on in silence for a few seconds.

"Your turn," said Francesca.

Ivan sat up.

"No major drama in my life," he said. "Although the early years were somewhat melodramatic. But my own life, so to speak, my adult life, has been mainly characterized by mediocrity, drifting, flabbiness."

Francesca had spoken for three minutes. Van was verbose.

Was it out of recognition toward her, or to show a sort of allegiance to her simplicity and her courage? He spoke for a long time, slowly.

At the age of twenty he had broken off all ties. He no longer saw anyone from his family—a poor family, very small, he said. He had studied English, and Chinese, and he thought he might become a teacher. He claimed to be a follower of the libertarian school of nineteenth-century utopians. The educational authorities had a different idea of what school ought to be, and his career as a teacher did not last longer than two years. So he left for the United States, where he devised literary tours to places that great American writers had loved and sung the praises of in their works.

"I got the idea from their books. I devoured writers like Whitman and Thoreau. That year, I began to read a great deal."

He was also reading French novels. He missed France, and he went home. He found work with a budding publisher of comic books who soon became famous thanks to a best-selling author. "Let's call him B.," he said. "B. Editions, after the owner's name. Everybody knows him."

Heffner's expression told them that he didn't know him. Van wondered if he was one of those readers who was too passionate about prose ever to open a comic book, and concluded, no, that he was sincere, and went on with his story. He worked as a rep for the publisher. He went around the bookstores in the east of France selling comic books. And that is how one day he became a bookseller, just by chance, a fairly happy twist of fate.

One day in Strasbourg he was canvassing a fairly inactive bookstore. The books were displayed in the annex to a restaurant. The manager had bought the bookstore with the restaurant. It is not infrequent to find gourmet intellectuals who think that there must be plenty of people around like themselves who enjoy fine dining and books, and who think putting the two together is a good idea. In Strasbourg, there must not have been enough of them, and the business flopped. The new owner didn't care about anything but the restaurant. Books were piled up in cardboard boxes, it was a mess. I'd like to sell them, said the restaurant owner to Van. I'm prepared to sell the whole lot for fifteen thousand francs, the bookstore and the books.

Van didn't have a penny. He tried to get a banker interested, in vain. He talked about the business to B., who signed the contract right away, and asked him to revive the bookstore.

"That's how I got my start in the business," he said. "It didn't take very long for me to feel like a fish in water."

In those days, there were bookstores for sale all over France. B., who had turned out to be a good entrepreneur, bought up a dozen or so of them, one after the other. Each time, Van was delegated to get the business going again. He might spend six months selling books in Vichy, six months in Marseille, and so on.

"We were more or less specialized in comic books," he said.

He was running a bookstore in Briançon when all of a sudden B. decided to sell off all the businesses, and he fired Ivan without any respect for convention, let alone any sort of compensation.

"After everything I'd done for him, it really pissed me off," said Van. "But taking him to court would be a hassle, and I was in a hurry. To be honest, I didn't really think it through. I still had my Simca, the company car. One night, with the rear end of the car, I smashed through the door at the Briançon store, and drove away with a whole bunch of vintage comic books that I had haggled for myself, so I knew how much they were worth. In those days, they didn't reprint comic books once they went out of print, so the old albums were worth a lot of money. Just to make my point, I left the dented Simca there. I had come with a friend. We loaded my booty into his car. B. didn't take me to court, either."

Ivan then moved to Pantin as a rare-book dealer, special-ized in comic books because there was a lot of money in it, but all the while his taste in literature was developing. He had a stand at the flea market in Saint-Ouen. He earned a lot of money in the space of a few years. He knew all the wealthy col-lectors. When he turned up a sought-after album, he would call four or five collectors who were ready to pay anything to get their hands on it, and he would give them an appointment in his little office and auction off the comic book.

But business, to be honest, bored him. One day, with his pockets full, he dropped everything and went off to bum around Asia. "I was thirty-six," he said. "I was on the road for a bit more than five years.

"You get bored with pure leisure like with all the rest," he continued. "Or maybe it was great novels that I was missing: I didn't find anything particularly good in the stations where I stopped. Suddenly I'd had enough, and I came back to France.

"I had no particular place to call home. In the few months I'd lived in Briançon, I'd fallen under the spell of the moun-tains. Coming home, I felt cleaned out. I was broke no matter where I went, so I figured that at least in the ski resorts in the Alps I might find some seasonal work. So I bought a train ticket for Chambéry."

In Chambéry, yet another coincidence, another twist of fate—walking past the employment office, Ivan went in. Among the jobs on the board he saw one advertising a position for a bookseller in Méribel. There were thirty candidates, but in the end, Van was the only one who'd had any experience in books, so he was hired. That is how he ended up at Bono's, two days after his forty-second birthday.

"So many chance occurrences, fortuitous ones," he observed, as if to himself. "You really could say I became a bookseller by accident. You could even put accident in the plural—and then you start to wonder if it really was by chance. You could even say it was out of necessity. And I'm amazed by how stubborn that necessity has been, every time I happen to think back, like just now, on the twenty years leading up to the opening of The Good Novel."

Heffner was looking at him.

"But to be exact," continued Van, "when Francesca came on the scene and talked to me about her project, I was still in the frame of mind that yet another chapter of my checkered existence was ending in failure. And whatever I might have shared with her of my life thus far was hardly of the bet-on-me-and-you'll-win variety."

"That's true," said Francesca, turning her head. Because she was speaking to Van, not to Heffner, or even for Heffner. "You came across as a born loser. But there was something else you said, I remember it very well. For the first time in your life you wanted to do everything you could to succeed. I can hear your words: I've spent twenty-five years settling accounts—with my father, with the authorities, with society, and I've never taken care of the rest; I've been searching in vain for what to do with myself; I've been self-destructive. I can no longer afford to waste my time. I'm forty-five years old. I have to devote myself to something that's bigger than I am, and it has to be a success."

"And do you remember," asked Van, "how you replied? I can recall what you said, too, word for word. You said: To say the same thing in a fairly naïve way, I too want to do something worthwhile in my life, at last."

16.

Van had decided, long before their conversation on the seventh evening. He had given his consent to Francesca already on the first evening, and had handed in his resignation to Bono the very next day. He stayed ten more days at the bookstore, while waiting for the replacement Bono had found. On the very last of those ten days he saw the penniless student from the valley once again.

So many things happened that winter, he could not get over it. He told me that the following day, for the first time in his life, he bought a magazine on astrology, because he was curious to see, since it was early in the new year, what the stars had predicted for him. But, ever faithful to their habitual anthropomorphism and housewifely worrywart proclivities, the stars predicted nothing more than a nagging sore throat.

During the weeks that had preceded, Van had thought about the young woman every day, dismayed that he did not know how to reach her, imagining himself sending a letter to "Little Anis, Department of Social Sciences (Sociology), University of Grenoble"; all that he had to cling to was the affectionate tone he had used in asking her to stop in again.

And lo and behold, on the stairs leading to the cellar, there appeared first a pair of brown rubber boots, followed by a gabardine, a red scarf, and smiling lips which then went on to say, Good morning. I'd like you to look up all the titles of works by a young author by the name of Noëlle Revaz.

Van was due to leave the mountain the very next day; his bags were packed. Francesca had gone back to Paris a week earlier. When he called her, in order to justify coming twenty-four hours late Ivan invoked a parting that mustn't be rushed.

He had groped about for a way to put it that wouldn't be a lie—he was not about to start telling fibs to Francesca. And yet the following afternoon, during the two hours he spent with Anis in Grenoble, more than once he wondered if, where formal partings were concerned, he wasn't doing exactly the contrary: he was trying to create a bond as quickly as possible, regardless of the usual propriety.

Anis had offered to show him around the old center of Grenoble. Sleet was falling, discouraging any walking around outdoors, so they went from café to café, comparing the aroma of their mulled wine. Van grew more talkative with every street. Loyal to his vow of secrecy but without hiding his enthusiasm, he explained why he was leaving Méribel, Bono, his little cellar, and the extraordinary opportunity that had been given to him, through the grace of a person like no one he'd ever met. Anis looked at him with her eyes wide open. What a dream, she said softly, more than once.

Night was falling, Van glanced at his watch.

"Not right away," said Anis. "you've got too much rum in your blood to sit behind the wheel. And I have an operation to perform on you. Come and drink a tea."

They sat down at the back of a café. From her pocket she took a small cloth bag and said with a smile, "Take your clothes off." Van removed his parka, his scarf, and his sweater. He was in the mood to take everything off but Anis raised her palm to him, like a traffic policeman, and said: "That's enough."

From the little bag she took a big needle and a length of navy blue wool.

"I've always seen you wearing this sweater," she said to Van, spreading the sweater onto the table. "And there's always been this hole in the left elbow. It's true that I've only seen you three times, including today."

"Does it bother you, the hole?" asked Van. "It's true, Bono already told me I had a hole in my sweater. I knew it, I didn't argue the fact, but I've never understood why it's a problem."

They had a discussion about the clothes that you must cherish more than others, because you never tire of wearing them.

"If we didn't have to live in society, we'd wear nothing else, frankly," said Anis.

"No matter how worn out they are," said Van.

"That's why, from time to time, you do have to intervene. Otherwise, someday, the hole will get too big, or the tear will be too visible. Reform is inevitable. I can see two options, you choose. I can fill up the hole. You can be sure it will come back. If you like it the way it is, I can also leave it that way, just reinforcing the edges."

"Fill in the space," said Ivan.

The young woman did not react. She did not say, It will come back, Van noticed.

He watched her stitching. In three minutes she had finished.

"Do you know what invisible darning is?" she asked, raising her eyes to meet his gaze.

"No idea."

"It's when you cannot see it's been darned. Look."

"I can see nothing else," said Van, "and I'm not about to let it out of my sight."

He had been hesitating for quite a while. The moment seemed favorable.

"Come to Paris with me," he said.

Anis stiffened: "No. That's not possible."

"And why not, why isn't it possible?"

"I won't be pinned down," said Anis, shaking her head. She had grown pale: "We'll write to each other. Is that all right?"

She took a receipt from her pocket, turned it over, and wrote a few words on it.

"Here. That's my address."

"You remind me of a fairy tale," said Van, "the princess who vows not to change her shift as long as her fine husband is away at war. I shall make a vow to wear this sweater every day until you come to join me in Paris."

Van was looking straight at Heffner.

"I'm a bit nervous telling you all this," he said. "My taste for old clothes may seem antisocial, or even subversive, in this era devoted to consumption. But you'll have no difficulty ascertaining that Anis and I have stayed in touch, and that she is a salaried employee at The Good Novel. I suppose she will be part of the investigation. I prefer to introduce her to you as she is, that is, the way she introduced herself to me."

Van's behavior was not exactly subversive, Heffner would say, much later on. It was maternal, rather, or even possessive, he thought, for he was someone who had never been able to stand being manipulated and he was hypersensitive to any sort of emblematic gesture of women's power. He could picture the little hand with its needle sewing its mark on the sweater, like an embroidered signature. He could hear her fresh voice saying, You decide, after she had given him the choice, either I sign this way, or that way.

"So you came to Paris," he said. "In early February, 2004."

17

P utting the committee together was neither a lengthy nor difficult process. Francesca left Ivan alone on the front line. "Introduce yourself as the one who is launching the bookstore," she said. "It is the truth, after all."

She preferred to remain in the shadows.

"My name already has such a connotation about it. As for my husband's, it's even worse."

Ivan apologized: "I might seem indiscreet, but you have to tell me a bit more. All I know about you, in that respect, is that you are Francesca Aldo-Valbelli, residing at 30, rue de Condé. I can see that your name has an Italian connotation, no more than that. I don't even know whether that is your maiden name, or your married name, or both."

"Let me explain," said Francesca. "Then we won't need to talk about it again. I don't like to discuss my pedigree. But of course I owe you a minimum of explanation. Aldo-Valbelli is my maiden name. It is rather . . . well-known in Italy. In the old days, my family had a huge estate—land, and so on. They were totally unable to keep pace with the modern world. Those of them who did feel the winds of change, in the nineteenth century, lost their way, almost as if they'd planned it: they wagered everything on sectors that were swept away thirty years later by technological progress. Nothing brilliant remained about the name, except, like a dead star, an illusion. I'll get back to my grandfather, Stefano Aldo-Valbelli. He's the only one who deserves any attention, a true prince. My parents lived way beyond their means—perhaps they were unaware of what they were doing, or were incapable of understanding that times had changed, and they could not admit that their fates might be the same as everyone else's. They died fairly young, both of them, my father from illness, and she— she died of coldness, I believe; her heart dried up. They left me a few houses, nothing else.

"But my grandfather, on the other hand, left me a great deal. I don't mean money: he kept nothing. Neither of my parents could stay in one place, and they were not at all attached to me. I wouldn't go so far as to say my grandfather raised me, but it was only with him that I felt good. He was a famous historian, and had also written three charming novels, because literature was his true passion. I'll talk to you about him again. I owe him a great deal. And even quite recently he gave me a royal gift, from the beyond.

"My husband's name is Henri Doultremont, and he is the CEO of the Cinéor Group."

"Quite a responsibility," Van said politely.

"That's an understatement," corrected Francesca. "Responsible for having made cultural demagogy into an economic system. Do you know what they do at Cinéor? They make blockbuster movies that neither you nor I can stand, run television channels we would never watch—games, videos, magazines: 43 percent of the radio and television revenues in France. The funds that I will invest in the bookstore belong to me personally, and I do not want my husband's name to be associated with The Good Novel. Because my connection with him is public knowledge, the less visible I am, the better. Believe me, it would be better if you approached our potential committee members on your own. Not to mention the fact that you will be better at it than I would. There are certain circles where I feel somewhat awkward."

"You, awkward?"

"I assure you."

"Writers don't tend toward circles."

"No, but they do all tend to think that they have been the authors of their life just as they've been the authors of their texts: they tend to look down on people like me who have inherited, I don't know, a name, a position."

"What you say only applies to writers who've been success-ful. And the writers who are dear to us aren't that successful, on the whole. Don't go thinking I'm questioning your strategy. If you prefer, I can present myself as a bookseller who is fed up with the way his profession is going these days, and who wants to try something else."

Ivan made ten phone calls, and three appointments. The large office on the rue Dupuytren was at his disposal. On the ground floor, work had started. It was only renovation, noth-ing that would stop him from beginning work upstairs.

At the end of February, the committee had been set up. Larry de Winter, Sarah Gestelents, and Gilles Evohé had wanted to meet Ivan in person before giving their reply. What sur-prised Francesca was that only those three asked for a meeting. Out of the first eight Van had approached, only two declined, Pierre-Alain Oslo, who was in the middle of a depression and who moaned on the phone: I don't know what writing means anymore, I haven't written anything for four years, I can't stand to think that others have been writing or are writing; and Marthe Chavert, who refused to commit unless she was told who the other committee members were. A collective is a col-lective, said this woman of principle, who had served her apprenticeship with the Maoists. The six others, to Van's utter surprise, each exclaimed: The ideal bookstore, that's an idea I've had for years. I've been dreaming about it!

Van and Francesca did not hesitate for long over the two miss-ing slots. They had the consent of Paul Néant, Ida Messmer,

Armel Le Gall, Sarah Gestelents, Gilles Évohé, and Larry de Winter. Then came Jeanne Tailleberne and Marie Noir, whom they admired nearly as much as their eight favorites. From all those who had been kind enough to consent, Ivan requested a list of six hundred titles, to be handed to him in person before the beginning of May. And he explained the rules of the game: they would not receive a cent in payment, there would be no trace of their work, since their names would be kept secret and their lists destroyed, and they would have no say in running the bookstore. A free, invisible contribution that would never be made public. At last something that looks like a truly disinterested position, said Winter.

Up to that point Francesca had been putting Van up at the Hotel Louis II on the rue Saint-Sulpice; now he used the few days of relative leisure that followed to look for an apartment. He found one that he liked on the rue de l'Agent-Bailly, a little street in the Rochechouart quarter that was astonishingly quiet, not at all what it seemed. This old, cobblestoned cul-de-sac slumped in the middle like a donkey's back, and behind the imposing porte-cochères there were long courtyards, the likes of which one might not have imagined in Paris, former postal inns or convent gardens.

The three hundred square feet that were available for rent were on the top floor of an unprepossessing building. By the looks of it, particularly the way it faced north, it must have been an artist's studio once, unheated and poorly insulated, but endowed with a bay window looking out onto an immense maple tree, and beyond, onto an ocean of slate, zinc, and chimneys that Van immediately referred to as the North Sea.

It would be wrong to say that he wasn't thinking of Anis when no sooner had he visited the studio than he signed the rental agreement. The first thing he did in his new house, once he had received the keys, was to take from his briefcase a postcard of the

Place des Victoires and write: *Here I am, I have my own address. As of two minutes ago I live on 6 rue de l'Agent-Bailly, Paris, 9th.* As a postscript he added: *The guardian of the peace Charles Gaston Bailly passed away in 1901 for having tried in vain to rescue a woman from drowning. That was all I could find out about him on the Internet; but it's something, and it's not bad.*

He went no further for the time being. He was well aware that he had been asked to be neither authoritarian nor intrusive, and that he had been given an address, and not a telephone number.

Francesca and Van did not phone each other either. They shared the same irrational fear of being overheard. Everything was off to such a good start.

In the beginning, they did not see much of each other. Francesca let Van get organized the way he liked. He did not have to report to her. She left him the big office upstairs. But Van quickly noticed that she did drop by the bookstore at the end of the morning, just to keep an eye on the renovation work. He got in the habit of being there at the same time, so he could talk to her. Why don't you come upstairs, he would say. It's quiet up there.

He was the one who expressed the wish for Francesca to have her own table and files in the big office. "You can't leave me all alone," he told her. "I constantly need your opinion. What we're doing is not cut-and-dried." He was sincere.

So Francesca moved a desk into one end of the big room, at the opposite end from Van. Between the two desks she placed three armchairs and a coffee table.

"Should we get a bigger table?" she asked. "Like a conference table? And chairs?"

"What for?" asked Ivan. "We'll never have meetings here. Or elsewhere, for that matter. For the two of us these armchairs will be perfect."

They sat down, and talked. Ivan, who had not earned this much money in a long time, often brought a bottle of kefir or muscat wine with him in the morning. Francesca liked hot drinks. She had a small kitchen area which she called the pantry set up on the landing. There was a small fridge, a hot plate, an Italian coffee maker, a tea kettle, a juicer, glasses, cups, and an antique hat rack which made a perfect supply cupboard and which was always filled with amaretti, short bread, chocolate, and dried figs, and soon other basic items turned up there, who knows how.

As is often the case with thin people, Van snacked from morning to night. He drank a lot, primarily milk. Francesca ran on tea and coffee, irrespective of the time, alternating back and forth. She taught Van how to make tea Indian style, without a drop of water (boil milk for a long time, into which you have placed a lot of excellent tea, sugar, and spices).

"The name of the street, rue Dupuytren, reminded me of something," said Ivan one day. "I've just found it. In 1919, at number eight on this street, Sylvia Beach opened the first Shakespeare & Co. bookstore. And when she moved into the premises on the rue de l'Odéon, one of Gaston Gallimard's close friends, Gustave Tronche, took over her spot with another exceptional bookstore, the Nouvelle Librairie Bibliothèque. And which, you'll note, was so successful that he soon opened six others."

As the owner of both the walls and the business, Francesca took care of all the administrative formalities with the labor office, tax authorities, Social Security, and the office for disability.

"I'd like to go with you," said Van.

"Whatever for?"

"For the pleasure."

"The pleasure? These are chores."

"For the pleasure of being with you."

Francesca had a fondness for going everywhere on foot. And I adore Paris, she explained. Van walked for miles by her side. He noticed her preference for flat shoes that allowed her to take long strides, and shoulder bags that were big enough to hold two or three books, and her perfectly cut clothing of a sobriety that was almost austere, and her shawls and scarves that she only ever wore over one shoulder, allowing them to drift behind her. She was nothing if not striking, with her wide forehead, high cheekbones, rapid gait, and tall, slim form. Yet you would have said she was completely unaware of it. Van never saw her look at herself in the mirror or a shop window. He understood that if she were to make the people she passed in the street turn around and look at her, she would need that "delighted to be herself" side, of the woman who is on a quest, and who sees her reflection with delight in windowpanes, is enchanted by her lovely figure, her hairstyle, or the vibrant sway of her hips. Van found her extremely likable, and that's what he said when trying to describe her a few words. And people would make him repeat what he said: likable?

"Yes," he said ardently, "in addition to being beauty itself and elegance personified, and generosity, and ardor, she is simple, she is good, she is as nice as can be."

One day at the beginning of March as they were leaving the labor office on the rue Montmartre, at one in the afternoon, after they had spent the morning waiting to see someone, who turned out to be a young woman sharper than a kriss, who notified them in less than a minute, after she had taken them into her office, that they had been given the wrong directions and had to go to a different office, both of them suddenly found themselves running on empty in a nearby square, an extension of the rue du Louvre, a fairly ugly and windswept place, but it was bathed in sunlight. An optimistic café owner had put two tables, four chairs, and a parasol out on the sidewalk.

"I'm hungry," said Francesca. "To be honest, I need a good lunch to offset this dreary morning. Oysters and chilled wine would put me right. Shall we sit down here?"

Van liked seafood—he liked the word, above all, he said—but he thought that sauerkraut would be a more serious counterweight to their administrative hassles.

"Do you know that at the end of her life, Karen Blixen ate nothing but oysters?" he said, handing a chair to Francesca.

"Some people think it was out of snobbery, particularly when you know she only drank champagne. But in fact, it's because she was sick. She was famous, and celebrated on both sides of the Atlantic, but she was syphilitic, skeletal, perhaps happy at last. I love her tales passionately."

"Such grace, indeed. So much elegance in her distress. She said one of the most desperate things I've ever heard. When she married Bror Blixen, loving him no more than he loved her, she made him agree to leave Denmark, where neither of them had any real reasons to remain, and she said to him—I'm quoting from memory—'At least we'll have done that, we'll have gone away.'"

Francesca was silent. Seeing how thoughtful she was all of a sudden, as if she were elsewhere, Ivan was struck by her resemblance with Karen Blixen at the same age. And he thought, petrified, that little Violette too had wanted to go away, desperately, and she had gone away.

Francesca must have read his thoughts, because she smiled to him, with obvious effort, and asked him, "Have you ever been married, Van?"

"Never."

Van did not particularly like personal conversations, but in this case he was quite happy to change the subject.

"God knows I love women, and that I have loved women and some of them did not want to leave me. But I gave none of them enough hope to dare to speak to me of marriage—or even think of marriage, simply living together. And when I say hope, I'm expressing myself poorly: I should say substance, constancy. What I have to offer is not substantial enough for a woman to imagine she could do something with it—let alone build anything on such a fragile foundation. To the few who looked at me, I always offered more instability than security, all soap bubbles and no real plan . . . magic tricks that I could perform for them the whole night through, but as for children, I never wanted any.

"Living together, and everything it implies, is not a path I can see myself heading down. I'm not proud of that. It's not a choice on my part, but an inability, perhaps some sort of phobia. I know only too well that I would disappoint any woman who placed her trust in me.

"I was very marked by my early years, my attachment to my mother. That's banal. But what is banal about a person is also what is strongest, isn't it? I once referred to having had a miserable childhood. It was above all on the emotional level that I'm using the word, and emotional misery was my mother's fate more than my own. My mother had two long relationships. At the age of nineteen she married the man who had gotten her pregnant, my father. No point in saying anything more about him. He dropped us, both of us, the year I turned four: just late enough so I could know what having a dad was about, and what it would cost me. My mother went under. She had no family, no support, she worked in a factory.

"I was seven when she met the man who became her companion. Seven years old: the very age when you find out to your horror that you're not enough for your mother, and that she prefers someone else. Never mind. That guy was a gentle sort. A worker, like my mother, ugly, puny, full of talent—he was a marvelous singer—good as good bread. I think he gave my mother what she expected, unconditional affection. But after five years, he died. He had been deported as a young man, in

1942—he was twice my mother's age. He came back worn out from Germany, and he never really recovered. He died at the age of fifty-five. My mother was annihilated for a second time. Without ever saying so, without even knowing it, perhaps, she counted on me to fill the void of her life. I wasn't up to it. I dreamed that she would be happy, but the idea that it might be my responsibility—something inside me rebelled. I did just the opposite of what I should have done. I didn't work at school. In the evening, I was never home. At the age of twenty I left, slamming the door.

"She died two years later. I hadn't seen her again. I used to call her on the phone, from time to time, and every time it went badly. In her voice there was so much need, although there was nothing she reproached me with, she asked for so much that I was distant, evasive, and I hung up as quick as I could. Not once did she tell me she was sick.

"Something terrible has come of all that: I don't want anyone to rely on me. Because I know I'll run away sooner or later. I say it, right from the start. I'm not up to taking care of a woman.

"And I've organized my life a certain way, I can see that. I fall in love every six months. In my way, I adore women. When I fall in love, it must be visible. They encourage me. I let them get closer. I love them for as long as they want nothing from me. But if we're arm in arm and they stop outside a baby store, or give me a ring, or worse still ask me for one: then I do a U-turn. I put my hands on my ears and leave at a run.

"So you see. Love at first sight, serenades, trills and cooing. And then I get completely fed up, it's my fault. Full speed reverse. Tears and reproaches on her part. And on mine, regret, shame, relief. A great deal of relief."

While he spoke, Van had been staring into space. Now he looked at Francesca.

"There are happier love stories. I consider myself to be romantically challenged."

Francesca said nothing. They had finished their meal and sat on in silence for a moment.

"Do you want anything else?" asked Francesca. Van shook his head. This was not the first time that Francesca's words seemed to have several meanings.

18.

The first list came in at the beginning of March, the second ten days later. Jean Tailleberne and Sarah Gestelents had not wasted their time.

"I had no choice," said Tailleberne. "It's not the easiest selection process in the world. Titles and authors kept running through my head, day and night. I could do nothing else."

He was a tall, handsome man of forty, blond, with lavender eyes, shy and smiling. He lived in Maule, to the northwest of Paris, but he was working that winter at the National Library of France. Van had invited him to lunch wherever he liked, in the neighborhood, and Tailleberne had suggested a local restaurant he knew nothing about, but the name intrigued him, Vila Real.

Van had insisted that Francesca come along. Subsequently, each time they received one of the seven other lists, he wanted her to be present. Given the rules of the game imposed on the electors, it was unlikely they would ever have another opportunity to meet them. Francesca had accepted, provided Ivan drop half of her name, and introduce her as Francesca Aldo, co-manager of the bookstore, nothing more.

Vila Real was a Portuguese restaurant, and the specialty was cod. Francesca ordered brandade, Ivan ordered cod with mussels, and Tailleberne had cod *acras*, perhaps because that was the first time he had heard the word, he said. Thereupon he took a manila envelope from a black nylon sleeve.

"We're dying to have a look, but we won't in front of you," said Francesca, her eyes shining.

"Nor will I comment upon it to you," said Tailleberne.

"You remember what it says in the contract," said Van. "We won't discuss your selection. All the books on your list will be on sale at The Good Novel. You remembered not to put your name on it? As soon as we have all the lists, we'll combine them into one, and that way we won't know who suggested what."

They talked a bit about the future, moving in, the calendar. Van confirmed that the store would open in September, if there were no hitches. Jean Tailleberne volunteered his promise to remain as silent as the tomb.

"By the way," asked Ivan, "have you come up with your pen name?"

Tailleberne gave a childlike smile.

"The Red," he said.

"I see," said Francesca. "The name of your ancestor Erik."

Van mentioned *Ada,* whose characters have coded names, in the spirit of the one chosen by Tailleberne, a sort of schoolboy reference to historical figures or the heroes of novels. Tailleberne seemed delighted: "On my list, you will find every novel by Nabokov."

"You see!" said Francesca. "When you agreed to be on the committee, I reread all your novels. They made me think of a certain tone, a certain author, and I couldn't remember who. Of course, Nabokov. It's the way you write that has echoes of his style, that sad, cruel irony, the virtuosity, the charm."

Tailleberne was bright red: "You have made me very happy saying that."

Two hours later, the three of them were still talking.

"We could hardly be more discreet," said Francesca, on giving the signal to leave.

"Don't you think that in France, at every meal, in every restaurant, there is at least one table where people are talking about literature?" asked Tailleberne.

"That's our wager," said Van, "our conviction, our hope."

"Nor could you have found anything to say that could make us happier," said Francesca, holding out her hand. "I hope we meet again someday."

"We can't be sure of that," said Van. "The Red, I won't call you unless it's absolutely necessary. As for you, you know how to reach us. You have my phone number. Beware of the Internet: it's like shouting from the rooftops. It would be better to use your cell phone."

"I see," said Tailleberne. "In a word, I will avoid making myself known."

Francesca had put his list in her handbag. She waited until they were back at the rue Dupuytren to take it out again. With the envelope in her hands, she paused: "I have an idea," she said. "Wouldn't it be better for us to look at the eight lists all at the same time, the day we have them all, so long as we make sure we don't know who wrote them? That shouldn't be impossible. We asked them not to sign their lists."

Van agreed.

"It will make us lose a bit of time, since we're going to have to wait for all the lists to start our orders, but you're right. We can only gain in objectivity, discretion, and rigor."

"You'll see," said Van, who, for his part, had already seen. "Sarah Gestelents is nothing like her name."

Francesca pictured a tornado, a jumping jack, a cannonball. She discovered an extremely thin young woman, boyish, her flat butt squeezed into dark-gray jeans, with a hoodie, and very short hair. At first glance, she seemed to correspond fairly well to what she wrote: nervous, not an ounce of fat, a very contemporary roughness.

She declined an invitation to lunch and suggested, rather, tea at the Dunes, an Oriental café in the south of the 11th arrondissement. She lived near there.

"I thought about Quicksilver, Bleak, or Grasshopper," she said the moment Van and Francesca had recognized her. "I wanted a pseudonym that would be just the opposite of my name. And then I thought that would be too easy to decode. What do you think of Green Pea?"

They sat down on three pouffes around a low table with straight legs and mother-of-pearl inlay. Sarah Green Pea had brought with her ten sheets of typewritten paper, without an envelope. Van immediately folded them in two, while Francesca was explaining their recent decision to read all the lists on the same day, without trying to identify the authors.

"When I sat down to do the lists," said Sarah, "I thought it would take me two or three hours, at the most. I must have spent two weeks on it. Are you also on the committee?"

"Upon careful consideration, no," said Van. "There's something we like about the idea of honoring the choices of readers other than ourselves. We feel like we are serving the novel."

Green Pea frowned.

"There are those who say I'm rigorous," she said. "Some might even say rigid. Well, I would find it a pity if you don't intervene, to some degree, by adding this or that title that you hold in high esteem if it isn't on one of the lists."

She left again after they had talked for a quarter of an hour. Van was captivated: "What a woman! She's rock solid. How old do you suppose she is?"

"What do you think?" asked Francesca.

"Thirty-five."

"She's actually a year younger than you. Her biography on the Internet doesn't hide it. She has written thirteen novels, published over a period of twenty years, beginning in 1984."

"And is Gestelents actually her real name?"

"Yes. Or at least so she says. I'm a bit lost, I won't hide it, between real names that seem false, the pen names that some have already adopted, and the pseudonyms we are asking everyone to provide. To find my way, I took a file card and wrote down all their names and pseudonyms, in three columns."

"Francesca, Francesca," said Ivan, with a half smile.

Francesca went pale.

"Oh, what an idiot I am. Van, how can someone so serious be so stupid? I'll go home and destroy that paper right away."

Van was perfectly calm.

"Do you have a lot of papers relating to The Good Novel at your house?"

"A few, in my desk. Ivan, before the evening is over, I'll have burned them all, I promise you."

"What an ingenious idea Green Pea had," said Van the next morning. "If *La Princesse de Clèves* is missing off any of the lists, of course we would have to add it."

"Or *Le hussard sur le toit*."

"Or Borges's short stories."

"Let's go one step further. To save time we could begin by buying all the most famous great novels. Stendhal, Dostoyevsky, Conrad, Proust, Woolf, Faulkner, all the giants."

"You mean the ones we are almost sure will be suggested, and which should be at The Good Novel no matter what?"

"Yes," said Francesca. "The obvious list. Of course. They've nearly finished the work at the bookstore, we can begin."

This meant informing publishers of the bookstore's opening in September. The sales reps would begin to come.

"It's a bit early," said Van.

"Let's stay a bit vague about the opening date. Let's just say we're opening at the end of the year, and tell them simply that we are beginning to put together our stock, starting with the classics."

"Go for it. So, paperbacks or no paperbacks? If we start buying, we'll have to decide."

They had often talked about it. Ivan didn't like paperbacks. Francesca liked nothing better.

"We need both," she said. "Hardbacks are to read at home, paperbacks for the train, or the beach."

She refused to give in.

"Well, all right," relented Van. "But in that case, why not have reference editions for the office? Like La Pléiade volumes and so on?"

"It's a deal," said Francesca. "For the most famous books, we'll have several editions. And for the others, the first edition and the paperback, whenever possible. We'll have plenty of room, and we may assume we'll have customers of all sorts, penniless, wealthy, scholarly, newly converted, obsessive . . ."

The renovation work was almost finished. Nearly two-thirds of the space on the ground floor had been redecorated. They had not yet decided how to use the rest. It could be put to use if The Good Novel expanded. In the meanwhile, Francesca figured that they could make a small conference room: there might be requests for readings or presentations. Unless they kept the remaining third for a stock room. They would see.

The bookstore was very attractive and seemed enormous without the books. In the beginning it might even seem too big for the four or five thousand volumes they had planned, so benches had been installed along two of the walls. A large fig tree in a pot filled one corner. Francesca had ordered some magnificent tables from a young cabinetmaker who, for several years, had been working in squares—square bases, multiple squares, rectangles resulting from two squares put together, four squares forming another square. Squares, not cubes, insisted the young man, in a fundamentalist tone of voice.

"Tables, tables," objected Van. "And what are we supposed to put on them? In ordinary bookstores, they put the new books on tables: the regular stock is on the shelves, against the wall. But we are not going to have very many new titles."

Francesca had thought about this.

"I suggest we put our favorites on the tables, yours and mine. Whether they're ten or a hundred years old, or whether they've just come out."

"But, by definition, all the books at the store will be our favorites."

"But not necessarily all the same. Among your favorite books, there are some I prefer to others. And you know what it's like with fads, things come and go. We'll rotate the books on the tables."

Van began to send in orders to the publishers. Books arrived. To Francesca, each box seemed like a present.

The six months which preceded the opening of the bookstore would remain, in their memory, a sort of long springtime. Everything seemed simple, happy, strong and necessary, bound to become superb.

"I see," said Heffner unexpectedly, in a tone that made you think he was talking to himself. "One of those springtimes you have only once or twice in your life."

19

V an was growing attached to his studio on the rue de l'Agent-Bailly. He could not imagine living anywhere else in Paris. By the bay window he placed the first piece of furniture he had ever bought in his life, an armchair of an uncertain age, with such wide armrests that there was room not only for your elbows but also enough sustenance for several hours, five or six books on either side.

The knowledge that, in all likelihood, he was living in a place where there had been a great deal of drawing and painting going on gave Van an idea, somewhat in the manner of stubborn lingering traces of turpentine that eventually go to your head. He wanted to paint a décor on the two walls of the studio that had neither windows nor doors, and which happened to be contiguous and therefore would allow him to create a painting that could continue from one wall to the next, fifteen feet long and six feet high, roughly.

He had reached this stage of his project—it was not even conception, let's call it the conception of the conception— when he got a reply from Anis.

It was in May, 1901. Officer Gaston Bailly was on guard duty outside the National Assembly when a crowd of people suddenly rushing onto the bridge near the Concorde incited him to leave his post. A young girl has jumped in the water! shouted the onlookers. By temperament or conviction, Bailly was the sort who would think, that's her choice. But the crowd was of a different opinion. We have to get her out of there! they cried. Jump, officer. Bailly was a reasonable man, he did not hurry. Where is she? he asked. I don't see her. Jump, jump! shouted the crowd, not answering his question. The desperate woman was no longer to be seen, already drowned or carried away. Bailly placed his kepi on the parapet, held his nose, and jumped. The water was freezing, and he was not a good swimmer. Only with difficulty did he reach solid ground, five hundred yards from the bridge, at the port des Invalides. The crowd was already there, waiting for him. They were pleased. He's a hero, they said. Hot coffee, blankets.

Officer Bailly received a medal and had a street named after him, and never knew who the young woman was to whom he owed them, nor why she had jumped. He dreamt of her so often, that he eventually sank into melancholy, and no doubt through some sort of sympathy, he was pulled under. He spent the thirty remaining years of his life in the asylum of Sainte-Anne, with a sad smile and a drowned gaze.

To end her letter, all Anis had written, above her signature was, "Yours." Van read it as an invitation to accept or reject her story, and he answered right away.

Anis, your trust in humanity is touching and worrying. Your version of the facts does not work. How could you think that Officer Gaston B. would be celebrated simply for having tried to save a woman from drowning? If he survived the failure of his attempt, the crowd would have heckled him. I expressed myself poorly in my letter. Officer B. is remembered by posterity because he died in vain attempting to assist a desperate woman. It is their wedding of death that moved their contemporaries; it is because he died with his arms around her, struggling to save her, and they sank together.

And it suddenly occurred to me: posterity remembers nothing about the young woman, which is a bit unfair if you consider that if it were not for her, Gaston Bailly would also be forgotten. Anis, you have just shown me the way to remedy the injustice. Thanks to you I have found the way to honor Officer Bailly for-ever, as well as the drowned woman, whom I shall now remove from her anonymity. I am going to paint their beautiful sad story on the walls of my room. I see green, black.

Your turn. Give me, if you will, the name, age, and any other information about the young woman. And come to see, if your heart so moves you, my tribute to Gaston Bailly and the undine of his life.

Van got to work right away. He would get up early every day and work on his painting for an hour or two.

He began by pinning huge sheets of paper on the wall. His idea was to paint the story in three views: the young woman jumps, the officer jumps in turn, urged on by the crowd, the young woman and the officer drown with their arms around each other. Van was not very good at drawing, but he had painted from time to time, and he was told he had a sense of color. He decided to devote a large part of the picture to the surroundings—the banks of the Seine, the buildings, the river, which he would paint green—and to represent the final moments of Officer Bailly on a very small scale.

Within a week he had completed the preparatory drawing on paper. Van removed the big sheets from the wall, which he covered with the necessary coating. He copied the sketch out with a charcoal crayon. Then he bought his paint, black and white for the grays, yellow and blue for the greens, a little bit of Sienna for the officer's mustache, and carmine for the lips of the desperate woman, and he began to paint.

Anis's reply arrived very quickly this time.

The young woman Gaston Bailly might have saved? Yes, I've found some information on her.

She was twenty when their paths crossed. That year, she was devoting most of her energy to trying to extricate herself from a childhood in Belgium which, frankly speaking, had not been a gentle one, in a milieu of very small farmers who were being driven off their land. The familiar refrain: the stepfather who stank, the mother who did not work and lived vicariously through the photo romances she read and where, among other matter for daydreaming, she had found a fussy name for her only daughter.

Said daughter, at the age of fifteen, found a suitable nickname and, at the age of eighteen, went away as far as possible, using as a pretext the fact that university studies were free in France. She landed by chance in Grenoble where, through a process of elimination, because she was neither of a literary nor a scientific bent, she enrolled in sociology. She was living on a scholarship so modest that once she had paid for her garret room, the university cafeteria, and a few reams of paper, she could not afford anything extra, neither clothes nor theatre nor movie tickets, let alone skiing lessons in the mountains around Grenoble. She didn't mind such hardship. She had never been so happy. She could breathe. Every moment she felt the euphoric joy of being whole, autonomous, with everything there for her to learn, to read, and her life ahead of her, her body which asked for nothing other than to be amused, her hair flowing freely down her back and a terrible hunger several times a day. Not to mention that it turned out she had a sincere interest in sociology.

She had friends, comrades, young people from comfortable families actually, or at least normal families, who could not even conceive that someone in their midst could really live with as little money as she had. One feature they had in common astonished her: not one of them, it would seem, tried to find out more about her than she was prepared to reveal: the fact that she was fresh, even-tempered, and always willing to share with her fel-

low students who did not attend class or go to the library the notes she took in class or when reading.

But there was a certain charm to her lightheartedness. The young woman discovered that there are friendships that require nothing of one but which have their purpose all the same. For example, without even trying, she had found herself among a bunch of friends who often went skiing in the neighboring resorts, with a preference for Méribel. She was delighted to get out of Grenoble, but she had never skied. She invented an aversion for sports in general and skiing in particular, and a passion for sitting reading at the back of a café—and gradually this became reality. And her bunch of friends could hardly fault her for it. One of the good skiers in the group, a certain Antoine, even told her sometimes that he admired her free spirit, the way she was able to resist the obligation to go skiing in the resorts.

Perhaps it was rather silly, but it was infinitely preferable to any Whys or How can yous.

One day after she had been reading all day like that in a café in the resort, and had finished earlier than planned a long South African novel she had borrowed from the library—and for good reason; she was so bored, at the end she was only skimming— she went to kill some time at a sort of local newsagents' next door to the café. In the basement, she discovered a bookstore of unimaginable variety, and in this treasure cave, the pure masterpiece of a novel by a début author whose name she was not about to forget, Noëlle Revaz. She read the book in one go, then, raising her eyes, adrift, she saw the bookseller was watching her with a smile of complicity. She apologized. As did the bookseller, for the fact that she might have thought he found something reprehensible about her behavior. They conversed with a rare ease and pleasure.

She had to meet her student friends at the car at five, and said goodbye. She would have liked for the bookseller to ask to see her again. But no, he let her leave without saying anything like that.

Two months or so went by before she went back up to Méribel. For three hours she hesitated, then finally she went back to the bookstore. The bookseller greeted her with a joy that seemed authentic, but then told her immediately that he was leaving the Alps the very next day to go and settle in Paris.

She was able to arrange a meeting for an hour the next day, upon his departure, since he had to go through Grenoble. And so they did meet, indeed, and it was more like two hours than one. In his mind, the bookseller had already left. He had just met a fairy godmother who was offering him the dream of a lifetime, that of running a bookstore in Paris, where only masterpieces would be sold. He had had dinner with her seven days in a row, and this woman, he said, was supremely beautiful, aristocratic, sensitive—in short, an exceptional creature of the kind you only see in films.

A month went by before she received word from him. All he could find to write was a few lines about a woman, a century earlier, who had drowned because of a man who was in no particular hurry to rescue her, a man who subsequently left his name to the street to which the bookseller had moved.

The student had shivers down her spine. She let a few days go by, the time to let the hurt subside, then she replied in a letter which she sought to make crystal-clear. She implied in her letter that one can also, inadvertently, let slip an opportunity to love.

The bookseller replied with a note that showed he had not grasped her allusion at all. He returned to the story of the drowning, adding complacently that the man who hadn't given a damn about trying to bring the unfortunate woman back to life had also drowned. The student read between the lines: that is what is beautiful. Indeed, the bookseller informed her that he was going to paint the story on the walls of his room, that he would use a lot of green, and gloomy colors. Worse than that (how is this possible?), he was inviting the young woman to fuel his inspiration by telling him the story of the drowned woman, and coming to see his painting. In Grenoble, the abandoned girl spent a sleepless night. She could detect, in the bookseller, a penchant for anything unfinished, in the realm of love, a preference for rough drafts. With a final burst of energy, she wrote his rough draft for him.

Your turn?

Anis

When Van got home one evening and read this letter, it was half past midnight. He went slowly up the stairs, reading more and more quickly. Once he reached the fourth floor, he folded up the letter and continued on his way four steps at a time. As soon as he got into the studio, he reached for the telephone, without even closing the door. He did not know Anis's number. He tried desperately to find it, exhausting the telecom employee who, after repeating to him ten times that he could find no one by that name in Grenoble, eventually hung up.

Van went back out of his building in a whirlwind and, still at a run, searched the neighborhood for his car; he hadn't used it since he arrived in Paris. He went round and round for half an hour, on the verge of tears of rage, and eventually came upon the jalopy by chance, in a dead-end street around the corner from his house.

It took him six hours to get to Grenoble, and he arrived before dawn. That was what he intended. He climbed the steps up to Anis's garret, then curled up on the doormat outside her door and, contrary to all expectations, fell asleep.

When Anis opened her door at a quarter past eight and saw him, she stood still for a few moments, then climbed over him without waking him up. There must be a patron saint for those countless lovers who do not know what they want—a little saint, from among the lowest-ranking in the crowd of the blessed, little-known but very busy, and working for himself, by definition. Van was roused from his sleep by a noise that grew gradually fainter as it went down the stairs. Anis was able to keep her heels from striking the steps, but she could not hold back the huge sobs that were shaking her body. Van hurried down the stairs, nearly came to grief on two occasions, but when he got to the entrance of the building, there was no one there. He hurried outside and saw Anis at the end of the street, springing away like an escaped prisoner, her books and binders in her arms, her raincoat flying open. He caught up with her, embraced her, almost knocked her over and nearly fell himself, causing her books and binders to go flying. She was in tears. If they both broke their neck, that would not be so very different from drowning, she hiccupped, turning her head away to avoid his kisses.

How do I know these details? Van often related the episode to me, beating his breast every time and berating his own blindness, his clumsiness, his selfishness.

Anis stepped back. He picked up her books and wiped them off.

"I have to go," she declared, taking her books.

"I'll come with you," he said.

"Leave me alone," she moaned.

"Only if you tell me where and how I can find you during the day."

She seemed to be caught in a trap.

"I don't know," she mumbled.

"Back here, at four o'clock?" ventured Van.

"Okay, then," she said in one breath.

"I won't move from here!" he shouted, watching her as she walked away in a zigzag, without turning back.

He was trembling. It's the cold, he decided, but he wasn't fooled. He had said he would not move, but he had to react. Across the street, the employee of a little hotel was emptying a bucket of water onto the pavement just to the right of the entrance.

Van took a room, explained that he was going to sleep, and asked them to wake him up at three o'clock in the afternoon, without fail. He threw himself fully clothed onto the bed. When the ringing of the telephone roused him from sleep, his plan of action for the hour that was about to begin sprang to mind at exactly the spot where he had paused it the second he fell asleep: take a shower, send a fax to Francesca from the hotel, telling her roughly, "I've been called four hundred miles away by an urgent need for clarification and action, I'll be back," grab a bit to eat, and finally, find a bouquet of knock-out flowers—when a sudden thought froze him in his tracks. Anis could very easily not come back. She could hide somewhere—at that ridiculous Antoine's place, for example—the time it took to find another room, and she would never reappear. She could even go and live at Antoine's. Van would never find her.

He spent the hour leading up to their appointment in a state of terrible anxiety. He kept assiduously to his plan, except that something made him give up on the idea of the flowers: something like the idea that you don't pop the cork on the champagne before the victory.

At ten minutes to four, he went to stand on the sidewalk at the very spot where he had caught up with Anis that morning. At five minutes past four, he was all alone, moaning to himself among the pedestrians going to and fro. He shoved his hands in his pockets to keep from slapping his own face.

At seven minutes past four, Anis arrived, looking even more lost than he did.

"Hello," said Van, like a fifteen-year-old boy.

"Hello again."

"Would you like some mulled wine?"

"A tea, rather."

No alcohol, translated Ivan. No excitement, no dream. No laughter, no plans.

They went into the nearest café. Van felt as if he had made a huge leap backwards and this was his first meeting with Anis.

"You smile at me, I invite you," he said, "you turn me down. I try not to think about you too much, you contact me again, and it's to say: no, still nothing. I'm finding it hard to understand."

"And do you think," said Anis, rocking the upper part of her body nervously, "do you think I understand everything?"

They spoke for a quarter of an hour that seemed like an hour, without even touching fingertips.

"Okay?" asked Anis eventually, getting to her feet.

"Okay for everything," said Van also standing up. "For what you want. Whatever you want."

"Well then," said Anis, "sit back down. Let me leave. I promised you I wouldn't move. You wait for five minutes and then you drive off again."

She pressed on his shoulder to make him sit back down, and placed a childlike kiss on his cheek.

"See you tomorrow," said Van.

"See you tomorrow."

Five minutes later, Van was headed toward Paris. No matter how he had begged, describing the mural fifteen times or more, the way he saw it now—the young woman falls from the bridge, the officer jumps and catches her in flight before she touches the water, and the two of them fly away together above the roofs—Anis had not wanted to leave with him.

"Is your degree more important than everything?" he asked rebelliously.

When he saw Anis's expression of pale incomprehension, he backtracked.

"Of course your studies are important. Very important. They are. But you can, well, study somewhere other than Grenoble."

"I'm enrolled here."

"I get it," said Van, changing tack. "I'll get a room in Grenoble. I don't want to lose you."

Anis said straight out: "If you drop The Good Novel, I won't speak to you again."

She too had to get back to work. She had a whole series of midterms in April.

Ivan would not have left if she had not made two promises for the future: to call him by phone morning and evening, by means of a little cell phone he had given her; and to move to Paris herself as soon as possible.

"As possible," she emphasized. "I have to finish my year. After that, I would still have to find a room in the Latin Quarter, and I know that's not easy."

"The 9th arrondissement is so much better," suggested Van. "Not to mention that it's almost in the Latin Quarter, the New Athens. And in the 9th, I can find you a roof right away."

In vain. Anis would not budge. She agreed that Latin Quarter did not mean a great deal and could refer to a larger area in general, but never mind, she would enroll at the Sorbonne for her Master's, and she wanted to be able to walk there, she would live on the Left Bank, in the 5th or the 14th, or the 13th at a push.

20

The six remaining lists arrived throughout the month of April. Ivan and Francesca met the six electors one after the other. They saw Larry de Winter and Gilles Évohé —whom Van had met in February—in Paris, as well as Marie Noir. Paul Néant, Armel Le Gall, and Ida Messmer preferred to have them come out to them *en province*.

Larry de Winter was tall, thin, and gracious; you could have sworn he was an aging dancer. He had been a diplomat and knew literature from all over the world, with a preference for the least known.

"Maybe I'll win the prize for the most unexpected list," he said. "Let me beg you in advance to forgive me for the trouble you're bound to have tracking down some of the titles— Indonesian or Nigerian, for example. I must confess, however, that to my astonishment I put far more French authors on the list than I thought I would when I started out. I'm not being biased, believe me. But there are some young French authors who are extremely gifted."

He had suggested to Francesca and Van that they come to his house, on the rue de Beaune. In his little apartment, everything was just as he was, on first glance classical, but in fact, unexpected, so they told me later on, with his 1950s furniture, his books with Art Deco bindings, his enigmatic curios, his English-style full-length portrait of a gentleman in a park, who resembled him in every feature.

When de Winter saw that Van had noticed the resemblance, he spread his hands, the way one does to show that one has nothing.

"A few mementoes I've inherited from my mother. She had incredible taste, and money from her banker family. She was deported in 1943. I was nine. I had already been in boarding school in Switzerland for two years."

He spoke the way he wrote, a very precious French, precious in the sense that a fine jeweler might use—extreme rigor in the choice of materials, color, shine, the interplay of shapes and juxtapositions, extreme precision in the cut, intense dislike of ostentation. Van and Francesca could have listened to him for hours. He alluded to the print runs of his books that remained poor because his publisher simply expected correspondingly poor sales.

"But we don't care about that, do we?" declared Francesca eagerly.

Winter gave her a lovely smile.

"I have never dreamt of either success or money. I don't think about it. It is elegance that interests me. I mean elegance in the broadest sense—intellectual, moral, physical, elegance in one's relations with other people . . . I was sixteen years old when I heard a quote on the radio by the painter Martini, a quote that left its mark on me for life. Simone Martini said that his aim was to attain 'perfect elegance'—or was it the commentator who said that Martini was aiming for 'perfect elegance'? Either way, the two words went straight to my soul. They expressed exactly what I aspired to, without knowing how to describe it. I too wanted to aim for perfect elegance, in life and, of course, if possible, in art. With such a purpose in life, the goals of success and money, obviously, become relative: they belong, rather, to the things one must avoid."

He poured out a new round of aged, golden whiskey.

"Still on the subject of greed," he said, "a sort of degradation of literary morality is under way. It could well be that your project, in itself, simply by the light it will cast on the arena of literature, will show how pathetic this drift is. What I'm referring to is the way that authors, nowadays, live for rivalry, going so far, I am told, as to write with the sole purpose of crushing their rivals. Literary prizes bear a large part of responsibility in this respect. Writing solely to outdo another writer—what a paltry ambition. Cultural creativity is beautiful and special because it offers a place to everyone. And to think there are people who would like to restrict it! They've made a covered market of literature, where a few best sellers take up all the room. By 'they' I mean the major publishers, the journalists who act like sheep, the wholesale distributors of culture. Ah, I much prefer the world of those who care for literature—mind, I did not say the old world, or the little world."

He had placed his list in a little cardboard binder, closed with a ribbon.

"A pseudonym?" He raised one eyebrow higher than the other. "I forgot to think of one. Choose what you like, apart from Summer, a nickname that spoiled my high school years."

"Balanchine?" suggested Ivan.

"I'd prefer the opposite, a name that might make you think of Brezhnev, or Francis Blanche. What about Magot? Call me Le Magot. It's an Intelligence Service sort of name, it will remind me of my years at the Quai d'Orsay."

Gilles Évohé got around by bike. "Whatever the weather, thanks to my diving suit," he said, after climbing off his bike in front of Francesca, who was sitting on a bench by the banks of the Canal Saint-Martin, where he had suggested they meet. While talking, he was pulling off a sort of bronze-green overall.

"Actually—" He stood stock still. "I actually had no idea for a pseudonym, but that's just given me one. Scaph."

"Very good," said Ivan and Francesca.

"With a ph or an f?" asked Francesca.

"With an f," amended Évohé. "That's better, Scaf it is."

Short, brown-haired, nervous, he looked like Michel Rocard. His short stories and novels, on the other hand, were like those of Alexandre Vialatte. Évohé was his real name. He had worked for forty years at the CNRS as a researcher in mathematics. His specialty: corner variables, he said. Very amusing stuff. He hadn't come up with much, he added, with a note of forced cheerfulness.

He was very enthusiastic about the idea of The Good Novel. Did he have a cell phone? He did, yes, why? Really? If he had something to say, he would prefer to stop off at the bookstore. It wasn't far by bike. No? That wasn't a good idea?

Van and Francesca walked by his side for over an hour, along the Canal Saint-Martin, from République to the Place de Stalingrad and back. When they left him, they had been won over by his vitality, full of hope. Francesca did not understand what suddenly came over Ivan at that moment, for he turned around and ran after Scaf, who was already on his bicycle. She saw him come back waving in his hand a yellow and red plastic bag with the name "Nicolas" visible from far away. The list, he explained. He forgot to give it to us.

Marie Noir was a soft, round woman who, visibly, had remained faithful to the clothing style of her twenties, concluded Ivan, identifying the hand-woven alpaca poncho, the natural leather sandals burnished by age, the Indian cotton shoulder bag, and the braid down her back, now salt-and-pepper: he recognized them with a certain emotion, and a feeling of complicity. Like Francesca, he knew that Marie Noir was an authority on a pre-Columbian art, and he listened with amazement as she spoke, her eyes shining, about fair-trade jam and the incomparable vegetables you could find thanks to the Association for the Support of Peasant Farming. For Marie Noir's novels, while they had their moments of pure splendor, were dark as stone, filled with a cynicism that nothing tempered, not even the childish figure of an angel, silently present in a different form at the end of each of her novels, where they were invariably sacrificed.

"A pseudonym? Quinoa," she said.

"That's nice," ventured Francesca, unsure if it was a type of prehistoric kitchen knife or a funerary musical instrument.

"Above all it's good, and healthy," said Marie, "and no more difficult to prepare than rice. One of my favorite books is a little masterpiece from the sixties entitled *A Thousand Types of Rice, a Thousand Recipes with Rice.* In a manner of speaking, a thousand. You learn that rice comes in all shapes and colors, and there is an infinite variety of ways to prepare it. In a Bengalese novel that I love, *The Night on the Shore*, the author devotes twelve pages to a description of the preparation of a traditional rice dish for weddings. It's an unforgettable passage."

By the looks of it, this woman maintained no hierarchy of pleasures. Perhaps she did not even make any distinctions among them. The rules of the game imposed on the committee members seemed to amuse her—clandestinity, secrets, dispossession.

"And what about new books?" she asked. "All the books that come out in the future? Who will select them?"

Van explained the option they had chosen with Francesca: complete indifference to the fact whether a novel was new or not.

"We'll leave the new books to other bookstores," he said. "In this respect at least, our competitors should look upon us kindly. After the fact, of course, we will include the new novels that seem to deserve it. I think I already told you, our electors will be asked to add to their initial selection every year. At the time of the yearly addition we can include recent books, ones that are almost new."

Marie Noir did not agree: "Imagine some wonderful book comes out in the fall and goes unnoticed. It happens every year: one or two or sometimes three remarkable novels are buried in silence and go to the bottom of the pile. Maybe you think that doesn't matter and it's enough to go and get them from the bottom of the pile eighteen months later. I think it would be better, for the book and for the author, and for the reader, if you had these books in stock as soon as they came out."

"Who could make the selection that quickly?"

"You two. That selection is the job of the bookstore, after all. I would even go so far as to say that, in line with your intuition, it is at the heart of the bookseller's profession. And if you really want to, you could always have your additional choices approved by the committee."

Van and Francesca talked about the issue for a long time. Francesca would have liked, to a greater or lesser degree, for the public image of the store to be: at The Good Novel, you don't go looking for the books that everyone is talking about. She would not have been opposed to a fairly strict principle, something like: none of the novels in our shop are less than a year old. "I grew up loving books," she said, "guided by a passionate reader. But in his house, and in my own, I don't recall ever seeing any new titles."

Van, on the contrary, could see Marie Noir's point. The idea that they might miss out on a worthy book, and fail to support it, bothered him.

"Particularly nowadays, where the fate of a book is decided in the space of the few weeks following its publication. And when you know that a bookseller who really loves a novel can sell five hundred or a thousand copies."

But he knew better than Francesca the price to pay.

"If we plan to choose books from among all the new ones as they come out in the fall, practically speaking that means we have to tell the publishers in May or June that we are going to open in September; we will have to hide our decision to refuse their automatic shipment of new books, we will have to get all their fall catalogues, and a maximum number of ARCs or uncorrected proofs, and read all summer long. That is what I did in Méribel for years: read five or six hundred books, and in the end keep only ten of them."

"There are two of us," said Francesca. "We could each read three hundred books."

"Let's be honest, we can make a serious selection without relying on all the books from A to Z. For 80 percent of them, reading the first twenty pages will suffice. Regular book browsers know it well: what else are they doing, when they're browsing? The remaining 20 percent will have to be read carefully. That leaves only one hundred and twenty titles to be shared. Francesca, you just referred to the love of books that was handed down to you. Were you referring to your grandfather? You were going to tell me more about him."

"My grandfather Aldo-Valbelli is the man who has counted the most in my life. I would have preferred it if someone else could have taken his place. But that's the way things are. My love for him is boundless, and he made me who I am.

"Certain reputations don't cross borders, even between countries as close as Italy and France: that was the case for him. In Italy, he had a great deal of prestige, both as an intellectual and as a militant. He was a famous historian to begin with, one of those people who are erudite in a way people were in ancient times, of the sort you find only in Italy nowadays, as eminent in philosophy as they are in letters and science. His work as a historian is what made him known. But for me, and I am not alone, his novels are just as remarkable. But his prestige as a great man is something he owes to his involvement with his time. He was one of the first opponents of Fascism, one of the most courageous. And he paid the price. He was persecuted, really persecuted, and his academic career was threatened. He ran an entire clandestine network during the war. When peace returned, almost in spite of himself he was granted great moral authority as a senator, and he served several times as a minister—in short he was one of the founders of modern Italy. When he resigned from all his political mandates in order to return to his work as an intellectual he was still young, and he embarked on a third chapter of his life that was long, since he lived to the age of eighty-seven."

"Were you close to him?"

"I was twenty when he died. Yes, we were close, the two of us. We did not live together, but we weren't far away, he was on the second floor, and my parents and I were on the third in the same house in Rome. My parents did nothing but travel. He was working like mad. At the end of his life, when I was a teenager, he no longer left his office.

"He had a remarkable library—not huge, he was not a bibliophile, and I can still hear him saying, There are not so many brilliant books in the end, don't believe everything you hear. That must have had something to do with the genesis of The Good Novel.

"He gave me novels, sometimes just after he had discovered them himself (he wasn't the type to hide the fact that, despite his age, he had just read for the first time books as well-known as *La Duchesse de Langeais* or *Jean Santeuil*), a lot of foreign novels, all the classics, but also some novels that no one reads. I liked to talk with him about our reading. He let me take the initiative. He would never say: Well, what did you think of that book? If he happened to leave Rome, then he would write me long letters, exactly as if he were writing to a cultured friend his own age.

"He left me his entire library in an article in his will; I learned after his death that he had decided this on the day I turned ten. Nothing was removed from the collection. I created a foundation. The palazzo, with the library, is now a little research center.

"My grandfather left me a great deal more—a passion for literature, and something additional, fundamental: the conviction that literature is important. He talked about it often. Literature is a source of pleasure, he said, it is one of the rare inexhaustible joys in life, but it's not only that. It must not be dissociated from reality. Everything is there. That is why I never use the word fiction. Every subtlety in life is material for a book. He insisted on the fact. Have you noticed, he'd say, that I'm talking about novels? Novels don't contain only exceptional situations, life or death choices, or major ordeals; there are also everyday difficulties, temptations, ordinary disappointments; and, in response, every human attitude, every type of behavior, from the finest to the most wretched. There are books where, as you read, you wonder: What would I have done? It's a question you have to ask yourself. Listen carefully: it is a way to learn to live. There are grown-ups who will say no, that literature is not life, that novels teach you nothing. They are wrong. Literature informs, instructs, it prepares you for life."

Francesca fell silent. She was moved.

"You told me one day that your grandfather had spoken to you . . . from the beyond," said Ivan softly.

She nodded.

"He pulled me out of my depression, five years ago. And brought a soft golden rain down upon me."

Upon the death of her daughter, she had desperately invoked the old man, suffering from his absence even more than she had ten years earlier, when he had passed away. She sought by every means possible to speak with him, to get help from him, to hold tight to his strong, old hand as she went through hell.

The simplest way turned out to be also the only activity that might possibly ease her suffering: she decided to read the manuscripts her grandfather had left to her. Shyness, modesty, anxiety: until then she had never opened the cardboard boxes, carefully filed and put away for her. She discovered notes, projects for books that her grandfather had abandoned—he explained why—drafts, thousands of letters, and a journal consisting of one hundred and eleven notebooks of identical format.

The journal covered sixty-three years, from 1914 to 1977. It was characterized by such precision and depth that it constituted an extraordinary history of the period in Italy. The notebooks for the period 1939 to 1945 in particular could be read like a great novel—the maquis, the campaign for Italy, the end of Fascism.

Francesca herself transcribed the entire journal. The Milanese publisher to whom she sent a thousand pages or more published them enthusiastically.

"That was nearly four years ago," said Francesca. "It was quite a success. They sold over a million copies. There were slews of articles. It has already been translated into twenty languages."

There had been talk of it in France, Van remembered now.

For the first time in her life, Francesca had money. Van asked her to repeat what she had just said.

"I had never had any income of my own," she explained. "It's one thing to have two or three houses, another to be married to a man who makes a good living, and yet another, very different thing, to suddenly earn a lot of money yourself.

"I suddenly had an idea that would not leave me: do something with that money. An obsession: do something worthwhile. I'm repeating myself, forgive me, I have no other words for it. I had that big space on the rue Dupuytren, so I converted it into the gallery. You remember the rest. Death interfered with the project."

She looked at Ivan: "A bookstore is better. It's more in keeping with the man himself and his life as a patron of the arts."

She pointed to the heavens.

21

Paul Néant had suggested they meet in Chambéry at a café near the station, La Chartreuse. It had been raining since morning; on the train, Francesca had been reading a small book with a gray cover and what seemed to be very fine laid paper. Van, from his seat opposite her, noticed that the book was entitled *L'Eclair,* but that there was no author's name.

"What is it?" he asked Francesca, at a point where she had interrupted her reading and was looking distractedly out the window at the Burgundian landscape.

"You don't know it?"

She handed the small volume to Van.

"You are about to read the most beautiful love story that I know in French."

"Not until you've finished it," said Ivan.

"I know this book by heart! I read it several times a year."

"Who is it by?"

Francesca showed him, on the title page, two initials in the place of the author's name.

"P.N.!" Van was surprised. "You say it's a love story? I thought I had read all his books. There is always desire, the thousands of forms desire can take, from the most luminous to the darkest but, as far as I know, there is no mention of love in any of them."

"This book talks of nothing but love," said Francesca. "A love with neither hearth nor home, without a name, without a future, without a witness. It is the story of a man who is crazy about a woman—a mature man, a very young girl, who disappears one day. The story of the man's long struggle with his passion, when he does not understand, and knows nothing, and waits for years. I won't tell you the end, here, read it. This was Paul Néant's first book. Even if he had never written another line, he would not have lived in vain."

"No one ever lives in vain, Francesca," said Ivan.

Francesca looked away, out the window streaked horizontally with the pouring rain, whipped by speed.

The train arrived late in Chambéry. Néant did not get up from his chair when he saw Van and Francesca. He was not in a normal state. Van pretended not to notice, and spoke to him as if nothing were the matter. Not wasting a moment in prevaricating, he got the list from him—a schoolboy's notebook— his pseudonym—Brother Brandy, and another appointment. Eight days from now, mumbled Néant with difficulty. Same place. I'm here every Wednesday.

Francesca remained silent. Néant had not looked at her even once. Didn't sleep all night, he said in the end, swallowing his words, as if to excuse himself, when Van looked at his watch and asked Francesca if she wanted to drink something before it was time to leave again.

"And me," murmured Francesca, "do you think I sleep, at night? For six years, I have never slept more than one or two hours uninterrupted."

But she wasn't saying that for Néant's sake, and she looked at her hands under the table. Nor was she speaking to Ivan who, at that moment, had his eyes on her, waiting for her answer and, seeing the ravaged expression on her face, understood that she had not heard his question.

The second meeting was different. Ivan went alone. Paul was sober. And apologized, soberly. They agreed on the absolute need for discretion, on what would be the best way to communicate, and on the caution which meant they must destroy any written traces of their dealings. "Other than your list," said Van, "which we will ask you to enrich every year in the future. Be careful. Find a hiding place. Don't write anything on it that might lead to The Good Novel."

In comparison, the round-trip Paris-Saint-Brieuc was a delightful outing. The weather was fine that day, a turquoise breeze, a sky freshly washed. Le Gall had asked Francesca and Van to meet him at a fish restaurant in the port.

He had initially invited them to his home, for a simple home-cooked meal.

"That's impossible," Van had been forced to say. "It is out of the question for your wife to join us, and we cannot tell her why."

"Maïté spends more time down on the shore than at home, but you're right," Le Gall eventually agreed. "She decides how to spend her time, and often at the last minute. Let's meet somewhere besides Ploulec'h. That way I won't have to tell fibs about you. I'm a very bad liar."

They shared a dish of young turbot steamed in seaweed vapor.

"There are good things about secrets," Le Gall pointed out. "At home, we would have eaten coalfish poached in broth, with boiled potatoes."

He was happy as a boy to be associated with the founding of The Good Novel. He swore not to mention it to anyone, not even Maïté, who would have been delighted. He had his list.

"Quite a few Scandinavians," he announced, pulling a gray-blue envelope from his pocket, "Americans, Chileans, a bit of everything in fact, French writers too, you'll see. Six hundred, that was tough. You get there very quickly. I had to limit myself."

He suggested Ballon d'Alsace as a pen name. "Just to get any snoops off the track," he said in an accent that suddenly sounded Germanic to Francesca until she realized it was a Breton accent.

There was one thing that worried him, all the same.

"It can't be all that straightforward to suddenly set yourself up as a bookseller," he said as gently as possible.

Van apologized for not having told him anything about his past career, and reassured him: "I do have a certain amount of experience in the business, and I know the pitfalls of the profession, so that will help me. I know exactly what I no longer want to do."

"Van's not telling you everything," added Francesca. "He already had an ideal bookstore, not so long ago."

"This might seem awkward to you," Le Gall said slowly. "Forgive me. I don't know how to put it. I don't have a great deal of money, but . . ."

In short, he wanted to invest in the business. Francesca did not rule it out: "Someday, who knows? For the next eight or ten years, the funding has been taken care of. But this is an adventure, and maybe down the road we'll be glad to be able to count on you."

When Ida Messmer called Van, she told him that the easiest thing for her (she did not say why) would be to give them her list at Montsoreau. Yes, at the château of Dumas's *La Dame de Montsoreau*. "There's a little terrace, all the way at the top. Let's meet there, you'll have no trouble finding it. And you won't regret coming all the way."

Van and Francesca drove there in Van's jalopy. The closer they came to Montsoreau, along the road following the Loire, the less they spoke, captivated by the beauty of their surroundings.

They reached the terrace twenty minutes before the appointed time. It was indeed a remarkable location, like a crow's nest in the wind, overlooking the confluence of the Vienne and the Loire rivers. The weather was icy cold, the sky a hard blue streaked with the flights of wild birds. The water glittered among the brown forests.

At the appointed time, Francesca and Ivan saw a sudden apparition in the light. Van has described it to me at least ten times, and he is always moved. You have to imagine the most tender of creatures in the blonde-beauty category: a little girl's windswept curls framing a tiny pink and white face. And an adolescent's body wearing the usual outfit: tight jeans, a jacket, big clumpy shoes.

She had her list, rolled up in her hand, and she showed it to him without handing it to him right away. There was a pseudonym, Strait-laced, and a constant worry—that was the expression she used. She worried that despite the double screen of her borrowed name and her pen name—which was how she was known—someone might still manage to discover her true identity.

"It's a miracle thus far," she said, "but nobody knows, except for someone I will tell you about, who Ida Messmer *really* is. I took a risk by agreeing to meet you, a limited risk, because I'm not going to tell you my true identity, after all; but it's a necessary risk, because before I give you my list, I wanted to see who I'm dealing with. I'm weighing my words. Seeing you should tell me enough. Knowing is something else. I love your plan. I already told you, it's the stuff of my own dreams. I already admire you for wanting to go ahead with it. But it's a magnificent undertaking, you mustn't compromise it. And it is dangerous. Is your heart pure enough, since that is the crux of the matter, the question that is asked of the heroes of fairy tales before their trials begin?"

They spoke for an hour, the usual instructions about the telephone and the time frame, but also about what was at stake, risks, folly, reasons for living. No one came up to disturb their discussion.

"Right, I get it," the young woman said abruptly. "I see."

She fell silent. An anxious expression flickered on her face. The three of them stood in a corner of the terrace, overlooking the point where the two rivers met. The young woman stood up straight. She looked at Ivan and Francesca.

"I must ask you, I must beg you not to try to find out the true identity of the woman who writes under the name of Ida Messmer. She cannot run the risk of being identified. She would shatter into pieces, and Ida Messmer along with her. No one knows that she writes, and she writes for one person alone—to be exact she writes to someone, they're in a sort of world of their own, exclusive and precarious. If other people discovered their wavelength and came to interfere with their conversation, everything would come to a halt. If anyone were to find out that they are two in one, for the love of that other person, who means everything to each of those women—the woman who writes behind Ida Messmer's faceless mask and the real woman whom no one knows is a writer—they would both perish in the same instant."

"We promise," said Ivan.

Francesca repeated, "Promise."

The young woman handed her list to Francesca, a scroll attached with a short length of yarn.

"Well then, farewell," she said.

She asked to leave the terrace before them, and that they wait five minutes before leaving. Just before she vanished into the stairway, she turned around—her hair was dancing around her face—gave them a marvelous smile, and called out, "You do understand that I am not Ida Messmer? I mean, I am not the woman who writes under the name Ida Messmer."

And she disappeared.

Van and Francesca did not say a word, in the five minutes

that followed. They looked straight ahead, at the rivers meeting, with their islands, and the treetops where the first green of spring was quivering. They left the château without saying anything else.

"What do you think?" asked Francesca, once they were in the car, before they set off.

Van leaned back against his seat.

"I think we have met our match in terms of smoke screens," he said.

"Not so sure," said Francesca slowly. "Something makes me think that we were indeed dealing with the woman who writes what is published under the name of Ida Messmer."

"That would be even better."

"I get the impression there is more fragility than strength in the matter, more madness than mastery."

"That can all go together."

"Yes, but for how long? What frightens me is how disembodied it all seems—I'm serious—she scarcely weighs ninety pounds. That such a frail and tender girl could be so devoted to something you have to call a cult, to the point of walling herself up mentally, celebrating with so much violence—you know what she writes—there's something unbearable about it. I'd have great difficulty in explaining why. It's a bit as if she were walking on a wire between two skyscrapers blindfolded. The least little misstep, or mistake with her balancing pole, would be fatal: I mean mentally, something inside her would break."

"And now," said Heffner, "do you know who you saw at Montsoreau?"

Francesca looked at Van questioningly.

"We're getting there," said Van. "We're still only as far as April, 2004."

22

I van," said Francesca in the car, shortly after they had passed Tours, "we've agreed to transform the eight lists into one, without reading them. Now we have to decide who to entrust the typing to."

She had a plan.

"I'm not sure it will work. I'd like your opinion."

She was thinking of taking the eight originals to her notary and asking him to transcribe them into a single typewritten list, in alphabetical order by author's name, being careful not to omit any titles, and above all not to delete any of those that might turn up more than once.

"What you think? I don't see any risk. Each time an author gave us his or her list, we made sure that their names were not on the list. The entire list can stay on a computer hard drive, and can be passed around: it will never be anything other than the list of books you can find at The Good Novel."

"I see just one flaw," said Van. "The handwritten lists mustn't be photocopied behind our back, because somebody could, potentially, some day, identify the author through their handwriting."

"Indeed," said Francesca.

"There is one way around it," continued Van. "Before we take the eight lists to your notary, we could have them typed up, or retyped, one by one, at eight different typing agencies."

So one morning—it was already the beginning of May—

Ivan went around the typing agencies on the Boulevard Saint-Michel and the rue Saint-Jacques. He dropped off the lists one by one, and each time insisted that he was in a hurry, and he went back to pick them up one after the other before lunchtime.

That same afternoon, Francesca hand-delivered the eight lists, now all typed up, to her notary. "I could have typed the final list up myself," she said to Van, "but there was a risk I might recognize each of our eight electors by their choices."

She carefully explained to the notary, that if a same title showed up in all eight lists, it had to be typed eight times; it has to show up at eight times in the final list, on eight lines one after the other. By the same token, if the title was mentioned twice, three times, four times . . .

On her way back, she went by the bank to lock the eight original lists in her safe deposit box without looking at them. The next morning, the single list was ready. Without looking at it either, Francesca brought it to Van at the bookstore.

The list was one hundred and seventeen pages long. Two hundred and ninety-six titles had been mentioned eight times, three hundred and fifty-nine seven times, four hundred six times, four hundred and fifty-one five times, three hundred and seventy-eight four times, four hundred and fifty-two three times, four hundred and sixty-nine twice, and five hundred and four just once. Van picked up the pile of white sheets, and feverishly started organizing tables by country, author, title, and genre. He crossed things out, started over. In all, counting as one book the titles that had been mentioned several times, that came to three thousand, three hundred and nine titles. Novels represented 97 percent of the total, of which more than a third were French. There were some astonishing omissions. Only one Victor Hugo, only one Heinrich Böll. Nothing by Jules Vallès, or Joseph Delteil, or Evelyn Waugh, or Anna Maria Ortese.

Two books by John Berger, but not *Pig Earth*—and *Pig Earth* is a marvel, as Van has always told me.

"Is Pierre Bettencourt's *L'Intouchable* on the list?" asked Francesca worriedly.

"Vasily Grossman's *Life and Fate*," said Van, searching.

"All of McCarthy, I hope . . ."

"How many by Nicolas Bouvier?"

"*Be-Bop*, by Christian Gailly?"

Van abruptly put the list down on the coffee table, and pushed aside the papers covered with numbers.

"It's our turn now."

"You mean to correct the obvious omissions?"

"To fill in the gaps, yes."

"And what criteria should we use?"

"Only one, and you know it well, the only possible criterion: our innermost conviction that the book is worthy. It's simple. If it's obvious to you that *L'Intouchable* must be sold at The Good Novel, and it is not on the list, then you add it. Don't go looking for any guide other than your own discernment."

"That reminds me of Christian Dior's definition of taste."

"And what's that?"

"'To have taste, is to have mine.'"

"Precisely. But in our fashion house, there are ten designers, Christian Dior, but also Schiaparelli, Grès, Balenciaga, Givenchy, Saint Laurent, Lacroix, Gaultier . . ."

". . . and the two of us. How many additions should we allow ourselves?"

"It doesn't matter."

"We'll add them up after the fact. The logical thing is not to go beyond six hundred each."

"If you like."

"As a start."

"Francesca, it was a foregone conclusion: a certain number

of these titles are out of print. I've come up with almost one hundred and fifty. What shall we do?"

"Let's find them in a used edition. I imagine that's what you've been thinking yourself. Let's sell used books in addition to new ones. Is that a problem?"

"No. Except that used books are often more expensive than new ones."

"Do we have a choice?"

"I don't think so. At least not in the beginning. If we can get forgotten books back into circulation, we can't exclude the possibility that the same publishers who buried the books might look into reprinting them."

"That would be magnificent."

"I know an excellent network of used book dealers. I'll get in touch with them, and get them to find us those unobtainable books."

"It wakes me up at night," said Francesca. "God knows I sleep little enough as it is. I open my eyes, and I immediately know why. I switch on the light. I have a pad of paper on my night table. And last night, at three o'clock in the morning, I wrote down *Le Muet*."

"The what?"

"*Le Muet*, by Béatrix Beck. It's not on the list. *Léon Morin* has been mentioned three times. All the novels Béatrix Beck wrote about her double, the character she calls Barny, are on the list, except *Le Muet*. We have to have the entire cycle of Barny novels at The Good Novel. And *Don Juan des Forêts*, which comes after. And *L'enfant-chat*."

"Hello? Francesca? Listen to this. It's incredible. There is not a single book by Jean Rhys. I thought I was mistaken, I read the list over twice . . ."

"Van, for ten days we've been hunting for serious omissions. We're exhausted, let's stop. If this or that extraordinary book cannot be found at The Good Novel when we first open, we will apologize profusely, and order it. That's inevitable. The main thing is not to have *all* the good novels, but to have *only* good novels. And in this respect, we are extremely fortunate: our electors have not chosen anything we find subpar."

"What's wrong, Van? You're making a face."

"Nothing serious, just a little backache. I've been carrying too many boxes."

"September booksellers' syndrome . . . take a few days off. Please."

"Where we're lucky is that we'll only have this tidal wave of books once. We're filling up, and after that we can restock on request, in small quantities."

"And high quality."

"Need we be reminded?"

Francesca collapsed in an armchair.

"Maybe one of our electors should have been a foreigner . . . maybe we are too French."

"Less than half of our books are French. I thought there would be more. Francesca, the bookstore has only just started, it's going to expand. We'll add new titles all the time. Let's just open, to start with."

"I know what might reassure me. We've left one-third of the ground floor unused, and the basement is as it was. We should do something with all that. I'm going to start the next stage of remodeling without waiting."

"Personally, I think it would be really a good thing. I was just thinking about that, while gauging the exceptional quality of the stock we will have on offer, and dreaming that the service at The Good Novel will be equally exceptional. I could put those empty rooms to good use just as soon as we open the bookstore.

The great luxury, for a bookseller, is to have enough copies in stock of all the books on offer that you never run out. In general, that's impossible, because there's never enough room in the bookstore. But since we are lucky enough to have some space available, I really would like to order several copies of our books, at least the most famous titles. That way if we manage our stock well, we won't run out of things."

"You've just raised an issue that I hadn't thought of yet. What do you think we'll sell the most of, famous novels or the other ones?"

"I bet we sell the less famous ones. In all likelihood, our customers will be the sort who are passionate about novels and who've already read everything, that is, all the really well-known works."

"Tell me, Van. If you use the empty space for reserve stock, how can the bookstore expand?"

"Don't worry about that. Reserve stock stays in boxes, it can be piled up. One cellar will be enough. Maybe two."

"I'll calm down, Ivan. I'm going to calm down. Keep reminding me that we are not obliged to have everything on the shelf from the very first day."

"Francesca, as far as the bookstore is concerned, things are looking good. The store is magnificent, the books are irresistible. Our big problem is going to be closing in the evening, you know. The customers won't budge, they'll shout, Another hour! Some will just be impassive: Go ahead, close. I'll spend the night here, see you tomorrow! I am not at all worried about what we have on offer. If the bookstore were to open in two days, as far as I'm concerned we are ready. But on the other hand, it's time for us to look at our opening strategy. Thus far, we've only been thinking about secrecy. Now we have to think about the moment when we are going to go out into broad daylight. It's May, we have four months left."

"Let's stay in the shadow for the summer, Van. Let's set an

opening day in September—why not September 1? Everyone in Paris will be getting back to work. So we can make our entry with a bang."

"Even a bang needs preparing. You have to work on it. You need to put someone in charge, you need someone to light the fireworks, you need rehearsals."

"Van, as you know, my husband is in business. Every time I talk to him about The Good Novel, he has only one idea in mind, the launch. If there is one thing he is very skilled at, it is setting up businesses, and everything you need nowadays—marketing, advertising campaigns, business strategy. I don't know anything about all that. I listened to him thinking out loud there in front of me. He had me meet with some experts. But it's getting late. Aren't you hungry? Let's go have dinner, and I'll tell you my plan."

Ivan and Anis no longer wrote to each other, they telephoned. They talked a lot. They left even more messages.

The moment her alarm roused her from sleep, Anis heard her little cell phone ring. In fact, she used the cell phone as an alarm.

"It's seven o'clock," said Ivan. "I couldn't wait any longer."

"Just a second," interrupted Anis. "My alarm is ringing ten inches from my ear. I can't hear you."

Ivan wanted to be less formal with Anis, and call her *tu.* Anis was against the idea.

"But why?" insisted Ivan.

"I don't think it's an improvement," repeated Anis. "It changes nothing in our relationship, but it does make conversation seem more ordinary, not just to our ears, it flattens it on a deeper level."

"If it changes the tenor of the conversation, that means it changes the relationship," said Ivan.

"Indeed," agreed Anis. "That's precisely what I'm saying: it's better to stick with *vous*."

Van had stopped painting.

"That's stupid," said Anis the day she found out. "You can't leave that décor uninhabited. The Seine, the riverbanks, the buildings: without passersby or police officers or swimmers, it will seem dreary."

"There are no more swimmers in my story, I've told you again and again," moaned Van. "The young woman no sooner touched the water than the officer swept her up. They are flying above the rooftops."

"I'll believe you when you've painted them."

Van picked up his paintbrushes.

One evening when they had talked about this and that, Van had said, tired, "When are you coming?"

He used *tu* on purpose. He was well aware that he was provoking her, but you have to know what you want, he figured, and what he wanted was to give Anis a shove, so she'd fall into his arms.

"I don't know," Anis had mumbled. She was crying. Without adding a word she hung up. Van had not dared call her back.

From time to time she asked him how the mural was going.

"The wings aren't easy to do," he confided one evening.

"Remove the wings," she said. "That man and woman are not angels."

"There," he was finally able to say in April, "everyone is in place. The young woman and the officer are supremely happy, in a sky that changes from gray to pink. The crowd on the bridge is watching them. They all have their heads thrown back and smiles on their faces. I started with the last image, as you can tell."

"And the two earlier ones?"

"I don't feel like painting them anymore."

"What do they do between earth and sky all day long?"

"They talk. And when they stop talking, they don't notice. They think about what they're going to say to each other."

"Do they say *tu* to each other?"

"Not yet. He would like to, but she's reserved. And basically, he doesn't mind."

They talked about novels, literature, poetry. On that subject, Van got the impression she was listening, without reticence.

He sent books to Anis. She read all of them. "I'll never set foot in Méribel again," she said. "Or in any other ski resort. I've ended up believing what I pretended: that I don't feel like learning how to ski."

In May, Ivan noticed an imbalance. It was very worrying. He was the one who always got her on the phone or called back—not that Anis was not loyal to her promise, she called him every morning and evening. But she made sure she got his answering machine. It was as if that is what she preferred. She knew that Van was working a great deal, roughly office hours. She called the studio on the landline at a time when she was almost certain not to find him in. She left cheerful messages that said nothing about her. Something prevented Ivan from asking her to try to reach him rather on his cell phone—something like a fear that her tone would no longer be so cheerful.

It was almost June. Van no longer spoke of Anis moving to Paris. Nor did she.

23

Spring was turning to summer. The month of June was dazzling. Van didn't mind having to wear his votive sweater over his shoulders, casually, or tied around his waist: not one single day had he broken his promise, and the sweater now had holes again in both elbows. Francesca had put away her shawls and her greatcoats. In light, sober, almost severe outfits—never any prints, noticed Van, always plain fabric, very simply cut—she seemed even taller. She had the legs of a young girl, in her flat shoes, a raw-boned young girl with almost no calves.

"Ivan," she said one day, "the bookstore is huge. I'm a hope-less saleswoman. I don't intend to spend my days at the store, once it's open. I'd make us go under. I'm going to hire someone to give you a hand."

Van had already thought about it.

"I'm hesitant," he said. "Yes, the bookstore is huge, but let's not exaggerate, the stock is not that big . . ."

"It's going to get bigger."

"And it won't be crowded, in the beginning."

"I insist on it. In October, November, we'll have to be in two places at once, and we'll no longer have time to hire some-one in optimum circumstances. Would you prefer a man or a woman for an associate?"

"A man, please!" Van gave her a sad smile: "I've already told you, women turn me upside down."

Francesca knew no one who might suit the job. Ivan had in mind a friend he'd made the year he'd been a bookseller in Marseille, a likeable Kabyle who was a poet, insatiable reader, and unparalleled salesman. But no matter how he searched the Web and the phone book, or questioned his contacts, he did not manage to find him.

Francesca talked about placing an ad in the newspaper. "But five hundred candidates will show up," said Van.

They went through the job seekers in the professional publishers' journal. "I'll let you interview the candidates," said Francesca. "I'm terrible at screening people, I'd fall for the very first person."

Van interviewed eleven candidates. He decided without hesitation on a young man of twenty-four who had already worked as an editor and bookseller.

"One failure after the other," said the young man; his name was Oscar. "That's what you call experience."

He was ready to start right away. But happy all the same to have the summer.

"I have a novel to finish," he explained.

Francesca offered him her chalet in Méribel, and he accepted, modestly.

"Ivan," asked Francesca, "would you like to meet my husband?"

They were busy filling shelves that smelled of fresh pine and wood glue from a box full of used books that had arrived that very morning, putting each book in place according to century and country. It seemed obvious that they shouldn't keep the used books separate from the others. They gave the shelves the cozy look of a family library, with one or two well-worn books sitting among the others in perfect condition.

"Of course I would," replied Van. "I'm passionate about everything to do with you."

"I'd be very surprised if you were passionate about Henri," said Francesca, without bitterness, merely stating a fact. "He's not your style, at all."

"The way you are warning me against him I am sure I will find him very agreeable. But that's not the issue. I suppose you only want to introduce me to him to have my opinion. Don't count on me to give it, either. Where did you get this idea, to want to introduce us?"

"I can't decide whether he's on our side or not. I mean, whether he's in favor of The Good Novel or not."

"What have you told him about it?"

"More or less everything. Not the makeup of the committee, obviously, but the principle behind the bookstore, the method for selecting our books, our discussions, how many titles, where to set up, paperbacks or no paperbacks . . . I've talked to him about you, too. He asked me a few questions. Quite recently, at his request, we talked about the launch, strategy, advertising. He has shown an interest in the business, but I'm not sure what sort of interest. I'm not sure his curiosity is that of an ally. Perhaps he's pleased that I'm busy, because he'll get something out of it. Or perhaps he's looking forward to seeing me fall flat on my face. You'll be able to see that more clearly than I can. Perhaps you'll even get him to speak his mind."

They had dinner together, all three of them, one evening at the rue de Condé.

"Do I have to dress up?" asked Van when Francesca invited him.

"I've always seen you dressed," she said.

She blushed to her temples and then specified, "Dress however you want. Henri is very classic, in that respect, but it's more a question of convenience than choice, I think. He only knows one way to dress. And basically, he doesn't really care what other people have on their backs."

"But he's not totally insensitive to your elegance?"

"No, I don't think he is sensitive to it. He must think it's normal. All the women in our circle are elegant. To be honest, he doesn't look at me often. Let me be clear on that, we don't see each other very much."

The apartment on the rue de Condé was very stylish, with its high ceilings, tapestries, and fine furnishings. No sooner was he in the vestibule than Van felt relieved that Francesca had never brought him here before. He was well aware of all the distance such a décor could have put between them—a distance it would have taken time to overcome, but which by now was not an obstacle.

Francesca led him into a small living salon, cozy and comfortable to the point of being somewhat ordinary. Henri Doultremont was there. He spared his guest the act of the overworked businessman who is clearly making an exception from his usual agenda. He did not talk about himself to Van, nor did he question Van about his own life.

Ivan imagined that the apartment must be huge, but he only saw this small living room, and a dining room that he assumed must be the small dining room, as opposed to the large one. Francesca had kept things simple. She herself served them a glass of port, then a cold dinner already set out on a sideboard.

Doultremont did not lack culture. Already before dinner, he eagerly shared his discovery that winter of Kipling, and his admiration for the stories and *Plain Tales from the Hills*. Van did not think this was so conventional. While it might have seemed so at the end of the nineteenth century, at the beginning of the twenty-first there was something almost eccentric about it.

Francesca told them the dinner was ready. They sat down, and Doultremont said, "Let's talk about this bookstore."

Van met Francesca's gaze.

"Go ahead," she said.

"Things are coming along as planned," began Van. "I am struck by the positive echoes we are hearing."

"Have you got ten people involved?" asked Doultremont.

"What do you mean?"

What the businessman meant was that, among the few literature nuts like themselves, Van and Francesca were sure to hear good things, but that true success would be something else altogether.

Many unknown factors remained. How many people would really support the store? Were there enough of them in Paris? And how could they be mobilized? All together, what was their purchasing power? In other words, how many books would they buy each year at The Good Novel? And would they remain loyal?

"There is no way to find out other than to go ahead with it," remarked Van.

Doultremont was uncertain whether a bricks-and-mortar bookstore was called for. For him, the future was in online sales.

"One does not exclude the other," said Van. "Francesca must have mentioned it to you. Of course we plan to have our own Web site, and we'll use that channel for sales. My plan is to spend the summer finalizing that very aspect of our sales strategy."

Francesca listened to him, astonished. This was the first time Ivan had mentioned the subject in her presence.

"We'll take orders online, and ship out the books," he said as if it were a matter of course. "Nowadays a bookstore cannot overlook Internet sales."

He changed his tone: "Of course, what will make us special is our catalogue. Our particular stock will be our image, whether on the Internet or on the rue Dupuytren. To be honest, we are aiming to reverse the precedence between supply and demand. It's not demand that is going to lead, but offer. People will come through the door of the bookstore because they know they can find a rare selection of novels there, in addition to any particular titles they might be looking for. And they'll visit the Web site in a similar frame of mind."

"They'll trust us," said Francesca.

Doultremont grew animated. "The contradiction," he said, "is that your offer is both very limited and very diverse. Success nowadays obliges you to choose. Something becomes a hit either because it's a unique product, one that people like, such as crème de cassis in Asia, or on the contrary because there's a huge offer, like the IKEA catalogue for example, or even Amazon, which has thousands of books available online, of every type and for every taste. Whereas you aren't choosing: you are both little, and multiple. That won't work. You're harnessing two horses to a carriage, and they're pulling in opposite directions. The use of the singular in the name of your shop is significant. The Good Novel: You think the choice is going to be simple, but in fact you're faced with a very complicated choice."

"Our aim has never been to make a hit," said Van.

He found Doultremont's tone peremptory, his categories hazy.

"I'm not sure we need to oppose simple and multiple," he said calmly. "Our bookstore is more like a rebellious fashion designer who's had enough of shapeless rags and sinister colors—so he launches a line of clothing which is all elegance and fun."

"No," Doultremont flung back. "The difference with you is that the designer offers clothes which are all alike and go together. He's got what you call a style. Whereas you, behind the appearance of a line, you are offering a hodgepodge of books, each of which is fundamentally different from all the others. Your products have nothing in common."

"Our glasses are empty," Francesca pointed out softly.

Doultremont served some more wine and continued, "Not only are you not the first people to open a bookstore, but you are running headlong into a sector that is in difficulty, where a lot of people are losing hope."

"I hope you don't support the idea that books are finished?" objected Ivan.

"Not at all. I am merely saying that your type of business is a thing of the past."

"Have we ever considered this to be a business?" interrupted Francesca.

"You said it," Doultremont pointed out. He turned to Ivan. "Francesca must have told you, none of the experts I had her meet with would bet a brass farthing on your business."

It was Ivan's turn to be astonished. "The experts in marketing and business promotion?" he asked, as if he were talking about mad scholars.

"The very same," said Doultremont, who had missed his irony.

Van raised his palms and leaned back.

"I will grant you that neither Francesca nor I know the least thing about sales or business," he said. "Our concept is radical. It is a revolution in cultural behavior. Everybody nowadays agrees that too many uninteresting books are being published. We think this phenomenon is like a pollution of the mind, and we are simply saying: enough. Let us refuse to see our taste polluted. Let's refresh the air. Let's breathe. We think we have a good chance of finding followers."

He smiled. "You've made me think of something. We are trying to make something happen that actually did happen with tobacco, in a way that was as spectacular as it was unexpected. Ever since cigarettes became available to everybody, let's say over the last fifty or sixty years, people have been smoking, fully aware that they are poisoning themselves. There were plenty of Cassandras out there shouting Danger! But to no avail. And then suddenly, God knows why, in the final years of the twentieth century, something happened to the mass of smokers, a wave that went right around the planet, and every-body decided they'd had it with tobacco. It can happen very quickly. People's minds suddenly open. They become aware that their consumption is harmful, and in the end does not even bring them much pleasure.

"As far as literature is concerned, we believe that a similar awareness can be raised. And that The Good Novel, on little rue Dupuytren, could be the spark that will start to turn things around."

"I agree with everything Van has just said," said Francesca, "but personally, I don't have such ambitions. I just believe that in a city like Paris and a country like France, there will be ten thousand people who will be glad to see The Good Novel open and who will buy their books there and nowhere else."

Doultremont was thinking.

"You've also made me think of something. I'm afraid that novels may be more like wine. Do you remember the film *Mondovino*? Wonderful *appellation contrôlée* wines are being sidelined by the wave of American-style wines that are uni-form, not bad, sell well and are formidably promoted by an ultra-powerful marketing machine. Your AOC novels are no different. They can't compete against global bestsellers like *Harry Potter* and *Da Vinci Code*. You have almost no chance."

"It's the almost that fascinates us," said Van.

When she met him the next day at the rue Dupuytren, Francesca gave free rein to her surprise:

"You never told me about your plans for the Internet?"

"Your husband did us a great favor. He's absolutely right. We have to have a presence on the net. I'll spend the summer working on it, I wasn't lying. I absolutely have to learn how to design a site and run it. But you surprised me, too. The sales experts you saw were skeptical, you say?"

"Does it matter? I didn't want to burden you with their

doubts, because they didn't convince me. I got the impression I was talking about old lace with ironmasters. They're completely clueless. Speaking of lace, here's another example of an unexpected reversal. Thirty years ago the lace industry was dying, until two or three clever souls, for a laugh, and because it was something they liked, launched a line of old-fashioned lingerie trimmed with lace. Women, who at that point had been wearing nothing but gymnasts' panties, adored it. They went back to everything that their older sisters had burned—silk, satin, petticoats adorned with lace. The industry got going again.

"The comparison with tobacco can fill you with hope. But the one with lace, fills you with dreams. Those two or three clever women didn't have to fight, they didn't have to play Cassandra, they didn't say 'Stop' to anything. All they did was make their little luxury lingerie available, pretty pricey stuff at that, and the fashion took off. A powder trail. Maybe all we have to do is open the bookstore, and the taste for literature will spread."

". . . like a wave of pleasure," concluded Van, upbeat.

"Tell me. Your opinion, about Henri. Is he with us, or against us?"

"Neither," said Van hesitantly. "Francesca, I don't want to hurt you."

"Go ahead."

"I am convinced your husband does not believe, and never has believed in our project, but above all, he doesn't give a damn."

Heffner was nodding.

"It's an important point," he said. "Would you still say the same thing today?"

"Are you wondering whether Henri is our enemy?" said Francesca slowly.

"I'm convinced he isn't," said Ivan.

"I'm not so sure," said Francesca, her voice muted.

24

Francesca brought up her husband twice in the days that followed. Both times, it was when they were standing in front of the shelves, in the Italian and then the English section.

She had just put *L'Iguane* in place, with the care she would have taken to add a flower to a bouquet in a vase, and next to her Ivan was opening a box, when she suddenly blurted, "Don't ever marry a foreigner. Henri speaks excellent Italian, and I learned French at the age of two, but in spite of all that, we have never really understood each other."

She could not forgive her husband for having said "the shop" and "your business" when referring to The Good Novel.

"If a failure to understand was due to a difference in languages, it would be obvious," said Van. "No. I wonder if we ever understand anything about other people. What I mean is, even when you do have the same mother tongue, the same culture, the same age."

He was trying to sound casual.

"When you're in love, not only do you think you understand each other, but you have the impression you've known each other forever. And when suddenly you don't understand anything, other than that you were full of illusions, it means that you no longer . . ."

He met Francesca's panicked gaze, and tried to backtrack: "It's that things have—"

She cut him off. It was so unlike her that Ivan was sure she was doing it to prevent him from getting himself in any deeper.

"Precisely," she said, in a muted voice. "When the fog of illusion has lifted, when you see the other person for who they really are, and you no longer hold them responsible for your own errors of appreciation, when you're cold and you ache all over, aren't those the conditions that make it possible, finally, to understand each other? Should you not be able to begin some sort of mutual understanding?"

"You have to want it to begin with," said Van.

But he himself desperately wanted to understand what was making Anis tick, and he couldn't. He took back his words: "No, wanting isn't always enough. Maybe both of you have to want it, and both at the same time, each of you trying to understand the other and helping at the same time, by giving the other person the key, for example."

"The keys," said Francesca.

The next day, while she was adjusting the English novels on the shelf, she began to talk about her husband's predictions again.

"You get the impression he doesn't care about the store. All things considered, I'm not so sure. I think he wants us to fail and he was all the more agreeable with you because he has only one idea in his head, to destabilize us. He's the one who runs things, the business world is his chartered domain. He's jealous because I'm opening this bookstore, even though it can't possibly offend him in any way, just the way he would be jealous of a love in my life that would take nothing away from him, since he hasn't loved me in a long time.

"You don't know him. He is filled with that particularly French nastiness, the cruelest of all, after English nastiness—well, it's far behind, that's true."

The time had come to begin reading the September novels.

"The Himalayas," announced Van. "Four hundred and forty French novels, two hundred and twenty foreign ones."

"Are they already in print?"

"Nearly all of them. Fifteen or twenty years ago, books were sent to the critics in July, sometimes even in August. But paid vacation time has doubled, they have to find time to take their vacation, the problem is the same for everybody, including critics. Concierges have put the word out that they're fed up with having to stack in their loges piles of packages sent in July to the rather taciturn gentleman on the fifth floor. Over the last three or four years, press kits all arrive at the end of June, before the critics leave for warmer climes."

"We haven't received anything."

"It's because we haven't asked for anything. Don't forget, when we began to submit our orders, we said we'd be opening at the end of the year. It's time to call the publishers back. We have to let them know that The Good Novel will be opening earlier than expected, in September, and we'll ask them to send their press kits so we can learn about the books that will be coming out in the fall."

"Will they do it?"

"I doubt it."

"How so?"

"We will say: Our bookstore is opening in September. It will be very literary. They will have interrupted us already: We'll sign you up for the automatic shipment. No, we'll say (I can take care of the phone calls, I know the palaver, I played the role for years in Méribel). No, we don't really want the automatic shipment. What we would like, would be press kits—or proofs would also work—in order to choose the books we'll have in stock. The word 'choose,' which may seem perfectly legitimate first off—believe me, Francesca, it always makes them go silent at the other end of the line. There are two possible reactions. The first, the most favorable, they say to us: Fine, we'll send somebody over. So along comes a rep with the printed catalogue, and we have to ask him again how to go about selecting books we haven't read, and he sees no better solution than the automatic shipment, and we have to ask him to stop playing deaf . . . Best-case scenario, along come a few press kits or uncorrected proofs.

"The less favorable reaction is polite. They take note that the bookstore will be opening. And they say: You know how to go about placing orders, you know our distributor."

"Is it absolutely out of the question for us to subscribe to the automatic shipment?"

"There's absolutely no point for a bookstore like The Good Novel. For a general bookstore maybe, at a push, insofar as new books make up 8 percent of sales. You have to pay for the automatic shipment within ninety days, at the end of the month, but any unsold automatic books are sent back to the publisher at the bookstore's expense, and in turn this can't be done before ninety days, and the returns are reimbursed in the form of a credit given at the end of the same period; in the meantime, along come new automatic shipments . . . This is all a bit technical, you just have to remember that given the significant amount of returns, it's a way for publishers or their distributors to get some money in their accounts. The automatic shipment is convenient for bookstores where they sell everything that comes out and where they know they won't have the time to read even one one-hundredth. Don't forget, times being what they are, The Good Novel is going to be a specialized bookstore."

"We'll refuse the automatic shipments, they send us hardly any press kits, or none at all." Francesca smiled. "I'm going to call Lancre and Bonlarron."

"I was thinking of that," said Van, who knew the names of all the critics; he had been wondering for a long time whether Francesca had any critics among her friends.

They divided the chores among themselves as a matter of course. Ivan got in touch with publishers and distributors, received the reps. He remained perfectly vague regarding the bookstore's drift. Literary, he said. He detected a great deal of irony in the response of those to whom he repeated that he planned to do without the automatic shipment, and once or twice some compassion.

Francesca called her critic friends. "A bookstore?" they exclaimed one after the other. "Are you out of your mind? Well, if you think it's amusing . . ."

Would they pass on their press kits to her? As many as you like, they said. Whenever you want. I'll give them all back, promised Francesca.

Thierry Bonlarron insisted upon it, but Jean-René Lancre, who had built his reputation on his nastiness, humor, and a very idiosyncratic way of snubbing eagerly awaited novels in order to exhume obscure works that were all but self-published, acted as if he were angry: "And don't you dare send any back to me! I make that a condition of our agreement. It would be too easy to dump them on me. Figure it out, burn them, toss them into the Seine. I don't want to see a single one back at my address."

Van worried about the actual opening. He wanted to be sure that information on The Good Novel would spread rapidly as soon as the store was opened, and that the bookstore's singular philosophy would be clear right from the start.

"I think we should have eight or ten press luncheons," said Francesca. "As in, we invite in succession the journalists in charge of the arts or book sections of the major newspapers. When I say we, I mean you. If I were there, it would spoil everything. I have a disastrous image. Rich women, in France, are thought to be uncultured and ditzy. I know all about it. If at least I were on the left, it would be different. Notoriously on the left. Or dead, obviously: in that case, everything changes, you become 'the famous patron of the arts,' 'the great friend of culture.'

"You, Ivan, can take care of the journalists. On my side, I'll look after the business end of the launch, advertising, that sort of thing. After a few months have gone by, we'll have to think about giving a press conference, in order to release our initial results."

"Spectacular."

"Naturally."

"At that point, you can come out of hiding."

"No, it would be counterproductive then just as it would be now. Success doesn't change a rich woman's image, on the contrary."

25

On June 30, slightly before midnight, Anis telephoned. Van was at home; she must have suspected as much. "Well. I'm in Paris," she said.

"Where in Paris?" asked Van eagerly.

"At home."

She had a room in a university dorm in the Latin Quarter, she said, without elaborating. Van was careful not to reproach her in any way.

"That's wonderful. Will I see you again?"

"Yes," said Anis. "Now it's possible. The room wasn't in good condition. I've been sweating for ten days to make it look nice. It's all done. I finished this morning."

Ten days, and all that time, every time they talked, in addition to the sixty times where Van listened again to the messages on his answering machine, he had imagined her in Grenoble, in her garret room, or on her way to class, or in one of those cafés with their unforgettable mulled wine. This I know because he told me.

She was provoking him. He decided to risk everything: "I haven't unsaddled my pony yet, I've just come in. I can be at your place in a quarter of an hour."

"Your pony is like me, he can't keep his eyes open," said Anis. "So take his saddle off. It's late. I've found work, and I have a very early start."

Van said nothing for ten seconds.

"Call me back when you've got a few minutes," he said finally, somewhat mechanically.

"And don't you think," said Anis, "that it doesn't make much sense, now that I'm in Paris, for me to call you every day, morning and night?"

The next morning, July 1, and the day after, Van did not hear from her at all.

She called the studio on Saturday the third at ten. Van had figured that she would wait until then to send him a message that would be all the more affectionate if she could leave it on the machine. He let her begin talking, then he picked up.

They met early afternoon on the Pont Marie. It was her idea, because she didn't know Paris well, and wanted to start with what she knew best.

"The most famous ice cream shop in Paris," said Van, "is Berthillon. There, look."

They ate pink and white sorbet, walked around the two islands, down onto the banks, on to the Square Vert-Galant; they wandered through Notre-Dame, rested their legs sitting side by side on a concrete bench outside the cathedral.

"I feel so good without my navy blue sweater," said Van. "I was suffocating. I've thrown it out, I feel alive again."

Anis acted as if she hadn't heard.

"There's a place where I'm dying to go," she said. "Can't you guess?"

"Every time I think I can guess what you're thinking, I'm mistaken," winced Van.

"Go on . . ."

"The bookstore?"

"The Good Novel?" Anis gave an open smile. "No, I've already been there. You lose."

"I've been well aware of that for a long time, believe me. I won't say another word."

"These riverbanks, these bridges . . . can't you guess? It's fairly obvious, though. I would like to see the décor of your studio, after all."

"Tomorrow," said Ivan hastily, without knowing what had prompted him to answer like that.

When she entered Ivan's studio that Sunday—it was three in the afternoon—Anis looked at the walls in silence, gravely. Only then did Van understand why, the day before, he had delayed the exam. Something decisive was at stake, that seemed patently clear to him, as did the naïveté of his painting, so he went to stare out of the bay window, incapable of doing anything other than count the terribly slow beats of his poor heart.

"I like it very much," said Anis, from behind him.

I like you very much—Van knew perfectly well that this was the formula people used when they wanted to tell someone they didn't love them; he had used it himself on more than one occasion.

But Anis was already asking to compare the work to the original.

She stayed all of five minutes, Van calculated, as he descended the stairway behind her. He had polished his lodgings until late at night, and prepared a tray of pastries like the ones in the childhood song (the lover is a pastry chef, who weeps with frustration at her hard heart, while he still "loves her like a cream puff").

The weather was glorious. They walked as far as the Pont de la Concorde, along the rue Montmartre, the *grands boulevards*, the Madeleine. From the bridge, Anis looked at the Seine flowing, heavy and slow.

"Where is the Port des Invalides?" she asked.

"I can't remember!" said Van. "That's all in the past, for me. I never go over there. No, for me, the part of Paris that is interesting nowadays is the Latin Quarter."

"By the way, do you know if the chapel of the Sorbonne is

open on Sunday? This week it was closed. I thought that maybe, on Sunday . . ."

Van didn't have a clue.

"Let's go see," he said. "The most direct way from here, for the Boulevard Saint-Michel, is to take the Bateau bus."

The most direct, not exactly. But definitely the slowest. They waited for the Bateau bus in the sun, with the Breton scent of harbors, stagnant water rising.

"So you've been to see the bookstore?" asked Van.

"Fortunately the rue Dupuytren isn't very long, and there's only one store being remodeled. From outside, with that whitewash on the windows, you can't tell what sort of shop is going to open. When do you lay your cards on the table?"

"When we open, the beginning of September. We'll raise the banner, The Good Novel, at eight o'clock, and at ten we'll open."

He took a deep breath, then exhaled.

"If you like, I'll show you around. Whenever you like."

"I'm going to wait for the opening, like everybody else."

"Francesca's not there at all during the day. And even if she were, she would give you a friendly welcome. She's a fairy godmother."

"I see," said Anis. "I'd rather wait."

The Bateau bus was coming, white and shiny like a new toy, instantly recognizable among the filthy barges and old boats. It pulled alongside with the gentle touch of an engine remotely and expertly controlled.

The sun was setting. Light drifted on the water.

From the Port Saint-Michel, it took them ten minutes to get as far as the chapel of the Sorbonne, along sidewalks cluttered with slow-moving tourists, and when they got there, it was closed.

There was nothing posted on the door, no opening times, or any information.

"I wonder if it's no longer used," said Van.

"Would you like to see my room?" asked Anis. "It's right nearby."

"Why not? That way, I'll know your address."

When Anis laughed, she had a dimple on her left cheek, but not on her right.

"I'll stay five minutes," Van told her. "I'm like you, rooms . . . Life seems a bit narrow between four walls."

Anis did not comment. Her room was at number 44, rue du Bol-en-Bois, on the fifth floor of a gray and blue glass building constructed in the seventies: a light room, that smelled of fresh paint, despite the fact that the glass door leading to the balcony was wide open.

Van went out onto the balcony at once, intrigued by the foliage he could see. There was a little garden. Anis followed him, and she leaned against the railing next to him.

"I've been incredibly lucky, no?" she said.

"You should have left Grenoble earlier, you see. You're much better off here. With my perch overlooking a maple tree, and yours above the elms, you might think Paris is a park."

He took note of the distance between his left elbow and her right one, which must have been about three feet. The last time he had found himself anywhere near that arm, on the concrete bench outside Notre Dame the evening before, the distance between them had seemed roughly the same.

Let's stay positive, Van reasoned. If he looked closer, he could see that the distance between Anis and himself had decreased by a good millimeter in twenty-four hours. At the rate of one millimeter a day, he calculated that it would take a thousand days to reduce the three feet to nothing. He recalled a remarkable short story by Paulhan called *Les coeurs changent.* Albert and Rose like each other, they roll around in the bed right away, and then with the passage of time, they grow apart, and take years to get closer again. Van could remember the final sentence. Albert is trying to take Rose's hand, and she protests, "My friend, what do you want from me?"

A thousand days, or slightly more than three years. Van

thought he might try to arouse Anis's jealousy, and he began talking in a great hurry about all the women who filled the streets of Paris. He pictured Sarah Green Pea, quicksilver, a spark of sex, or Marie Noir, heavy lava, volcanic.

"What are you thinking about?" asked Anis.

"About women, certain women who move quickly in matters of love," said Van, trying to adopt a tone of despair and realizing he only sounded bitter.

"Men don't like that sort of woman," said Anis calmly. "Why don't we go have some dinner? Aren't you hungry? I haven't eaten since yesterday."

Van suggested the Centre Pompidou.

"It's a bit far, but from the restaurant on the sixth floor you have one of the finest views on Paris, in my opinion, neither too high, nor too low."

"I'm sure I can't afford it," said Anis.

"Well it's my treat, obviously."

She sighed.

"*I would prefer not to.* I've never known a boy to invite a girl without expecting a return on his investment."

"There, now you've hurt my feelings. I have no intention of buying you."

"Why should I believe you?"

"How can I prove to you that I am disinterested, other than to spoil you as often as you'll let me? I have an idea. You let me invite you for coffee from time to time, let me send you a poem, a few flowers, and every time I give you something, that means I can think of you, and you can think of yourself, as being freer; and we'll know that you are freer."

"There must be a catch," said Anis, dreamily.

"There isn't one! I defy you to find one." Van bristled. "I'm really being stupid. Probably you would prefer if I insisted that I am interested in you to the highest degree. It would be the truth, after all."

They had dinner in a run-down Tibetan place on the rue des Fossés-Saint-Jacques. Anis chose it because she didn't know anything about Himalayan cuisine.

"I don't know anything about it either," said Van, sitting down opposite her. "We are taking a considerable risk. What will we do if the only thing to drink here is tea with yak butter?"

"We'll make like Tintin," said Anis. "Either we're adventurous or we aren't. Let's try it."

They had some fairly ordinary Chinese beer, and stir-fried vegetables that were difficult to identify. Ivan talked a little bit about Asian cooking. He liked Thai cuisine.

"So," he asked during a pause, "how's work?"

"It's okay," said Anis.

Van counted mentally to three.

"What are you doing exactly?"

Anis looked him straight in the eye: "It's just to make money."

Van decided not to ask any more questions. Already he no longer discussed Anis's desiderata, and he took no more initiative, and he wasn't expecting anything more, since he didn't know what to expect. For all that, he couldn't be sure that this was what spiritual masters would qualify as pure love.

He walked home from the rue des Fossés-Saint-Jacques to the rue de l'Agent-Bailly. He must have reached his tenth mile of the day. He walked slowly, mulling over what Anis had said to him. How calmly she had said, Men don't like women who rush things. How confident she was.

Van suddenly felt as if his ears had come unblocked. Those are the very words he chose to describe it to me. He stopped short. All that confidence had a hollow ring to it! It sounded more like a question: Do men not prefer women who don't rush things? What an idiot he had been. Anis was expecting him to reassure her, to tell her that she did not fit in the usual categories, and that he wasn't comparing her to anybody. But he hadn't said a thing.

He took out his little cell phone and, walking on, he dialed her number. He got the answering machine. "I don't like things always in a rush, either," he thought. "I'm not in a hurry. My favorite short story by Jean Paulhan is called *Les coeurs changent*. It's only one page long, but it makes you think. I'll send it to you, and you'll tell me what you think.

"That is, if you want me to," he corrected. "You don't have to talk to me about it, obviously."

26

And indeed, Anis did not talk to Van about Paulhan's short story. She responded to his letter containing the story right away, also by mail.

It's a good story, but it's not finished. And what interests me is what comes after. Will Albert be inspired enough to calm Rose? Because he thinks it's the passage of time that has changed the way the young girl feels: and what if he asked himself what it is that's holding her back? If she has her own reasons? As for Rose, will she manage to leave her ambivalence behind? Because Paulhan, with his last sentence, is making fun: he turns her into a little Victorian ninny instead of trying to understand how a sincere girl can both look at a man tenderly and be unable to do anything but withdraw.

A.

The only signature was her initial. Van told me he was hurt. He read it as if she were taking her distance, eroding any affection she might have for him. He clearly did not have much confidence in himself. He might have read it as a kind of familiarity, as if she were saying, It's me, who else could it be?

They saw each other seven or eight times over the summer of 2004, sometimes in the evening, sometimes on the weekend. Please no appointments, said Anis, that's just too much. And not every weekend. Van would have said the same himself if it had been up to him to choose the rules of the game. But this time, he was not the one calling the shots (though in the past he had often called them by pretending not to call them, initially letting the young lady step forward and think that she had the initiative, and then gradually he would tilt the balance of power until, becoming vague and evasive, he was actually the one setting the pace, slowing things down, and deciding when it was over). No, with Anis he asked for nothing more. He never found out what sort of work Anis was doing, it lasted for three weeks in July and then stopped, and then she started something else—but Ivan only learned about all these changes after the fact, and he didn't know what her second job was, either.

"Considering what you told us about your inability to commit," asked Heffner, very neutral, "am I wrong, or did you at least find the slowness of this affair interesting enough to give it a chance to last?"

"I don't know," said Van. "No. You are not wrong. Most certainly not."

Van himself was very busy. Books were beginning to trickle in, and he still had a lot of orders to place. He was taking a class on how to be a Webmaster, a class he enjoyed and took very seriously. And he was reading his share of the fall novels which Lancre and Bonlarron were constantly dropping off at the rue Dupuytren. He went through ten books a day: he would keep one, and read it right away. Because the next day, it all started again: ten novels out of which, thankfully, very few were worth reading all the way through, and even fewer worth promoting.

Among the books he wanted for The Good Novel were *Dernier amour,* by Christian Gailly, which, blown away, he mentioned to me; *Sous réserve,* a first novel by Hélène Frappat; and, among the foreign novels, short stories by Roberto Bolaño. Francesca liked *Tristano muore* by Antonio Tabucchi, *La réfu-*

tation majeure, by Pierre Senges, and more than anything, Segalen's complete *Correspondence,* published at last.

Ivan hadn't told her that Anis had come to Paris. He had not planned to go away all summer but, if he had made any vacation plans, he would have canceled everything. As for Anis, she did not rule out the idea of going for a break at some point, or so she said without being more specific, and Van expected that any day he might find the bird had flown, leaving a kind note for him in the concierge's loge. She had decided to continue her studies in the fall, and he had not dared ask if this would be in Paris.

He spent several hours at the end of every day at the bookstore. Nearly all the novels that were on the long list had arrived, many of them in two copies. All that was missing were twenty or so books they could not find. Francesca was having the extra space in the bookstore remodeled. On the ground floor the unused area was painted, nothing more, and in the basement tiles were laid and the walls were whitewashed.

At the end of July all the work was done. Surplus stock of the books was stored in the basement. Francesca left for a few days on the Island of San Giulio, Lago d'Orta, where she had a villa she needed to air out, she said. "I'm joking," she amended. "It's a house where I used to go on vacation every year, as a child. I cannot spend a whole summer without at least sleeping there for a few nights. The villa is by the water. From my room, all night long, I can hear the lapping of the lake."

She was going to open up the house for some English friends who would spend the summer there. "In a manner of speaking," she said. "It's a pretext. The house is always open."

She came back to Paris on Monday, August 16. The bookstore was scheduled to open on the thirtieth, also a Monday. In the meantime Francesca wanted to make sure that nothing would hold up the opening, that there would be no hitches.

"When should we have the press lunches?" asked Ivan. "Since we have to do it."

"I've been thinking," said Francesca. "I can't really see you talking to journalists anywhere other than at The Good Novel, and even less so if it's before the bookstore opens. What we have to offer is a place, a living place, the spirit of a place. In other words, I can't envisage holding those meetings anywhere other than the bookstore, once we've opened."

Van looked puzzled.

"Let me take care of it," said Francesca. "I know what I want to do. Will you trust me?"

There was one word in Anis's letter about the Paulhan story that Ivan thought about incessantly, the "reasons" the disconcerting young girl must have had. Imagining her as a little girl, with her child's cheeks and eyes, he thought he had found the solution. Fear. The age-old fear of the wolf, so normal, so difficult to confess at his age.

One evening in mid-August when he was walking her back to the rue Bol-en-Bois, her entire person seemed to be telling him that he must stay there, outside, on the threshold to her building (after showing him around that first time, she never invited him in a second time), he took her in his arms, held her close, and said, "It's not fear that's holding you back, is it? I'm not the first man who's ever wanted to be close to you?"

A choking sound made him step aside. "No," she said, between two sobs, as if to confess as much would have been terrible. He tried to console her: "It's no big deal." She looked at him, her eyes full of reproach.

After that, he would wonder relentlessly what she had to reproach him with. "The reasons," he told me, "the reasons why she would leap back from me, and I still couldn't understand why."

On Monday, August 23, Oscar arrived to start work at The Good Novel. He was very excited about the project. He knew many of the books on the shelves, and it was his intention to read all of them. He did not seem to be intimidated by Francesca, even though he was four inches shorter than her. Van preferred not to ask him how his novel was progressing.

Francesca hired one more person for the bookstore. They needed someone to do the cleaning every day, or rather every night because it could only be done once they were closed, preferably before eight o'clock in the morning, given Ivan's morning habits. Francesca found just the person—a forty-year-old Iraqi with the handsome, emaciated face of a serene intellectual. Before the fall of Saddam Hussein, this man had been a university professor, a specialist in medieval music and poetry. He had been forced to go into exile, and, after trying to live in Damascus, then London, he had found refuge in Paris, with a cousin of cousins who was better at making his way in life, and who ran an oriental restaurant near the La Fourche Metro station. This cousin had hired him for next to nothing to give his establishment a cultural veneer by hosting musicians, dancers, and storytellers; there were many of them in the diaspora. Yassin al-Hillah was in sore need of additional income, and when one of his friends, an oud player who happened to be the brother-in-law of the concierge in the building where Francesca lived, had told him they were looking for someone to do the maintenance at a bookstore, he had immediately presented himself.

Francesca cried out in protest when she saw whom she was dealing with. She could not hire a man of letters to do the housekeeping. Yassin explained to her in his flowery French that one of the greatest torments of his life in exile was that he rarely had access to books anymore—books in any quantity, he specified. And he had suggested a contract made to measure.

He would take care of the two hours of daily housekeeping required for the bookstore, before eight in the morning, that they agreed, but he just asked for permission to come well before six o'clock in the evening to the premises to be able to read. I don't need to be paid in any other way, he said. But on that point, Francesca was adamant.

Van had prepared Francesca.

"I'm counting on a success, you know; I've often said as much. And I'm still confident. But I'm not sure the success will come right away. It's almost certain it will take us some time to become known. The first few weeks will probably be very quiet, maybe even the first few months."

"Are you forgetting my plans for the launch?"

Ivan smiled, wrinkling his forehead: "I don't have much faith in modern promotional methods, I've also told you that several times. For this type of undertaking, it seems to me that the real promotion will take place by word of mouth, slowly."

"Is there no such thing as fast word of mouth?"

"To be honest, I don't know. I've never thought about it."

"If we make word of mouth the decisive factor, can't you apply what you know about good novels to The Good Novel: I mean the way in which the buzz around a book is created and gets progressively louder?"

"Most probably, yes."

"But you haven't forgotten that sometimes it can go very quickly. Some bookstore hits are made in the space of a few weeks."

"Publishers had been beating the drum for months."

"Not always. Listen, Van, we'll soon find out. What does that change for us? What I want is for The Good Novel to become known, and known for what it is, for its particularity, the challenge it poses. But whether it takes three months or six, I don't care. What about you?"

"The same. I just wanted to warn you. What day is it? Thursday? In four days, we open. Monday at ten o'clock, you will physically open the door. And nothing will happen. That's what I want you to be prepared for. No one will come. Imagine the scene. The weather is fine, here we are in the bookstore, the two of us, overexcited. We haven't slept all night. And no one shows up. I'm exaggerating, eight or ten curious shoppers will cross the threshold, like tourists. Three or four will buy a book. One or two will ask us in what may seem a very disappointing way, how long have you been open, don't you sell DVDs?

"The day will go by. If we close at ten o'clock, as planned, the evening will seem interminable. When we say goodnight we will both have heavy hearts, and what will fill our lungs will be the impression you get nine times out of ten when you're finally living a dream you've waited such a long time for—a feeling that neither you nor I will express, on the contrary—of something banal and tragic: is that it?"

On Friday the twenty-seventh, Ivan got up early. There wasn't much left to do at the bookstore, however. Everything was in place, the books, the benches with their horsehair cushions, the big plants, the cash desk near the door and, underneath, on shelves, wrapping paper and gift envelopes stamped with a handsome logo that Francesca had pulled out of her bag one day. But Van could not imagine possibly being anywhere else except at The Good Novel, on the day before they prepared to do battle, physically present at the bookstore, ready to take up the daunting challenge.

He got to the rue Dupuytren at eight o'clock and ran into Yassin, who had just finished work, then he looked on the Internet to see what they said about *Madame Solario* (Where do you file a book when the author is anonymous? He finally put it under England, 1950s), and opened a few packages,

October novels that were already trying to worm their way into the September crop.

At nine o'clock, Francesca came out the door of the big office, golden in a white dress, her arms full of newspapers.

Van stood up: "Today?"

In response, Francesca put the pile on his desk. Van understood. He went straight to the page where the advertisement for The Good Novel was displayed in all the dailies: on the same page, he noticed, with the simplest slogan of all the ones they had considered, "You'll find good novels at The Good Novel," and three lines of explanation (great literature and nothing else, Monday, rue Dupuytren in Paris—with neither the street number, nor the opening times), against a background of a magnificent wash drawing, by Victor Hugo, of a legendary castle on top of a cliff.

Van acted astonished: "I saw this volley was planned for Monday."

Francesca was radiant: "I wanted to keep it a surprise, all the same," she said, "so that the launch wouldn't seem like a film you've already seen. We've talked about it so much. And you had ten ideas or more for superb slogans, we couldn't just choose one and throw out all the others."

"What you mean?"

"You'll see."

Van had guessed. On Saturday came the second salvo, the second slogan. A full page, in all the papers: "All the books no one is talking about," this time against a background of the type of Restoration painting that is often too hastily described as "a minor oil": a patch of Roman countryside with a Tilbury briskly trotting by and in its window you would recognize, if you had any literary background at all, the profile of Stendhal.

On the façade of the bookstore Francesca had placed panels to mask the entire shop front, identical on Friday to the

Victor Hugo page, and on Saturday to the Stendhal page. The door was hidden. The Good Novel shingle had not yet been hung.

It went up during the night on Sunday.

PART THREE

27

Monday, at eight-fifteen, Francesca found Ivan sitting alone in the bookstore on one of their lovely benches. "Have you seen this?"

She had brought the newspapers. Van was dazzled by her dress, a lavender blue shirtwaist dress with a wide belt, a snug bodice, short sleeves, and a flowing skirt that danced to the rhythm of her steps.

"The newspapers? No," he said. "I was waiting for you."

He was about to get up, but Francesca stopped him, her hand on his shoulder, and sat down next to him.

"I was thinking about today's rite of passage," said Van. "Our dream"—he made a circular gesture with his hand to include the entire bookstore—"now we'll be sharing it with strangers who have the power to make it a reality, but they don't know it yet."

"We'll tell them! You know what they call accompanying publicity?"

"More or less. We also need to put the Internet to good use. On the Web you can reach thousands of people."

"In the meanwhile, what do you think of this morning's volley?"

She placed the newspapers on Ivan's knees. This time the slogan was replaced by a long quotation from Michel Leiris, an excerpt from *Aurora:* "A man who heads off into icy regions in order to hunt furry beasts does not forget to take with him for heat a nickel-plated cigarette lighter of a delicate perfection, and he is attached to that lighter more than anything, because he knows very well that if he loses his way and is far away from any other human being, he will have to build a fire, and camp out in the snow, if he does not want to become stiff as a log in very short order. That woman was that cigarette lighter. A clock that is about to chime midnight in the air cleansed by drought will only do so if its two hands, hour hand and minute hand, coincide with the vertical radius of the upper half of the clock face. That woman was that coincidence . . . In winter, when the thaw begins, they smash the ice in the river with their pick axes, so that the rivers can carry those enormous fragments with a minimum of risk for sailors. That woman was each blow of that philanthropic pick ax, and yet she helped to accelerate the breaking of the ice."

There was a photo in the background, the full-length portrait of a woman of a rare beauty, in profile, in the foreground of a landscape of snow and forests. And in the three lines of information, on that Monday, there was the exact address, The Good Novel, 9 *bis*, rue Dupuytren, 75006 Paris, as well as the opening times, from 10 A.M. to 10 P.M.

"And a hundred posters were put up this morning, very early," said Francesca, "in Paris and the surrounding region. These posters are very basic, you see the façade of the bookstore, with the name in big letters, and the books are very visible in the windows and beyond. It's a montage, obviously, we had to make it up ahead of time. And all the slogan says is, 'At The Good Novel, we sell good novels, nothing else.' Ivan, I get the impression there are more people in the street than usual."

"If you like, we can debrief our impressions this evening."

"You're right. I'll leave you now. What time does Oscar get here?"

"I asked him to come a bit before ten."

Francesca got up, swinging her skirt from side to side.

"I'm off. You won't see me again until this evening."

"Do you think you can resist the temptation to come by?" asked Van, also getting up.

"If I do come by, I'll stay in the street, I won't come in."

"How are you going to spend the day?"

"I have Volodine's novel to finish, and Serena's to begin."

"Are you okay, Francesca?"

"This morning, yes. Last night, I had a rough moment. Henri had gone out. He left a note on my desk, I don't know what time it was, I found it at midnight, just one sentence: 'Obviously, you can do what you like with your own property, but to squander so much money on a total loss is not very glorious.'"

"Did it hurt you?"

"At the time, yes. But fairly quickly, his poor use of language cheered me up. I always find it entertaining when people are redundant. You can't squander your money in any other way than on a total loss. On a more serious note, I am convinced that what we are doing is right. And I can prove it. I proved it to myself between one and two o'clock in the morning, and so I got back to sleep. If I spent my money restoring a Roman viaduct or any other masterwork of our heritage, everyone would think it was a very worthy cause. What we are doing is no different. We are investing our time and money to support and enrich our literary heritage, which is being threatened by forgetfulness and indifference, not to mention the disarray in taste. Our cause is undeniable."

Her eyes were full of tears—her magnificent blue eyes, which were so fascinating that you could only look away after she had revealed herself to you, and then, when you thought of her, that is what you saw—her extraordinarily brilliant eyes, like the sapphires used for irises on certain statues.

Ivan took her by the shoulders. She stepped back. When she had closed the door, there was a scent in the air that made you think of lavender, or the sea.

Oscar was amazing. You would have thought that the inauguration of an unusual bookstore was something he had experienced a hundred times. People who like good novels know how to read, and they started arriving at ten o'clock. At eleven o'clock they were numerous, and remained so until evening. Most had come to have a look, and they could not believe their eyes: for years they had been dreaming of a bookstore like The Good Novel. They all said the same thing. They only read novels, and it wasn't that there was any lack of them, they had a whole pile waiting by their bed, on their night table, under their desk, or on the sofa in the entrance. But they felt ill at ease in bookstores, and most often they went back out feeling unjustifiably low, and they hadn't even bought anything: they'd had trouble breathing, something wasn't right, or they didn't know which way to look—it was very strange in any case, for people who liked nothing better than to read their fill in the evening in silence, released from all awareness of time, and they might think back on the time they broke their ankle and the two months of immobility that followed as a golden era, because there were novels to console them for everything, yet they rarely went into bookstores.

"It's the same for me," said Oscar, "and Ivan, too. We've opened the bookstore that was missing."

There was something irresistible about that boy, and it took Van all morning to figure out what it was. It wasn't just that he was slim, and wore his hair tied behind his neck, and that the white tunic he had on this morning contrasted with his brown skin. No, Van realized in a flash, it was that he didn't care about selling. To be honest, he didn't even think of it. If a customer concluded a long conversation with, I'll take this one, a bit as if he he'd say, I'm sorry I have to go, Oscar seemed to wake up, and smile, and he said: I love that one.

There were people until evening, people of all sorts, men and women of every age, with something in common that it took Ivan all day to identify, in fact. Something which explained why they remained calm, even when they had to step back to let their fellows pass them in the aisles, or wait to have their turn at their chosen shelf, or stand in line at the cash register: their relationship with their purchase had very little that was pecuniary about it, because their expense was not an expense and seemed deceptively like a reward, like at those good-cause flea markets where you didn't go to spend as little as possible but, on the contrary, to rid yourself of the heaviest part of yourself in the hopes of attaining pure joy.

Anis came by in the afternoon. Van did not see her come in. He was at the cash register, and suddenly there she was, adorably young and pink, holding in her hand *Enormous Changes at the Last Minute*, by Grace Paley.

"Would you like a frequent-buyer's card?" Ivan heard himself ask.

He had forgotten to have any in stock, and had just thought of it for the first time, but this afternoon he felt like he could make them appear from his fingertips.

"Oh, those things," said Anis with a tender laugh. "You never have them on you when you need them. You cannot remember where you put them. I don't believe in them."

Scratch of a nail on the bark of an oak. Van didn't feel it. Gravel tossed against a wave. The bookstore was rustling soundlessly like a forest, people did not speak or spoke very quietly, the tide rose, ebbed, rose again.

"Have something to drink," insisted Oscar. On the counter he had placed a tray with glasses of fruit juice, and a plate of fresh macaroons which, for several hours, no sooner had it emptied than it was filled again. Ivan never understood how the miracle occurred, but it no longer really mattered.

Not once did Oscar seem to be overwhelmed or running out of steam. He wore a constant, fairly disarming smile of triumph on his face, and at around nine in the evening, when there were fewer customers and Ivan wanted to congratulate him while he happened to be standing next to him, Oscar beat him to it: "You know the impression you've made on me all day?" he asked. "You were like a musician who's been waiting for his chance for years and finally one day he finds his audience, plays to perfection, and has a moment of euphoria, aware that his life from that moment on will never be the same."

At night, slightly before ten o'clock, Francesca appeared. Van noticed her browsing through a book. She looked like one customer among the thirty or so passionate readers who were lingering and did not seem the least bit ready to move. She came to the cash register, paid for *En silence*, by Daniel Arsand, which Ivan had strongly recommended to her the day before, and said to him in a murmur, "Eight or ten journalists will be coming in a quarter of an hour. Don't close, and above all, don't kick anyone out, they will mingle with the customers who stay behind. Anyway, some of them came by during the day, for the atmosphere, upon invitation from a press attaché. A caterer will be coming in five minutes to set up a buffet, over there, between Sweden and Albania. I'll be here, but as a customer. I'm not going to say anything. Don't speak to me. You know what the atmosphere is like on an opening night at a gallery? Things will be just as simple and relaxed. Whenever you like, make a gesture, I don't know, clap your hands. Introduce the bookstore in a few words, and tell them you'll be happy to take questions. There will be a few. The publicity campaign was effective. You'll recognize the reporters from their self-confidence, but if customers ask questions, so much the better, answer all of them.

"There will be piles of press kits on the buffet, they are very well done. Make sure everyone takes one. The same press kit was sent out earlier in the day to two hundred editorial offices, in Paris and elsewhere."

When he saw the maître d' come in, look around the bookstore, count the number of people present, go back out and return three minutes later followed by a young team who set up tables and covered them with hors d'oeuvres of all colors in less time than it takes to describe it, Van remembered the story of *Riquet à la houppe*. (He had added a copy of Perrault's *Contes* to their stock.) He felt as if he were the dreamy princess in the middle of the woods who suddenly sees a crowd of kitchen boys, cooks, and other officers spring from the earth.

He stood in front of the buffet and invited the visitors to come closer. They formed a circle. He spoke for two minutes about the bookstore, and then came the questions, one after the other, as expected. What percentage of new books will be stocked by The Good Novel? How were the books chosen? Why all the secrecy around the identity of the committee members? What might prevent them from the likely outcome of going bankrupt? Was there a group, or a corporation behind the business?

Van had no trouble answering. His answers were clear and precise. He invited everyone to take a press kit, and if anyone wanted additional information they could come up to him whenever they wanted.

It was nearly eleven o'clock. Hébert, from the *Vieil Observateur*, applauded as he said goodbye in a rather formal way, and everyone imitated him, but without the gravity. The caterer and his magicians took five minutes to make their gear disappear. When the last one had gone out, Van realized that he had not seen Francesca in the bookstore for a while.

He pushed the button that brought the blinds down, and the narrow slats of silk collapsed in a breath, isolating the bookstore from the rest of the world.

Oscar slumped onto a bench, his arms and legs hanging. Van massaged the back of his neck.

"The greatest day of my life," breathed Oscar.

"It's not over," said Van in a toneless voice. "For me, at any rate. What takes longest is to make up the list of titles sold. I wouldn't be surprised if we sold over five hundred volumes."

He was swaying slightly on his feet.

"We have to restock by tomorrow morning. Imagine if we get that many people."

He stopped, his voice interrupted by an apparition. Francesca was coming down from the second floor—she must have sought refuge up there during the press meeting. Her amazing skirt bloomed on either side with each step. Oscar got up, his eyes on her.

She went up to Van, took both his hands in hers, and raised them to the height of their faces so that they were very close to one another. She took a step back, lowering her hands. If this were a film, the next gesture would be to bring their two bodies close together again, this time in an embrace. Francesca let go of his hands and stepped back again, and Van thought that probably it was up to the hero to take the initiative of the third movement, and he swore to go back to the movies just as soon as the bookstore was autonomous.

"We need to talk about word of mouth again," he said, in a tone that he hoped sounded contrite but which was so full of regret that he was aware, a bit too late yet again, that he also thought up expressions with double meanings.

Their little ballet had not lasted twenty seconds. Oscar was reeling on his feet, like a child who is dreaming. Francesca went to kiss him with a gesture of camaraderie so sweet and straightforward that, far from feeling jealous, Van was filled with joy at the thought that he had never been gratified with the sort of little meaningless kiss that merely proves in plain language that such effusiveness will go no further.

"A celebration," said Francesca, her arms widespread.

"With a perfect finale," said Van.

"Totally improvised, at the beginning of the afternoon. When I saw what was happening at the bookstore, I felt instinctively that it would be better to give up on the idea of several press luncheons and, rather, invite the journalists to come and see what was happening on the spot."

"Did I dream it, or did you mention a press attaché?"

"No, you understood correctly. As I already explained, I did not want to be in the front line. The advertising agency has a public-relations department, a beehive of very lively young women for whom an hour of lead time is an unheard-of luxury. At the beginning of the afternoon, between two and three, they got hold of the journalists, told them about what was already happening at The Good Novel—something unusual—and suggested they go along incognito to have a look for themselves, and return at closing time to ask their questions while sipping on something."

Well, it wasn't enough just to congratulate each other. Half an hour from now, The Good Novel would be starting its second day. They had to make sure they did not lose their momentum.

Van was already sitting at the computer at the cash register. "Restocking takes priority," he said.

Francesca had been acquainted with him long enough to know that in booksellers' jargon restocking meant replacing the books sold, and that doing it quickly was synonymous with customer satisfaction, for customers do not appreciate it when they can't find what they're looking for, and most often they show it by leaving empty-handed.

The printer was churning out the list of books sold that day. The sheets fell in a flurry.

"Seven hundred and eleven," announced Oscar.

Two-thirds of the titles were in stock at the distributor's, the computer informed them.

"I'll take care of them remaining third," said Francesca.

28.

Van had provided her with the addresses of the publishers and wholesalers. She spent the entire day Tuesday driving to their warehouses.

Some publishers still had stores in Paris, and Francesca began with them. Every time she had more than fifteen books in her possession, she would swing back by the bookstore. She felt as if she were carrying gold nuggets around, and you can imagine that with fifteen or more gold nuggets in your possession you're complicating your life somewhat, and you are overly on the alert, and you get the impression that traffic lights stay red longer than green, and you can't get out of your car without walking around it twice to make sure the doors and windows are locked, not to mention the hatchback.

Once she had done a first round, at two o'clock, Francesca headed for Ivry (Volumen, Sodis, Union-Diffusion). She came back to the rue Dupuytren, then popped over to Vanves (Hachette), then back to the Odéon, once again.

Whenever possible, while she was at it she would take four or five copies of the title to be restocked. Eduardo, one of the Cinéor drivers whom she had requisitioned for the occasion, wasted his breath telling her what he had heard from Oscar that very morning, that she would only have to do this once, because as of the next day all the restocking would be taken care of automatically on a daily basis, and the books would be delivered by couriers. Francesca wanted to do her best, and her best, on that particular day, seemed proportional to her happiness, which was abundant.

How thin she is, thought Ivan, watching her climb out of the car outside the bookstore for the fifth time.

At the end of the afternoon, she left again for Arpajon, where a friend of Van's, a retired bookseller, had put together an incomparable stock of old books, which he only sold reluctantly when it was absolutely necessary. For the first time in a long while, as she drove through the dense green meadows and the yellow fields of wild mustard, she felt as if she were no longer being supported but was being drawn by something powerful, she was full of volition, against any temptation to let herself sink. Her strength, she would tell Van much later on, was nothing more nor less than the hope of, at last, attaining that goal which had become so important for her—not to succeed in doing something, but simply to do something good.

Every time she went by The Good Novel, the bookstore was full, and corresponded almost exactly to the vision she had had in her most confident moments, with its contemplative readers, capable of remaining motionless for an entire half a day, immersed in their reading, next to each other in silence, often standing—out of choice, since everything at The Good Novel had been arranged so that people could sit down, unless they had merely become distracted—and only the touch of madness in their eyes, characteristic of their addiction, betrayed their euphoria when, as it came time to leave, their gaze met that of one of the attendant priests, and whether their arms were full of books or their hands quite empty, they could hardly keep from dancing the moment they went out the door.

By the end of the third week, the bookstore had already found its clientele. From the first to the last day of autumn, it was never empty.

Right from the beginning of September, encouraging articles appeared in the newspapers, but the opening of a bookstore is not exactly headline news, and however laudable an undertaking it may be, and however risky, it is usually described in economic rather than lyrical terms.

What was decisive, something that neither Doultremont's experts, nor the advertising agency, nor the quivering press attachés had foreseen, was how much was discussed on the Internet. Right from the opening on Monday, and never letting up thereafter, a powder trail led from blog to Web site and from chat room to forum, presenting The Good Novel in terms so passionate that readers were bound to be taken by an irrepressible desire to go and see for themselves. *It's marvelous, Go check it out right away, The secret we are burning to reveal*: the panegyrics bordered on literary criticism in their form, accumulating the most conventional clichés in their own way. Basically, they all shared the same idea: At last! *At last a bookstore where only superb novels are to be found. At last a real choice. At last you can be sure you won't be disappointed.*

By then—mid-September—the press was treating this development like a news event. Radio stations broadcast their reports, and then, always last, television channels ran images that showed strictly nothing, and Ivan's sentences were amputated of their beginning and their end, not to mention every nuance, so they no longer meant a thing.

Nevertheless, the effect was positive. Sales continued to increase. The accompanying advertising that Francesca had planned turned out to be unnecessary. Oscar was a virtuoso on the Web, and by the end of the month he had taken charge of online sales and orders. He became the champion of restocking—so quick and precise at recording orders and sales, so friendly with the couriers, who were an essential element of the circuit and well aware of it—and he used the space on the rue Dupuytren to such good effect, that very rarely were they out of anything. During these first weeks, Ivan recognized among their customers four of the Parisian members of their commit-

tee, who had come incognito to see the results of their contributions, to see what success, something they did not know,
looked like. Ivan, who was usually so naturally friendly and
cheerful, found himself face to face one day at the cash register with Larry de Winter, and he would not smile: after the fact
he realized he'd been afraid he might give something away. But
he could not restrain a fit of giggles when the older gentleman
gave him a very amateurish wink, so exaggerated that his head
and the top of his body jerked forward, as if someone were
pushing him roughly from behind.

Many of the buyers became regulars. Oscar and Van
noticed the ones who came several times a week. The member
cards that Anis had inspired were printed up. (In fact, the
good customers seemed to think of them as an accessory, and
never remembered where they had put them.) Van came up
with the idea of opening accounts, the way people used to in
the old days in grocery stores. The initiative was a great success. As people signed up, they introduced themselves. Names
were exchanged. The appellative "Mr. Georg" began circulat-
ing. Call me Ivan, said Van. Oscar was immediately baptized
"Mr. Oscar," as his Malagasy name was too difficult to remember. Just Oscar, he said graciously, and from time to time you
heard people call him "Mr. Justoscar."

Other customers adamantly refused to give their names.
They were well-known writers or literary commentators that
nearly everyone in the bookstore could identify the moment
they came in, having seen them in photographs or on television. Bertrand Poirot-Delpech, for example, came every other
day at the end of the afternoon, and he immediately stood out
because of the way he tried to go unnoticed. One time he came
upon Bernard Frank and both of them, visibly thinking no one
had recognized them, laughed hysterically for a good quarter
of an hour, side by side, leaning over Evelyn Waugh's *Decline
and Fall.*

Customers soon began to suggest missing titles. Often it was disappointment that drove them to it: I can't find *Au pays du matin calme*. And yes, it's a magnificent novel. Would you care to order it? asked Oscar (or Van). But most of the time the customers who suggested a title did not want to buy it, they already had it. They just wanted to point out something that did not seem normal to them.

It's one thing to order a book for a customer, another to have it permanently on the shelf. However, when customers couldn't find a novel and ordered it, even if they did not explicitly suggest it be added to the stock, the issue was raised at the store all the same. Finally Van and Francesca decided to share with the eight committee members all the titles that people were surprised not to find at The Good Novel. Let the committee decide. All that was needed was for one elector to approve the addition for it to take effect. But if the eight of them disapproved, then the novel was not added to the bookstore's permanent stock.

Among those who made suggestions there were certain customers they quickly recognized, although they never gave their name. The authors. You could tell them from the very first words they uttered. Because their tone of voice was not neutral, but vindictive, painful, disillusioned, even hurt. They did not pronounce the titles normally, they whispered, and for good reason: they had devoted more time and care to choosing them than they had to choosing names for their own children. These authors never bought anything. Their suggestions were transmitted in the same manner as the others. Francesca and Van had hesitated, but what else could they possibly do, at this stage?

Others intervened in a more direct fashion. Publishers called, and they were not always diplomatic: you think it's right not to have a single book by Henri Troyat? They gave the same answer to all the publishers: send us a letter, or an e-mail. We will pass it on to our committee.

Numerous suggestions came in via the Internet, too. Van spent two hours every evening reading the day's messages. To those who suggested titles, he sent a stock answer explaining the rules of the game, how they referred to the electors, how each one of them had the power to add a title, but not individually to block a title. (Is there a word that signifies the opposite of veto? asked someone on the Internet. Bravo, added someone else.)

Some suggestions or remarks were worthy of debate. Van got in the habit of writing a brief every day, where he would note down an idea, emphasize a point of view, or share some information. This daily communiqué ended up as a newsletter and, for lack of a better name surfacing any quicker, it was soon referred to universally as The Newsletter.

Doultremont grew more distant than ever when reality went against his predictions. Francesca hardly ever saw him during those first weeks of The Good Novel. Not once did he mention the bookstore to her. He would not set foot inside— at least as far as Francesca could tell. She wished she were mistaken. He probably went by without drawing attention to himself, she told Ivan, and he did not have the heart to contradict her. "Yes," he said, "I'd be surprised if he could contain his curiosity. He could easily have found out that I often left the bookstore in Oscar's hands, while I went to work upstairs."

But that all time, it would have taken more than his lack of interest to destabilize Francesca. She had things to do. Questions without precedent were being asked every day at The Good Novel, and they needed to be dealt with. They had to think about the upcoming months, too. For Francesca, that fall was a turning point in her life. The obsessive thoughts of her loss now created a barrier to new experiences; Violette no longer held her back.

The customers acted like associates. One of their most loyal customers was a press cartoonist who, when his day was over at around two o'clock, and he had submitted his drawing to the daily paper where he worked, was in the habit of coming to hang around The Good Novel until evening. So when Ivan told him one day that the word "customer" did not seem right to designate the support they were receiving from people like him, Roselin Folco (his name was an echo of his Provençal origins) suggested he refer to them rather as friends. The Friends of The Good Novel, said Ivan slowly. No, corrected Folco, the Friends of the Novel.

They kept the name to use as a title for the forum where loyal followers met on the Web, at any time of day, but naturally mostly at night.

Another passionate reader, a dark-haired young woman, (oenologist by profession, who had discovered The Good Novel while attending a Salon du Vin in Paris, since she lived in a village on the slopes of the Jurançon), asked during her second visit whether they could mail her three novels from the stock every month. You choose, she said. If I've already read them I'll reread them, or give them as gifts.

She was the first to take out a subscription of a type that would become extremely successful not only in Paris, but throughout the entire Francophone world, and which, according to a friendly gentleman who they later learned was a professor at the Collège de France, was the revival of an old publishing practice from the time when most publishers were also booksellers. Oscar improved on the formula by coming up with the idea of tailor-made subscriptions. You signed up (Subscriptions to the Novel), and you could receive the number of novels you wanted, as often as you wanted, and you could ask that for the duration of your choice—a month, six months, a year—one particular author be favored, or a century or a country, or on the contrary, that all the genres and the origins be mixed up.

By November it had become clear that the Friends of the Novel could generate enthusiasm for a long-forgotten title, and in eight days they might exhaust the tiny stock at the publishers and in the week after that make all the online booksellers rich—until the publisher reprinted the work and the press finally reported on the rediscovery of an author like Eudora Welty or Patrick White.

By the end of the year of the publishers had got it. They would stick an intern six hours a day in front of a computer, with the instructions never to leave planet The Good Novel (the Web site, the newsletter, the forum), and to note down any spark of curiosity for a title or an author, and inform them of it that very day.

Gradually, without realizing it, Van was becoming a bit of a celebrity. Truth be told, he was great on television. For someone who was so neglectful of his appearance, and did not know how to dress, and never combed his hair, and refused point-blank to wear makeup before going on the air, he was perfectly natural onscreen and far more confident than in everyday life. He expressed himself with simplicity, precision, and humor, and talked about the books with so much enthusiasm that, in the days which followed, the ones that he had mentioned sold like hot cakes. He was the ideal incarnation of The Good Novel's plan to invite everyone to dine on the best and most agreeable literature. With his allure of an inspired dunce, bird-catcher, and friend of fairies, he enchanted the viewers, and they asked for more. The television people could not get enough of him, but Van only accepted if it was to talk about literature, and he never spoke about anything else, so without even trying, for those few months he became an unexpected star of television, the man who transformed cultural programs into large-audience programs.

Francesca had her eyes on Van; she was vibrant, serious, smiling now and again as he evoked a name or an anecdote, and then she was illuminated in one instant, the way a gray day is illuminated when, without warning, the sun shines through and changes it entirely.

To describe certain phenomena, there is only one possible metaphor, thought Heffner who, for the entire hour he had spent watching Francesca, had already thought of this metaphor several times. That's the way it is.

Francesca was looking at him now. "Thus, there are times," she said slowly, adopting the tone you sometimes use to tell a story to a child, "when in love stories, after a very long ordeal (shock, observation, despair, guesswork, calculation, hope), an accelerating impulse arrives (accident, decisive gesture, tears, declaration), and at that moment, contrary to the dark predictions that were all one had remembered, no doubt to prepare for the worst, there is an immediate agreement and shared jubilation. And then comes a period where one goes from bedazzlement to bedazzlement with stupefying ease, so much so that one regrets having waited so long to take the plunge. Afterwards, one remembers this succession of blissful moments as if it were a marvelous story that had happened to other people."

29

L et's talk a little bit more about the end of 2004," said Heffner, as if to prolong a happy chapter of the story.

"Winter came fairly quickly," said Van.

He turned to Francesca: "Do you remember Christmas Day?"

Francesca had organized a meal in a hunting lodge in the middle of the forest of Marly. A crisp snow covered the ground. After lunch, they had walked through the immense silence, among the gigantic black trees, cracking the frozen ground beneath their feet.

"Were there many of you?" asked Heffner.

"Ivan and myself," said Francesca. "Oscar was celebrating Christmas with his family. He has four sisters and a gaggle of nieces and nephews. Henri apologized for his absence."

"In fact," added Ivan, "Francesca had offered to take everyone to Méribel for a week." But he didn't see how they could close a bookstore for that long when it had only just opened.

"And as for asking Anis to come along for lunch in the forest, no," he said, "that wasn't possible."

Anis had not been back to The Good Novel since it opened.

Van would have preferred it, however. He no longer had a minute to himself. Anis was also very busy, ill at ease with the change of scale, the vast number of students, the way classes and workshops were scattered all over Paris, and she was disappointed to realize that not everything at the Sorbonne was as she had imagined it would be.

She called from time to time, left breezy messages that Ivan found terribly stilted, such as: Have you read *Gardens in Spain,* by José Cabanis? It's a trilogy, not very long. Written to perfection. There's an extraordinary female character, her name is Gabrielle, and she makes the narrator suffer a bit.

Ivan read the trilogy that night. He then understood that the message was anything but breezy. Gabrielle appeared and disappeared. Above all, she disappeared. She was flighty, well, you couldn't be sure, the further you went in the book the less you knew. What Gabrielle wanted was something you discovered gradually, but that was the whole point, that you didn't know, that she remained mysterious, elusive.

To the rue Bol-en-Bois Van sent novels of shared love, stories that were not necessarily simple (*Pride and Prejudice*), or explicit (*L'ouverture des bras de l'homme*), but which all concluded in mutual agreement. It took a lot of time to find stories that ended well. Almost all love stories are wrenching, and he knew there were not very many happy ones, but he had been far from thinking that it was so to such an extent. In each of the books he sent her, he slid the same bookmark, a sheet on which he had written: Can we see each other? And they saw each other, three or four times, on Sundays. Anis wanted to walk around Paris, so they visited Balzac's house and Odilon Redon's studio, and they went up to Belleville. As tourists, thought Ivan, that's no good. Anis gave him the impression she was being cautious. She asked him about the bookstore, and he wondered if she was jealous.

It rained a great deal, eight days in a row. All the leaves that still remained on the trees fell all of a sudden. Twice Anis said mysterious things, quickly and softly. One day: I've just got out of prison. Another day: I'm not free. And when Van urged her to explain, she clammed up. She means to discourage me gently, she wouldn't go about it any other way, Van sometimes thought. And other times: she's a lost child.

Ten days before Christmas, he invited her to the cinema. They were showing a revival of *Xica da Silva*. He remembered the film as being an injection of vitality, and he called Anis and suggested they go see it the next day.

At the last minute she canceled, saying, I can't, in such a way that Van did not even try to understand. His reaction surprised even him—he was completely discouraged. It's up to her, he thought, either she comes or she doesn't. As far as he was concerned, he was giving up. He would make no more efforts in her direction, no more calls, no more invitations, no more books. She could let the silence between them expand until they were well and truly apart, or the contrary—it was up to her.

That is why on Christmas Day, Francesca and Van walked for an hour after lunch, beneath a sparkling sun, across a frozen ground, without talking, each of them repressing a terrible desire: Francesca to hold Ivan's elbow in both hands and walk shoulder to shoulder, and Van to take Francesca by the hand. Their silence, walking side by side, did not bother them, and both took note of it deep inside. But they realized they were not strictly behaving like the founders of a newly hatched enterprise, triumphant in its early days.

30

In the week that followed, that very special week between Christmas and New Year's Day, when many city dwellers are on vacation yet stay at home, overcome by somewhat regressive desires such as sleeping more than is needed, or drinking hot chocolate at four in the afternoon, Francesca, going against the current, made the necessary arrangements for overhauling that part of the ground floor that was still unused on the rue Dupuytren. There would be no conference room, and it didn't really matter. They had to enlarge the bookstore. In the four months since they had opened, over twelve hundred new titles had been added to the stock. And above all, The Good Novel was thronged every day. Adding an extra third to the existing surface would hardly be too much.

The fitting out was fairly simple, the same wood shelving that they had already used, the same tables, benches, and lights.

Ivan was counting the days. He was waiting so impatiently for a sign from Anis that he had to admit to himself that his way of letting go was not really a letting go, but a classic maneuver: given the fact that he had made no gesture in her direction, he now expected, of course, a virtually automatic readjustment in the romantic order, which holds that you are never viewed with greater interest by the person whom you have dreamt in vain of attracting than when you resolve to look elsewhere.

On Thursday, January 6, in the day's press, both weeklies and dailies, there was a new page of advertising devoted to the bookstore.

In a few lines and bold letters, the team in charge of The Good Novel bookstore—no other details, no names—thanked both their readers and buyers who, over the last four months, had helped to make their undertaking a success. At the bottom of the page, a photo showed the interior of the bookstore on a busy day, with its El Greco colors—blues, carmines, and astonishing backlighting. The results of their activity were given in a few figures—average weekly visits, accumulated total over four months, curve of their progression; for sales, the same thing, two figures and a chart, daily average, overall total, and the curve, superb.

At the bottom of the page was written: "The bookstore is already turning a profit. But that's not the most important thing. The Good Novel is much more than a business, it's a movement."

Was this their mistake? All these signs of success, that only seemed to be growing: was it too provocative? Was there something unbearable about their heralding a fundamental movement?

The reaction was not long in coming. It took various forms, so clearly incremental that it quickly became obvious that they were deliberate.

A new type of customer showed up one day, not even taking the trouble to pretend to look for a book: he, or she, went straight to the cash register to protest: I don't see anything by Helen Fielding (Dan Brown, Danielle Steel). Van and Oscar were prepared. They knew that a bookseller does not have the right to refuse to sell a book that is available. We don't have everything on our shelves, they said. Would you like to order it? Each time the answer was yes.

Some of these buyers had a title in mind. Others asked for

paperback editions of a certain author, then hesitated, took their time, and spoke loudly. Oscar (or Van) was unflappable.

Fairly quickly, these particular customers increased in number. By the end of January, there were fifteen or twenty of them a day. Van (or Oscar) saw similarities among them. They were people whom, at first glance, you might not be able to tell from anyone else, people who were crazy about fiction yet showed no external signs of madness, youngish, men and women alike. But no sooner did they open their mouths than you sensed the same absence of conviction in their request—it was as if they were reciting something by rote—you could tell they lacked culture, they massacred the author's names.

"We would ask them a trick question," said Ivan. "For example: which Danielle Steel are you referring to, the American or the Australian? They were incapable of answering. They were probably hired through a classified ad."

In February it became clear that these pseudo-customers were not coming to pick up their order. When someone from the bookstore called the number they had left, it was always a cell phone. It was a wrong number, and they disturbed someone who didn't know what they were talking about. And the cost of the books, some of which had been hard to find, now had to be borne by The Good Novel. Oscar (or Van) finally resolved to have customers leave a deposit: the number of deadbeat customers diminished spectacularly, and they eventually disappeared.

At the same time, at the beginning of 2005, The Good Novel forum on the Internet began to receive messages where the tone was nothing like that of the previous posts. Which is an understatement. Some of them tried to sound like vaguely formulated criticisms: *There is nothing snobbier than this so-called Good Novel. It's the most middle-class choice of books on earth.* But most of them were downright insulting: *Bunch of*

*reactionaries! And what if I happen to like Dan Brown? What
you're doing is just trash, you are bound to fail spectacularly.*

There were threats: *We'll slash your throats, you stuck-up
jerks. You should hang, fascist pigs.*

It wouldn't have been anything to worry about if the messages hadn't arrived in the hundreds, repeated ten or twenty
times over without the slightest variation, provoking in response
hundreds of protests as well, a flood of incoming and outgoing
messages that saturated the network and the inboxes, wrought
havoc on the subscriptions, and took up time that Ivan could
have spent much more fruitfully.

Van had tried to hide from Francesca what he now considered to be organized attacks. With Oscar's complicity and
some luck, he had managed to hide the systematic ordering of
blockbusters. Poisoned darts arriving over the Internet, that
was another story. Although Francesca came as rarely as possible to The Good Novel during the day, she was in the habit of
spending long periods of time at the computer: she was
responsible for follow-ups that took hours, one thousand seven
hundred subscriptions, and almost daily suggestions for new
titles (it was she who passed them on by telephone to all the
committee members). She became aware of the change all by
herself.

"What is going on?" she asked Ivan at the end of January.
"Is the tide turning?"

At the beginning of February, she got an embryonic reply:
"Something is going on."

31

On Thursday, February 17, after a hasty late lunch at the Comptoir, a café at the Carrefour de l'Odéon where, every time he went there, he recalled a sentence by Jean Echenoz on the paradox that in this very windy spot in Paris, fairly ugly and quite polluted, the sidewalk cafés are always packed (a sentence he unfortunately did not have the time to look up in order to quote it literally, because in literary matters it is not so much the idea that counts as the manner), Ivan, before heading back to The Good Novel, bought *Le Ponte* at the kiosk situated below Danton's outstretched bronze arm, near the métro station. It had been ages since he could read the papers every day. He bought individual issues, once a week, on the day when the literary supplement was included, and he went through the Book pages of the weekly magazines on the Internet—and as he did so he jumped on his chair, grumbled, and abruptly left his computer, reinforced in his conviction—happy overall—that The Good Novel was on the right track. He had felt obliged to subscribe to the weekly *Livres Hebdo*, and read it out of professional conscience. To be honest, he knew of only one publication whose Literature pages were impeccable, and that was *303*, the fine quarterly journal published in the Loire Valley.

On his way to the bookstore, from the pile the vendor had handed him he removed the few pages of literary supplement, apparently designed for this purpose, since not only was it detachable but had already been detached and, as was his usual habit, he left the rest of the papers on a bench.

Before he had reached the corner of the rue Dupuytren, he stopped short and stood motionless in the street, with that paper open in front of his face. On page two, over four columns, the wink-wink headline made him forget the place, the time, and to make a long story short, everything that was not The Good Novel. "The Commissars of Literary Worth." By the bottom of the first column, he got it. They were bringing out the heavy artillery.

The article was signed by one Jean-Brice Abéha, assistant professor of political sociology at the University of Paris IV. "In September a bookstore opened in Paris, with considerable means behind it and the shameless intention of selling only great novels." Ivan read as quickly as he could. "The advertising for the launch of the bookstore was unequivocal . . . Nobody thought it worthwhile to be alarmed. This, however, is nothing more nor less than a totalitarian undertaking. Individuals who have been careful to keep their identity a secret have claimed the right to decide for others—worse, to decide for everyone—which are the great novels, and to push aside those books, far more numerous, that they happen not to like . . . What does *good novel* mean? Who are these kapos who have the nerve to place their seal of approval on this book and not that one? Where are they coming from? What gives them the right?"

The article concluded: "We all know where lists lead. The next stage is purges. The bonfire of forbidden books is not far behind."

Van raised his head and once again became aware of the boulevard, the cinemas, the sun veiled in a grayish white light, and his own pulse, which seemed to be racing. "Where are they coming from?": he thought he was hearing those Saint Justs in jeans perched on the soapboxes of action committees in the 1970s, the violence they displayed to discredit everything that wasn't *them*, their grotesque phraseology, their methodical bad faith. This has gone far enough, he thought. But at this point, far did not mean a great deal.

He folded the supplements and mentally smoothed his face before going through the door at The Good Novel. Once he was inside, back in the silent and vibrant atmosphere of the busy time, for a moment he had the impression he had woken up from a nightmare. But alas, the attack did exist, it was under his arm, black on white in the daily paper considered to be the most serious one in France, and the dream might instead be this ideal bookstore.

He would wait a few hours and think about the best strategy before calling Francesca. He sat down at the cash register, behind one of the computer screens, and looked on the Web to see what he could find out about Jean-Brice Abéha. He found nothing. Among the entire faculty at Paris IV, there was no one by that name.

Folco, the cartoonist, came in with *Le Ponte* in his hand. He went straight to Van: "Have you seen this?" Van placed his hand on Folco's arm: "Let them talk. There are always people who, the moment they see a rose that has just bloomed, feel like crushing it into a million pieces."

But five minutes later, Francesca called. She wanted to show him something. She was at the stop of the number 63 bus, outside the École de Médecine.

Ivan wasn't sure it would be about today's *Ponte*. Francesca never read papers when they came out. She was both more and less detached than he was where newspapers were concerned. She had subscriptions to a dozen publications—*L'Idée*, *Le Ponte*, *Esprit*, *Le Débat*, *La NRF*, *Les Inrockuptibles*, *Le Matricule des Anges*, *Critique*, *Art Presse*, *Cahiers du Cinéma*, *Alternatives économiques*—which she never read when they came out and later only partially, but she leafed through them from A to Z. Every time she had a fit of reading, she would devote two or three hours in a row to pruning the pile of printed matter she had allowed to accumulate, transferring everthing, after a quick look through, from the magazine rack where they were stacked to the firewood basket that was always kept by the fireplace in her study at the rue de Condé.

Van saw her waiting at the number 63 stop, sitting on a bench beneath the shelter. She got up and came to meet him.

"Have you seen?" she said.

"Yes," said Van. "We might have expected this. Good old lefty criticism is alive and well. Anything that is not their style they call fascism. But tell me, that's not like you to read *Le Ponte* on the day it comes out."

"Someone shoved it in my face."

"In your face?"

"Haven't you seen?" said Francesca again.

She made Van turn around and led him to the Odéon métro station. On the façades of the buildings between the shop fronts and the window displays, on the back of the newspaper kiosk, on the two low concrete walls on either side of the métro escalator, on the municipal panel with the map of the neighborhood, the article had been glued, at eye level, thirty or forty times over.

"I've come here from Saint-Germain," said Francesca. "It's everywhere, in front of the church. I love dazibaos. It seemed that this one had just been put up, so I went to read it right away."

"When I saw the same posters here, in the métro, I popped over to the Place de l'Odéon. Same thing over there. They're all around the theatre."

She squeezed her shoulders, and continued, "I feel a chill in my spine just to think that someone bought a hundred copies of the *Ponte* the moment it went on sale, put them in his car and, in one hour, stuck them up all around the bookstore. Someone who knew the article was going to come out."

"I picture it differently," said Van. "I picture maybe a dozen or so young guys each of them given ten articles already cut out, and told which is zone of action and be quick about it."

"What's the difference?"

"We're no longer dealing with some bilious individual like the author of the article, but a whole commando. Concerted action."

"Do you think they're keeping a watch on us, even here? That they're getting a kick out of seeing our faces?"

"It could be. Let's not stay outside."

"I'm going to call Tourterelli."

"The publisher of the *Ponte*? Don't do that. That's giving too much importance to an unfair article. What we have to hope is that a lot of the friends of The Good Novel will respond to that Abéha article through the newspaper."

"And what about us, should we respond?"

"An open letter, yes. They attack us, we defend ourselves. You want me to draft a response?"

"Would you? You'll do it with more restraint than I would. Van, I can't stand the idea that someone might be watching us, I'll be off. Call me."

Van shut himself in the big office on the second floor. Half an hour was enough. He put forth two sorts of arguments, which made up the two parts of his reply.

First of all, the article was full of falsehoods. Van had never hidden his identity, his name was in the paper when The Good Novel opened, it had been heard on television, and you could find it on the bookstore's Web site ("Who are we?").

He was not assuming the right to decide on the quality of the novels: it was a committee of experts who selected them, in secret, in order to avoid any pressure. This procedure had also been described on The Good Novel's Web site, and at great length in the newspapers.

And did he need to point out that there was nothing totalitarian about their project? Given the fact that they were one bookstore among thousands in France who were biased toward a certain type of novels, and not an exclusive authority, a State, or a monopoly?

Secondly—Van's pen hurried across the paper—selection is a common practice where culture is concerned. Museums, art galleries, theatre festivals, and movie theatres all make their choices. As for books, publishers choose—to publish or not to publish—and literary prizes have selection as their vocation; the literary sections in newspapers are nothing other than selections, and do not cover even one tenth of the fiction published overall, and the bookstores that have always been qualified as good bookstores are the ones that make no secret about what they prefer. In all these spheres of cultural life there comes a moment of "this, yes, that, no," which means, "we think this is good, but not that."

It was four o'clock. Ivan called Francesca and suggested he show her his draft. She asked to meet at La Grille on rue Mabillon. She did not want to go through the neighborhood. She did not have the heart to see that article again, multiplied by thirty.

Van was about to leave the office when suddenly it occurred to him that the name Abéha sounded like the initials A.B.A. in French. He sat right down behind his computer, and went back to the Web site of the University of Paris IV. Once again he scrolled through it, department by department. There were two professors with the initials A.B.A., Anne-Brigitte Acker and Alain Bernard-Amont. In addition, if he were to believe the telephone directory, there was no one in Paris or in the region with the last name Abéha.

Francesca thought it was pointless to investigate the two people with the initials A.B.A. or to write to them. Both of them would say, it's not me.

Other than the fact that she thought it was necessary to add that Abéha was by all appearances a pseudonym, she did not want to change a single word in Van's draft.

"The tone is perfect. Not the least bit aggressive. The truth, nothing else. Do you mind signing it?"

"Not at all, it will be an honor."

"What should we do? Send a letter to this Abéha?"

"Yes, but an open one. A reply to the signatory but addressed to the *Ponte*, and we'll ask them to publish it."

"Shall we send it by mail?"

"No, that would take too long. I'll hand deliver it."

"Let me go. You have things to do at the bookstore. Type the letter, and sign it. It will take you quarter of an hour. I'll wait here. Send me Oscar, I'll stop in at the newspaper. By the way, Ivan, where exactly is Paris IV? Which faculty is it?"

"It's the Sorbonne," said Ivan.

When she saw Oscar coming, Francesca hesitated, then asked him, "Have you heard?"

"Yes," said the young man calmly. "It's hardly surprising. The Devil only ever attacks whatever is beautiful and pure."

He smiled.

"In his place, I would do the same. As for the rest, everything that's really ugly, everything that's wrong on earth, that's up to God and his saints to fix."

Francesca thought about what she had known that was most tender and pure: Violette.

"Sit down," she said. "Do you believe in God and the Devil?"

"I can see how someone might not believe in God," said Oscar, "although for me personally, that's difficult. But not to believe in the Devil, that I find very hard to understand. You have to be really distracted, and be totally unaware of what's going on around you."

"What worries me is the terrible struggle between the powers, I mean the fact that the struggle is unceasing, there's never a victor, there's never an end, and we are just terrified playthings."

"I see things differently. I don't believe we are on the sidelines. I don't think that's even possible. We are in one camp or the other, sometimes first in one then the other, in succession, and I'm afraid that most often we are in one and the other at the same time, because we are ambiguous by nature. But we are not doomed to ambiguity, we can escape it: that's what we call making progress, I think. And of course the struggle will end. One side will be victorious."

"For someone so young, you have made a lot of progress."

"Young? I'm almost twenty-five."

"An age when people think they've been around a lot, that they're mature. Later on, you'll see, you realize that you don't know much, you discover that you are a novice, and then a beginner. You realize that you're going to spend your entire life practicing scales."

"What a gloomy prospect!"

"Do I seem gloomy?"

Oscar hesitated. Francesca expected him to say, not all the time.

"Not only," he said.

"How is your novel coming along, Oscar?"

"I'm letting it settle, get some air."

"Have you finished it?"

"I finished a first draft before we opened the bookstore, in Méribel, at your place. For the time being I have other things to do. And it's good timing, I had planned to put the manuscript aside for a while, to forget about it, and then reread it with a fresh gaze, a reader's gaze."

"Well, that certainly is wise. And what's it about, your novel?"

"Everything we've just talked about—God, the Devil, the great cosmic struggle, the weak and the strong, faith, discouragement . . ."

"All that!"

"What else should I write about?"

"Is there a plot?"

"Ten plots. And, above all, it's a novel with a country."

"Madagascar?"

"Yes. It's a political novel. But I'm wasting your time. Ivan asked me to give you this note, and he told me to be quick."

Francesca looked at her watch.

"I'm not sorry we had this conversation, believe me," she said, getting up. "We'll continue it someday, if you like."

She went on foot along boulevard Blanqui, to the editorial offices of the *Ponte*, by way of the rue Monge and the avenue des Gobelins. A half hour more or less made no difference. In any case, Ivan's response would not come out the next day. And she needed to walk. All afternoon she had imagined those little brutes hastily gluing their filthy article on the walls. Striding now through the fifth arrondissement, she was looking out for angels. But it is always difficult when thinking of angels not to have a stereotyped idea, and Francesca had in mind long tall creatures with coffee-colored skin and very black hair tied at the neck.

Oscar was right, far too often we forget the Devil, and we are wrong to do so. When Francesca went home to the rue de Condé, it was eight o'clock in the evening. From the streets outside her building, she could see light in the windows. That was unusual for that time of day. She found Henri in the living room and immediately saw *Le Ponte* spread out on the sofa where he had been sitting.

"You should have told me you were having dinner here tonight," she said. "I would not have made plans to go back out."

Two minutes earlier all she had wanted was to lie down—she was exhausted. But the prospect of a tête-à-tête with Henri was beyond her strength. No sooner had she seen him than the words "go back out" had sprung to her lips.

Doultremont had been able to read as much on her face.

"I'm going back out, too," he said. "But I wanted to tell you how sorry I am, after such a terrible blow."

"The article in *Le Ponte?* A blow below the belt, more like."

"Terrible and below the belt."

"No. Such a rotten trick is not necessarily terrible. We'll let it crawl along on the ground, and go around it, and go on our way."

"Are you going to respond?"

"With composure, yes. We won't use the same tone."

"Do you know where the article came from?"

"No, and I have no intention of trying to find out. It comes from spite, envy, and mediocrity."

"Well that's already not bad."

Francesca thought of Oscar.

"Not so bad," she said.

Doultremont folded up *Le Ponte* and took it with him.

"Fine," he said. "I'm on my way. I was afraid you might be upset, but I see you are holding up. I feel better, knowing you're going out. I wish you an excellent evening."

Francesca raised her eyes to look at Heffner, who was listening carefully.

"Showing off, playing tough, was probably exactly what one shouldn't do. I must have provoked him. God knows that was not my intention. I had only one desire, to get away. To escape from a tête-à-tête where I would only take a battering, in spite of appearances."

"Go on," said Heffner.

32.

Ivan's response could not be published, not the day after, nor the next. But it had better not to take too long, he said. "How long should we give them?" asked Francesca.

"I suggest we wait until Monday. If there is nothing in Tuesday's paper, I'll call the editor-in-chief's office. I'll insist on our right of reply."

By Thursday evening, however, the net surfers had mobilized. Things got very heated that night, and in the days that followed. Several hundred messages came in support of Abéha. *Literature for lords, thanks a lot! Beware of order in the kingdom of letters, Readers, toe the line! Still the same old notion of wanting what's good for us, rubbish ideas that we now know lead to nothing but domination and repression.*

Francesca was despondent. Nothing but platitudes! How could such hackneyed slogans still be so active? It would seem that nothing takes longer to wear out than a cliché.

Ivan saw a certain similarity to all these invectives.

"Did you notice? There are no more than fourteen or fifteen formulas. It wouldn't surprise me if they were all by the same person."

"It's very easy to program these mass mailings," explained Oscar. "Above all, don't go thinking there are a hundred people behind all this. It's done automatically. It's elementary electronic boorishness."

Messages supporting The Good Novel were far more numerous, and infinitely varied—it was clear each message had its own author. *It never fails, the moment you are demanding, they accuse you of elitism, What is totalitarian is the reign of marketing and mass-market books for the lowest common denominator, At The Good Novel we can breathe, Read and let read.*

At eleven o'clock in the evening on Thursday, Van wrote a few lines for the Web site Newsletter and signed them *The Booksellers. Everyone is entitled to express their opinion,* he wrote, *but let's have fairness and honesty preside over the debate. Anonymous invectives are unworthy. Mr. Abéha, if you are anything other than bitterness in disguise, show your face and introduce yourself. Our forum is open to you. Let's talk.*

The opposite camp was ready. Five minutes later, the forum was flooded. Messages signed Abéha were arriving by the dozen. They all reproduced, word for word, excerpts from the most accusing passages in the *Le Ponte* Op-Ed piece. Oscar's reply went out in successive salvos. *Time to go to sleep, or better yet, to go and read.*

On Friday morning at seven, Ivan signed yet another message in the newsletter, in the form of an appeal. *There is virtual, and then there is real,* he wrote. *What is real is the bookstore, and the purchase of books. The number of our customers and our sales figures will show us how much loyal support The Good Novel gets.*

There were a lot of people at the bookstore that Friday. People were talking. Basically, they were all saying: we are here. One young man stood out in the street, in front of the window, holding against his chest a big sign on a pole, where it was written: HAPPINESS. He stood there all morning. He did not find it necessary to introduce himself or to ask for permission. A woman brought a big blank book. Without saying a word, she wrote a first message of support and left it open next to the cash register. By the end of the day the book was full. The woman was the very discreet sort (Gray hair? Glasses?

After the fact, no one could say, she had been through there so quickly) and the first message was the longest:

"... 'I took from the reading-room Eugène Sue's *Arthur*. It's enough to make you vomit, there are no words for it. You have to read it if you are to feel pity for money, success, the public. Literature has an ache in its chest. It is spitting, spewing, it has blisters that it covers with pomaded taffeta, and it has brushed its head so hard that it has lost all its hair. It would take the Christs of Art to cure this leper.' ... —Flaubert. Letter to Louis Bouilhet. November 14, 1850."

At midnight, Van was able to announce in a newsletter: *Record sales at the bookstore. One thousand one hundred and two books sold today, Friday, February 18. Friends, you are magnificent.*

Since the publication of Abéha's article, Francesca had changed her habits, and she bought *Le Ponte* just as soon as it was on sale, to leaf through it within the quarter of an hour. As for reading it, no: she couldn't.

On Saturday, Van called her late in the morning. "When you go out, be sure to pick up *Le Bigaro*."

"Don't tell me they've started again!"

"Alas. And it's urgent."

On the Op-Ed page of the daily, taking up the entire width of the broadsheet, was an opinion piece entitled "Scorn," signed by the Executive Director of VLAM. The "people's press" had a soft spot for this Mr. Grantarroi, a former socialist who was now a liberal, well-known for his fondness for big cigars and bigger motorcycles. "It would be excessive to speak of totalitarianism," he wrote. "But for over forty years, in the VLAM bookstores (of which there are one hundred and sixty at present), we have offered the greatest number of books possible, and our goal has been to have the largest range and the greatest diversity. We do not have a great deal of sympathy for the opposing policy adopted by The Good Novel. We detect a certain amount of class condescension in their agenda.

"Our idea of culture and democracy makes us wary of any kind of effort to create standards. We prefer to leave our readers free to decide for themselves what is good for them.

"There are some people whose taste goes toward Bernard Clavel rather than Thomas Pynchon. That is their right. It is above all their pleasure, and we will not allow ourselves to criticize that right. We have to ensure the life of a popular culture which has given us great works. Some of those works, which were looked down on when they were published, are now unanimously revered, such as works by authors such as Alexandre Dumas, Jules Verne, or Hergé.

"The essential problem raised by the notion of literary value is that this value changes with time. A work that might have been hailed by its contemporaries seems trivial a hundred years later, perhaps even thirty years later. Inversely, another work that was judged unpleasant or uninteresting may now be praised to the skies.

"Our love of the novel and of the book is so great that we cannot see why, or even how, one could exclude, by means of a selection process, 99 percent of the titles available. Our passion, and our cause, is to respect the diversity of cultures, and the diversity of individuals."

Francesca was just arriving at the bookstore when she saw Ivan coming out, putting his jacket on.

"I was sure you wouldn't wait," he said. "And yet there was nothing urgent."

"What a load of sophistry."

"Do you think? What is good, is that they dislike us on both sides of the political spectrum. First *Le Ponte, Le Bigaro:* it's just as well that way."

"I feel like answering back with a page of advertising where we would just list the books sold at The Good Novel that originate in popular culture. There are loads of them, from Henri Pourrat's tales to *Marie-Claire* by Marguerite Audoux to *Le Dernier des justes* by André Schwarz-Bart."

"That would be an elegant way to go about it. But to respond to an article with a page of advertising—that would only earn us sarcasm, such as, all they have to offer in response to ideas is an ad worth €10,000. Francesca, can you spare an hour?"

"I'm free as a bird, Ivan. Unfortunately."

"I beg you, don't let this get you down. These attacks are very unfair, but they are still within the realm of ordinary debate."

Van pointed in the direction of Saint-Michel.

"Why don't you come with me to an appointment that ought to be fairly pleasant. Someone has offered to respond to Grantarroi's article for us. I got the offer by phone, just before I called you. He's waiting for us."

"Do I know him?" asked Francesca.

Ivan wasn't sure. He told Francesca that among the regulars at The Good Novel, one of the first to show his enthusiasm was a jolly, rosy-cheeked man in his seventies, who bought a great deal, and struck up conversations with everybody.

"But not just idle chit-chat," he specified. "He suggested several titles to add. He's very well-read. He is the one who made the connection between our subscriptions and the monthly shipments publisher-booksellers used to make in the old days."

"Do you know his name?"

"Not yet. I asked him just now, on the phone. He told me to meet him at the Balzar, and he'll introduce himself there."

"But that's Armand Delvaux," said Francesca when Van pointed him out, sitting in a corner of the brasserie.

"The medievalist?"

"I'm sure of it."

Van apologized to the historian for not recognizing him earlier. "And yet I'm very familiar with your work."

Delvaux lifted his hands from the table: "If only you could say, I know your novel! I did write one, thirty years ago, I slaved over it and it went nowhere."

He turned to Francesca.

"Ivan Georg and I have known each other since the opening of The Good Novel," he said, "but I don't believe I've seen you at the bookstore. I would not have forgotten."

"Francesca and I are associates," said Van, hoping that her first name would suffice for Delvaux, and that he would not wonder why they did not explain the association further.

Delvaux did not seem troubled by Van's vagueness, and without further ado he took from his pocket a sheet of paper folded in four and already covered on one side with what seemed to be an outline.

"I have an idea," he said. "Just one. It doesn't happen every day. I'd like to write an article and run it in Le Bigaro. The paper has a weakness for institutional old fogeys like me, and a rather nice typeface for captions such as 'Professor at the Collège de France.'"

Delvaux's idea was that you cannot oppose popular literature and elitist literature, that there is in fact no point in trying to distinguish them, never mind the fact that it can be difficult. Both types of literature include a quantity of insignificant books, and a few masterpieces, and the only worthwhile distinction is to promote great books, some of which are very simple while others are difficult.

"Since the purpose is to defend you," added Delvaux, "if you'll allow me I'll go even further. I would like to write that, on the contrary, treating mediocre books as if they were equal to good ones, and placing everything on offer as if everything had equal value, has a great deal to do with scorn, because it's demagogy. And demagogy holds that what is common will always be common."

"How can we thank you?" said Francesca.

"By not changing a thing at The Good Novel. And having no doubts about its principle."

Delvaux suggested they have lunch together. "The oysters are very good," he said. "It would be my pleasure to invite you."

If they continued their conversation, Francesca knew that sooner or later he would ask her how she had gotten involved in the bookstore and, one thing leading to another, who she was. She declined the invitation: "I'm busy, and very sorry to be, believe me." But with just a glance of her eyes, which could be extraordinarily evocative, she was able to convince Van to accept. "I'll let Oscar know," she said.

When she stopped off at the rue Dupuytren she saw there was still a good crowd in the bookstore. She almost offered to help Oscar at the cash register, where there was a long line. But the people who came to The Good Novel did not behave like ordinary customers. Five minutes more or less did not matter to them. If they had to wait for a while, they showed each other the books they had chosen, and talked about them amongst themselves.

That evening when Francesca went back to the bookstore a few minutes after closing, as was her habit, she ran into Oscar, who was exhausted by the end of the day. She questioned Van: "Delvaux must have asked you who I am."

"Not at all. He asked me about the business partners. I said they were private. That seemed to be enough for him. Francesca, I understand that you don't want to run the risk of introducing yourself. Don't you think you might be going too far? Sooner or later, you will have to make an appearance. Why are you so nervous about it?"

"I'll try to explain."

She was frowning.

"It must not be easy to understand. We've already talked about it, I think. I've always had a desire to do things. But the moment I undertake something, people look at me askance, with condescending irony, not because of what I'm doing but because of who I am. The worst of it is that what I am doing becomes part of their foregone conclusion. You'll see, when they discover my role in The Good Novel, there will be twice as much criticism: they will discredit me, and the bookstore along with me, as if it went without saying. In France, intellectuals or even simple cultural entrepreneurs must come from a modest background and make their way alone, through their work, to be considered deserving. A woman like me, particularly if her studies were fairly insignificant, has no legitimacy in the cultural world. At best they will let her be a patron of the arts, on condition she remain invisible. Sign the checks and be quiet.

"The worst of it is that if all I did was to show myself in a haute couture gown at gala openings, that sort of tribunal of merit would find nothing to criticize. They would leave me alone. Everyone in their place! Look at the paradox: if I do nothing other than play my high-society walk-on part, all is well; if I get involved, invest a lot of money, I'm ridiculous and my motivations are suspect."

Van said nothing. Francesca was grateful that he did not dispute her analysis.

"But still," he said, "I wonder if I haven't made a mistake by letting you stay in the shadow up to now. Sooner or later, people will wonder why. Perhaps we should have de-mined the territory by making the first move."

"I am prepared to say in public what I have just tried to explain to you as best I could."

"I hope it won't come to that. We're not being dragged

before a tribunal, after all. Anyway, be prepared to be unmasked at some point."

They had had another remarkable day as far as sales were concerned. Van got the impression that there were newcomers among their regular customers.

"And guess who came by at around three."

"Tell me."

"The Red. With a beautiful smile on his beautiful face. He came through the door and walked straight over. To keep him from talking I had to give him a cold stare and say in this ridiculous way, Can I help you sir? so that he'd come back down to earth. He mumbled, Do you have any books by Nabokov?"

"And we had specifically asked him to be discreet. I can still hear him saying, it's perfectly simple, I'll avoid coming round."

"I took him over to Nabokov's novels, and he couldn't help but say, I am very close. I told him curtly, don't be too close.

"And an hour later, there was Scaf sending me a text message, clear as could be: *Behind you with all my heart.* I replied, *Condolences pointless. Prefer silence.* To be on the safe side I sent the same warning to the other six."

In the notebook that was later found in Francesca's desk—and where only a few pages had been filled, seven to be exact, with her large upright handwriting that was so like her—each entry is carefully dated. The most touching, I find, is the one from February 19, which was the Saturday when Grantarroi's article was published. Francesca wrote down her dream.

We are in a room where there are a lot of people, I don't know where. I am so troubled by your presence just two steps away that I cannot look you in the eye. I look at your feet, always the same beige lace-up Clarks.

Then you do something which astonishes me. With one foot you step on the toes of my shoe, hard, deliberately.

You are standing next to me and I still don't dare look at you. You are pressing your body against mine at the same time that behind my back, you take hold of my wrist and squeeze it in your hand, fit to break.

It is obvious that behind us, every one has seen your gesture.

It didn't take me long to understand who was meant by "you." Everything written in the notebook has to do with Van. Although he is never named, the host of details make it clear.

33

A t *Le Bigaro* they were very decent. The response that Armand Delvaux had hand-delivered in the middle of the afternoon on Saturday at home to the assistant editor, who happened to have been his pupil, appeared in print on Monday morning.

And on Monday afternoon, *Le Ponte* published Ivan's article, cut by a quarter, and flatly entitled, "Totalitarian, you said?" But it was in the right place, on the Comment page.

"Thirty-all," said Francesca.

"What?" asked Ivan.

"Two points each."

On Friday, however, in *L'Idée*, a Collective of Free Booksellers whom no one had ever heard of delivered their blow. "These magnificent premises by the Odéon, a part of Paris where housing prices are among the most expensive: to whom can they belong? . . . A bookstore that is anything but commercial must cost every day more than it can possibly earn. Who is paying? . . . This business is doomed to fail, by nature it is not viable: who is behind it? Who can be sinking so much money into an enterprise whose aim, clearly, is to undermine the fragile publishing economy by discrediting its players? . . ."

"This is terrible," said Francesca. "All we care about is literature, to glorify and defend the novel, why do they have such violent suspicions? Who can want to harm us like this? Who could possibly feel threatened by The Good Novel?"

"Plenty of people," said Van. "To begin with, all the authors whose books are not on sale at The Good Novel."

"Their books are on sale elsewhere! Everywhere, in twelve thousand other bookstores."

"I don't think it's the likes of Jean-Christophe Grangé or Marc Lévy who could get so wound up, authors whose books sell in the millions. They can't possibly be affected by one bookstore that ignores them. Although I don't know a single best-selling author who isn't convinced of his talent. But we must have some enemies among all the others. Because rich and famous novelists are not the only ones who think they are excellent. Unknown authors are equally convinced of their own talent. The ones that success ignores have one element of genius, at least: they know how to come up with perfectly good reasons for their misfortune: they're too refined for the common herd, they're ahead of their time, they're rowing against the tide, their books are not the kind that critics like, not the right format for the price . . . The worst is that there are some in the batch who should be celebrated, who are unfairly neglected. Not many, and I'm sure that they were overjoyed when we opened. But as for the others, no. All those authors of 'books not worth bothering with' do not have a warm spot for us in their heart."

"Nor do their publishers."

"Nor do the bookstores where they sell their books, fully aware of how pointless they are."

"Nor the journalists who shower praise on them to follow the crowd, or because they're lazy, or because they're hoping for some favor in return from the publisher . . ."

Francesca asked again and again the question that was nagging her: "Do you think these people are organized? In a word, is there a conspiracy?"

"I'm not sure at all. Maybe that first baring of their fangs— the so-called Abéha's article—unleashed the spite of a whole bunch of people who thought, Hey, let's go for it, without necessarily consulting each other. But I don't know. I have no idea. One thing is sure, though, this Collective of Free Booksellers did not exist before late February of this year. As for finding out who's behind it, I've been searching, to no avail."

A letter arrived in the mail at the rue Dupuytren, addressed to "Mr. Georg." It was signed by B., from Alsace.

These attacks against a model bookstore, which has harmed no one, make me think, relatively speaking, of what I went through when my first book came out. I had worked on it for years, and all I wanted was write a book that would be as good as possible. Success came quickly. And, to my amazement, attacks came just as quickly. Too working class, too conservative, I heard it all. Here I was delighted to be in touch with my readers, and I didn't want to get in anyone's way, just to be a new face in the crowd, and for the first time in my life I found I had enemies, I was being ripped to pieces by the press, and looked down on by people I didn't even know. Let them say their piece, concluded Ballon.

And the following week, it was *La Turbine* that published an article that was neither for or against, entitled "Who is behind it?" and signed by an in-house journalist. Perfectly legally, the newspaper had got hold of details from The Good Novel's registration at the Registry of Businesses and Companies, and it published them in full. The reader was informed that The Good Novel was a simplified joint-stock company, with an executive officer named Ivan Georg (born in Asnières on September 5, 1959, residing at 6, rue de l'Agent-Bailly in Paris, 9th arrondissement), an auditor by the name of Jean-Marc Aubert, and the capital of the company was divided between the civil society Epicéa (99%), and Mr. Georg (1%).

Nothing terribly worrying there, nothing that any ordinary person couldn't find out through the commercial court. But a short paragraph above the body of the article fuelled the mystery in terms worthy of a second-rate television series. "The Good Novel Bookstore, at the Odéon, provokes questions and rumors, with its provocative stance of offering nothing but 'great' literature, most of which was published long ago. But bookstores are unanimous in saying they cannot survive if they do not devote most of their stock to new books, including best-sellers. Who is defying the book world in this way? Who owns the civil society Epicéa?"

"What a load of bull," said Van. "It reminds me of something Pierre Lazareff is rumored to have said. When he was the boss at *France-Soir*, he worried that no one was reading the business pages, and supposedly he said to his reporters, 'Let's show some tits and bums in the economy.'"

Francesca looked at Heffner.

"From that point on, you see," she said, "I stopped believing in what Van continued to maintain, that the people who were annoyed by The Good Novel were going after it individually and independently from each other. The fact that the malicious articles were coming out in various newspapers, and among the best-known ones, would give anybody the impression we were being universally repudiated—and I continue to believe that the succession of articles was orchestrated with this in mind. But it made me feel like I was being surrounded. I could not see anything other than a campaign. And it was all too obvious that whoever was targeting us had both the means and the savoir-faire."

She fell silent, then continued, "It was at that point, I think, that we began to call them 'the brutes.'"

"I did not share Francesca's theory," said Van. "But I also thought that was the appropriate word."

On the Web, swords were crossed. Among the more notable contributions on The Good Novel's forum was one from the actress Audrey Doudou:

I'm not very cultured, I didn't go to university, and what I want to say is perfectly simple: Reading is very important to me. The cinema is a tough world. You expose yourself, you are open to blows. Audiences think that making a film is all fun and games, but I think it's very difficult, sometimes really trying. In my life, and in particular when I'm on the set, reading is my recreation. I mean this literally: I re-create myself through reading, I find new strength. But often my recreation was dreary, and I've had a lot of disappointments, reading books that people had told me were very good.

One day, out of curiosity, I went into The Good Novel. It was crowded, and no one recognized me. I stayed there for several hours, and didn't see the time go by. I wanted to read all the books.

See for yourself. You will leave The Good Novel the way I did, dizzy with gratitude. How can people attack a place that is so good for you? That's what I don't understand.

Dear Audrey, replied Ivan in his newsletter, *you cannot imagine how happy your words have made us. You appreciate everything we have tried to do at The Good Novel. I never went to university, either. Bit by bit I came to appreciate novels, as easily as the cinema. At one point I realized that beautiful novels were indispensable to me, like air, or food. I would like The Good Novel to be a place where others will find what I needed and enjoyed so much myself, nothing else.*

The following Sunday, March 1, the phone roused Ivan from his sleep. Anis's little voice.

"The chapel at the Sorbonne is open today."

"You want me to come to Mass with you, is that it?" Van said slowly.

"You're making fun of me."

"No I'm not, Rose. Rosette. I was dreaming. I imagined you with a violet and some silk gloves. What time is it?"

"It's almost nine. Did I wake you up?"

"I think you did. And I'm really surprised. I don't usually sleep this late. It bothers me. Something must be going on. I've always noticed that during rough times, I sleep like a dormouse. But tell me about yourself. I'm so glad to hear your voice."

"Later. Are you worried?"

"I don't know. No. Maybe. Did you say that big café on the place de la Sorbonne is open? Give me an hour, I'll be there."

In his mind he always pictured the young woman to be taller and more confident than she was, and now she looked quite helpless.

"I wanted to tell you," she began, "all this fuss about The Good Novel . . . I'm so sorry that you're having such a rough time of it."

Disarming, rather, thought Van.

"Have you seen the papers?"

"No. I followed everything on the Internet. Did it begin with the newspapers?"

"Not exactly. It came from several directions at once. First there were the pseudo-readers at the bookstore, who came to bother us, then aggressive people on the Web, increasingly numerous. Then one, two, three articles demolishing us in the major papers."

Anis listened, with her eyes on him. He wanted to take her cheeks in his hands.

"I didn't know you spent time surfing the Web."

She adopted a casual tone that sounded completely false:

"There's a cyber café across the street from my house. I spend a lot of time there."

She blushed: "In the evening."

Van didn't have much left to lose.

"Maybe I could meet you there. I mean on the Web, not the cyber café. Do you have an e-mail address?"

"Anis@free.fr."

"Anis free, that's a fine name. I'll try that kind of message. Traveling butterflies, they won't make as much noise as the ones I used to leave on your answering machine. And you shall be even freer not to answer."

Van wrote to anis@free.fr that very evening:

Yes, it's a rough time. Our success was too brilliant, no doubt. They want to run us into the ground. Anis, the truth is, however, that you only notice me when I'm weak. You noticed me because my sweater had a hole in the elbow. And now you're speaking to me again because I'm being mistreated. Must I hope I shall be totally discredited? I would consent with joy if my disgrace could be dissociated from the fate of The Good Novel. What should I do?

Your old friend Corneille—worried and tired.

Anis answered the next day at 21:20, according to free.fr:

Indeed, I am not attracted to strong people, unlike most girls my age. I might even say that I can't stand them. Should people hold it against me? I think that The Good Novel is hard to swallow for a reason that goes far beyond its success: because it foreshadows and has launched a reversal among the habits of book buyers. Throughout history there have been groups of humans who seem to be used to being oppressed yet they managed to make an effort and set themselves free. Almost always, all it took was one or two militants who made them aware of what was weighing upon them, and above all that they could set themselves free. If you leave The Good Novel, if you back out even the tiniest bit, I won't see you anymore. I've told you already.

Chimène

Told him already? Perhaps. Ivan could search his memories later. All he saw now was her signature, Chimène. His heart fluttered with joy. Chimène, or procrastination, inaccessible Chimène. Chimène divided, contradictory, Chimène opening her arms to the man she does not want to see, closing her eyes as he kisses her—the one might explain the other.

34

In the days that followed, Van and Oscar were constantly brought up to date on the latest developments in the controversy. The media is an echo chamber, or even a recording studio. Magazines and radio stations were asking the same questions, over and over: is it a legitimate practice to sell only great novels? And how should one go about it? Who knows what literary value is? Who is behind The Good Novel? Who is financing it?

And then the controversy receded. One piece of news replaces another. The fourteen members of the IOC Evaluation Commission were in Paris, in order to study the city's candidacy to organize the Olympic Games in the summer of 2012—all forecasts agreed that Paris had the best chance of all the candidate cities. Public debt in France had now passed 65 percent of the GDP: the media had suddenly noticed this. The cost of oil was nearing $57 a barrel, which was unprecedented. Russia was condemned by the European Court of Human Rights for its crimes in Chechnya. As for the crimes committed by the Sudanese state in Darfur, they would be dealt with by the International Criminal Court.

The Good Novel, like any cultural innovation in France, had survived the ordeal having gone through the typically French ideology wringer, as violent and conventional as it was approximate and inconsequential, and one might have logically concluded that the matter was closed and the bookstore would be left alone to go on its merry way. But on March 17, a Thursday,

Le Poing published three pages entitled: "Great Literature and Little Deals," with a subtitle: "Our investigation into the star bookstore at the Odéon."

Henri Doultremont showed the article to Francesca the very same day. She had been getting ready to go out, at around ten, when a driver from Cinéor called her from his car: There's an envelope for you. Francesca found the weekly magazine in the envelope, and stapled to the cover was Henri's card, on which he had written: pp. 52-53-54.

"The fair-eyed bookseller, the fine man of letters with his air of a moonstruck Pierrot denying, hand on heart, the accusations leveled against The Good Novel, is no angel.

"Ivan Georg cannot see why anyone might find fault with the superb bookstore that opened six months ago with, as its motto, Here we only sell great novels, which elicited a substantial tide of interest and sympathy before raising a number of questions. No, he has never made a mystery of his identity. Yes, you can read everything about the rules which govern the store's selection on their Web site. No, their high standards do not reflect any cultural elitism, it is the honor of the bookstore (see *Le Ponte,* February 21). Moreover, Mr. Georg has moral support, from none other than Audrey Doudou, which is no small accomplishment, but also from the historian Armand Delvaux, professor at the Collège de France (*Le Bigaro,* February 21), not to mention hundreds of sycophants and anonymous readers, but also teachers, writers, and intellectuals of varying degrees of notoriety who have lent their support to The Good Novel on the bookstore's Internet forum.

"This defense seems altogether vague, and protestations of virtue are quite general. Ivan Georg will tell anyone prepared to listen (and film him at the same time) about his passion for literature and his disinterested intentions; he will say nothing about himself. He does not say a thing about how he came to be at the head of an establishment which clearly will not turn a profit yet has considerable funds behind it; not a word about his background, if any, in books, not a word about his past. This shadowy zone seemed worthy of further exploration; rightly so, as it proved.

"The fact that a bookstore that places labels of quality on its novels is run by a man who has very little education is not alarming in and of itself. It is a well-known fact that the selection of books has nothing to do with Mr. Georg but is made by a committee of experts, and he is only too eager to vaunt their competence while fiercely hiding their names.

"No, that Mr. Georg himself is not an authority in literary matters is not particularly alarming. What is, however, is the life as an adventurer he led before he landed at the controls of The Good Novel . . ."

Francesca was skimming. She wished she could toss out the magazine and never open it again. Yet she had to find out what to expect, how and where the next blows were going to be dealt. She read every other word, but the argument was clear. There were three charges against Van, in three paragraphs: "The teacher removed from his students," "Bookseller and tough guy?," "Prison."

Investigators had found pupils' parents who remembered the troubles Mr. Georg had had, twenty-five years ago, with his superiors. It didn't last long, they said. "Before long, he was no longer around." Had someone filed complaints? "At the time, it wasn't as frequent as it is today." "But anyway, the school district must have known what it was doing."

Comments were couched in the interrogative. "Could it be that . . ." "How can we not surmise that . . ." Bastards, thought Francesca, furious. Cowards. They were protecting themselves against a lawsuit. A lawyer must have read their text.

In the paragraph about the years during which Georg had been a bookseller, moving from town to town, Francesca recognized everything Van had told her. But the story was no longer the same. A rather odd story, don't you think, about a little employee who spent only a few months in each town . . . was he just a subordinate, or was he up to something fishy? Small businessmen obliged to sell for peanuts businesses that immediately afterwards turned out to be flourishing . . . And to conclude—Francesca was reading quickly—there was the quarrel between the principal and his agent. And his crime. The police archives were perfectly clear on that matter. One night in 1990, Georg had smashed through the door of a bookstore in Briançon with a car before making off with valuable merchandise and vanishing into thin air. "I did not press charges," declared his erstwhile employer, the publisher Béraut. "I was disgusted." That, too, seemed strange to the investigators, the man's reticence to elucidate.

Thirdly, the most troubling incident. A few years later, there was our man in prison in Ankara. Evidence is lacking in this case, there are no archives. But at the prison at Ulucanlar, the guards remember there were numerous charges: drug trafficking, shady dealings in antiquities, fake papers . . .

The phone rang. Francesca's eyes were full of tears. She walked over to the phone saying hello out loud, to steady her voice. It was Van.

"Oh, Ivan," she said simply.

"What's wrong? Is something the matter?"

His tone was that of someone who knows nothing.

"Van," said Francesca, "can you come to my place? We have to talk."

He was there within a quarter of an hour. When she saw him, Francesca knew that he hadn't read the article.

"This time, they've really struck hard," she said, showing him the magazine.

"Against you?" asked Van.

"Against you, me, all of us. You haven't seen *Le Poing?*"

"Are they at it again?"

"Here."

She went to heat up some coffee, leaving Ivan to read unwatched. When she came back into the little sitting room, with a tray in her hands, he was standing, looking out the window. He turned around.

"That's the worst they can do," he said. "Pure slander, but each time there is an element of truth."

"Don't tell me any more," interrupted Francesca.

But, on the contrary, Ivan wanted her to know exactly where the truth left off and slander began.

It was true that he had belonged to a movement of libertarian teachers, he said, who had been inspired by sacred texts such as A. S. Neill's *Summerhill*, as had a good number of teachers in the 1970s. It is true that he had been barred from the roster of National Education teachers. "I think I told you this. But it's not true that it was about morals. It was political, and I'd asked for it. I didn't apply one quarter of the regulations or decrees. I changed the programs. I gave the inspector a hard time."

And as for the dirty work he performed for B., from one town to the next? "If you recall, I was reviving dying bookstores. It's true that we bought them up for a song." It was true that Ivan had never spent more than six months in one town. It was true that his relations with his boss had soured—"He fired me, without a penny"—and that one night, in Briançon, Van used the company car as a battering ram to get his hands on a stock of valuable books. "Oddly enough," said Van, "those shit-stirrers didn't turn up anything about my subsequent activity as a comic-book seller. And yet there's a gold mine of facts that would have been really easy to travesty, with any amount of little nuances and insinuations."

"And finally, Turkey," he said. "And there I must apologize to you. I kept quite a few things from you."

It was true that he had been in prison. For nearly a year, he explained. In terrible conditions. "I don't like to remember it." He must have been trafficking something, anything. "I had spent all my savings, and I planned to go home when I had nothing left. No need to tell you they pinched it all from me in the can." And why had they put him in prison? "The most ordinary thing in the world," said Van, "and the most pathetic. I'm not proud." He had cannabis in his pockets. Truth be told, for years he'd always had some on him.

It had been Francesca's turn to look outside, while he was talking.

"What shall we do?" she asked. "Personally, in a case like this, I think we should get a lawyer."

"That's not my style," said Van. "The less I see of anything resembling a lawyer or a policeman, the better I feel. It's an old flyweight leftie knee-jerk reaction. In this case, I'm afraid a lawsuit might simply reinforce the gossip."

"And I feel just the opposite," said Francesca. "Getting a lawyer and going to court has always seemed the simplest solution to me, and a perfectly ordinary thing. My grandfather was often slandered during his public life, and he never let an uncalled-for adjective go by him. Henri always has one or two lawsuits in progress. He usually wins, you know."

"I don't really believe in justice, in the case in point," said Van. "Don't you see, vague allegations, about matters that are fifteen or twenty years old. Some of them in Turkey . . . The investigation would get lost in the sand."

He sounded bitter.

"Maybe you think I'm trying to hide things that are even worse than what those cretins invented."

"Please don't think that, Van. If you are my friend, please banish that idea from your mind."

Ivan needed a few hours to think. He went back to The Good Novel and forced himself to go back to work. But the words of support from customers, many of whom had come on purpose to speak to him, hurt him as much as they helped. He went upstairs to the office and closed the door.

He found an e-mail from Anis, sent at noon. She told him that she had read the article in *Le Poing*, and had left him a letter in his mailbox on the rue de l'Agent-Bailly. She had immediately noticed something unusual about the street, it seemed more animated than usual. Passersby were reading fliers on the walls, and she knew what must be going on. The three pages from *Le Poing* had been glued thirty times over on the walls, at eye level, on either side of the street. *There is nothing left,* said Anis. *It didn't take me long, I tore everything down. That's how I know exactly how many copies of the article had been stuck up.*

Where are you? wrote Ivan in response. She did not reply.

He had made his decision. He would respond to the slander via Internet. That seemed the simplest and quickest way. He spent an hour and a half drawing up, chronologically, the exact details of the facts that had been distorted by the pseudo-investigators at *Le Poing*.

Name: Ivan Georg
Date of Birth: September 5, 1959
Place of Birth: Asnières
1977-1980: First year undergraduate degree in English at Nanterre and first year of Chinese at the National Institute of Oriental Languages and Civilizations.
1981-1982: Ecole Normale.
1982: First year as substitute at elementary school.
Van left no blanks in the sort of resumé he was drawing up.
1984: Barred from teaching by National Education.
1985-1986: Employee, Emerson Trust, Virginia, USA. Tour guide, accompanying tours inspired by the life and works of great American authors.

1987-1992: Salaried employee at Béraut Publishing. Sales representative in books.

1988: Bookseller in Strasbourg (salaried employee of Béraut Publishing).

1989: Bookseller in Vichy and Marseilles (salaried employee of Béraut Publishing).

1990: Bookseller in Vendôme and Rennes (salaried employee of Béraut Publishing).

1991: Bookseller in Charleville-Mezières, and in Vizille (salaried employee of Béraut Publishing).

1992: Dismissed by Béraut without motive; no severance pay. Appropriated, in kind, one half of the indemnity owing.

November, 1992: Settled in Pantin as secondhand bookseller (specialized in comic books).

1996: Left for Asia, road trip.

He hid nothing.

2000-2001: Detained eleven months in the prison of Ulucanlar, Ankara, for possession of thirty grams of cannabis. Charges were not brought formally; no legal assistance, no trial.

September, 2001-January, 2004: Employee in a newsagent's/bookstore in Méribel.

February, 2004: Salaried employee of The Good Novel.

August 31, 2004: Opening of The Good Novel bookstore.

Van passed his draft on to Francesca, and at five o'clock in the afternoon the chronology was online in The Good Novel's newsletter, without any form of commentary other than a two-line introduction: *We will respond to slander with the facts.* Signed, *The booksellers.*

On his way home that night, Ivan turned into his little rue de l'Agent-Bailly with, for the first time, the painful impression that he was being watched. There was no one around at that hour, other than a man walking his dog, and Ivan refused to look at him because he knew that if he did, it would not be without harboring some suspicions. Little Anis had done a good job. Van felt a rush of gratitude. There were no more posters on the walls, and you would have had to been as alert as he was in order to detect here and there a scrap of glued paper.

He felt relieved to be home. I must be frightened then, he was thinking, when he noticed that on either side of the door to his building, the pages from *Le Poing* had been posted, three on either side. Without thinking, he ripped them off. They had been poorly stuck with scotch tape.

So they had been here at least twice. Or someone had come back. Or that someone did not leave the street, saw Anis tearing the posters down, let her do it and leave, and went to get two more issues of *Le Poing* to finish his little job.

Van couldn't sleep. Could it be that the two series of posters had been independent of each other? Could two people who did not know each other have had the same idea of sticking the slanderous article up at the rue de l'Agent-Bailly, one of them focusing on repetition, and the other on precision?

He jumped out of bed and threw his parka over his shoulders while he was opening the door and hurtling barefoot down the stairs. Anis had mentioned a letter in the e-mail she had sent him. Ten times that afternoon Van had wondered whether, yes or no, she had eventually dropped it off.

Yes, because signs of friendship are more welcome than ever on a day like today. No, because her message had been written before she discovered the posters in the street, and it was no longer suitable.

It was yes. Van tore open the envelope as he headed back up the stairs.

Anis had written only one line, between quotes: *"What is essential is constantly threatened by what is insignificant."* René Char.

How like a young woman, thought Van. How earnest. He had hoped for something like, I hold you in my arms.

But was it really so different, what Anis had written? Did Char's lovely sentence not mean: I am with you, in other words, I am close to you, in other words, I am kissing your eyelids?

No, Ivan eventually conceded. She meant, You are right, these slanders against you only confirm as much. Hang in there. Not: I dream of being in your arms. No.

In the days that followed, the newspapers rehashed Ivan's biography, almost every time with the same agenda in mind, comparing word by word the allegations in *Le Poing* with the booksellers' defense. All in all it seemed clear that *Le Poing* was coming out the loser. And as always in such cases, the one who suffered the most from the whole business was Van: his public image, and even more so, his own self-image.

All through those days expressions of support flowed into The Good Novel in every form imaginable—letters, e-mails, faxes, bouquets of flowers, hugs, handshakes.

Iannis Arban, the filmmaker, whom they had never seen—or, at least had never recognized—at The Good Novel, wrote an op-ed piece for *L'Idée*, without informing anyone at the bookstore. In his piece he drew a parallel between The Good Novel's difficulties and those of La Joie de Lire, François Maspero's bookstore in the 1970s and 1980s. "Each generation sees the birth of a bookstore that is unlike others," he wrote. "No doubt it is too appealing, too successful. Very quickly it becomes subject to attacks, occasionally frontal but more often hidden. The point is that too many people have an interest in bringing it down. The conspiracy of mediocre and envious people has only one strength: they are innumerable . . . They managed to sink the Maspero bookstore. We must not allow them to destroy The Good Novel . . ."

No matter how Ivan tried to put on a smile before each of these gestures of support, he was more affected than he himself realized. Just knowing this made Francesca suffer. A sort of sadness had come over them, which did not show when they were apart, but it seemed to be kindled the moment they were alone together. God knows why each of them tried to hide it, making a forced effort to seem pugnacious and ferociously cheerful.

A registered letter arrived at The Good Novel, from a major law firm. In two pages the Nada Publishing House, through their attorney, Mr. Kipper, accused The Good Novel bookstore of business practices that were equivalent to a refusal to sell, and they summoned their director, "or his usual counsel," to contact said Mr. Kipper within the week; failure to do so would leave the attorney free to instigate legal proceedings in order to see that his client's rights were respected.

"Well, well, so they're waking up," said Francesca. She was of the opinion that they must treat this summons with disdain and refuse to answer. "We can't start taking into consideration all of the nonsense people are saying about us."

Van managed to make her relax her position. "You are my usual counsel," he said. "I hear what you're saying. But we don't have a single book published by Nada on our shelves, and I'll bet you anything we never will. Put yourself in their position."

He waited for nine days and answered in a few words. He maintained that they had never refused to sell any book at The Good Novel. *Of course we don't have all the works available in the bookstore. But we do know our obligations. We always offer to order a book that is requested. We defy you to prove that we ever failed to do so. All of your publications can be bought through The Good Novel.*

He was no longer invited to go on television. "It was about time that stopped," he said. "Fortunately media buzz never lasts more than a season. No matter how lightly you take that sort of invitation, it uses up more energy than you'd think. It preys on your mind to excess."

He regained both his energy and his composure. "You know," he said to Francesca in mid-April, "our sales have not gone down. I've done the figures, comparisons, there even seems to be an upward trend. There are still just as many people at the bookstore, and just as many sales online. We can't exclude the fact that we may have more customers, buying less per person—that's impossible to verify: who knows whether it isn't the same people who are coming more often and spreading out their purchases? To know exactly, we would have to associate each purchase with a buyer. You can do that when they pay by credit card or check. But 80 percent of the purchases are made in cash."

All the controversy over The Good Novel and the repercussions that followed for weeks thereafter had the additional effect of making the bookstore's whole concept, and its principle, seem remarkable to a number of people, fiction-lovers the world over, inspiring them to launch similar undertakings. In April three requests for information arrived, from Berlin, Milan, and Buenos Aires. They were very precise requests (profit margin, financial results, cash flow) from private individuals who seemed virtually determined, each of them in their respective city, to open some sort of Good Novel bookstore.

Van was wary.

"Anything we tell them could be used against us. I don't feel like answering. They know enough to get started without us."

Francesca, however, cast a favorable eye on these potential offshoots.

"If we are really dreaming of a veritable movement, of an about-face where book buyers' behavior is concerned, well, then we need look no further! Can you imagine the day when there will be a Good Novel bookstore in every major city? The change that that will represent?

"And then, don't you remember, in Méribel, that week when every evening we thought about the bookstore of our dreams, what it might be, we even broached the idea that to really do things properly, there should be an English Good Novel in England, an Italian one in Italy, a Spanish one, a German one, each with a different selection of books, and each one would be focused on a particular linguistic zone and literary heritage, just as here at the rue Dupuytren, we have favored books in French."

She did not see any danger in talking with strangers about the way The Good Novel was set up.

"Obviously, we won't divulge anything that must remain secret."

Van agreed, on condition that the interested parties come to Paris, so that they could get to know them, and get them to talk, as well.

"So that we can be sure they are our brothers."

It was on that day in mid-April, when he had given into Francesca's reasoning and her enthusiasm, and was just finishing his sentence, and the sound of his final words—"our brothers"—still echoed in the ensuing silence—a somewhat unexpected silence, and a rather long one, that Van looked up and saw Francesca's eyes on him, particularly anxious, and he heard her say, Van, do you realize that I no longer look upon you as just an associate? That was the day when he spoke to her about Anis for the first time, telling her that their affair was not straightforward, and that he didn't know where it was headed. Francesca looked like a child caught with her hand in the cookie jar: beautiful, incredibly beautiful, in a light woolen dress of a slightly rough texture, almost white. She had stopped abruptly, with words that Van had difficulty understanding, and she changed the subject, mentioning that perhaps Anis would like to work at The Good Novel. "I'll ask her," said Van.

He did not ask her that very day. He was also rather upset during the hours which followed. He kept seeing Francesca's worried eyes, hearing the words she had used to stop herself and that he didn't really understand—I didn't have anything to tell you, don't get me wrong, I'm not expecting anything from you. Her offer to hire Anis was really typical of her—excessive, emotional. Ambiguous? Van didn't think so.

What he could not see was how to convey the offer without Anis realizing he had spoken about her to Francesca. How would she take it? Her feelings toward Francesca seem to be divided. Van remembered her reaction: I know, a good fairy. Should he remain vague and simply not tell her that it was Francesca's suggestion? But if Van explained to her, as if it were a perfectly simple thing, that they needed more people at the bookstore, that they were going to have to hire someone, and that he'd had the idea to talk to her about it, Anis would turn on her heels. Van could already hear her protest: what makes you think I was looking for work?

She spaced their meetings methodically. She only wanted to see him on the condition that she took the initiative. How could he imagine she might agree to work at the same place as him? Worse yet, to work with him?

Van spent two days thinking about it, went through a dozen scenarios, then finally took the plunge. It was better to save handwritten letters for words of love. Telephone? He would find it hard to take if he left a message and there was no response. He couldn't explain it, but when she failed to return his calls it was more painful than when she didn't write back to his e-mails. He spent three quarters of an hour behind his computer, unmoving, came up with a dozen ruses, a pseudo want ad, a pseudo message from the university, a pseudo heads-up from a pseudo student, and in the end—it was midnight—he decided to go for broke, as directly as possible:

When Francesca was getting ready last August to hire someone in addition to me at The Good Novel, as you can imagine, I thought of you. But that was when you had just gotten to Paris. Paradoxically, we were meeting less and less often. I didn't dare talk to you about the position at the bookstore. You would have thought I was up to some trick. I was too afraid you would laugh at me.

Now Francesca would like to hire a third bookseller. She's leaving it up to me to find someone. Maybe I shouldn't have mentioned it to you?

Van hesitated for another good quarter of an hour, how to close the message. He finally decided just to click "send." At that moment he saw he had forgotten to sign. He sent a second message, writing *P.S.* in the subject line, and in the body of the message, just one word, *Ivan.* Drained, he went to bed.

Anis's reply arrived calmly through the same channels a day later.

No, of course you had to mention it to me. It is a dream job. But need I remind you that I'm terribly short on time?

A.

Van didn't get it. The best he could think of was to show the message to Francesca.

"How do you read it?"

"I read, no, mention, dream, terribly, time, and finally the letter A. With something private about it. It's fairly clear."

"You think so?"

"Don't you? And yet it's perfectly comprehensible. Translation:

Right now it's impossible, however much I might want the job. I'm working on overcoming my fears. Give me some time. Talk to me."

"But why? Why is it impossible and why does she need time?"

"Ivan, that's the riddle you have to solve if you are to get anywhere. You and you alone. For me, it's much simpler. I will maintain my job offer to our little sphinx. A few weeks more or less won't make any difference. We can wait. But you would do better not to tell her that. Don't answer. Above all, don't insist. Don't even mention it. I wouldn't be surprised if before too long she comes up to you as if it were no big deal and asks you if the position has been filled."

36

Van asked for nothing better than to be counseled. His own modus operandi was so chaotic. He would even have been pleased to have directives. He complied, and was all the more grateful: he had been trying for a while already on his own to stick to the line laid down by Francesca.

He spent his days at The Good Novel and, in the springtime he even spent the night there occasionally. At eleven o'clock or midnight, he no longer had the courage to head back to his attic room, so he fell asleep in a heap, flat on his back, on the sisal carpet.

At the bookstore an atmosphere of effervescent calm, the intense complicity still reigned. Things had gone back to normal, and customers were sparing with words, as usual. Signs of support were no longer explicit, but could be perceived in discreet gestures—a certain smile, a way of shaking hands with the booksellers—something which is not usual in Paris—and exclamations of Hang in there! said fervently, in the place of goodbye. Francesca never mentioned to Van the so-called revelations in *Le Poing*. Van referred to it once, at his own initiative. Oscar had arrived early that morning at The Good Novel, still in shock after reading Ageyev's *Romance with Cocaine*, which had kept him awake most of the night. As it should be, confirmed Van. And it's not a book you're about to forget.

Francesca had not read it, and she asked if they should add it to their list.

"There's something mean-spirited about the story that I don't like," said Van. "But that's not a proper criterion. I'll submit it to the committee. Francesca . . ."

He hesitated.

"I owe you an explanation about something. Ageyev's book made me think about it. I told you that for years I could not do without various toxic substances. That is no longer the case."

"I haven't asked you anything about that," interrupted Francesca.

"Yes, and I noticed, and I'm grateful. But I'm asking you to listen to me. Two minutes. I've often wondered why people feel the need to take drugs. In my case, it was self-disgust, I suppose—to avoid my own self. I always had to have something on me in order to be able to make myself scarce, like a guarantee that I would be able to *leave myself*, do you see what I mean? Just leave myself behind. In person, I was weaned off it by force, cold turkey. It was terrible. I thought I'd go crazy. Then I regained a sort of equilibrium and, after a few weeks had gone by, I realized that I could stand myself. Once I was back in France, I went on living *without it*."

Francesca didn't say anything, she just looked at him. Looked at you. Whomever she has ever looked at in that way—me no less than anyone else—has been unable to forget the way she would let her gaze light upon you, her passionate, sad eyes so full of expression even though they were always somewhat veiled, changing, so special.

Don't get me wrong, I'm not expecting anything from you, I didn't have anything to tell you: Van often thought back on the strange way she had stopped abruptly after confessing something that sounded like a strong emotion. And every time he recalled these lines by Laforgue that he loved more than anything:

"Ask for Nothing with soul . . .
and conclude the craziest of sentences
with: My God, let us not insist?"

And all the while, if those who had Francesca in their sights, adjusting their aim, if they had gone near her, if just three feet away they had met her gaze, would they have pressed the trigger?

The page about Francesca that came out in *Le Ponte* on April 20 was entitled "Truly Literary Chic." It was signed by one the of their foreign correspondents who was also a fashion specialist. "We have found out who is behind the civil society Epicéa, the owner of The Good Novel," began the article. "This civil society belongs exclusively to an heiress." Then followed information that was more or less exact about the Aldo-Valbelli family, the condottiere, Renaissance bankers, seventeenth-century ship builders, eighteenth-century paradise, nineteenth-century industrial barons, twentieth-century personalities, the woman who swore only by underground theatre in London in the 1960s, the man whose passion for race cars had precipitated into the Adriatic from the height of a narrow winding road, and of course the great anti-Fascist historian who died in 1977.

From this point on the article struck a different tone, changed register. The newspaper had uncovered a photograph where Francesca, in a long dress, her shoulders bare, a champagne glass in her hand, was laughing against a background of Italian balustrades and Riviera. To sketch her portrait, additional information had been provided: casual assertions couched in hollow formulas, clichés, trivia. A golden youth, no university studies, gallant knights. No profession—why bother? Marriage to a French captain of industry who, even though he headed Cinéor (television, studios, films) was not exactly what you would call a man of culture. This lady had no experience of either publishing or bookselling. "Endowed with the cultural veneer of a major snob more likely to quote Henry Fielding than Helen Fielding, even when she has only read Helen." An inability to see anything that is not great—"one is either haughty or one is not"—the haughtiness of every instant, every gesture, every word.

"If she were a bookstore? It could only be The Good Novel. For the lady has her crushes, she has had many, and she is fickle. As someone close to her has said, 'She has passing fancies that last a year or two; she showed an interest in the foundation to the memory of her grandfather, and in the Palazzo Valbelli on San Giulio Island on the Lago d'Orta, which she has restored to perfection; then there was a Norwegian sculptor, then there was her daughter. Last year, she gave herself a bookstore that couldn't be like any other, that had to be the most beautiful, the most elegant and the most elitist bookstore on earth.'"

"Water off a duck's back," said Ivan. "It will pass. It's the sort of thing that leaves your skin raw, but gradually you get scar tissue, and it doesn't hurt so much. No, I don't think it will change anything as regards the image of the bookstore. The article is light years from what anyone who has ever set foot in The Good Novel knows to be the truth."

Francesca disappeared for two days following the publication of the article. "I was writing," she said to Ivan. "I was desperate, I had to find a way to respond and not be reduced to ashes. It's not what the article says about my family that hurts. What drove me out of my mind was one word."

"Yes," said Van.

"Her daughter . . . she showed an interest in her daughter, by the way, among other passing fancies, in the simple past: it's finished. They could not have hurt me more if they had tried. Such a brief semblance of tact ('we won't mention the tragedy'), but it implies, very precisely: because of her frivolous nature, this woman was harmful to her daughter. That's what people will remember, even if they know nothing about my life. It's nothing less than planting a white-hot needle into my heart, and I would rather not know the identity of the close person that they mention, if he or she exists.

"I wrote for a long time about the truth, who she was, the Violette I loved. For hours, without taking my pen from the page, over a hundred pages.

"And then as the hours passed, I realized that the article in *Le Ponte* was more than just the portrait of some ridiculous high-society woman, it was a really nasty blow against the bookstore. Attack the major snob, and while you're at it you devalue everything she touches. I knew this would happen, don't you remember? (I had not expected it to be so cruel.) Basically what they're saying is that it's all just frivolous, it's all just incredibly elitist.

"And I began to write something else. What I had written about my daughter, thinking I might make it public, I will keep to myself. It's not for other people to know. But what I wrote afterwards, I would like that to be read. Here."

She held out a few handwritten sheets to Ivan.

"Where did you go?" he asked.

"There is a little Benedictine monastery in Montmartre . . . they've taken me in before, when I was in a bad way."

Francesca's text, which she signed, was published in *Le Ponte* a week later. The newspaper acted as if they were being very fair and above board, they must have decided that it was preferable to publish Francesca's lines in their own pages rather than to read them elsewhere.

"Last year, Ivan Georg and I opened a bookstore in Paris that we called The Good Novel, to make its raison d'être perfectly clear.

"And people understood our intention, which must have responded to a need, because success was immediate.

"Who can this bookstore possibly be overshadowing? Who begrudges us our existence to the point of wanting to destroy us? For four months now we have been subjected to violent attacks, both in the media and on the Internet.

"To denigrate us, our attackers have invoked our so-called elitism, our bias in favor of literary quality, which they term reactionary; they invoke a doubtful connection between the bookstore and big money, and most recently, they have implicated Ivan Georg and myself, delving accusingly into our private lives.

"They have fundamentally misunderstood what we are trying to do, and what The Good Novel aims to be.

"For as long as literature has existed, suffering, joy, horror, grace, and everything that is great in humankind has produced great novels. These exceptional books are often not very well-known, and are in constant danger of being forgotten, and in today's world, where the number of books being published is considerable, the power of marketing and the cynicism of business have joined forces to keep those extraordinary books indistinguishable from millions of insignificant, not to say pointless books.

"But those masterful novels are life-giving. They enchant us. They help us to live. They teach us. It has become necessary to come to their defense and promote them relentlessly, because it is an illusion to think that they have the power to radiate all by themselves. That alone is our ambition.

"We want necessary books, books we can read the day after a funeral, when we have no tears left from all our crying, when we can hardly stand for the pain; books that will be there like loved ones when we have tidied a dead child's room and copied out her secret notes to have them with us, always, and breathed in her clothes hanging in the wardrobe a thousand times, and there is nothing left to do; books for those nights when no matter how exhausted we are we cannot sleep, and all we want is to tear ourselves away from obsessive visions; books that have heft and do not let us down when all we can hear, over and over, is the policeman saying gently, You will not ever see your daughter alive; when you can no longer stand looking all over the house, all over the garden, in a mad frenzy for little John, when fifteen times a night you find him again in the little pond lying on his stomach in ten inches of water; books you can take to your friend whose son hanged himself in his room, two months ago, two months that seem like an hour; books you can take to a brother who is so sick you no longer recognize him.

"Every day, Adrien opens his veins, Maria gets drunk, Anand is knocked down by a truck, a twelve-year-old Chechen or Turkoman or Darfurian is raped. Every day, Véronique dries the eyes of a condemned man, an old woman holds the hands of a horribly disfigured dying man, a man takes in his arms a dazed little child from among the corpses.

"We have no time to waste on insignificant books, hollow books, books that are here to please.

"We have no time for those sloppy, hurried books of the 'Go on, I need it for July, and in September we'll give you a proper launch and sell one hundred thousand copies, it's in the bag' variety.

"We want books that are written for those of us who doubt everything, who cry over the least little thing, who are startled by the slightest noise.

"We want books that cost their authors a great deal, books where you can feel the years of work, the backache, the writer's block, the author's panic at the thought that he might be lost: his discouragement, his courage, his anguish, his stubbornness, the risk of failure that he has taken.

"We want splendid books, books that immerse us in the splendor of reality and keep us there; books that prove to us that love is at work in the world next to evil, right up against it, at times indistinctly, and that it always will be, just the way that suffering will always ravage hearts. We want good novels.

"We want books that leave nothing out: neither human tragedy nor everyday wonders, books that bring fresh air to our lungs.

"And even if there is only one such book per decade, even if there is only one *Vies minuscules* every ten years, that would be enough. We want nothing else."

37

Francesca's answer had considerable repercussions. Her text was picked up by over a dozen newspapers and magazines, and hundreds of Web sites.

Immediately afterwards, a flyer came out, where only the second part of the text was printed, "we want necessary books . . ." This manifesto circulated for months. It was printed in a variety of ways, always with care, sometimes on very fine paper. Most often, the page layout was in the form of a poem, with a new line for each "books":

books that will be there like loved ones . . .

books for those nights . . . when we cannot sleep . . .

books that have heft . . .

and a new line for each "We want":

We have no time to waste . . .

We have no time for . . .

We want . . .

You could see this page posted everywhere, in libraries, at the entrance to cinemas, in café windows, and in many bookstores. *I always have a pile in my bag,* wrote Anis in an e-mail to Ivan, *I hand them out to everybody.*

Francesca's profession of faith was even published in the form of a tiny ultra-flat book, remarkably beautiful, with a short preface summarizing the context, and several blank pages that immediately made you want to write down quotations and titles, in a soft blue cover stamped *The Good Novel.*

Francesca received the booklet through the mail, addressed to her, at the rue de Condé. She was troubled.

"So does everyone know where I live? Why isn't there a note with it?"

"Well, that there is no note, I can understand," said Van. "Forget it. It must come from an admirer who wrote forty drafts and didn't keep a single one. Or a neighbor, I don't know, a young man of thirty who's known you for a long time."

Francesca shook her head.

"Everything makes me nervous, now."

"That's normal after an attack. I'm not afraid anymore. I am convinced that your text put a stop to everything. Controversy of the type we've been mixed up in can stop all of a sudden, you know, it happens a lot. People get all excited, and then they weary. Current events give them something new to get heated up over every month."

Sure enough, there was no more discussion in the media about The Good Novel. What else could be said, anyway, that had not already been said, thought Ivan, who also had his share of dark hours.

On the Internet, the controversy had also died down. People began to talk about books and literature again, in the forums related to The Good Novel. Jane Austen had a sudden surge in popularity, since two of her novels had just been made into films, very successful adaptations. Anna Maria Ortese was often mentioned for a novel she had written two years before she died and that had just come out in French, *Alonso e i visionari,* a journey into Italy's "years of lead," in her typical style, both fantastical and despairing. Admirers of Christian Oster hailed the publication of *L'imprèvu.* A newcomer, Stéphane Audeguy, had received considerable attention for his début novel, *La théorie des nuages.*

In spite of everything, Francesca was not relaxed. She could not see why the enemies of The Good Novel would have given up. First an ideological verdict, then an attack on individuals: what does a brute do next? Physical aggression? Blackmail? Assault?

She had a dream that left her feeling anxious for days. Someone had set fire to The Good Novel. Everything was burning and, like in a dream, everything was collapsing, reduced to ashes, in a great silence. Nothing was left of either the walls or the books.

Ivan was worried about something else. Even if the controversy had died down, he worried that perhaps the slander had actually done what it set out to do. The idea came to him in reaction to a declaration by the Minister of Culture—it was not any kind of formal position regarding The Good Novel, just a few words at the end of a press conference on the budget for culture, when he happened to be taking questions about books, an allusion to "people in the bookselling profession who would like culture to be only what is sublime." "If there are summits," said the minister, enjoying his metaphor with the headiness of end-of-banquet political pronouncements, "it's because there are mountains. Culture contains everything. There would be no peaks without valleys, gentle slopes, and meadows, at lower altitudes. The genius of democracy is a love for everything, to offer everything, value everything, and let individual freedom express its preferences here as elsewhere. I personally, for example," he had concluded, carried away by demagogy, "like adventure books and costume drama because they're en-ter-tain-ing! And the key word, where culture and art are concerned, is pleasure!"

Van remembered his words, which under normal circumstances would have made him shrug because they reminded him of so many others. Several times already customers at the bookstore had told him about people who screwed up their face when The Good Novel was mentioned.

"Oh yes, that intellectual bookstore . . ."

"So austere . . ."

"Old-fashioned . . ."

As controversies deepen they always leave a negative impression on people: I know, that doctor who had problems with Justice. What's his name? That novelist who was accused of plagiarism? (Even when the doctor was exonerated and the novelist was proven innocent.) Something of the same order must be going around about The Good Novel, a provocative, simplistic cliché: Oh yes, those wet blankets, those complete bores . . .

Francesca forgot an appointment. Van found the way she walked had changed. He did not dare ask her whether Doultremont was being friendly toward her.

One day when he was talking to her, he realized she was not listening, and he placed his hand on her arm: "What's the matter? Have you received any new tributes from anonymous admirers?"

"You are the kindest one I know," said Francesca with a smile.

Tears were running down her cheeks.

"No," she continued, "there's nothing new. I'm just sleeping poorly, that's all. I'm used to that. It's not important. I have no exams to take, no decisions to make. You take care of everything at The Good Novel."

"I'm nothing without you."

"Go on, I'm the one who should say that."

"You inspire me."

"And you inspire me, too, and give me energy."

"I don't wish to be indiscreet, but your husband . . . does he show you at least a tiny bit of solidarity?"

"In his way. He said, 'That's what business is about, my darling. Sometimes it's very exciting, it's always terribly brutal. It toughens your hide.'"

One Thursday in May, at the beginning of the afternoon, she drove to the Hôtel Drouot, where a great bibliophile's collection was being auctioned. It wasn't the rare books she was interested in, but the other ones. For sale that day, next to priceless editions and rare bindings, were several hundred novels in ordinary editions, which were surely those that the bibliophile had actually read. In the list of lots, Van had noticed some titles that were out of print, and difficult to find.

Francesca was able to buy nearly everything they had picked out. All of it filled three cardboard boxes, and one of the deliverymen helped her carry them to her car, which she had parked on rue Laffitte. Just as she was about to get behind the wheel, as she was opening the car door, she saw a white paper folded in half under the windshield wiper. An advertisement, she thought as she unfolded it, unconcerned. An ordinary white sheet, and across it was scribbled diagonally in very big letters: *You here?*

"It means I was followed. Someone saw where I parked."

"Or someone recognized you. It's not hard, you know. You are a noticeable person. Nor can you exclude that it might be an error, and the note was intended for someone else."

"In that case they would have signed, even just an initial. Save your strength, Van. The note was for me, and it makes perfect sense, you have to admit. It's made to measure. 'You here': in a different context, these two words would have been friendly, playful. Here, what they mean is, every time you go somewhere, we're aware of it, we have our eye on you."

"Yes, they did find the right formula. If you show this paper to a policeman, he'll laugh in your face. It's like a love note."

"It doesn't take much to spoil someone's life . . . it can go so quickly. And it's so simple. Two words on a piece of paper, not even threatening, and you become wary of everything, you have to disrupt your most ordinary habits, you stop using your car . . ."

"You must resist, Francesca. I beg you. Don't change anything in your life. That would only be showing them that the arrow struck home, and letting those brutes know that they've scored a point. You don't want that?"

"No. You are right. I didn't use my car much as it is, so I won't take it any less often, or more. I won't leave Paris, I won't suspect my concierge, or Oscar, or Henri. And hey, look, I'm going to cancel this note. Reduce it to nothing."

She tore the sheet into tiny pieces.

"How stupid I am," she said. "I should have done that on the rue Laffitte. They must have been watching me. That is what I should have done."

"Did you really tear it up, that paper?" asked Heffner.

"In tiny pieces. Was it a mistake?"

"A handwritten note can always be of interest. But maybe you have other ones?"

"I don't think so," Francesca said slowly.

"No," said Van.

38

There was a period of beautiful weather, day after day of clear skies. Winter was over all of a sudden, the endless Parisian autumn and winter, shunted aside by a truly lovely season, like one act in a play following on another. All the buds in Paris opened at the same time. At the rue Dupuytren, the tree in the courtyard was covered with cream-colored blossoms.

The bookstore stayed pleasantly cool. Francesca set out huge Baroque bouquets, white lilacs with green roses for the two weeks or so the lilacs were in bloom, then the branches off the chestnut tree in flower, and irises the color of tobacco, and Chinese peonies, all the flowers set among foliage that seemed to have been created by an extravagant feather-maker.

Ivan wondered how he had been able to live for such a long time in complete indifference to flowers. He asked Francesca who her florist was. A magician, said Francesca. You are not the first person she has awoken to flowers.

She was a very old Turkish woman who had been a florist for over fifty years, in a sort of warehouse behind the Place Maubert. She was a genius of floral composition, but had no store. She worked for individuals whom she swore to secrecy, never to reveal her name. She insisted on choosing her own customers. Candidates were presented to her one by one. The interview was held at the Jardin des Plantes. The old woman never took more than five minutes to make a decision. Eight times out of ten, it was a no.

Francesca had her meet Ivan at the spot at the top of the maze where she herself had been approved that winter, and she left the two of them alone.

"Tell me about this young person," said the old woman right away, staring harshly at her candidate.

"She's small and pink, incredibly moving"—Ivan felt fifteen years old—"She's tender, she's tough. Incomprehensible."

"I see," said the florist with the sharp authority befitting a hospital executive.

She had already turned around, and she said nothing more. Ivan followed her into her lair. Without asking his opinion, she immediately pointed to a small tree in a pot, covered with golden flowers that seemed about to take flight.

"This tree has done extraordinary things," she said, explaining, "there's the smell, it's something like magicians who share their secrets without giving away a thing."

Van gave her Anis's address. The old lady had a Laotian delivery boy, who drove a three-wheeled cart of his own invention that looked like a little itinerant wardrobe the size of a large bouquet.

Van waited for a sign, a breath, finally a miracle. He lasted two days, then could take no more. Why this time? Why the evening of the second day? If anyone ever knew, he surely didn't. The florist, perhaps? He heard nothing more, had no hope, just a sort of indefensible certainty, a summary, imperious, This can go on no longer.

The strategic systems that love inspires—among the most sophisticated of systems—can, on occasion, break down altogether, for no good reason, without warning, just like that. Unless they are obeying the order of a virtually conscious desire for catastrophe.

One evening, at seven o'clock—the sky was a bluish pink—leaving the bookstore to Oscar, Van went over to rue Bol-en-

Bois at a run. There was no answer at Anis's door. She's not back yet, confirmed the superintendent.

There was no turning back. Van stationed himself at the door. If Anis were to turn on her heels on seeing him, he would catch up with her, take her by her hair, twist her neck.

She arrived an hour later, so lost in thought, gazing so persistently at the ground that she only saw him at the last moment, suddenly there three feet away, motionless. She did not step back—or forward, nothing.

"Little miracle," he murmured.

"Is something the matter?" she said, turning very white.

"On the contrary. You are here now. I can breathe."

"Shall we go for a walk?" she asked, on the alert.

"Short one, long one, as you like," said Van, taking her arm.

They walked back up the rue Claude-Bernard, golden with sunset, and the deserted rue des Feuillantines. They did not speak. Van felt how tensely Anis held his arm, and he would have liked to be made of feathers, leaves, smelling of bergamot and acacia.

They came to the avenue de l'Observatoire, where evening was slipping among the tight rows of chestnut trees. And there, suddenly, something occurred to Ivan, an idea which without thinking—he who had analyzed Anis's every word, every gesture—he delivered to her as if about to share a discovery, throwing caution to the wind: "It's my age!" he said. "Maybe you don't want to get involved with someone who is old enough to be your father."

As he said this, he let her go and turned to face her. When he saw her expression, her eyes filling with tears, he suddenly made the connection between the words he had said, your father, and the words she had written in her long letter, a year ago, about her "stepfather who smelled so awful."

He took her in his arms. She pulled away forcefully. "Age,

again . . ." she spluttered. "It's your eyes . . ." She was crying, and shouting, without looking at Van: "I can't stand . . . blue eyes . . . No, I can't bear to have . . . blue eyes . . . come anywhere near . . . my face . . . I mean . . . My stepfather is a horrible man, he stinks . . . He has little blue eyes, that's all I could see . . ."

She ran away from him. She was zigzagging, Van was afraid she might trip. He could have caught up with her in two strides, but at that moment all he could think of was to reassure her that he would not try to hold her back, that he was letting her go, and would cherish her from afar.

He went home on foot, as night was falling. By the time he got there, his letter was ready. He wrote it in one go.

My age and my eyes are two things about myself that I cannot change. The thought that I am tormenting you is unbearable. I love you and I am letting you go. Ivan.

He fell sound asleep, woke up in the dark, rewrote his letter mentally and finally changed nothing, and went back to sleep. He woke up when the birds began to chirp noisily on his tree, put the note into an envelope, and went to drop it off with the porter at the student dorm, on the rue de l'Enfant-de-bois.

He went through his day as if it were the day after someone's death, working relentlessly, attentive to everyone who spoke to him, to the least little word that was said. He went out of his way not to look at the flowers. He had no more imaginary space, nowhere he could escape to, no more expectations, all he could do was make himself available to the present moment, to what was immeasurable, the terrible profusion of moments that make up a day.

That evening, he let Oscar leave earlier than usual. "I have plenty of time," he said, telling himself that this was one of the saddest sentences there is. At that moment he recalled that this poverty was also Francesca's daily lot, and had been for years. He thought of calling her to say, Well, now I too am free as the air. But he didn't feel like talking about himself. He had a long discussion with a young man about syncopation in Christian Gailly's prose, then, with some difficulty, he replaced the water in the flower vases the way the old florist had told him, locked up the bookstore, and walked home. It never even occurred to him anymore to take the métro or any other means of transport.

Little Anis was sitting on his doormat, leaning against the door. She got up when she saw him, placed her index finger against her lips, her eyes pleading, and then threw her arms around his neck. They stood there, embracing, for an eternity, until a swaying movement overcame them, and nearly made them fall.

Ivan opened his door, held Anis with one arm around her hip, put his other arm beneath her knees, and set her down among the books, on the only armchair in the house. No, she went, shaking her head. He picked her up again and put her down on the night blue batik he used as a bedspread, she had closed her eyes, he went to draw the curtain and open wide the bay window, so that the moonlight would come into the room. He did not dare turn around, he was afraid, like Anis he would have liked never to have to speak again in his life. When he came back to kneel by the bed, his eyes level with hers, he saw that her eyes were still closed. He waited for a few moments then had to accept that she was sleeping.

It would be an understatement to say that the next morning she found her voice again. She talked for two hours without stopping. She placed her fears one after the other into Ivan's hands: the predator's approaches, eyes that do not see your face, hard fingers, smells that cling to your skin for days and days—childhood terrors that never left her and prevented her from growing up: she handed them to him. Van would take care of them, he swore. She wanted to believe him. She talked about the flowers with the extraordinary scent on the potted tree that had been delivered to Bol-en-Bois three days earlier, and she had swallowed them one by one, hoping to die—from the sleep into which this precious comfort immersed her, from despair as she awoke, from the inability she'd had for months now to work on her thesis, from her little underpaid jobs late at night and early in the morning, from fatigue, and hunger.

Van listened to her, spreading her hair across the pillow to make rays of sunshine around her head.

"You have to finish your thesis," he said.

She laughed. "My studies, you know . . . If you only knew how little I care, now that I'm a bookseller."

She had been dreaming for so long of the job at The Good Novel. She would start the very next day, this afternoon even— well, as soon as she could.

"Fly, love!" she said, going naked to place her cheek and the palms of her hands against the wall, beneath the place where a young woman and a man in a kepi, neither of whom had wings, were somehow floating through the sky all the same, with smiles on their faces.

Van confided that he was madly happy about something in her, and he would tell her what it was if she promised to change nothing about herself. She promised. He pointed out to her that she was no longer saying *vous* but *tu* to him. She hadn't noticed. And he didn't know when it had happened. He liked it better this way: finally something was happening that neither one of them had decided upon. Naturally, he didn't dare say as much.

How do I know all this? It's very simple. I didn't make any of this story up. Everything I am relating here, I heard from Ivan.

39

Go back to sleep," said Van. "I'm off to the store. I'll call you."

He could not wait to tell Francesca how inspired she had been to give Anis time to think about the job, since in the end she had said yes; how inspired to have trusted her and to have agreed with what he had not said, that this little stranger was the best person in the world for The Good Novel. He could imagine the spark of friendship he would find in Francesca's eyes.

But Francesca was not at the bookstore that morning. She only came in long after noon.

"I was waiting for you," said Van.

She understood at once.

"Is it settled? Will she accept the position?"

Van squeezed her hands so hard it hurt.

"It's not that she was hesitating," he explained. "She told me she'd been dreaming about the job."

"Careful," warned Francesca. "Now it's no longer a dream but a daily bookstore. Breathing the same air as you every single day, between the same walls, isn't it going to be too much at once?"

"For her, maybe."

"Ask her."

"I'll be back," said Van.

He came back with Anis. The young woman shared Francesca's opinion, she was a bit afraid she might suffocate.

"From two to six, the afternoon?" suggested Francesca. "How would that suit you, to get started, the slack time? And during those hours, we'll oblige Van to go and read. Since he's been here, he hasn't read a tenth as much as he used to, that's unacceptable."

Anis looked at her watch.

"Go on then," she said to Van, shoving him in the back. "It's time."

Van went upstairs, collapsed into one of the big armchairs, and closed his eyes to view again, in slow motion, the hours that had just gone by, and he fell asleep. During that time, Francesca showed Anis around the bookstore. She told her the story behind it, taught her the geography.

After an hour had gone by, she said, without finishing her sentence, "This is definitely a lucky day . . ." Anis looked at her questioningly. Francesca told her that her handbag had been stolen that morning, and then found again. Only two hours separated the two events, and nothing had been taken from her bag except a little bit of cash.

"What the hell is going on?" grumbled Ivan. "I didn't hear anything about a theft. You didn't tell me."

"You had significantly more important things on your mind."

"I was intoxicated, that's true, and had no strength left at all. Francesca, tell me the truth, did you mention the theft and I didn't react?"

"I did indeed. But it was no big deal, either."

"Tell me about it," said Heffner.

On the morning of June 8, said Francesca—the day where she saw Anis for the first time—she left her house and went up the street when she heard a motorcycle behind her. In a split second she was knocked in the shoulder, she panicked, staggered, grabbed at the wall, saw a motorcycle roar by, there were two of them, and she realized that they had just stolen her handbag. She still had her keys in her pocket, so she went back upstairs, called her bank and told them to stop payment on any withdrawals from her account. Then she went to the police station on the rue Bonaparte, where she reported the theft, but hesitated to talk about The Good Novel and all the attacks against the bookstore over the last three months. She decided to go ahead for fear that if she said nothing it might seem strange, and they might think she was trying to hide something. So she was surprised when the policeman taking her deposition showed very little interest in what she had to say. Handbag thefts—we get ten a day in this arrondissement alone, he explained, as if they were talking about the average rainfall in Paris.

An hour later—Francesca was back home—there was a call to tell her that her bag had been found. Someone had picked it up by the door to a restaurant on the rue Dauphine, and taken it to the police station.

Nothing had been taken, except for the €30 in her wallet. Francesca was surprised they had left her credit card, for example. "Let me explain," said the policeman who was every bit as blasé as his colleague who gave her back her bag. "Everyone knows what they can do with the contents of a wallet. A credit card, if you don't have the code, is more complicated. You have to have a certain amount of training. And above all, nowadays the guys know that it leaves a trail. They don't like that."

"Are you sure?" interrupted Ivan. "There were no withdrawals on your account?"

"None at all."

"Then why didn't you tell me that?"

"I tried, Ivan."

"You should have forced me to listen!"

Francesca didn't answer. She shook her head gently, looking elsewhere, then said, "maybe you'll recall," she said, "that not long afterwards, I had to leave for Orta?"

"They had called you there, I remember. Some emergency: a thunderstorm had caused some damage."

"A thunderstorm, yes," repeated Francesca.

She winced, imperceptibly.

"When I got there, the view on the mountains around the lake was so beautiful, the blue of the water is such a . . . consolation: I was terribly tempted not to budge from my island. I had the pretext that there was major repair work to supervise. And I knew that everything at the bookstore would go along in the same way whether I was involved or not."

"May I?" interrupted Heffner.

He turned to Francesca.

"I know that six months down the line you won't find it easy to answer my question, but do you remember what was in your handbag on the day of the theft?"

"Well, would you believe I can tell you quite easily. I change my handbag fairly often, depending on what I'm wearing. And for years, I've had a habit that simplifies my life. No matter what handbag I take to go out, I always put in there, in addition to a book and magazines, a little black pouch shaped like an envelope that I never empty out, and that contains all my ID papers, my credit card, my wallet and my diary."

"Out of all that, in the bag," asked Heffner, "is there anything that might have been used against you?"

"No, I don't think so. What bothered me the most was that they had taken my ID card. But I got it back."

"And in the bag, did you have anything that might have been used against The Good Novel?"

"I wondered the same thing myself for a few days, you can well imagine. I don't think so, no. There were a certain number of notes about the bookstore in my diary, on the pages for the weeks that had gone by, and I read them and reread them:

lists of titles I couldn't find, appointments with book dealers, that sort of thing. I don't see anything that could have been used against us."

"It might not be a bad idea if I have a look in your little envelope-shaped leather pouch."

"Whenever you like," agreed Francesca. "Right now?"

"No," said Heffner. "Let's go on rather. We were in June . . ."

"In mid-June, 2005," said Van. "You know what a lull can be like: in the beginning, you hardly believe it. But an entire week went by without a snag, and then another. We began to wonder if the worst was not behind us."

"The weather was beautiful," said Francesca. "I was beginning to think that perhaps we had earned the right to work the way we wanted to—and, if not approval, at least a certain respect."

They still received some nasty messages via the Internet, malicious gossip about The Good Novel, but these were sporadic, and did not seem to be part of a conspiracy.

And then there was the unexpected tribute from Peter Carey in a long interview he gave to *Le Vieil Observateur.* The novelist was on a book tour in Europe to promote the publication of *My Life as a Fake* in translation, in several languages. The enthusiasm was unanimous, and some papers did what they could to give a certain angle to their approach. The journalists at the *Vieil Obs* questioned Carey about why he had left his country and settled in New York. And in lieu of an answer, the Australian novelist used the occasion to praise a certain French élan. "Nowhere but Paris," he asserted, "does there exist, nor could there exist a bookstore as unlikely as The Good Novel. In no other country in the world could a patron of the arts have the idea to devote their fortune to such a gamble. What's more," he insisted, "I was able to spend hours in that dream of a place without anyone recognizing me."

"I remember thinking one day: that man looks like Peter Carey!" Ivan confirmed. "But there you are: even if I had the proof that it was Carey, I wouldn't have done anything more. I would have left him alone. At the most I might have said to Francesca the next day, Peter Carey was here yesterday afternoon, he spent almost two hours over in the Central European section."

"As for me, I would have written to him the next day," said Francesca. "Just a few words: 'We are happy and honored to have seen you at The Good Novel, and we hope you enjoyed your visit.'"

Yet something had changed in the nature of Francesca's commitment. To Ivan, it was obvious. He wouldn't have gone so far as to say she was dissociating herself, that would have been wrong. She remained passionate about the cause, as she called it. But she no longer came to the bookstore every day. She was no longer attentive to everything. She assigned tasks to others, or said, "Ivan, don't you get the impression that . . ." or, "Could Oscar . . ."

We talked about it to ourselves. "Don't forget what she said, that she's afraid of everything now," Oscar reminded him. "If she's afraid, I think it's no longer for her own sake," said Van, "or not only. No, I'm afraid she's gone back to her old notion that The Good Novel has more to lose than to gain if she is visibly involved. In my opinion, if she's distancing herself, it's out of a sense of duty. She must think she brings bad luck."

On one point, moreover, Carey was wrong. The Good Novel was born in Paris, but it remained a firm possibility that it could be reproduced elsewhere. The project for a store in Berlin was taking shape.

Van had replied to the three individuals who had expressed their desire to open a similar bookstore: "Let's talk about it. We'll be waiting for you in Paris."

Max Frucht spent an entire day in the store, observing everything, then he sat down that evening with Ivan and Francesca in the big office. He was a thirty-one-year-old trader who'd had enough of finance—physically, a tall blond and pink fellow in an expensive suit without a scrap of elegance. In ten years in New York he had earned a packet, and he didn't want to leave it idle. Several of his colleagues, like himself, their pockets full by the age of thirty, were making a complete break with their life in suits. Some of them were going into humanitarian work, others into art. "As far as I'm concerned," said Frucht, who spoke excellent French, "The Good Novel offers a bit of both, art and philanthropy." Before working in finance, he had studied ancient history in Berlin for two years.

He did approach the issue as a manager, all the same. He asked to see the books, pulled out his calculator, scribbled down figures.

"Basically, it's fairly simple," he concluded. "The Good Novel, is doing well. Other than that, it's a bookstore like any other."

"You got it," said Van.

"The secret," said Francesca, "is a very rigorous selection of books."

"And an efficient publicity campaign behind the launch," added Frucht, "along with careful positioning on the market."

"The most sensitive question," added Van, "what takes the longest, is putting the committee together."

"And the hardest is to learn how to be thick-skinned when they start attacking you," said Francesca.

Van had his reservations.

"I don't like that Frucht guy very much," he said the next day.

"Don't you think it's prejudice making you say that?" asked Francesca gently. "A bias against anyone wearing a dark suit?"

"It's possible. The fact is I can't see anything good about the guy."

"Personally, I can't make up my mind about him. He is so conventional that there's something almost mysterious about him."

"As for the business," said Ivan to Heffner, "it was still looking good."

Sales continued to increase, as did the number of subscriptions. The only figure that remained relatively low was the online sales when compared to in-store sales. There were far more customers who stopped by the bookstore to choose their books than those who ordered them from a distance. Nonetheless, Internet sales accounted for 7 percent of total sales, a figure that was twice the average for French booksellers. It was not important. They had gone well beyond all their development goals.

Some publishers had begun to offer The Good Novel interesting business terms—nothing astronomical, just slightly bigger margins. There were two sorts of publishers: old houses like Gallimard, who had considerable funds, and at the other extreme, very small publishers, who frequently had just started up and were only publishing titles that were in the public domain. Both of these kinds of publishers were pleasantly surprised to see, prominently displayed on the tables at The Good Novel, forgotten books such as Marc Bernard's *Pareils à des enfants* or Stephen Crane's *The Open Boat and Other Tales of Adventure.*

"Little Anis was like a fish in water at The Good Novel," said Francesca. "Luminous, and efficient."

She hesitated.

"Van was less reliable," she said with a smile. "From time to time cloudy moments came over him. Anis got on extremely well with Oscar, and I sometimes wondered, when I saw the two of them become such fast friends, whether Ivan didn't feel he'd been relegated to his own generation."

"I did suffer from it, to be sure," said Van, honestly, "but there was something else. Anis and I were going through the difficulties of adjustment that always arise in a couple after they have finally gotten together. You see: you fall into each other's arms, you're happier than you ever thought you could be. And then you get your wits about you again, you get a grip and you have to ask yourself: what do we do now? For Anis there was never any doubt we would not do anything more."

Heffner looked puzzled.

"Let me be more precise," said Van.

For Van, when you got along as well as he and Anis did at that point, it was self-evident that you should live together. For Anis, it was equally clear that what you must avoid above all was to begin sharing living quarters too hastily.

"Your place is much too small," she said. "And mine is even smaller. Besides, I can't really see one of us moving in with the other. One would not feel at home at all, and the other would not feel at home anymore."

"Let's look for something bigger," said Ivan.

"I'll look into it," Anis assured him.

But she couldn't find anything. Or, to be more exact, she couldn't make up her mind. She visited apartments and found them shabby, or too dark, or too expensive. At ten in the evening, when the bookstore closed, there she was, all smiles, waiting for Ivan. She took him back to his place. Dinner? she said. Oh, no! She climbed up the steps four at a time, she wanted to try everything, learn everything, she had an inexhaustible imagination, and soon it was Van who became the apprentice. But as soon as he fell asleep, with her hand curled around her mouth she called a taxi. Van would protest, mumbling no, half awake and trying to hold her by the ankle in the dark—but she was gone.

The next day, Van would wake up alone, and get ready in silence. One morning he had a premonition. She is casting off her past with me, he thought, and after that she will leave me. She will be cleansed, healed, and at last she'll be free.

40

There's something else we've forgotten," said Van. "Well, something we haven't done quickly enough, and that is to pick a few novels from the ones that have come out over the last few months. There must be some good ones, in the lot."

"At least four," said Francesca. "*Un pedigree*, by Patrick Modiano; *Louis Capet, suite et fin*, by Jean-Luc Benoziglio; *Oreille rouge* by Eric Chevillard; and A.S. Byatt's *The Biographer's Tale*. I am also very fond of Eric Holder's book of short stories, *Les sentiers délicats*. People have already ordered it from us. The Good Novel's faithful readers have good hunches, and they are an enormous help."

To these titles Van added the reprint of Ivo Andric's *Chronicles of Travnik*, Saramago's *O homem duplicado*, and François Valléjo's *Le voyage des grands hommes*. Anis adored Marina Tsvetaeva's *Captive Spirit*, an anthology of the poet's personal prose.

"It's already July," said Francesca. "We have to remind our eight committee members of their commitment. Each of them must give us a list of titles from the books published during the year."

"We could have asked them earlier," said Van. "They gave us their first list in May, so it's been more than a year."

"Let's give them until August," suggested Francesca. "In France, the literary year goes from summer to summer. We can make that our reference."

Two weeks after he had come to visit, Frucht informed them that he would not be going ahead with the project. In an e-mail, without beating around the bush: *The return on investment seems insufficient,* he explained.

"I'm not surprised," said Van. "You see what he means: he was horrified to learn that he wouldn't strike it rich with a business like The Good Novel. You know as well as I do that what success means to us, in financial terms, is never anything more than a tiny margin, on low cost products, day after day. A guy who's been a trader for ten years is wasted on something like this. He would die of impatience. You might as well ask a professional poker player to go into the forestry business."

Winter sent them his list early, with a note that was typical of him.

It was hard for us, he said, *to witness daily the violence perpetrated against a business, in other words against people—people for whom we would do anything—and yet that was the very problem, we couldn't do anything, since we agreed in advance that we would not get involved. You will have noted the paradox: we are the only ones on earth who are forced to remain so inactive, and yet The Good Novel is like flesh and blood to us, in a way. I felt like a father watching his child be mistreated before his very eyes and who can neither scream, because he is gagged, nor interfere, because he is bound hand and foot.*

Don't be surprised that I've shifted from "we" to "I." It's not that I'm into using the royal "we." I'm speaking for myself but, although I have no idea who my other gagged alter egos are, I cannot imagine that anyone else in this situation would react any differently.

Le Magot

P.S. There has been so much support for The Good Novel from other literary people, it seems to me that if anyone could figure out who had abstained, they would be on to the best way of figuring out who is on the committee.

P.P.S. Wouldn't it be a good idea, therefore, for some of us to voice our support anyway, in order to cloud the issue? Would you agree to release me from my vow of silence?

"Under no circumstances," replied Francesca to Winter's answering machine, "my dear . . ." She held her tongue just as she was about to say Magot, and eventually said again, My dear.

What was new, all the same, between Anis and himself, was the fact they were saying *tu* to each other, Van reminded himself. Anis talked to him now, and answered his questions.

"It's hard to explain," she said, for example. "I don't want to be locked up. In Grenoble I only began to breathe when I had my own room and I was the only one with the key. For me, sharing an apartment means someone else has the key. I can't stand for anyone to have a hold on me."

Van didn't protest; he did not say, it's not the same for me.

"I have an idea," he said. "Keep your room on the rue Bol-en-Bois. We'll find an apartment that's bigger than my studio. I'll rent it, I'll move in there, and you'll come when you feel like it, and you can stay or not stay. You can fix it up the way you want, you can bring whatever belongings you feel like bringing. And if you want, I won't have a key, you'll be the only one to have one. We won't lock up when we leave, we'll figure something out, a magnet, something so that the door won't be wide open when we're not there."

Anis was nodding her head, silently.

"Take some vacation, Ivan," said Francesca. "Oscar will choose his dates depending on you. Go on a trip with Anis."

Van dreamt of it. I'm waiting for her to ask me, he thought.

"I'm looking for an apartment," he said. "It's taking a long time. I want to find something by September. And then, things are very fragile," he added. "With Anis. I'm in more of a mood to say, let's not go anywhere."

At that particular moment during the summer, Van had a professional reason to stay at the bookstore. The article that came out in June, where Peter Carey sang the praises of The Good Novel, had inspired an American woman in Houston to open a similar bookstore. This woman—a young voice—called one day in mid-July. Ivan couldn't hear very well, and all he had said was, *Come and see*, and he had given her his e-mail address. Nothing had happened after that, not even a message. But three days later, a jolly redhead had shown up at the bookstore: *Here I am*.

Her name was Ruth McCormac—Cormac! echoed Francesca—and she was overflowing with enthusiasm about The Good Novel, but her French was fairly limited. What she understood by "see" meant, basically, staying on as an intern, *Come and see*: come and spend a month or two with us.

Francesca would have understood the same thing. "It's perfectly obvious, an internship to start off," she said.

Ruth didn't ask for anything, but she was given a stipend that would enable her to live in Paris without having to pinch her pennies every day. She had arrived with her laptop slung over her shoulder, and that very evening she had found an apartment to share in Montreuil.

She had read a great deal, traveled all over North and South America, dabbled in cinema, and lived, very meagerly, from the theatre. She was plodding, thorough, a self-taught intellectual who didn't know she was one. But to see her in the bookstore, you would have thought she'd been a bookseller all her life. She spoke a very clumsy French, which annoyed her, so in conversation she often switched to English or Spanish and this often flattered the customer, who would try to go one better. Every day she managed to have a discussion with Ivan. She had no managerial experience. You can learn as you go, said Van, who knew what he was talking about. Nor did Ruth have a penny to her name. She left again at the end of August with a clear idea of what her initial investment would be and her two main objectives: find a financial partner (if possible an individual, if possible a handsome young man) and associate herself with someone who was good at bookkeeping.

41

When Ruth left Paris, Francesca had already been gone for ten days. She had left—to sleep, she said, nothing more—without giving any precise date for her return.

Nothing abnormal about that, Van thought to himself more than once. She was exhausted, he didn't want to tell her that she needed rest more than he did. He hoped, without really believing it, that she was simply at home in Orta. The bookstore had hit the cruising speed commensurate with the unavoidable drowsiness of August in Paris. Sales had dropped off by half—Van said, Only half! For August that's fantastic. Francesca could take some vacation, if the word even had any meaning for her.

One morning, however, it occurred to Van that she might not come back. He was crossing the Seine by the Pont Royal, on his way to The Good Novel. It was seven o'clock in the morning, and a lovely white mist was rising from the water, softening everything—lines, colors, sounds. Van was frightened. Suddenly everything seemed cold to him—the stone, the water, the sky. He thought about how thin Francesca had grown, particularly in July, and she smiled too often, and too rigidly. It would be just like her to bow out without warning, after secretly dealing with every last detail to ensure the bookstore's survival.

There were thunderstorms on the horizon nearly everywhere in the world. Iran seemed determined to acquire nuclear weapons, despite the glowering of all the great powers, who already had theirs. Every week or so, rickety boats full of twenty-year-old Africans capsized offshore near Lampedusa or the Mauritanian coast. Fires the likes of which no one had ever seen were ravaging the Portuguese forest. Nearly eight hundred people had drowned during the monsoon in the Mumbai region alone.

One day at lunchtime, Brother Brandy came through the door of The Good Novel, holding to the walls to keep from falling over. He had such difficulty finding his words that Van immediately took him by the arm and led him to Le Comptoir, a few steps down the street. He's brought his list, he thought. And no doubt Brother had also thought about it, because all he could do was mumble titles, looking Ivan straight in the eyes, *Terminal cargo. Terminal frigo*, corrected Ivan, yes, it's very good. *C'est . . . C'est égal*, by Kristova. You mean Kristof, said Van, Agata Kristof. *Europes,* you know, Reda, you know. Yes, said Van. And . . . *Terminal cargo . . .*

Ivan listened to him repeat the same three titles (which he noted down, admiring his choice) for five minutes, then he hailed a taxi, climbed in with him, and made him get out at the Gare de Lyon, where he waited without Van letting him out of his sight for the first TGV for Chambéry; Van only turned around once the train had left the station, with Brother Paul on board. But no sooner had he left the train station behind him he realized he'd been a fool. He could kick himself! Brother was uncontrollable, he might talk during the trip, tell anything to anybody. It would have been a better idea to lock him away somewhere, at the rue de l'Agent-Bailly for example, and wait for him to sober up before sending him home, once he'd made him write up his list, and given him a proper telling off.

Anis found a three-room apartment on the ground floor in Auteuil.

"Auteuil?" echoed Van.

"It's the best value for money in Paris these days," said Anis. "Don't you want to live out there?"

"Well yes," Ivan hastened to say, but to anyone else he would have answered, I'd rather die. "I'm not crazy about the sixteenth arrondissement, except that area around Auteuil. The rue d'Auteuil and the surrounding neighborhood, that's just as nice as, I don't know, the Contrescarpe. And then, in terms of distance, it wouldn't put me any farther away from the bookstore than where I am in the 9th, I could go on foot along the Seine. Yes, Auteuil would be perfect."

Anis burst out laughing: "April fools! Ivan's a fool!"

She put her arms around him.

"How could you possibly have taken me seriously? You think I'm that mean?"

On the Boulevard Saint-Marcel she had found a big two-room apartment just under the roof.

"You can also walk to work along the Seine from there."

Van moved in on August 25. He gave notice at the rue de l'Agent-Bailly without regret, happy he no longer had to look at the walls that he had painted, the way one is happy to leave behind a landscape associated with difficult moments. On all the windows of the new apartment, with some tacks pressed right into the frames, Anis had hung strips of golden yellow cotton netting. Sunshine no matter what the weather, she said.

In one of the two rooms, in front of the window she had placed her magic tree, a Japanese futon in the middle, and in a corner a basket full of clothing in a jumble. "If you don't mind, this will be my room," she said, making sure, this way, that one of the rooms would not gradually become the living room and the other one a bedroom for the two of them.

Van said yes to everything. He was careful not to buy for his own room the six-by-six bed that he'd been dreaming of, but to install, rather, a sofa bed for one.

He would have been almost happy but, as the days went by, he was increasingly worried by the lack of news from Francesca.

A book by Ida Messmer was published on the twenty-ninth, among the onslaught of autumn novels that came with the latest automatic shipment in August, but it was so different that already the critics were reserving a particular fate for it: they were both blown away and curiously unable to talk about it. It was an erotic story, with a lot of talk about books, since the entire story took place in a library over two nights and the day in between. An old-fashioned library, on the second floor of a provincial manor house, where the narrator, a woman, opened a novel, then another, half a dozen in all, and read passages out loud that were adapted to the narration at that point. When Van noticed what the novels were, a vein began to pound in his forehead, because all of them were available at The Good Novel, which would have had nothing alarming about it per se if they had been books that were as famous as *Juliette* or *La Vénus à la fourrure*, but in fact the author was playing with fire, because the titles were far more obscure, such as *Olympe* or *L'Ivoire*.

Francesca came back on August 30. It fell on a Tuesday that year, and she got to the bookstore shortly after noon, just as if she had been there the day before and the day before that. Ivan could not hide his joy.

"How could you think I might not be here for the first anniversary of The Good Novel," she said, and Ivan kept to himself the fact he'd been prepared for anything.

"I haven't planned anything for this evening," was all he said.

That could be interpreted in several ways, but Francesca acted as if there were only one possibility: "Thank you for trusting me," she said.

She was looking more and more like Silvana Mangano, the Mangano from *Death in Venice*, a thinner, less confident version. She did not say where she had been for two weeks, nor how she had spent her time.

Van did not tell her about Strait-laced's latest book or about the very visible hints it contained. The shot had been fired. Whether Francesca found out or didn't would change nothing regarding the impact it might have. Whereas if he told her, he would be forcing her to listen to the dull drum roll of something threatening, and you might wonder, if you had noticed that distant rumbling, whether in reality it wasn't several drums beating all together, and where they might be far away as yet, or already very close.

And on that anniversary day Van wanted to block off anything that might resemble the sounds of battle, and show nothing but a second year that was sure of itself, taking great forward strides, surrounded by friends.

He brought Francesca up to date about the bookstore's activity over the last two weeks—sales, subscriptions, and the latest hats off on the part of the Friends—the paperback edition of *Montano*, by Enrique Vila-Matas—and birthday wishes had been arriving in the hundreds over the last few days.

"A steady wind, smooth seas, regular speed," he commented.

"A truce," said Francesca.

"The fine weather has returned," corrected Van. "And . . ."

He hesitated. But he felt he ought to tell Francesca this too: "I—Anis found an apartment."

He could not manage to say "we." He fell silent. He didn't want to say anything more about it. He felt easy about it, he knew that Francesca would figure it out and would say nothing, no remarks, no questions. He looked at her—saw the saddest smile in the world and eyes as changing as the sea.

At night, once they had closed the bookstore, Francesca led Ivan, Anis, and Oscar on foot to the rue du Cherche-Midi, just beyond the boulevard Raspail. It was hot, and in the streets, there were few cars, and you could hear the laughter and tinkling of dinnerware coming from the restaurants. Francesca entered a code on a wall next to a large entryway. They went through a barrel vault and into an enclosed garden, no larger than a courtyard but full of beautiful trees and rosebushes. Beneath the roof of leaves, a table had been set, lit by globe lamps and two lanterns on either side of the stone porch of a small private residence with three French windows.

"A friend's place," said Francesca mysteriously, waving her hand in a half circle. "The house is empty."

And indeed no one came during the entire dinner. Everything had been prepared on a trolley—melons, a chaudfroid of poultry, figs, raspberries, and champagne on ice. They helped themselves, like at a buffet. It was then that Van noticed that Francesca was wearing her lavender shirt-dress.

Oscar and Anis were over the moon. Francesca got them to talk. Oscar had spent his vacation in Madagascar, accompanying a filmmaker who was making a documentary about Jean Paulhan's long stay on the island before the war, and his work as a poet ethnologist, collecting as many popular sayings as possible. Anis knew entire passages of Tsvetaeva by heart, excerpts from her letters to Rilke. "They never met," she said, a hint of wonder in her voice.

Ivan was quiet.

At midnight Francesca signaled that it was time to leave. "A car is waiting at the door, you three get in. I'll walk home. I prefer to, you know."

42

In the first days of September, the bookstore filled up again—the level rose every day—enough to make you think that as they tore the page September 1 from their daily calendar, the French must be thinking, "September 1? Good Lord, all the new autumn books will be in the store, better go have a look."

At The Good Novel, nothing had changed; they were no more interested in the latest in literary fashion than they had ever been. There were no tables at the bookstore overloaded with seasonal produce, just a few titles here and there rescued from the flood and displayed in their appropriate sectors: *Snow,* by Orhan Pamuk (under Turkey, twenty-first century); *The Great Fire*, by Shirley Hazzard (Australia, twenty-first century); *L'arte della gioia* by Goliarda Sapienza (Italy, twentieth century)—because the book, now in French translation, had been published nine years earlier in Italy, and written thirty years before that; and under France, twenty-first century, were *Magnus*, by Sylvie Germain, *Clara Stern*, by Eric Laurrent, and *Le Petit traité sur l'immensité du monde*, by Sylvain Tesson.

L'Idée devoted a full page to the bookstore's exceptional stance: "The Good Novel is the only bookstore in France where you won't find piles of Michel Houellebecq's latest novel." The tone of the article was ambivalent, a mixture of Bravo! and Still, what is this, they've gone a bit too far.

Some clients requested the Houellebecq—not very many, to be honest. The response was gracious: head in either direction when you leave the bookstore and you will find this book roughly every hundred meters. But naturally if you really would like to buy it here, we will order it for you.

Several of the regulars at The Good Novel mentioned independently of each other that they thought they could sense something new this autumn in the bookstores: not exactly a spirit of revolt, or even a clearly marked trend, no, hardly a breeze, a puff of wind—but there was a way in which, increasingly often, booksellers were somewhat peremptory with their clients, saying: Oh really, don't get that. Do you trust me? And instead, they would place in their hands a novel that the papers had not talked about, or very little, but for which they could willingly vouch.

Every evening Anis spent several hours in the apartment on the Boulevard Saint-Marcel, which she still called "your place" ("Van's place"):

"See you later, at your place, Van?"

"Van, I'll wait for you at your place."

She left the bookstore long before Ivan; he stayed until closing time. He liked the busy hours between six and eight, and then after eight o'clock the moments of calm and intensity that were so deep that by ten o'clock, in order to close, he had to go around among the stragglers, so immersed in their reading that they had lost all sense of time and space, and ask them one by one, in a low voice and in a way that apparently is still current in little scholarly libraries, to give some thought to their dinner and to getting a bit of sleep between now and tomorrow morning.

There were some very fine days in September. Anis had begun, like Francesca and Ivan, to walk everywhere in Paris. At the end of the afternoon, between The Good Novel and Boulevard Saint-Marcel, she would stop off at Place Maubert and buy something for dinner—something good, something cold, she said. Quality ham, quiches, cheese, fruit. For she had discovered that if you went up a small flight of stairs from the landing of the apartment, beneath the roof, and you pushed open a door on which it was written, "No entry. Danger," you came out onto the sky, onto a zinc terrace surrounded by a light railing. All you had to do was put the dinner basket on a canvas or a blanket to feel absolutely wonderful up there—in the twilight, with an impression of absolute luxury, because all you could see or hear from this crow's nest, as far as living creatures were concerned, were birds, and as for the rest, the view on Paris was magical, like in a film.

As the days went by, Anis began saying, unconsciously, not "at your place," but "on the terrace": Shall we meet on the terrace? When Van got there, at around half past ten, it was dark. Fairly quickly Anis got in the habit bringing up a second basket, full of cushions and homemade lamps, little glass pots with stubs of candle. She left to one side an enormous umbrella that would enable them, in case of a downpour, to finish their dinner without rushing.

In the beginning, every other day she would go back to her place early in the morning, but it was obvious she was forcing herself, and that she was doing so out of principle. Then she began to stay all night, two days out of three, then three out of four. Whatever the case may be, every time, keeping her room for her exclusive use, and frequenting Van's room in order to play with him, she would fall asleep on his narrow sofa, curled up against him, before adopting the position of a well-fed infant, on her back, with her forearms wrapped around her head. So much so that after an hour or two Van, who was reduced to placing one hand on the floor if he was to stay on the edge of the bed, his shoulder in pain and his calf paralyzed by cramps, eventually went into the room next door, where he spent the night on Anis's futon which, in the end, was only of use to him.

The next day, he would get up early, while she stayed in bed. He knew she liked to be alone when she woke up. He would roll up the futon without making a sound and head out to walk to the bookstore. He would also stop on his way, often on the Place Maubert, to have some breakfast with coffee and try to answer the question he always asked himself at that point, every morning the same question: in his entire life, had he ever been this happy?

"Where do you think Francesca went in August?"

"No idea."

"I wonder if in the summer she doesn't go on the sly with her husband to those really snobby places, like Gstaad or Marbella."

"She may well have been hiding out in a little monastery in Paris that she mentioned one day. Why don't you ask her?"

"I'm just afraid she'll tell me she's been on a pilgrimage to a place her daughter liked, or something like that."

At the beginning of October, Éditis got angry. A "free opinion" column appeared in *Le Ponte*, signed by the three directors of the publishing house. Their argument was monetary: "Ninety percent of the novels that are on this autumn's short-lists for literary prizes cannot be bought at The Good Novel. What is the point of that? How can such hatred of contemporary culture be justified?"

"They're exaggerating," observed Ivan. "Ten percent of the titles that are on the short list, that's already enormous."

"Let's be exact," said Francesca. "Of these 10 percent, two-thirds of them are foreign novels."

"So? Do we have to respect some quota of French titles? The same every year?"

"Of course not; and it's out of the question to respond to such an idiotic attack. But I can understand why we annoy people."

The controversy went no further.

"There are two possibilities," said Van. "Either everyone is tired of these non-stop trials against us, no one is up in arms anymore. Or they've heard the pleadings, and we have won. They'll let us carry on our business as we see fit."

He looked at Heffner: "How wrong one can be. Fifteen days later the first of the three attacks took place."

43

It was half past twelve. The history of The Good Novel's fifteen months had lasted two and three-quarters hours.

"In the beginning you mentioned three crimes," Heffner reminded them.

"And that's what they were," said Francesca sharply. "Crimes in the judicial sense, horrible crimes, not symbolic ones."

"Go ahead," said Heffner, his voice even.

Francesca looked at Ivan.

"Three members of our reading committee were attacked," began Van, "and with a touch that was borderline genius, I must say. They were given a glimpse of death. All three are safe—I wouldn't go so far as to say they are sound.

"I only heard about the first attack well afterwards, eight days ago, on November 20. It took place during the night of the seventh. The victim was Paul Néant. I found out about the two others afterwards as well. One happened on the fifteenth and the other over several days somewhere between the nineteenth and the twenty-fourth. I was informed yesterday and the day before. The day before yesterday, Saturday, I got a phone call from Ida, and yesterday, Sunday, from the victim himself, Le Gall."

"Let me interrupt you," said Heffner. "The members of your committee have pseudonyms. Are you deliberately giving me their names?"

"Yes," said Van.

"Things have taken a criminal turn, there are no more secrets worth keeping," confirmed Francesca. "We are going to tell you everything we know about the three people who were attacked and, to begin with, who they are. That goes without saying."

"Perhaps we will also have to tell you everything about the other committee members," said Van.

"You may well have to," said Heffner. "But let's start at the beginning. The first attack."

"You mean what happened?" asked Van.

"What they told you happened."

"You are right to make a distinction. All I know about these three attacks is what the interested parties told me. I didn't check or cross-check anything."

"To each man his own trade. Go ahead, tell me."

What Ivan knew about Néant-Néon, in fact, didn't go far. He was a great prose writer, and very depressed. Hounded all year long by his inability to write, goaded from time to time by a merciless inspiration. Very famous yet not very well-known—admired by the tiny literary milieu, but ignored by the crowd. Incapable of writing, incapable of doing anything else. In chains. A bear. Anxious and unsteady. A misanthrope, alcoholic. He had sought refuge in Les Crêts, a dreary alpine village two hours from Chambéry by road. Friends, in spite of everything, women. One of them very attached, Suzon. He was ungrateful, unpleasant, uncommunicative. He had been in a real slump for several months. Benders, lack of sleep. Impotence.

It took Ivan three minutes to describe the attack. They forced him to drink, but obliged him to hold the bottle in his own hands, he concluded. That is what he is most ashamed of now.

"And how is he, now?" asked Heffner.

"What he has cannot be cured. But the treatment is radical:

if he wants to survive, he must abstain from alcohol, forever. They won't keep him in Lyon for very long. A few more days, and they will send him back to everyday life. He does not know where to go. He cannot possibly go back to Les Crêts."

"There is a solution to that problem," said Heffner.

Never taking his gaze from his interlocutor, he had taken a few notes on a pad of paper, isolated words, it seemed, in close handwriting. He turned to Francesca.

"Do you have anything to add?"

"No. I'm not as well-informed as Ivan about this attack or the two others. He told me about all three this morning, after he'd heard from the victims. Néon is a sort of wounded animal, that's what I would say. He writes like no one on earth, but when he's not well, he can be despicable."

"The day he came by the bookstore, in August, he was really a nuisance," said Van. "I put him back on the train as quickly as possible."

"You told us about that a while ago," interrupted Heffner. "And the second attack?"

"Ida Messmer. Another story," began Ivan. "We had met Ida one time, at the château of Montsoreau. An extraordinary memory, almost fantastical."

Heffner pressed him, abruptly: "She called you on Saturday, you said?"

She had reached Van at the bookstore, speaking in a low voice and warning him that she would be brief. He had listened without interrupting. He was discovering an Ida whose existence he would not have suspected, a passionate, active, extroverted mother, surrounded by family and friends. An experienced driver, who was perfectly aware of how unbelievable her story must seem. Driving slowly, along a dry road. A bend she takes four times a day, twice in each direction. And on that day, November 15, at four-twenty in the afternoon, a huge sedan was blocking the road.

"Was she injured?" asked Heffner.

"Yes, and in shock. She has migraines every day."

"The third attack?" asked Heffner, displaying no emotion.

"I heard about it yesterday," said Van. "This time, it was Armel Le Gall who was targeted."

Once again, the attack was hand-tailored. Made to measure, proof that the attackers knew Le Gall very well, just as they had known Paul and Ida. On Saturday, November 19, Le Gall set off just like every day along a customs path above the sea. That morning, they were waiting for him, and again the day after that, and the day after that. Two men, not speaking, just looking at him. Made to measure, said Ivan again. They had struck Paul in his weak spot, and Ida at the heart of her daily life. Armel was trapped by the regularity of his routine. It must have taken them some time and a lot of observation to discover the particular vulnerability of each of these three individuals, with such different lives—alcohol, the road, the cliff. It had taken a Machiavellian imagination to find for each of them the trap that could be disguised as an accident, just in case it did turn out to be fatal.

"Good," said Heffner. "I'll have a talk with each of these three individuals."

"Thank you," said Francesca warmly.

"Just a second," warned Heffner. "I understand that you do not want to press charges at this point, to avoid any publicity. And I can do the spadework involved. It fits more or less with my job description, and I agree with you, I'll find out more if I act in secret. But I will not investigate for very long outside of a legal framework. If I find confirmation that there has been an intention to harm, we will have to revert to regular procedure, press charges, and everything that ensues."

He turned to Ivan: "You didn't tell me where the young woman is."

"And for good reason," said Ivan. "I don't know myself.

She called me from a hospital—in Anjou, she said. Nor do we know where she lives—in other words, where the accident happened."

"We can find out all that from her cell-phone number. She called the day before yesterday, you said?"

"Yes, Saturday the twenty-sixth, just before eight o'clock."

"Give me her number."

Francesca took out her notebook and dictated Ida's number. Heffner asked for Paul Néon's and Armel Le Gall's as well.

"One more thing," he said. "Néon, Le Gall, I realize those are real names. But Ida Messmer, if I'm not mistaken, is a pen name?"

"You are not mistaken," said Francesca. "Even we do not know Ida's real name. She asked us not to try to find out."

"We will find that, too."

Francesca frowned.

"But how is that possible?" she asked. "How can you go from a number to the subscriber's name?"

"You can't. For the police, it's very simple. The telephone company in question does not give out the names of their account holders to just anybody. But they are all listed, and the police have access to them, if need be."

"In Ida's case, that really worries me," said Francesca. "I would prefer to go and see her, and explain to her what is going on and ask her to reveal her true identity."

"All right, if you can see her quickly."

"As soon as we leave here, I'll call her."

Van had another objection.

"You said you would speak to each of the victims. There's nothing surprising about that. But they haven't been warned. So they must still believe they have to maintain the secrecy around The Good Novel. We have to let them know that an investigation is underway."

"I suggest we do it right away," said Heffner.

"Here?"

"Yes, right here."

Van dialed a number on his cell phone.

"How shall I introduce you?" he said precipitously to Heffner.

"Don't use the word police, at this point. Mention an investigator. Don't give them my name."

"Hello, Paul?" said Van, turning to one side.

In a few words, he explained that they would be conducting an investigation. He held the receiver slightly away from his lips and raised his head to look at Heffner: "Are you the one who will meet him?" he asked in a low voice.

Heffner nodded.

Francesca was very tense. The moment Van put down the phone, she asked nervously, "Did he get angry?"

"No. He made no comment. I get the impression he has changed quite a bit."

Then Van called Le Gall. He got his voicemail, and left his name. Le Gall called him back almost immediately.

Then Francesca got hold of Ida. She agreed to let her come and see her that very evening.

"Where is she?" asked Heffner.

"In Saumur. At the hospital."

Heffner gathered up his notes, silently.

"In your story," he continued, "several times you insisted on the fact that the names of your committee were secret, and that the secret was well kept. And now in the space of three weeks, three committee members have been attacked. Do you have any idea of where the leak came from?"

"No," said Van.

Francesca said, "That's the big question."

Heffner placed his hands flat on his desk and looked them in the eyes one after the other.

"I must still ask you to give me the complete list of the committee members, with their phone numbers."

"That goes without saying," said Francesca. "My God."

She was very fearful for the five members who had not yet been attacked, and was prepared to send them abroad, or take them in her own home, or elsewhere . . .

"You will let me take care of this?" interrupted Heffner. "There's no point getting them upset."

"Well," injected Van, "we will have to warn them, too, that you will be contacting them. What shall we tell them?"

"Be somewhat evasive. Tell them something like: we've had too many people interfering with the bookstore, we're fed up with it, now, and we've asked someone to start an investigation."

He turned a page on his pad, and smoothed the blank sheet with his fingers: "Do it during the day," he added. "Good. I'm ready for the names of the eight members and their telephone numbers."

Van had taken a piece of paper from his pocket.

"I got this ready for you," he said. "Here you have the eight names, the eight numbers, and seven addresses out of eight, since we don't have Ida's. This is, moreover, the first time that it has all been written down in black and white on one sheet."

Heffner also wrote down Francesca's and Ivan's numbers. "In case of an emergency," he said, and he gave them his number. "If anything comes up."

He turned to Francesca. "One more formality and then I'll let you go," he said. "You will have to trust me for a while with your leather pouch. The one you said is shaped like an envelope."

"I had forgotten," said Francesca apologetically.

"It will take me half an hour. You can wait here. Or I can have a courier bring it back."

"You don't need more than half an hour?"

"No, no more than that."

"Let's go with the courier. That will save some time. I have to arrange to be in Saumur sometime this afternoon."

From her shoulder bag Francesca removed a pouch that was indeed the size and shape of a rather large envelope.

"I'll just take out some money so I can get home," she said, as she reached into the pouch.

"And your keys," suggested Heffner.

He looked at his watch.

"You'll get the rest back before two. What is the code for your building?"

PART FOUR

44.

There was a train that left Gare Montparnasse at three o'clock and got in to Saumur at half past five. Francesca arrived at the Medical Center reception shortly before six. But instead of going up to the desk she turned around and, six feet away, dialed a number on her little cell phone.

"Ida?" she said, as quietly as possible. "May I call you that? It's Francesca—you know. Ida, I'm at the hospital reception, and I don't know who to ask for, to come to your room."

"Anne-Marie Montbrun," said a voice which, for the second time that day, Francesca recognized as that of the unreal creature from Montsoreau.

"So it's you," said Francesca when she had sat down. "Excuse me, what I just said is absolutely meaningless."

Anne-Marie smiled to her: "No, it's perfectly clear."

They talked for an hour. The sun was setting, the sky was pink. Anne-Marie's expression changed when Francesca told her that three of the committee members had been attacked. So, she concluded, this confirmed that it was her hidden self, the writer, who had been targeted by the accident. It was then, in her little hospital room lit up by the setting sun, that she confessed to Francesca her habit of writing in her parked car, in other words, that her car meant much more to her than it might to others. That was the only place she felt truly alone, in that parked car, wherever it might be. Alone and free, to be honest, released, unleashed.

"But nobody knew," she said. "You are the first person I have told."

Francesca stopped her.

"Allow me. I can tell that you are very upset. One of the reasons I wanted to meet you as quickly as possible is that I am going to tell you something which might reassure you."

The pseudo road accident elicited three questions, she said. How did they know that Anne-Marie wrote in her car? How did they know that she published under the name of Ida Messmer—since, in Montsoreau, she had explained how important it was for her to have this double identity, and how carefully she made sure no one knew whose hand signed this name? And, thirdly, how did they find out she was on The Good Novel's reading committee?

"I'm thinking out loud in front of you," said Francesca.

It was not at all sure, she conjectured, that their decision to attack Anne-Marie on the road meant that they knew her car was the bubble where she went for inspiration. After all, the road was also the only place where she exposed herself to danger on a daily basis, because driving was her only activity that was both regular and risky, so this allowed them to plan an attack.

Nor was it at all certain that the brutes could have known that Anne-Marie Montbrun was Ida Messmer.

"It was another committee member who came up with this hypothesis when he was talking with Ivan, no later than yesterday," said Francesca, "one of the two others who were attacked, like you. It's not a bad idea."

What was certain was that there were strangers who had something against Anne-Marie Montbrun, and it seemed very likely, given the fact that other members of The Good Novel committee had also been targeted, that it was because the strangers had found out she belonged to the committee. This did not mean that they knew Anne-Marie Montbrun was Ida Messmer.

"It makes all the difference for me," said Anne-Marie slowly. "For The Good Novel, it's very worrying that they attacked Strait-laced, as a member of your selection committee. It wasn't much fun for me either, but I'm telling you the way I feel, and it would be far worse if they had targeted me as Ida Messmer."

Francesca looked puzzled.

"It's hard to explain," said Anne-Marie, blushing. "But I've always been convinced that if anyone in my immediate circle found out that I write, I would no longer be able to do it."

She was silent for a moment, then continued, "That is, if someone found out, and they also knew who I write for. You will understand. I can tell you."

The person for whom Anne-Marie Montbrun wrote was also the person who inspired her.

"It's fairly common," said the young woman. "He is also my character, the you, the he, and the him in everything I write. I have been his wife for twelve years, and I only see him a few days a month."

Arnaud Montbrun's profession was the reason their married life was founded on waiting. They'd made the most of a tough situation, and in the end it had given rise to joy, said Anne-Marie. For her, rarity meant desire, intensity, invention. She put her brain to work, imagined décors, scenes, and she wrote. She sent, or did not send, what in the end were only letters, she said, a sort of long endless letter. Arnaud went along with it, he hardly had anything to lose.

"Anyway," said Anne-Marie, suddenly blushing, "you know my books. You understand," she continued, "that what I write writes itself. I never *wanted* to write."

And she had always had the intuition that if her modus operandi were revealed, if people around her learned that she was the author of the fairly unorthodox texts of Ida Messmer, if they knew the identity of the lovers in the story, and who they were "in real life," and how they wed imagination, eroticism, and discretion, the story could no longer be written. There would be nothing more, ever, signed Ida Messmer.

Since her accident, she felt amputated, and could not stop thinking about the life she had had, and that she could never have again.

"So, if you can confirm that although they found out that Strait-laced was Anne-Marie Montbrun, they didn't identify Ida Messmer, they missed out on Ida and her books, in a way, you have given me back my life. You are giving me back to myself."

"And Ida Messmer will pick up her pen," said Francesca.

She did not add what she was thinking. One question would remain unanswered, a fairly significant one, the third one: How did they know, who had discovered that Anne-Marie Montbrun was on The Good Novel's reading committee?

They were interrupted. It was seven o'clock, time for visitors to leave.

"We'll talk again about your latest book," said Francesca. "It is one of the few September novels that we have on sale at the bookstore. I didn't have anything to do with it, trust me."

45

I found out that Heffner started the investigation right away, even though he had other cases on his hands. I didn't know everything, but what I learned, I learned at the same time as Van and Francesca, although the beginnings of The Good Novel were told to me afterwards.

Of course there were certain things they didn't tell me. For example, for a long time I had no clue that I had been among those under suspicion for having discovered and handed over the eight names on the committee. It was the last thing I'd have imagined.

Heffner went to speak to Néon and Le Gall. Anne-Marie Montbrun gave her consent, and he went to see her as well. No doubt he met with other committee members, too.

Paul Néon wasn't proud of it, but he could not tell them a single thing about the men who had forced him to drink. The most he remembered was that the so-called filmmaker looked like your average Frenchman, not very tall, not very big, not very dark, no mustache or beard . . . He hadn't the slightest recollection about the other fellow. No doubt there is some connection, he said, between my inability to recognize them, if ever they came back through Les Crêts, and my terror at the mere idea of ever setting foot there again.

Heffner talked with him for a long time. It would not be hard to find him somewhere else to live, since no professional activity obliged him to stay in that part of the Alps, and he could settle anywhere. You are wrong, said Paul. He did not want to leave Chambéry.

When asked, he willingly gave the reason for his attachment. Heffner even got the impression that that was all he had been waiting for. It wasn't that he particularly liked the region, on the contrary, he couldn't stand average mountains, for the very reason that they were average, always somewhere between two grays, two clouds, two rainfalls. But for the last eleven years he had been bound by a commitment that he did not want to break. Every Wednesday he went down to Chambéry to look after children.

When Heffner heard these words from Paul, he wasn't learning anything new. Through Ivan, who had heard it from Paul himself, he found out who these children were and why they came every Wednesday from all over to a playground in a dreary housing project to the south of Chambéry. But he did not tell him that he already knew the story. For while he saw no reason to criticize—Paul read stories and lent books to disenfranchised children, as the facilitator of what the ATD Fourth World Association called a street library—he did wonder what sort of call of duty a writer as antisocial and misanthropic as Paul could be answering by devoting so much of his time over the last eleven years.

"You may wonder why this regular meeting with a bunch of snot-nosed kids is so important to me," said Néon that very moment.

Heffner nodded vaguely, without showing more interest, like a Freudian psychoanalyst at the very moment when he is certain that he and his patient have reached the crux of the problem.

"It's simple," said Néon.

Heffner, like a shrink, did not believe that anything was simple. But he said nothing.

"Eleven years ago," said Néon, "for the first time in my life I was carried away by passion."

A sixteen-year-old Gypsy had come up to him in the street. A dark beauty. She was offering her person for next to nothing—the only thing she knew, in French, was how to count—and she seemed to get extreme pleasure out of this commerce. At first Néon thought she was bluffing, that it was some sort of marketing ploy. But in the time it took to examine her mind somewhat closer, and make doubly sure there was no pretence about it, the careless man was caught in the web. Shackled. He fell madly in love, and suffered death and passion between two meetings.

The least one can say is that the passion was not reciprocal. Paul tried to teach the lass what love could mean. But that word, which he would later realize all sorts of little savages knew and used, was incomprehensible to this young girl. Mina—that was her name—did not even grasp what she might have got out of Paul's folly. At the most there were times, when she saw him kissing her hands, when she burst out laughing.

This man had made so many women suffer, because with each one, he very quickly realized that all he liked about her was her youth and femininity—but they realized this even sooner, those women, and in spite of everything they still loved the big guy, not because he was handsome or kind, he wasn't, but because he was unlike any other man. And now, for the first time, because of a brunette who couldn't even be bothered to find out his name, this same man had suffered the torments of being used solely as an instrument of pleasure.

"And a source of profit," observed Heffner.

"Hardly," said Néon.

The kid forgot the money, took it and put it back, in fact she didn't really seem to care. To such a degree that Paul wondered if she hadn't played the prostitute just to start a hassle-free relation without a fuss and attain her ends more quickly.

"I thought that Gypsy girls were supposed to be good," said Van when he heard the story, "married off at an early age, faithful . . ."

"I read that somewhere, too," said Heffner laconically.

Paul was not sure he had understood properly, but Mina had led him to believe that she had been married at fifteen, and that she had run away after two years of conjugal life. She talked about herself as little as possible. It would seem that she lived with a family that was not her own, who were not really a family, in the strictest sense of the word. People who were sedentary only part of the time, members of a clan who were beginning, after a fashion, to put down roots in this poor neighborhood in Chambéry.

After a fashion: because while some of them decided to stay, and agreed to be housed between four walls and send their children to school, others could never bring themselves to do so: they would stay a few weeks in Chambéry, then go away, then come back, then go away without warning, and when they were there, they refused in any case to be housed anywhere but in their own home, their caravan that is, in a large field near the apartment blocks.

One day, the young girl disappeared. Néon looked for her and learned that her band had left, nothing more. He waited, suffering more and more. He never saw Mina again. He had been waiting for eleven years.

At first he thought he would go crazy. Every day he went by the big field where he knew Mina had left from and where, in the beginning, he was sure she would return. For months on end he questioned all the gypsies he could, in vain. That is when he learned that they called her Mina.

No matter how often he told himself that if the little bitch had left to get away from him, then he had lost any chance of ever finding her again, since he had made it clear to her that there was only one place on earth to avoid if she was to be free of him: it did not work. Gradually he stopped wandering back and forth through that part of Chambéry, but he was never able to tear himself away completely. When a volunteer from

ATD Fourth World who had an office there asked him if he wouldn't like to join up with them, he accepted without hesitation.

Eleven years had gone by. While Paul no longer hoped to see Mina again, he could not stop missing her. He almost never wrote anymore—he didn't think that "it" would come back. He had reached a point where he called the missing girl and his vanished inspiration by the same name, Mina.

Then he no longer had hope? No, he did. Of course. It was no doubt because of his activity as an itinerant librarian and his regular contact with children, many of whom came from the Gypsy camp: he realized fairly quickly that Mina might have had a child by him. He even persuaded himself of the fact (and by extension, that she had run away to have the child all to herself). He had nothing but scorn for the passage of time, in a sort of desire for eternity—since eternity is not time that has become endless but the opposite, time suspended, non-time—and by reading stories to little Gypsies he was in a way preventing the embers from growing cold. He might be transmitting to an unknown son the most beautiful thing he knew and what was best about himself, his passion for words and sentences.

As he was listening to this confession, in the little room at the hospice in Lyon that was both badly and too well lit, Heffner—he would tell us the story later on—abandoned the distance befitting his position for a moment, and looked at Néon, his dilapidated body, his yellow skin, the bags under his eyes, and he thought, How young he is.

Le Gall had seen his aggressors four times, he recalled. But Heffner didn't think he could make much use of his descriptions. The two fellows were wearing ordinary clothes, parkas or fur-lined jackets, beige, brown, or khaki. They must have been wearing jeans, otherwise Le Gall would have noticed their pants. Well, something like jeans. They had heavy shoes, and their heads were covered (woolen caps, unless they had raised their hoods: a tight hood can look just like a cap), no gloves, their hands in their pockets, no glasses; but on this last point, Armel did not trust his own memory; he had been known to swear that a person he had run into the day before was not wearing glasses, when in fact they were—as if glasses were not clearly noticed by other people, or at least other people didn't memorize them as distinctive signs, particularly when those other people were the very same who had to wear them and who were convinced they were disfiguring.

"Same for their noses," said Le Gall. "In the middle of their faces, surely, but if I had to stare at them to a point where I could describe them . . ."

As for Heffner, he had known for a long time that people don't see much of what is there before them. It was all the more deplorable for the fact that it was in this vagueness of memory, in this impressionism, that it became his job to detect the exact observation which would allow him to identify, or connect, or deduct, the way from a tiny piece of column found among a hundred pebbles in the undergrowth one can reconstitute an entire temple; it was up to him to find the motive for the crime and the person behind it.

He's confused, he realized as he listened to Le Gall in the Le Grand Gallo bar, particularly dreary at the beginning of December, where they were sitting opposite each other. His memory is hazy; something must be blocking it.

And just as Armel was hesitating: "To be honest . . ."

Go on, Heffner pleaded.

". . . this is all very painful. In other words, I'm finding it hard to relive it."

Le Gall was humiliated to confess that he was having trouble getting over his misadventure. No matter how often he had gone back to the place at the top of the cliff since then, and found no one sinister-looking, and promised himself he would resume his habit of taking a walk by the sea every morning, he couldn't do it.

And the worst of it—but it was related—was that he couldn't get back to work on his book. He had stopped at the page he'd finished just before what he had come to refer to as his "huge scare." Only eight days had gone by in the meantime, but to spend eight days without writing, Le Gall no longer knew what that was. He had never had writer's block. He had read everywhere, in biographies and memoirs, that it is hell for an author, but he had never suffered from it. And now was not a good time, at the beginning of a new novel that he didn't quite have a grip on yet. He was struggling, he would sit down at his desk first thing in the morning, but nothing came. Not a word, not a sentence, not an idea. Nothing but disgust at his subject, at his work, and at the writing project in general, and after a while, the disgust won out over his will.

"I am paying for my cowardice," he said. "You know, writing, no matter what the subject, however fictitious you think it is, at best it's sitting down to face yourself, at worst you're fighting yourself, in any case you have to take stock of your limits. And this time that is all I can see, my limits. The man I have before me makes me feel ashamed.

"It's painting that's keeping me going," he continued. "An old tub. I'm acting as if. And it's a good thing the painting is working: I almost told everything to Maïté."

Heffner tried to convince him not to resist. "Go on a trip, get a change of scene, spend your time differently—well, take what we call a vacation. It is generally acknowledged that it can be good for you."

But the few times that Ivan—who was not supposed to be aware of Armel's distress—called him on the telephone, he found him at home, picking up the phone right away and going on and on, continuing the conversation and talking about everything except the very thing that was poisoning his days. And Ivan did not dare rub salt in his wound.

Heffner saw Anne-Marie. She had just gone home, and he was the first person to learn her address. I think it was to him—I can't remember, but it's not important—that Anne-Marie told him how one evening it came back to her.

She was still at the hospital, and it wasn't an ordinary evening, because Francesca was leaving. Anne-Marie could still hear Francesca's words, words which, she said, had done more to make her well than any doctor.

Her pain was subsiding. For the first time she could breathe without getting the impression that her broken ribs were piercing her lungs. She was alone. She looked out the window. The sun was setting and she saw a purple and yellow sky that gave her a craving for rose petals.

She closed her eyes. She saw him. A. smiling to her—the man Ida always called A. in her books. She went up to him, and placed her lips against the hollow behind his ear. She could feel the heat of his skin, his smell.

She was laughing as she told the story, it was a pleasure to see, it seemed. She lit her bedside lamp, sat up, pressed the buzzer next to her bed. When the nurse came, she asked, Could you find me some paper and a pencil? I can sit up now. And I have something to write.

46

Heffner went to see Doultremont in his office on the quai Citroën. He saw Yassin al-Hillah, the cleaning man, man of letters. He was working above all, at least so he said, on the trails left by every telephone, and all the Internet communications: there had been thousands of messages sent to The Good Novel, and posted All over the Web, about the bookstore. He took each of the bookstore's computers away in turn, and kept them for two or three days. Francesca brought him her personal computer.

She did not say much these days, early December; she hardly spoke. But you could sometimes see her moving her lips, silently. She told Van she could no longer look at the people who came into The Good Novel without suspecting them. She also told him that she would have liked to spend all her days at the bookstore, but she would not allow herself.

She could not understand why the investigation was taking so long, and she did not dare question Heffner. Normally so lively, so enterprising, she no longer took the initiative. I think she simply was afraid. Of what? Of everything, I imagine—to use her own words.

"Why don't you go up to Méribel for a while?" said Van. "It's been snowing, you'd feel good up there."

She gave a dissonant little laugh.

"The chalet has been sold," she said. "I emptied it in August."

Van didn't understand.

"Bankers can be very annoying sometimes," said Francesca. "There was money owing, I had to find some cash."

With a finger in front of her lips, she motioned to Van not to add anything.

"It's just as well," she said. "The only reason I still went up there was because Violette used to like the resort, and she often spent her vacation there. I had trouble letting go of it. Now it's done. It's not a bad thing."

Oscar showed himself to be an invaluable collaborator, efficient and discreet, particularly toward the end of 2005. Without saying anything, and perhaps without her even realizing, he did his utmost to take the work off Francesca's shoulders, particularly the subscriptions, of which there were now more than three thousand. It was Oscar, if I remember correctly, who noticed that the three attacks had all occurred right in the middle of the literary prize season.

"Oh, damn it all, the prizes," said Francesca.

When they mentioned it to Heffner, he was not so categorical. He had already made the connection. He came out with a well-turned phrase, such as: we can't not take them into consideration, and on the other hand one should never underestimate the element of chance.

But on December 13 nobody—not Heffner, nor any of those who were in on it—had much respect left for chance when they learned that Scaf had called Van in the middle of the morning, asking him to come over—"My place, yes, it's urgent. Yes, right away, can you?"—and that no sooner had he opened the door than he led him into the kitchen where, leaning against the refrigerator, was his bicycle.

Scaf-Évohé lived then, and still lives, almost all the way at the top of the rue Valette, under the Panthéon, in the building where there still exists, in the courtyard, hidden from the street, the tower that enabled Calvin to escape over the roofs one day in 1533 when he was about to be arrested. When Ivan provided this detail, I could envisage the place. In front of the main door there is a History of Paris plaque which tells the story, and which I had read.

Gilles Évohé lives in a three-room apartment on the top floor, not in the old building that gives onto the street but in a 1950s block in the courtyard, a fairly nice space where he is able to leave his bicycle in a corner of the storeroom, chaining it to a foot scraper with a bike lock.

On Tuesday 13, at nine-fifteen in the morning, with his backpack on his back he came down into the courtyard, sniffed the weather, gray and cold—well, that was normal—went into the storeroom and, before unlocking his bicycle, as he had promised, he took a good look at it.

Nothing unusual. Évohé unlocked his bike, went under the archway, and took the bike over the threshold. On the rue Valette, on the sidewalk, he gave the vehicle a forward thrust to check the brakes, holding the left and right handlebars at the same time, and he nearly fell over: both brake cables were flapping in the air like crazy antennas.

"The bastards did a good job," he said, showing Van. "Look. I would have seen that they had cut the cables if they had merely sectioned them in the middle. No, they cut them right by the handlebars, underneath the brake handles, and then they stuck them back together with some sort of invisible glue, some superglue."

He was still furious. A black-and-silver Peugeot that wasn't even two years old! In mint condition! It was a crime.

Van felt a wave of gratitude toward Heffner.

"Our investigator warned you?"

"Fortunately," grumbled Évohé. "To think that if it weren't for him, this marvelous bike could be history, by now."

Heffner had stopped by at rue Valette one week earlier. They had talked about literature—"He's got culture, your guy," said Évohé. "He'd read all my novels"—but also about bookstores, The Good Novel, and the threats they'd all received. That's when Heffner went into details, he talked about the three attacks on the three committee members, and he questioned Scaf at length about his lifestyle, his eating habits, his activities, his manias, where he spent his time. When he found out that Évohé got around by bike, and remembered that he lived on one of the steepest streets in the Latin Quarter, he didn't beat around the bush: he begged him to stop riding his bike and, since Évohé refused to do so, then at least to check his vehicle before he used it—examine it from every angle whenever he was getting ready to ride it, and not just in the morning, several times a day, if need be.

47

L et's stop everything," said Francesca.
It was noon.
"We're not stopping anything," said Van.
"That's what I just said."
"We agree on that."

"You have no other choice," said Heffner decisively as soon
as he joined them, ten minutes later, in the big office on the rue
Dupuytren. "You have to bring together your eight electors and
tell them everything—there were a number of details I didn't go
into—and you have to get them to agree to press charges and
you have to decide with them how to handle things from here
on out."

The eight electors: he's using our words, thought Francesca,
our expressions. It's an understatement to say he's with us. He
is one of us.

Ivan was gloomy.

"Press charges," he objected. "That means the investigation
will go out into the open: there are bound to be leaks, and the
names of the eight committee members will get around. The
very principle of The Good Novel will be compromised, that
the books are chosen by an anonymous committee. By coming
to you, we hoped to avoid initiating legal proceedings and
revealing the identities of our committee members."

"If you want to save the four electors who, thus far, have
been spared from an attack, then you have no choice," repeated

Heffner. "Revealing both their names and the threats hanging over them, that's the best way to protect them. It's fairly simple—you publish a communiqué in which you say, Those who have a bone to pick with us have gone too far, they've managed to find out the names of our committee members; four of them have been attacked. But we refuse to be intimidated. We are pressing charges, we are changing the committee. And then you reveal the eight names: they are respected writers, and it will be excellent for the image of The Good Novel."

"We would have had to set up a new committee sooner or later," said Francesca. "We never envisaged a permanent committee."

"Where were we?" said Van. "We get the eight together. To begin with, they will get to know each other."

"Is that such a bad thing?" asked Heffner.

"In fact," said Van slowly, thinking out loud, "there was one principal reason why we did not want them to get to know each other, and that was because we wanted the secret of their names to be kept as well as possible. Now that the secret is out, it no longer has any importance."

Francesca was giving little nods of her head: "If only we knew who gave the list of names, and who has it."

Heffner looked at her for a few seconds.

"I think I can throw some light on that," he said.

"What do you mean?"

"I don't know who has the list—although I'm beginning to have some ideas on the matter. But I think I do know how the list got into the hands of those brutes."

"Tell us."

"I've been hesitating to do so ever since I understood what must have happened. First of all, it won't change anything, the deed is done, the names are going around. And then there are two sides to the information. On the one hand, it should be something of a relief. On the other, it's going to set you up for a rather . . ."

"Go ahead," urged Francesca, without waiting to be told what would happen.

"The good news is that there is no traitor, I am nearly sure of that, now. Nobody deliberately gave out the names."

"And?"

"The news that you will find somewhat less pleasant to hear is how the leak came about."

When Francesca had her handbag stolen, at the beginning of June, she had not been the random target of an average pickpocket. Heffner did not have any proof, but he would have staked his life on it. They were targeting the owner of The Good Novel, they wanted her papers. And they must not have been disappointed. They got what they wanted, the list of the selection committee members.

"But that list wasn't in my bag!" protested Francesca. "I never wrote it down. I never had it on me."

"Indeed," said Heffner. "The thieves compiled it from your address book."

Francesca didn't understand. She had never written the name of any of the eight members in her address book—that was the most elementary precaution. Neither name nor pseudonym.

"Just their phone number," said Heffner.

"Yes, I'll say it again, there was no name next to it, no initial, nothing that could allow someone to connect the number to a person."

"That's what you thought," said Heffner.

There was not the slightest trace of smugness or reproach in his voice. It wasn't really an address book, he said, because there were only three or four addresses, and sixty-one telephone numbers, to be exact.

"Yes," said Francesca. "It's not really an address book, but a little removable index in a diary, you noticed? I write down the phone numbers that I need frequently. I use it a lot."

Of the sixty-one phone numbers, explained Heffner, almost

all of them corresponded to a name that was written on the same line. Almost all: eight of them were not associated to any name or address—nothing.

Francesca's features froze.

"Someone who found this notebook by chance would not notice a thing," continued Heffner. "But someone like me, who is carefully going through the list to try to find particular numbers, will immediately notice that some have been given special treatment. Eight is a good number, eight numbers connected to nothing, spread over several pages."

"I found my handbag again an hour later, and the notebook was there," said Francesca, "with all my papers."

"Elementary," explained Heffner. The thieves had set it up so it would look like an ordinary theft for money: pickpocket, handbag quickly abandoned, only cash disappearing—they had staged the most common scenario.

"When it was my turn to go through the contents of your little pouch, I gave myself half an hour, less than what your two scoundrels on the motorcycle had. It was more than enough to photocopy all your papers, including your diary and the relevant list, page by page. I did it myself. After that, you have all the time you need to study the photocopies."

"And here I thought I had been so clever by putting those eight numbers without names on the pages of the corresponding pseudonyms," said Francesca, her voice muted. "Sarah Gestelents's number under P. as in Green Pea, Évohé's number under S. as in Scaf, and so on."

"It didn't matter, as it happens. That didn't make it any less obvious that there were eight numbers without names. If the sleuths wondered why you had written them down on those particular pages, the question must not have preoccupied them for long."

Francesca looked down, then raised her head again.

"I'm not trying to get myself off the hook," she said with an effort. "My lack of caution was extremely foolish. But there is something I don't get. Let's put ourselves in the place of my thief. He has a list of eight cell phone numbers: what can you possibly do with it?"

"Don't you remember," interrupted Van, "we talked about it the other day, some people have no problem gaining access to the files of telephone companies, and to find out who the client is for each number."

Once they had the eight names, it was clear to them that they had put together the committee list, concluded Heffner. There was only one actual name that remained unknown out of the eight, that of Anne-Marie Montbrun. The seven other names were those of very well-known novelists, like Le Gall, or lesser-known authors who were well-respected in literary circles. (Néon, Néant, you could figure out it was the same person.)

"Which would go to show that the brutes belong to those circles?" asked Van.

"It's a definite possibility," said Heffner.

48

Francesca immediately started work on organizing the meeting. "Let me do it," she said. "Please. To try to make up for some of my stupidity."

"Just one thing," said Heffner, "to save some time. Your electors all have new numbers."

And, forestalling Francesca's question: "They all have new telephones, yes. I thought it was preferable."

He handed her a piece of paper.

"I wrote down their numbers."

"Shall I learn the numbers by heart and then swallow the list?" asked Francesca.

"Just put the paper in a place where no one will think to look for it."

"In the tea jar?"

"For example."

Francesca slipped the paper between her watchband and her wrist.

"Temporary hiding place," she said. Then, changing her tone, "Did you tell us that Anne-Marie has gone home?"

"Yes. She can travel by car."

"And Paul? Does he have permission to move around?"

"I was getting there," said Heffner. "He got out of the hospital last week."

Néon did not want to set foot in Les Crêts ever again. Heffner had convinced him to go back there for one hour, under his protection, at night, the time he needed to throw his work things into a suitcase. They would worry about his move later on.

Paul grumbled: "I'm not working on anything."

"Just take whatever is on your writing desk," Heffner told him firmly. "You have to get ready to get started again."

On the way back from this lightning visit to Les Crêts (the village was snowed under, and they didn't meet anyone; Suzon had gone by the day before to get the keys from L'Alpette and hide them on the windowsill of the garden shed), while he was at it, Heffner had driven Néon to his new residence.

"He's over by Maisons-Laffitte," he said. "Don't go thinking he's in Peru. I found him a detox center. It's going to be hard work for him. He has to learn how to feed himself all over again—and how to drink."

Francesca was able to set up the meeting for the following evening. She managed to convince everybody that it was urgent. "In a way," she told Van, "I'm glad I found out the leak beforehand. I'll tell all eight right from the start that I alone am at fault, and in no way are they under suspicion."

One of them did defect, however. Anne-Marie refused point-blank to take part in the meeting, or to show herself in any way, or to see her name mentioned. This was to be expected and, on the line, Francesca didn't argue. What it amounted to was that Anne-Marie was resigning from the committee. She had no objection to The Good Novel pressing charges—although she herself would not have done so—nor to the list of committee members being made public, provided she was not on it. But she did not want the name of Anne-Marie Montbrun, nor that of Ida Messmer, to be made public, nor that the strange accident in the bend at Les Galardons, near Saumur, be mentioned in any way.

She had to regain her freedom of mind. Arnaud wanted it as much as she did, and they were moving. They would leave the Anjou region. Anne-Marie asked them to forgive her, she had been passionate about The Good Novel, and remained so, but she preferred to keep the place where she would settle with her family a secret.

At this point, I knew about her double life. I shouldn't have, but the fact was that a few hours earlier, through Ivan, I had learned who hid behind the name of Ida Messmer. If Anne-Marie was leaving the history of The Good Novel behind her, and if future events enabled her to remain anonymous, there were still four of us who knew her secret: Francesca and Ivan, Gonzague Heffner, and I—four people who were firmly determined never to say a word about it.

All things considered, Francesca decided to accept Sarah Gestelents's offer to use her studio on the rue Alexandre-Dumas to hold the meeting. It was more discreet than at her place on the rue de Condé, or at Ivan's place, or in an ordinary restaurant.

I wish I could have been there. A lot was at stake for Francesca and Ivan that evening. They were the first to arrive, with a basket full of bottles. (Francesca had brought a bottle of port, a Grave, and some bourbon. When he saw this, in the taxi, Van protested that if people were drinking in front of him, Brother would have a hellish evening. He had obtained permission to leave the center, and it would be preferable to send him home in a decent state. Francesca could have kicked herself. She forced the taxi driver to accept the bottles of alcohol as a gift, then to drive by a grocery store that was open where they could buy some fruit juice.) It was a dark night, and it was snowing.

Sarah's studio took up the second and top floor of a tiny building opposite the looming church of Saint-Jean-Bosco, which looks like a reinforced concrete rocket. At first glance, the studio reminds you of the office of an architect who is just starting out: twenty feet by twenty feet, wide walls covered with shelves, jute flooring, clip-on lights here and there, a long, low mattress in the place of a sofa, two tables on trestles in front of the two windows, covered with papers and books and, in one corner, more trestles and plywood panels of various sizes so that a third of any size table could be built, if need be.

For nine people, they would need one of the big panels. Sarah brought in some folding chairs and a short-haired Moroccan blanket that served as a tablecloth.

Francesca had invited the six other electors to come between eight-thirty and nine o'clock, so that they wouldn't all ring the bell at the same time. Though it was a meeting held to deal with a crisis, it began like a game, as the various participants arrived, discovered who the others were, and realize with whom they had formed a team without knowing it. Some of them already knew each other. Armel Le Gall and Gilles Évohé had been friends for a long time. Marie Noire and Jean Tailleberne had sat together for three years on the Commission for the Novel of the National Center of Letters. Néon didn't know anyone; Winter knew everybody, with the exception of Néon, whom he knew by sight.

"We're all here," said Francesca shortly after nine o'clock. "Have a seat. Bring your glasses."

She began by relating the history of The Good Novel, something of which only she and Ivan had an overview. She reminded them of the bookstore's promising beginnings, then the succession of attacks and their variety. She explained, her voice less confident, how the brutes had stolen her bag—Ivan and I call them the brutes, she said—and identified the committee members.

"My handbag was stolen at the beginning of June. The following months must have been spent making lengthy inquiries. In November, one after the other, three committee members were physically attacked, and on December 4 one of them had a very close call that would have been disastrous had he not been warned—as you all were, I presume."

"It's probably not worth describing each attack in detail," interrupted Néon.

Francesca did not intend to do so, she said, nor to name the victims. If any of them wanted to tell the story of what had happened, they were free to do so, or to remain silent.

"Any questions?" she asked.

They all had questions. They talked about this and that for over an hour. They had questions about The Good Novel's stock, its image in the press, sales, support, the investigator who had suddenly showed up not so long ago, who asked a lot of questions but didn't give much away, and about the brutes, obviously—who could they possibly be?

Ivan put an end to the discussion to move on to the "action" items on the agenda: what should their response be? He had a plan.

"It's a suggestion," he said. "We'll discuss it. It goes without saying nothing will be done without your consent."

"Two things," he began. "First of all, we will file a complaint against 'unknowns.' Then, the same day or the day after, we issue a three-point press release: our decisions to take legal action, a summary outline of the succession of attacks that are the grounds for our action, and the composition of the committee at the same time that we announce our intention to dissolve it."

"Obviously," said Tailleberne.

Winter, slowly, as if to convince himself he was not having a bad dream, said: "The end of the committee."

Both of them looked distraught.

"I'm listening," said Van. "Already, one committee member preferred not to come this evening, in order to remain anonymous and take the initiative to resign. That is his—or her—right."

"So there were eight of us," said Marie Noir, although you could not tell whether the number surprised her, annoyed her, or left her indifferent.

"Please," said Sarah Gesteslents. "I have an idea."

She approved of the idea of filing a complaint and of going public with the makeup of the committee. She saw three advantages: they were not backing down, or giving in; denouncing the attacks was a way to make them stop; and all in all, the operation was bound to create a favorable buzz around The Good Novel, reinforcing the wave of support and sympathy.

"Personally," said Sarah, "you have my consent to give out my name. I have absolutely no objection to showing, at last, my solidarity with the bookstore."

She looked like a little stable boy from the Middle Ages, with her boyish beige and black clothing, her pageboy haircut, and her strong jaw set in her thin face.

"Here's my idea," she said. "Once we have dissolved the committee, there is nothing to stop us from setting up a new one where the incumbents could be secretly reappointed, a second time round, in a way. As far as I'm concerned, I would like to continue to work for The Good Novel. I constantly have new ideas for titles to recommend. My additional list for next year is already quite full."

She paused. Nobody said a thing, and then she asked, somewhat curtly, "Does that sound idiotic?"

"Not at all," said Jean Tailleberne. "That's fine with me. I'd be very happy to join a second time round committee."

"Me too," echoed Évohé, Néon, Le Gall, and Winter, who added, "There is no better way to remain unnoticed. Classic secret-service strategy."

Marie Noir had her reservations: "We won't work in the same way, now that we know each other."

The others did not share her opinion. Nothing would prevent them from remaining independent, or even breaking off all ties. Le Gall, however, did meet with the group approval's when he suggested that the committee ought to give itself a year. They all agreed that in the long run, it would be a good idea to renew the sort of clandestine management behind The Good Novel.

"I may withdraw my participation," said Marie Noir again.

Van suggested they move on to preparing the press release.

"It's going to take us a while to get it ready," he said, not looking at anyone in particular, "and that will give you time to think before signing. Today is Wednesday, December 14. Let's date the press release December 15. We have three items to announce, agreed? The summary of events, the decision to file a complaint, and the dissolution of the committee."

It was half past midnight when they adjourned.

"Let's all leave together," said Marie Noir. "We've had enough of being careful."

She had signed the press release along with the six others.

In the street, wet snow was still falling. Le Gall dropped back to talk to Van.

"So, I won't get to see Strait-laced?" he asked. "After what you told me the other day in Rennes, I had built up an exquisite image of her."

"What makes you think you didn't see her this evening?" suggested Van.

"I did not see any English roses. Those were the words you used to describe her."

"I'm afraid that neither you nor I will ever see her again," said Van. "She will now become one of all the Morgan le Fay and Isolde fairies of our dreams in the country of improbable creatures, unlikely ever to have existed. As for the fact that a touching person who was not the least bit strait-laced belonged to the committee: even now, I am no longer sure she ever did, and as for you, you would do better to forget it."

Obviously, Heffner remarked the next day, when he saw they were revealing the seven names, the brutes, who had been informed that there were eight electors, seven of whose names they now knew, would have no difficulty in pinpointing the identity of the eighth member not on the list. They could reveal what they knew very easily, through their own press release, for example—saying there was an eighth member, by the name of Anne-Marie Montbrun.

"But that would surprise me," said Heffner calmly. "They would have nothing to gain from it, and it could lead to their discovery."

Van had thought of this, and at length. He had lost sleep over it, the previous night, after the meeting. He had only managed to fall asleep once he had convinced himself that Anne-Marie had made an inspired move by bowing out, to hide both herself and her writing. In any case, if her name surfaced now, no one would be able to make the link between that unknown woman and the writer Ida Messmer.

49

Coverage of the press release varied in the papers; there was not a great deal. Two or three articles worthy of the name were published in literary journals or magazines. The daily papers printed only a brief paragraph, and the weeklies a line or two. Of all the radio stations, only Radio Libertarian devoted a news service to the subject, which turned out to be excellent. Television, once so eager to woo Van, seemed to have completely forgotten The Good Novel.

The literary gossip columnists were only interested in the names of the seven committee members. Others focused exclusively on the attacks: but as there were no details, they associated these new forms of intimidation with the harassment of the first six months, without really making any difference between the two. What we need is a dead body, said Heffner. Francesca took note of the "we."

In fact, the few journalists who showed up at the bookstore to investigate were quickly discouraged. Not a single word more was said about the recent attacks than what had already been in the press release. As for the seven electors, they had all agreed to refuse to give any interviews.

In addition, it was ten days before Christmas, and everybody was busy, media people no less than anyone else. (Not to mention that a flu variant was making progress: it had reached Africa, and there were two outbreaks in Zimbabwe. The Indonesian government had obtained permission from Roche laboratories to produce the antiviral medication Tamiflu. Ariel Sharon had been hospitalized following a stroke. Two million people were dying of hunger in Somalia.)

On the Internet, matters stood otherwise. Gossip and rumors proliferated, the best and the worst. Everyone was still passionate about The Good Novel. The worst: over-the-top conspiracy theories, virulent fabrications, sometimes incriminating Hachette, sometimes America, sometimes the teaching profession, sometimes the Islamists, and often particular individuals cited by name. The best: the support that arrived day and night. From empathy to suggestions for new leads for the investigation, from renewed friendship to subscription renewals, the full range of solidarity was voiced.

Oscar sent the same reply to hundreds of supporters: The best support is to shop from us. Come to rue Dupuytren. Place an order. Merry Christmas.

News of the dissolution of the committee led to a wave of congratulations proffered to the outgoing members. Sales of their books at The Good Novel increased dramatically. When the announcement was made that a new committee would be formed, applications came pouring in. One hundred and twenty-two writers volunteered, a tenth of whom were foreigners. Among them were esteemed authors with whom Van and Francesca would gladly have worked. But it was no easy thing to add newcomers to the committee. It would be impossible to bring them up to date on everything the original members already knew. It would mean creating two sorts of electors, and neither Francesca nor Van liked the idea.

They told their candidates the truth, that committee number two had already been put together, but they would note their interest and keep them in mind the next time the committee was renewed: there were no lifetime mandates at The Good Novel.

At the bookstore, things were going well. It was a good period. Like everywhere else, people asked for gift wrapping. But it was also clear that no one came into the store with the same aim as when they went to other bookstores. Oscar, all on his own, was selling thirty copies a day, on average, of a book that had been published in 1929. Over the last month, he had been discovering the novels of Marcel Aymé. He was familiar with Aymé's short stories, and had often praised the collected edition published by Quarto. One day in November, a customer came in looking for him, exhausted, gaunt, and radiant—the infallible signs of someone who has fallen in love. He had just read all five hundred short stories, one after the other, and had not slept a wink all night. He was eager to move on to Aymé's novels. Oscar simply gave them all to him. He didn't say anything about them, because he realized he hadn't read any of them, or maybe he had read *La Jument verte*, years ago.

In the days that followed, Oscar made up for lost time. He delighted in *La Vouivre*. *Uranus* was incredible. But the one that he preferred, the one he read three times in a row—the first time for the plot, spellbound, to find out what happened, the second time very slowly, not to lose a word, and the third time taking notes, to try to analyze why the book was so powerful—was *The Table of Corpses*.

He gave it to Van, Anis, and Francesca to read (Yassin already knew it, and could quote entire sentences from memory). And to all the customers in the store that month of December, with shining eyes he asked the same question: Have you read *La Table-aux-crevés* by Marcel Aymé, who won the Renaudot prize in 1929?

Van did not want to be outdone. It was the Portuguese author Agustina Bessa-Luís whom he rediscovered. He had already read several of her novels. He was fascinated by their intelligence. This month, a bit by chance, he read *Le Confortable Désespoir des femmes*. It was pertinent, lucid, contemporary, and humorous: he sold many copies, to men and women alike.

Meanwhile, on the same day that Ivan sent the press release to Agence France Presse and posted it on the Internet, Francesca filed an official complaint, and Heffner informed his superiors.

There are several ways to file a complaint, depending on whether one is a private individual or a company, and whether one is in mortal danger or not—and Francesca felt that she was a bit of all that. She asked Heffner for advice. In accordance with what he suggested, and to save time, she did not go to the state prosecutor of the Republic of Paris but to the deputy state prosecutor in charge of criminal matters. They gave her an appointment that very afternoon, at three o'clock, at the Quai des Orfèvres (not at number 36, which was the criminal division, but at number 14, the County Court: Heffner had drawn her a map), and she met with a round, levelheaded woman who must have taken the matter very seriously because, at five-fifteen, an examining judge was appointed. What this lady, the state prosecutor, had done, in front of Francesca, was to call the most senior of the examining judges, who returned the call himself ten minutes later: he had appointed Judge Albéric Blin.

The very next day, one by one, Francesca, Van, Oscar, Anis, Yassin, and the former members of the committee—in short, all the principal players in the history of The Good Novel—were summoned by Judge Blin into his office, in the first section (General services), in the gallery of examining judges of the law courts. There they discovered a young blond man who did not mess around with procedure, nor did he ever once let go of his tone of authority and importance.

Francesca did not want to hire a lawyer.

"That is your right," said Blin.

"It doesn't change anything regarding the investigation?"

"No, it won't change anything regarding the pre-trial investigation."

That same afternoon, while Francesca was meeting with the deputy state prosecutor, and telling the history of The Good Novel from A to Z for the second time in a month—although she was the only one talking this time, and more concisely—Heffner informed his superiors. Despite the administrative stiffness of the habitual formula, very little formality was required.

Gonzague Heffner made a call to his immediate superior, André Marx, head of the criminal brigade, and fifteen minutes later they were seated on either side of a narrow table in the Marguerite, a café on the Quai des Gesvres they had chosen for the very reason that it was not the closest café to the Quai des Orfèvres. And now it was Heffner's turn to tell the story of The Good Novel, from its brilliant beginnings up to the attack against Scaf.

In fact, Heffner told him neither the entire story nor anything about the preliminary investigation he had conducted for eighteen days without authorization. He just told Marx enough to convince him that it was a criminal matter, that he had already cleared the terrain, and that it was obviously within his jurisdiction.

Marx was skeptical, but then, he always was. And he liked Heffner. When he had finished, Marx placed a hand on his arm:

"I think I get the picture. This afternoon or tomorrow, an investigating judge will call me. He is eager to deliver his letters rogatory, and is somewhat excited: a rather unusual matter, just imagine, the victim is literature. I act surprised, I listen to him without interrupting, and I hang up. And the most logical person for the investigation is Heffner, that goes without saying. He's perfect for the job, he always has a book stuck in his pocket. It's borderline, to be sure: only one of the attempted crimes took place in Paris. You'll have to work with the regional services."

He changed his tone: "Regarding literature, tell me: I nicked a book from my son and I'm finding it really excellent. *L'Organisation,* by Jean Rolin, have you read it? The memoirs of a veteran of the proletarian left, written in a crazy sort of style. I'd like to know what you think of it, since you're someone who's read so much. I get the impression it's very well written."

Heffner had not read *L'Organisation.* But when he mentioned it to Van—he had just filled him in on his conversation with Marx—Van came out with a very firm endorsement: "Well-written? It is admirably written, tell your boss. And admirably constructed, with a series of progressive revelations over a period of ten or fifteen years."

After he said that, Ivan moved away. Heffner was afraid he had annoyed him.

The bookstore was about to close. He had chosen that time to go by, knowing that usually by then only the last batch of hard-core customers were still hanging around, so deeply immersed in their books that they noticed nothing else.

But here was Ivan was coming back to him, a copy of *L'Organisation* in his hand.

"Here," he said. "Commissioner Marx is not just anybody. For a start, he doesn't seem to have been offended by the fact you opened an investigation without consulting anyone, and here he is, introducing you to the finest book published in France about the upheavals and consequences of May '68."

50

With all that was going on, Christmas somehow didn't seem right. Francesca confessed as much: "I'm tired. I can't see myself organizing anything. I'd be afraid of provoking"—here she hesitated—"a new attack."

Van swaggered. What was the meaning of this bad patch? "There's no reason to be worried. We are as strong today as this time last year, and we're hardened, less naïve. But if you feel done in, go get some sleep. I'll wake you up on the morning of the first, it will be a new year, and everything will be different."

A letter came that seemed like a good omen. Ruth had decided to go ahead with the business. She had found financing—not the broad-shouldered patron of the arts she had dreamt about, but a foundation, a trust of the sort of which there are thousands in the United States, set up by an oil baron in his will, a man who had never learned to read anything other than figures and, because he regretted it, no doubt, he had started a foundation in his name devoted to the promotion of literature.

The Good Novel Bookstore was going to see the light of day, in Houston. If everything went well, the foundation did not exclude the possibility of opening another one, a year from now, in Phoenix, and why not, over the years, new stores in other towns, either back East or on the West Coast.

On January 1, it snowed. The sky was white with a yellow light. Ivan called Francesca: "The forecast is good for tomorrow."

He had seen Heffner the night before, at the bookstore.

"He stops by sometimes. He has a look around, he buys a book. Yesterday we talked about Inoué and I nearly forgot that he's not just an ordinary customer. At the end, without changing my tone, I asked him if we could meet up—you, me, and him, just to bring things up to date. He's been on the investigation for a month already."

"Is that part of procedure?"

"Procedure allows for him to meet us as often as necessary, wherever he wants."

The three of them had lunch together the next day, in one of the biggest restaurants in Paris—biggest in terms of size, that is. The immense lobby of the Théatre du Rond-Point, on the Champs-Elysées, a place where the tables are spread very far apart and there is sure to be background noise, given the number of tables.

Heffner and his team had dug up a lot. Things which had no apparent connection, some clear, others vague, but they did all seem to converge.

They had managed to identify people. Thus, among the thousands of hostile posts that had rained down on The Good Novel's forum between February and June, 2005, they had identified a number of particularly active contributors, and after going through a considerable number of stakeouts, tailing people, and setting traps—done very much in the same manner on the Web as in real life, and by analogy as has been done for a long time on telephone networks—they had been able to put names on these anonymous shirkers. Names of companies, names of people.

Thanks to relations in the media and publishing—people who owed them, or were talkative, or plain stupid—Heffner had managed to find out who had run the article in *Le Ponte* signed Abéha, the first of the damning articles. It was neither of the two assistant professors at University Paris IV whose initials happened to be A, B, A (on that point, the newspaper had been taken in; one of the two professors had, moreover, written a letter to protest), but the secretary of a big shot in publishing, a network man, a major distributor of emoluments, an expert in corruption, well-known, for example, to have had supreme control for years over half of the literary prizes. (A friend of Heffner's who was herself an author had said to this publisher one day, about a novel he had published and that he was praising to the sky: It is really dreadful. And the answer she got was: My dear, that is not the issue.)

Ivan and Francesca knew of three publishing bigwigs who could fit the bill. Heffner did not tell them who he had in mind. "Obviously," he continued, "a person who submits an article to a newspaper can very well not be the person who wrote it. The publisher in question, moreover, did specify that he did not write the article. I think for once, he was telling the truth. And I have a theory about who it could be."

The Collective of Free Booksellers who had launched the attack in February in *L'Idée* was an empty shell. It had been created for the occasion. Behind the mask hid a television and radio host with a wide audience, a man who drew several salaries at once from several different publishers, a novelist in his spare time who bragged about taking two weeks to write his books.

One of the guys who had been gluing the dazibaos at the Odéon had been arrested at the time, by chance, caught red-handed. On the basis of his deposition, which was in the archives, Heffner had been able to trace right back to the man behind the posters.

He had located the informers of the two journalists from *Le Ponte* who had composed the portrait of Francesca.

"I beg you, spare me the names!" Francesca stopped him.

"You may have noticed that I haven't given you any," said Heffner. "I can't, at this point."

He knew who was behind the Minister of Culture's speech, written in the Minister's very office, where The Good Novel had been referred to in scarcely veiled terms; the man had whispered it to Heffner behind the Minister's back.

He had a photo of one of Le Gall's attackers on the cliffs at Ploulec'h.

"A photo?" echoed Van.

Heffner had shown over two hundred prints to Le Gall. In the lot, Le Gall had been positive, was a photo of one of the two musclemen who had stood in his way several days in a row.

Where did he get the series of two hundred photos? Heffner had put it together methodically, he said, according to a time-honored principle. He had compiled a list of everyone in publishing who stood to gain if The Good Novel disappeared. On the whole, this meant those who made a profession of publishing editorial rubbish, because they knew they could make money from it; whereas the The Good Novel's policy excluded them and their moneymaking schemes and, were such a policy to become dominant in the milieu, would forbid such schemes altogether. To the list of these literary money grubbers, he had added people who were close to them, who filled various roles as operators, chauffeurs, security guards, concierges, in short any position that could prove useful in playing dirty tricks.

But 80 percent of their questions still had no answer. And new ones arose all the time. On the door of the shed where Gilles Évohé stored his bike, the morning after the sabotage, when Heffner had come back on the scene so he could think about what had happened, he saw a message scrawled in chalk that he was certain had not been there the night before: "The Good Bicycle."

Other officers from the criminal division in the provinces were investigating the three attempted murders. They were on the verge of discovering who had called Anne-Marie on the telephone just before her accident. They would have to find out a bit more about Frucht, in Germany, and about Ruth in the United States.

Heffner counted on the Internet for a lot. Every night for several hours he ventured into the far corners of the Web. What he was looking for, above all, and had not yet managed to find, was the connection among those he called the "actors." He hadn't found anything resembling an organization or group. It would just take time, he was willing to stake his life on it. Someday soon, he would stumble upon a list that would include the names he had already identified.

"There is someone," he said, "a name that has cropped up several times—God knows that I have followed any number of trails. It surprised me. Apparently, this person moves in very different circles."

He paused.

"I could tell you a lot more. But for today I'm going to stop there. I have a theory, about the way that they mobilized against The Good Novel. It's more than a theory: assumptions, in succession. I have to keep at it."

"Have you been able to tap anyone's phone?" asked Francesca.

Heffner smiled, "Don't go thinking that. That's a device we reserve for criminal affairs."

"Isn't our affair criminal?"

"I've had difficulty in convincing the judge of that, I won't hide the fact. And even some of those who are on my team. It's a fairly conventional milieu. That must be why crime novels are often conventional. I prefer to work alone."

Francesca was astonished. Admiring, but above all astonished, she told Van.

"I get the impression he's like a fish in water in the publishing world. And yet, what he's looking into are not the elegant offices on the *piano nobile* of little old buildings in Saint-

Germain-des-Prés, it's the tiny rooms that no one ever sees, the unaired basements, backstage if you like."

"There are milieus that are more opaque. We're not dealing with the Mafia, after all. Heffner knows this little world."

"He's known it for a month . . ."

"Not at all. Didn't he tell you?"

After the two years he spent doing prep classes to try to pass the entrance exams to a prestigious college, Heffner had been uncertain of his future for a time. Finally he had enrolled in modern literature at the Sorbonne. Through the friendship of a professor, he had become a reader at the publisher Julliard. For a few years, before he started at the police academy, he had got to know publishing from the inside, as a dogsbody.

"He must have been writing," said Francesca. "Don't you think?"

"He hasn't told me as much, but I bet he was. Is he still writing? Has he given up? That's less obvious, it's hard to say. The only time he talked to us about his passion for literature, and his choice to go into an active profession in spite of everything, if you recall, he added that very soon his eventual choice no longer seemed very well-founded."

51

The new crop of books for January had arrived, five hundred new titles. Not the six hundred that arrived every September, but five hundred all the same. Jean-René Lancre had left Paris in mid-December for a minimum of six weeks "and more, if blessed with perfect happiness." He had gone to Réunion "on the heels of youth," he said mysteriously. His tastes were eclectic in such matters, and he chose to depart so as to waylay any third parties who would otherwise prance around Paris, spreading rumors of the "he has come back to us" sort. Just before he left, he opened a post-office box on the Rue Danton, forwarded his new address to his publishers, and gave Ivan a power of attorney. Since the beginning of January, Ivan had been stopping off every morning early at the post office, and would arrive at The Good Novel with a bagful of books on his shoulder.

Francesca, Van, Oscar, Anis: everybody liked Echenoz's *Ravel.* Van bent over backwards to acquaint people with Iegor Gran's *Les trois vies de Lucie.* A miracle, he said. A real literary conjuring trick.

Anis defended the toughest novel among the five hundred, *El pintor de batallas* by Pérez-Reverte. A weighty subject—form is not the only thing, after all, she said glancing toward Van, who claimed the contrary.

Van was amazed to find her so simple, after she had been so disconcerting. Amazed, and not disappointed. He hesitated, then he said to her—it was January 11—"Do you know that you haven't slept at rue Bol-en-Bois in three months?"

"Actually it was three months the day before yesterday," corrected Anis.

One of these days, dreamt Van, I'll find out that she handed back the keys to her student room long ago. But he lacked the self-assurance to ask her himself.

Francesca worried him. She looked as if she were always cold. Even when she was indoors, she never took her coat off, or hardly, though to be fair it was a particularly cold winter.

One day, when Van was having lunch with her in the bistro on the rue Mabillon where she was a regular, he saw she was just picking at her food. He questioned her: "Aren't you hungry?"

She gave him her radiant, heartbreaking smile.

"If you knew how tiring it is to eat," she said.

Just like every time he was about to go deeper into the question, "Are you okay, Francesca?" she changed the subject.

"I wonder," she began, "I don't know how long it's going to take Heffner to find out that Henri is on the Board of Directors of EIO."

"EIO?" echoed Ivan.

"The number one telephone operator in France. They have half the customers in France, I think."

"If the company is as heavy-duty as you say, Heffner must know who the board members are."

Francesca was looking down. Ivan saw a tear fall from her lashes into her plate.

"You love him!" he said, out of the blue.

"It's complicated," said Francesca, without seeming offended or looking up, or asking Ivan specifically whom he was talking about. "These days Henri is too tough, too attentive to destroy me. I would be lying if I said I loved him. I would be lying just as much if I said I despised him. I wish I could love him."

She raised her head, but her gaze quickly went beyond Ivan's shoulder.

"He was so . . . different when I met him. Well, maybe not that different. Of course, he was the same. That's the whole point."

This time, she aimed her eyes, shining with tears, straight at Ivan.

"I'm not explaining myself well. Let's just say that part of me lives in the light of the Henri I knew at the beginning."

"Does today's Henri know that?"

"He knows and he's not interested. That's what he's trying so hard to destroy. As for me, I am struggling to keep the tiny flame in me alive beneath the stones—so that at least I'll still have that. I'm afraid of the day when I shall have to admit that I've lost."

She suddenly seemed startled: "My God, how pitiful it all is."

"I don't think it's pitiful at all," mumbled Ivan, dismayed that he could find nothing better to say.

Because he did not believe what he said.

The suggestion of pity troubled him for a long time. It was exactly that, he told me. The last word anyone would have thought to use when talking about her, and yet it was the most precise, provided you paired it with another. Francesca was greatly to be pitied.

52

On Monday, January 23, in the morning, a shop opened on the corner of the rue Dupuytren and the rue Monsieur-le-Prince, across the street from The Good Novel. There had been renovation work going on there for a few weeks, behind a thick gray green tarpaulin that hid the ground floor of the building. That Monday the tarpaulin was gone. Van was headed toward The Good Novel from the other end of the rue Dupuytren, on the Boulevard Saint-Germain side. He did not even notice that the work had been completed.

It was Oscar, when he arrived, who took Ivan back out onto the sidewalk and led him to the building on the corner. There was a bookstore in the renovated space, and the shop sign read The Pleasurable Novel. The space was lovely and light, with a fairly classic decoration, as far as you could see from the outside. And in the middle of each of the two windows, both on the Monsieur-le-Prince side and the Dupuytren side, a big square banner proclaimed in red letters:

READ FOR PLEASURE
NOT ONLY WHAT IS GOOD FOR YOU

Ivan saw they were looking at Oscar and him from inside the shop.

"Let's go," he said moving away. Oscar followed him, but he wasn't sure he had understood.

"I thought you meant, let's go in the bookstore. Let's go have a look."

"Then I'd have said let's go in," said Van, annoyed.

"True. Excuse me. My mistake. Don't you want me to go and have a look, and see what it's about?"

"Wait," said Van.

He called Francesca.

"If you come to the bookstore this morning, come from the top of the street. On the corner, just across the way, you'll see that we have competition."

"What sort of competition?" asked Francesca, on the defensive.

"Very clever competition, at least on first sight. I haven't gone in yet."

"Why not?"

"I wanted your opinion."

If they didn't go in on that very Monday, it would be harder and harder to go in at all, that was Francesca's opinion. She arrived at The Good Novel very quickly. She hadn't dared go into The Pleasurable Novel, either, and she was mad at herself. She had noticed excitement around the new bookstore, people coming and going with a certain amount of ostentation.

Van still hesitated. He couldn't see himself showing up all on his own, the silence greeting his entrance—would he be recognized, welcomed by name, even? And as for going in as an envoy on Francesca's arm, that was something he had even more difficulty imagining.

At that moment, Armand Delvaux walked into the store. "I have been moping since yesterday evening. I have nothing left to read. Of course I should have reread something but, how to explain, I was in that sort of insecure mood I sometimes get into on Sundays, when The Good Novel is closed. So as a result, I went to the cinema."

He agreed without hesitation to go and scout The Pleasurable Novel. He came back after half an hour.

"It's ingenious," he confirmed. "Clearly, they took their inspiration from The Good Novel as far as the décor and the atmosphere are concerned. You've got the same kind of space, fine materials, a certain luxury. They sell only novels as well, French and foreign. But they've gone to no bother to make a selection. They have everything, above all new books, maybe all new books. With piles and piles of what's selling, Thingammy, Whatsit, well you know the titles better than I do."

"It's unfair competition," fumed Oscar.

Delvaux was not so sure.

"Not in the legal sense, in any case. The name, at a push: there you could, no doubt, make a point that it's a plagiarism."

But Francesca had no intention of going after them in any way.

"Besides," she said, looking at Delvaux, "if I follow you correctly, in this case we can't even talk about competition. We have nothing to fear."

"I'll be back," said Van abruptly. "Give me five minutes."

He came back with the newspapers. Francesca understood immediately. Every one of the morning papers had a quarter page of advertising: against the background of a reproduction of the astonishing *Woman Reading* by Jean-Jacques Henner— a redhead, flat on her stomach in a lemony light, leaning on her elbows, as absorbed in her book as she was peaceful and stark naked—were two lines: The Pleasurable Novel, the address, opening times, and the same slogan, give or take a few words, as in the two display windows of the bookstore:

READ WHAT GIVES YOU PLEASURE
AND NOT WHAT YOU'RE SUPPOSED TO HAVE READ.

At around one o'clock in the afternoon, Roselin Folco came into The Good Novel, as was his habit nearly every day. He had just spent three quarters of an hour, at his own initiative, browsing at The Pleasurable Novel. He wasn't worried. "Those plagiarists aren't going to convince anybody for long," he said. "Their business may look like quality, but it has neither the smell, nor the taste, nor the strength, nor the finesse. It's a very ordinary bookstore."

"Except that they do only sell novels there," remarked Van.

"Yes, but only very run-of-the-mill stuff."

No, in Folco's opinion, the new shop had only one serious advantage. "They have a far greater number of books in stock than we do. Three to four times as many, at a rough estimate."

"Well we're up to over eight thousand here, now," said Van.

"I wouldn't be surprised if they have around thirty thousand."

Two weeks later, exactly to the day, on Monday, February 6, on the sidewalk outside The Good Novel, 7, rue Dupuytren, another bookstore opened up. This one was called The Excellent Novel. This time, they had played the surprise card. Two days earlier, there had been a hairdresser's at this location. Between Saturday at four in the evening and Monday at six, in the morning, the entire interior had been changed, and in place of hair dryers and sinks, there were books against the wall and on tables.

It wasn't a very big bookstore. But it had been well-designed, using light wood, noble materials, and carefully conceived lighting—you might almost think the same interior designer had been at work both here and fifty yards away at The Pleasurable Novel.

There were fewer books at The Excellent Novel, probably about as many as at The Good Novel. But the resemblance stopped there. By the end of the week, an entire swarm of friends of The Good Novel had gone in, at various times, to have a look at what was on offer at The Excellent. They all said the same thing, they were selling exactly what The Good Novel didn't sell, all the slapdash novels that don't look dangerous but which were threatening to be the death of literature.

The designers of The Excellent had gone to a lot of trouble:

it would seem that they had not ordered a single one of the titles available at The Good Novel. "It's not stupid, either," said Van. "They're playing the it's-all-relative card. You claim to have a good choice? We say our choice is excellent."

No advertising this time around, no full-page ads in the newspapers or signs in the window. "I think I get it," said Van. "They're not counting on difference or superiority, but confusion."

He was disturbed by Francesca's reaction. You might think she hadn't noticed. She was behaving as if the new bookstore did not exist. If you mentioned it in her presence, she didn't hear you. If you went to her to ask her what she thought about it, her answer had nothing to do with it.

Watching her more closely, Van noticed that she was including the two new bookstores in her attitude of denial. She made no more of it than if they had been fashion boutiques.

Oscar, Winter, and a few others decided to get acquainted with the booksellers working at each of the two stores. They found clever individuals, who were somewhat well-read, and if you asked them what the principle governing their choice of books was, they would reply as if it were perfectly obvious: what was current. At The Pleasurable Novel, they met a round and good-natured sixty-something gentleman, with a perky brunette who introduced herself as a doctoral candidate in letters; at The Excellent a reserved man from the South, whom Winter supposed came from the Larzac region, and who informed him that he had always worked as a bookseller.

Folco sent his two daughters, that same day, to ask the same question in each of the two bookstores. They were twenty-six-year-old twins, devoted to The Good Novel, and ready to do anything to lend their support. Each one, at either end of the street, began browsing through books at the same time, asking questions about a particular title ("I've heard there's a biography of Dan Brown. Apparently his wife wrote it"), discussing the January publications, and eventually they asked: "Have you been open for long? I wasn't familiar with your bookstore," and finally they went on to query: "It's very brave of you to open a bookstore with the way things are nowadays—are you the owner?"

Mireille reported that the sixty-year-old at the Pleasurable Novel could not restrain a little smile. "The owner? No, it's not me," he said, in a way that made it clear he would go no further. Mireille played dumb: "Who is it?" she asked. And the reply: "An investor."

At The Excellent, the man who looked like a shepherd was more clever. "You couldn't tell a thing from his expression," said Magali. He looked the young woman straight in the eye and replied: "A collective, I think. Some sort of association. I was hired through an employment agency. I deal with the manager, a certain Pierre, or Paul Martin."

Van went to the registry of commerce to ask for corporate registration certificates for each of the two bookstores. The names of parent companies meant nothing to him. Aubert, The Good Novel's accountant, did some research. One of the companies was created in November and the other in December, he said.

The media were very quick to react. There's nothing like a play on words to get people's attention. The names of the two new bookstores went around the editorial offices as if they were some minister's latest sound bite, or publicity slogans transformed into proverbs within the week.

The newspapers may have been reluctant to report on the complaint filed against unknowns by The Good Novel, but they were only too eager to applaud the birth of what *L'Exact* called—and what everyone else would soon call—"good novel street." This time, word got around not so much through the daily papers but through larger audience magazines. The three bookstores, one after the other, were a dream subject for the Leisure pages, the Weekend sections, and the Paris supplements. There were any number of brief pseudo-special reports, with photographs of the three bookstores. No, bookstores were not being driven out of city centers. Yes, their proximity helped to increase demand: just as you might go to rue Montgallet to shop for computer accessories, or to the rue de Paradis to buy dishware and stemware, now you could go stock up on novels on the rue Dupuytren.

And what if this was laziness, or stupidity? We'll never know, said Van. But to add confusion to world chaos, well done, media people: always at the ready.

Van spoke sharply, because he was convinced they were dealing with a maneuver based on conformity and a lack of curiosity. He could just imagine one of the individuals Heffner had painted a masked portrait of—the blockbuster publisher, the media-savvy strolling player—inviting some department head from the Ministry of Culture for lunch, or calling a henchman reporter to brag about a program and, in the end, whispering, Oh by the way have you seen, isn't it amazing, on the rue Dupuytren at the Odéon, within thirty yards of each other there are now three exceptional bookstores. The Good Novel has acquired a following!

Van shared his conviction with no one but Heffner, then me, later on. To Francesca he only pointed out two articles describing the difference between The Good Novel and the two newcomers, a vitriolic note in *L'Humanité*, and a humorous column in the *Herald Tribune*.

But Francesca did not read them, Van told me, any more than she had read any of the pseudo-special reports on the so-called "good novel street."

53.

It was in mid-February, one early afternoon, that Heffner called Ivan on the telephone and invited him to come, with Francesca, to his office without delay.

They did not in fact meet at the Quai des Orfèvres. Heffner went out as soon as he had hung up. He was stamping his feet to keep warm on the pavement at the far end of the Pont Saint-Michel, and as soon as he saw Ivan and Francesca, he went up to meet them. He suggested they walk for a while. It was cold and gray, once again. They were expecting snow, once again. Straight off, Heffner headed down the Quai Saint-Michel toward Notre-Dame.

"It will take me two sentences to tell you what I have to say," he said.

He stopped, as if he meant to look at the Seine. Van and Francesca did likewise, and leaned with their elbows against the railing.

"The judge has finished," said Heffner. "For him, the investigation has lasted long enough. He is going to serve you an end of inquiry notice."

"And have they taken you off the case?" asked Francesca.

"There is no case. The investigation will stop there. The judge maintains that there are neither ample charges nor sufficient evidence to warrant setting the wheels of justice in motion. There will be no suit. No charges against anyone."

"The judge . . ." said Ivan. "Did you tell him everything that you found out?"

"Of course, I had to," said Heffner. "I saw him any number of times. He has all my notes about the investigation. He knows as much about it now as I do."

Francesca lifted up her collar: "And he does not think there's enough to warrant a suit? Everything The Good Novel went through—the verbal attacks, the slander, the physical assaults—for him that's all right?"

"He's not saying that. I asked him exactly the same thing in more or less the same tone, and his best and most learned voice, he uttered the conventional formula for motioning a non-suit: 'The investigation has not yielded sufficient evidence to charge anyone with attempted murder, as alleged by the civil party.'"

Below them, the Seine was running high and rough, the color of frozen mud. Van took Francesca by the elbow—he saw that she was numb—and turned to Heffner: "Let's go somewhere warm. Do you have a moment?"

They went into the first café they could find, on the corner of the Quai and the rue du Petit-Pont. The café was crowded. The floor tiles were dirty and wet. "This is perfect," said Francesca, forestalling Van's gesture to go back out again. "It's noisy, and smoky, and today that actually suits me."

"You can appeal Blin's decision," said Heffner when they had sat down. "I don't advise it. The way things are headed, you would gain nothing. But I am tempted to continue the investigation on my own."

"What's the point?" asked Francesca bluntly.

"To find out. To find out more."

He talked for nearly an hour. He had stored up a lot of assumptions, near proofs, things he was so convinced of that he would have staked his life on it, nothing blatant or irrefutable. Nothing solid enough for a judge, he said.

The people they were dealing with were very cautious, very careful to remain within the bounds of legality, and whenever they did go beyond those bounds, they were extremely careful to cover their tracks.

Heffner was sure of one thing. All the people who, for over a year, had been attacking The Good Novel had not found themselves involved in that undertaking by mere chance.

What Van had believed for a long time, and had been trying to make Francesca believe for even longer, was that the first punch—that first aggressive article—had released the pent-up spite and unleashed the fury of a large number of careerist authors, unscrupulous publishers, venal judges, critics so well-ensconced in their laziness and positions of power that they would never move elsewhere; Heffner did not buy the theory of an unorganized movement arising spontaneously in ever increasing waves.

Nor did he believe the conspiracy theory Francesca had suspected from the very first press campaign. The idea of an organized group methodically planning to demolish The Good Novel was not a script that would stand up to an investigation.

The truth lay somewhere in between, borrowing elements from both hypotheses. Heffner spoke not of a group but of a movement, and he did not think it was run by a cold calculating individual but by someone frenzied, at least at the beginning.

"Frenzied, literally," he said. "Because art and culture are the arena of insane violence. Everyone knows that there are no limits to passion where love is concerned. And it's easy to imagine that political life is awash with extraordinarily ruthless antagonism, where ambitious people are capable of anything. Or that in business you hack out your place with a machete. We know only too well that there's no longer much of a game where sports are concerned, that anything goes—lies, corruption, intimidation. But for vaguely idealistic reasons, we have not yet come to realize, and are loath to suspect, that artistic creation, and all the infrastructure surrounding its production and promotion, can also be an extremely hateful forcefield, impelled most often by envy and, in France anyway, the usual weapons of ideological discredit.

"The name of this frenzied individual is Eric Ervé. I found his trail nearly everywhere when I explored the places where the missiles against The Good Novel had been fired."

Ervé: Ivan and Francesca had run into him. They knew precisely where he was situated in literary circles. Fifty-something, once very handsome, growing fleshy. Twelve novels, including one big success, *The Glue*. A prize, in the early years, for one of his other books. A desk job at a publishing house that was struggling, its image tarnished by a series of second-rate books. A column in a mass-media weekly. A man who could be servile on command around anyone in power, in publishing, the media, television, academies, and beyond, with prize juries, advertising people, filmmakers, politicians, philanthropists, aristocrats, the jet set, and finally the truly rich. But on the whole, despite so much energy spent trying to please, manipulate, and slander, despite the favors and titles and innumerable interested friendships he fostered, all he gained was the reputation of a writer of no interest, astonishingly conformist and stable.

"When he saw he didn't have a single book at The Good Novel, he went ballistic," said Heffner. "He's a calculating bastard. He wouldn't go to the front. He pinpointed several dozen authors like himself, slightly famous, very ordinary, and who were not represented at the bookstore. He got in touch with them, one by one. He used them as his tools. The four or five of them who lived through the Internet—he got them all riled up, so they would communicate, propagate, influence, and denigrate through the Web, the way others used to do by phone, in an earlier generation. He came up with sharp jibes and whispered them here and there, and was never more pleased than when he could read them or hear others say them.

"Ten times people mentioned him to me. He found relays in the press: he's a genius for sniffing out who, in any social group, is the careerist who hasn't made it, or hasn't got as far as he'd like, dead drunk on frustrated zeal, shit-scared by the passage of time and the inexorable arrival every year of celebrated new young talents.

"He canvassed the publishers always looking for a hit, and frightened them. These are people who are well aware that they are supporting, incarnating and engendering impostors: no one fears more than they do that they might hear someone say, as they go by, The emperor has no clothes . . .

"Ervé also got in touch with the big chain bookstores. Times are hard as it is, he told them, the Internet is taking millions of customers away from you. So, just imagine that some sort of unscrupulous know-it-all is poaching on your territory, like some sort of Green movement for literary consumption, you see: it won't even take ten years for bullshit like this to create a planetary wave. Imagine the same thing happening to your products that happened to tobacco, and that could happen to junk food: imagine people turning away from it in the name of mental health and a refusal to pollute their minds."

Heffner had managed to trace the origins of the article signed Abéha, which had been the signal to start hostilities, thanks to the person in charge of the Op-Ed pages in *Le Ponte*. Nothing like a legal summons to loosen people's tongues, he said. The article had been written by Ervé and submitted to Malinovic, the great corrupting publisher. Ervé feigned modesty: It's a draft? You think it's good? How can I go about publishing it? Neither of us is in a position to sign it . . . Malinovic had taken care of it.

"Don't go thinking that I'm talking about the entire book business," said Heffner. "You know as well as I do that's not the case. Even here, we're talking about a minority. Altogether the ones I would incriminate, who I would say are part of a movement, cannot number more than a hundred. That may seem astonishing, if you put together all the writers, media people, publishing people, and booksellers. It's because some of them wear several hats, they might be writers, journalists, publishers, and judges all at the same time. Some of the novelists who were furious not to be sold at The Good Novel have long arms. They might, for example, be judges for a literary prize: so they have a hold over those journalists who are also authors and dream of winning a prize. Other novelists—or the same ones—have positions in the media. By virtue of that alone, if they find the least bit of favor in the eyes of publishers, they come first in line for the prizes—and we know that some publishers negotiate them with the judges. And to make sure they are compliant, the publishers will publish them no matter how second-rate their books are. So, we don't find their books at The Good Novel.

"The Good Novel has caused every element of a fairly limited socio-professional group to break out in hives. Far be it from me to suggest, let me say that again, that this group represents everyone in publishing, the media, or criticism, or bookselling. They are a sub-faction of people who share the view that a book is a product that can make a lot of money and that literature can be a rich seam.

"Ervé was the strategist, the spur. But he couldn't get very far on his own. And he didn't want to risk exposure. He masterfully manipulated those I will call "the thirty"—there might be twenty of them, or maybe fifty—fourth-rate authors who had not given up on the idea of making it someday, and who saw that marketing confusion could earn them more points every year, and they dreaded being left to stew in obscurity if ever The Good Novel was so successful that it brought about the unexpected rebirth of a practice you would have thought was timeless—the appreciation of talent at its just value.

"So it's perfectly clear," explained Heffner, "at the beginning of the anti-Good Novel offensive, you can see Ervé's hand or influence on any number of occasions. For example, he used at least twenty-five different e-mail addresses, in other words he had twenty-five identities on the Web. And then his signature became more rare, while his devoted henchmen's signatures appeared more and more often.

"With all due allowance, something happened here that is comparable to what happened with Al Qaeda and all its consequences. In the beginning, a hard-core cell attacks in strength. But very quickly the brain grows smart enough make use of propaganda in addition to pure action, so much so that he succeeds beyond all expectation: other cells are created, other cores.

"I'm not implying that Ervé brainwashed and held the hand of every single person who attacked The Good Novel, but I believe he convinced a certain number of people to act, people who were just waiting for the opportunity, and who now developed their own ideas for striking a blow, and who went into action, either directly or through somebody else."

"Give us some names," said Ivan.

"This will come as no surprise. Breigne, Jovis, Levron, Dabant, Piéfort, Marin-Larmier, hang on . . . The elegant Mr. Miguel, the suave Olivia Venette. A lot of Malinovic authors, a lot of scribblers you see regularly on television. A number of big shots from the major media corporations.

"In other words," continued Heffner, "the harder the strikes against The Good Novel, the more the responsibility is spread around; the greater the number of instigators, the more intermediaries there are—and the harder the investigation. To find out for sure who designed the attacks against the electors, who planned them, and who carried them out, would take weeks of investigation.

"The acts for which I had evidence for the judge were not the most serious: harassment on the Internet, bribing of journalists, spreading slander—the judge calls that freedom of expression, lobbying, normal competition . . ."

"How simple it is," said Francesca. "One hundred determined people can shape opinion, influence the media, turn falsehood into reality, designate scapegoats . . ."

"Nothing new under the sun," said Heffner.

". . . Raise funds," continued Van, "get the frustrated people all riled up, then go into action . . ."

". . . And reward them," said Heffner. "Reward them for their contribution. Nothing new, you know. The mechanisms of violent action are always the same. They are denounced when they go beyond legal bounds—provided you can identify them. But as long as they stay within those bounds, there are tolerated, by definition."

"All the same, tell me," asked Francesca, "who has the means to open bookstores in the Odéon?"

"Hundreds of people, dozens of companies," said Heffner. "I'm surprised you ask. Here: you, your husband, any number of people who are not criminals but who want to defend their interests. You're bound to know a few."

54

On February 20, another Monday, a new bookstore opened right next to The Good Novel. A huge medical bookstore, at the bottom of the rue Dupuytren, had been transformed into a general bookstore. They had gone straight to the point, baptizing the bookstore For Every Taste.

And that's what it was—a new concept, a third sort of banana skin. The huge premises had been divided into four sections, which they had carefully ensured were not isolated from each other. The first section was devoted to good novels, the second next to it to all the others. You had to spend a certain amount of time to figure it out. There were no barriers, even anything as symbolic as a row between stacks, and no signs. Simply, as the twins and good old Delvaux, who had been to scout the premises the first day, explained, in one spot you want to buy everything—you would think you were at The Good Novel—but in another, a bit further along, it was the contrary.

The third section was devoted to essays, and the fourth to everything else—graphic novels, manuals, encyclopedias, art books.

It went without saying that the interior design and the decoration were very stylish. The furniture and woodwork were red, in lacquered wood, with an oriental touch, the color of blood, both stimulating and gentle. Down the middle, five sofas and a circle formed a sort of roundabout. There were large bonsais in varnished pots. And already on Monday the twentieth, a good crowd.

That very day, from several acquaintances who all thought this was the opening of an annex of The Good Novel, Francesca learned that invitations had been sent out, a mass mailing, it seems, with red, lacquered cards proclaiming: "The street of really good books is getting longer. It now has its prestigious bookstore. A prestige within everyone's reach."

"Pure propaganda, a smoke screen, conjuring tricks," fumed Oscar. "Prestige: I hate that word. You can wrap anything up in prestige paper. Come this way, you suckers! At The New Luxury, there's no difference between cheap and quality."

The media were not hard to please. They applauded, meekly. Everywhere you could read the sentence from the invitation: The street of really good books is getting longer, another superb bookstore is opening.

On the following Saturday and Sunday, rue Dupuytren was spectacularly busy. It had snowed. It felt like Christmas eve. People were wandering around the bookstores. A lot of them came into The Good Novel, often for the first time.

Armand Delvaux was preoccupied.

"The real plus at that For Every Taste bookstore is that it is spacious. If they have thirty thousand books at The Pleasurable Novel, at For Every Taste they must have double that. You go into those big bookstores to take a look. You've heard about this or that book, you may have no intention of leaving the store with it, but you do want to browse. Particularly as you may decide not to read it after all. There is a pleasure to be found in bad books, a sort of hasty reading, not unlike gluttony. Who has never indulged in it? It doesn't mean, of course, that you will buy it."

"Of course," said Van. "You don't go sniff a book in one bookstore, then buy it elsewhere. Particularly if in the same bookstore you can find everything, the worst and the best. We don't have that kind of loss leader in our store."

At The Good Novel, the doors were banging from morning to night. Francesca would appear and disappear, in her beige and white woolens, her gaze lost and smiling. Either she was brazenly putting on the dog, or she refused to be bothered by it all, or she could not see the change. I don't like this, said Van.

He took a dim view of all these newcomers at The Good Novel. He did not *recognize* them. It was irrational, he said as much to himself, you can't see these things at first glance, but he did not see the signs of complicity in these buyers, anything that made them true readers, friends.

I tried to reason with him: they're not just puppets, after all. They're not being manipulated.

"Well they haven't exactly been paid to go around all the bookstores on the rue Dupuytren. But let's not be naïve, all consumers are manipulated nowadays. As consumers, we are all manipulated."

In fact, Ivan had his reasons to be worried, and I learned this after the fact. He hadn't said anything to anyone: reasons based on numbers, figures. Sales at The Good Novel had dropped off dramatically. The reversal had become noticeable in mid-February, and the decline was growing by the week.

Van could not bring himself to tell Francesca. But he would have to at some point. One day soon she would ask him. It would be better if he made the first move. The longer he waited, the harder it would be.

On March 1 he gave himself a week. The weather was still just as bad. One day it snowed, the next day it rained.

On March 8, it was pouring nonstop. Van's worst fears were realized. As he was leaving the bookstore that night, Francesca said, her tone ambiguous, one of sad gaiety: "All these people, all this animation, it must be good for sales?"

"No," said Van. "I wanted to talk to you about it."

It was not a good time for a talk. There were still people in the bookstore.

"No," said Van again. "Business is not very good. We're going into a difficult period. Francesca, let's set a time to talk about it. Would tomorrow be all right, at lunch?"

Francesca was still smiling. She nodded. Van was nearly certain that deep down he hadn't told her anything new by telling her the truth.

The next day it was still raining. Francesca didn't come to the bookstore. At half past twelve, Van called her at the rue de Condé. It took a while for her to answer. "I was asleep," she said, her voice flat. "I took a . . . tranquilizer at six o'clock in the morning, it was kind of late."

She had said "kind of" instead of "rather." That wasn't like her.

"Is something wrong?" asked Van.

"Yes," she said.

For a moment Van thought she wouldn't say anything more. But then she went on, still in this flat voice, her words painfully detached: "At midnight, I had a conversation with Henri . . . wasn't easy. It must be . . . what kept me awake the . . . rest of the night. It's funny, coincidences. He was just getting home. I didn't want to talk to him about The Good Novel, after what you . . . told me. He was the one who came at me: it must be a hard blow for The Good Novel, all these bookstores in the neighborhood. I don't know why, I answered: it is indeed. I got the impression that . . . those three words opened a valve.

"He adopted his superior air and said, 'I told you so. It was a foregone conclusion. If I've learned anything in thirty years of business, it's that quality doesn't win, in the long run, only trash. You can see it in every domain. Low-end electrical appliances, dirt-cheap clothing, journalism that's increasingly hollow, that's what wins. Publishing is no exception. Look at who

the stars of the novel are these days . . . There might still be a few
starving aristocrats who wear the colors of Lady Literature, your
beloved Bergers and Bouviers. They camp out on deserted territory, and they won't last for long.'"

With his ear up against the receiver, Ivan lowered his head
so he could hear her better.

"What hurt the most," said Francesca, "was his delight. In
his eyes there was such a glow of triumph that a question
crossed my mind—and the same glow kept me from asking it.
Was he, is he in any way complicit in the attempt to drown us
in this junk culture?"

Ivan insisted on having lunch with her. "I'm not in a hurry,"
he said. "I have things to do at the bookstore, I'll wait for you."

And he added, "We're not the first people who've had to
deal with a drop in sales. I have ideas on how to fix that."

He was sincere.

"Give me an hour," said Francesca. "I'm coming."

An hour later, she still had not arrived. Van waited another
half hour, and called back. There was no answer.

He thought that Francesca had gone back to sleep, and in a
way he was glad. When she sleeps, she's at peace, he thought.
Then he corrected himself. There was a greater chance she'd
be at peace asleep than awake. (Later, he would think back
with horror at this false conjecture, which was not so far from
the truth.)

He went out for a bite. The rain had stopped. At the
Carrefour de l'Odéon, a crowd was dispersing. The lane which
led from the boulevard Saint-Germain to the rue Saint-Sulpice
was closed to traffic. At the bottom, a policeman was redirect-
ing cars. A bus had stopped in the middle of the street, slightly
at an angle, next to a police car. Half a dozen people were rushing about, some of them in uniform, others not, telephoning,
taking measurements, taking notes.

The bus, a number 63, was empty. Even the driver had left his seat. As he drew near, Ivan could see that at the front, below the right front fender, in a quadrilateral made by plastic ribbon, between four poles, there were chalk marks on the asphalt.

This time, the investigation was conducted right through to the end, and it was rapid, we had our dead body. It was an accident, without a shadow of a doubt. The driver of the number 63 had seen Francesca step out in front of him as if the bus were invisible. She was taking big strides, her eyes straight ahead, he said, indifferent to everything around her.

The unfortunate man could not get over it. He had blown his horn, but Francesca had already fallen. She spent the day in a coma and died that night.

Van was devastated. He was the one who had insisted she come to the bookstore. He held himself responsible for her death.

I told him, over and over, It was an accident. No one is responsible when it's an accident. And he would start over. If it weren't for him, Francesca would not have crossed that extremely dangerous intersection in such a trance. I told him again that he had nothing to do with our friend's deep weariness, nothing to do with the insomnia of her final night.

That afternoon of March 9 I saw him clench his fists at least ten times, without speaking. He thought of closing the bookstore, as a sign of mourning. He changed his mind. Francesca would not have approved.

He wanted to go and smash in the faces of the new booksellers on the rue Dupuytren: I stopped him. He said he wanted to slap red paint all over their windows: "On Thursday, March 9, at lunchtime, Francesca Aldo-Valbelli was assassinated."

But I was exhausted as well, and I could no longer respond.

I took him by the elbow, and put my arm around his shoulders.

Henri Doultremont would remain a mystery to us. Van saw him several times in the days that followed, and once he was alone with him. I saw him, too, at the bookstore, and then on the day of the funeral. And we both had the same word to describe him: the man was crushed.

His private conversation with Ivan took place the day after the accident. Doultremont showed up at the bookstore and asked to speak to Ivan Georg. I accompanied him up to the big office that Van no longer left.

The conversation lasted five minutes. Van told me almost nothing about it. Just a scrap, immediately afterwards: Doultremont had come to ask him to say a few words during the funeral mass, something about Francesca. Van declined. He knew he would be incapable of speaking in public, at that mass.

Several weeks later, he referred again to their private conversation. On leaving, Doultremont had muttered, Thank you. Van had stared hard at him: What for? The other man did not reply.

The bookstore closed only on the day of the funeral. On the front door was a sign: "Closed due to exceptional circumstances." Van objected to using the words "mourning" or "funeral." Oscar had suggested they write Francesca's name, and her date of birth and . . . Van had interrupted him: "I don't think so," he said, without explaining.

I did not see Doultremont again after the mass at Saint-Germain-des-Prés. What I mean is, I never saw him again.

There were a lot of people in the church, and just outside, standing in the rain. The entire committee was there, scattered through the crowd. Doultremont left right away. Rumor had it that he had a long drive ahead of him, because Francesca was going to be buried in Italy. A few of us knew exactly where, on the island in the middle of Lago d'Orta that she so loved, and where, today, I am writing the closing pages of this story.

No, I am not writing this next to her tomb, or in front of her house. I went to see the tomb and the house, which are both by the water, but I'm writing in the hotel, trying not to dream too much of Francesca's changing faces, because I am only here on the island for a few days, and I would like to finish here.

55

We had to return to the bookstore, we had to go on, to read, and talk about books, and speak with passion about the best ones.

I don't know what we would have done without Oscar. Van did not write a single line about Francesca on the Internet. He didn't want to say anything about her. He refused any interviews with media people. He said maybe ten sentences a day.

Oscar provided the necessary information through the newsletter. He put a photograph of Francesca online, a marvelous photograph that a stranger had sent to him, a wistful, sad profile against a background of clouds. Oscar answered all the questions that came in on the forum. Yes, of course, The Good Novel would survive. No, nothing would change regarding its approach. Everything would go on as before—the committee, the subscriptions, the Association of Friends. The team remained the same. The spirit of The Good Novel remained Francesca's spirit.

Van spent most of his time in the big office in the bookstore. We were determined to disturb him as little as possible. But we did have to talk to him from time to time. There were decisions to be made. Doultremont had not shown up, and we all hoped, without really believing it, that he would lose interest in The Good Novel.

Ivan organized a small get-together in the bookstore, one

evening after closing. We had to redefine our job descriptions—which meant distributing among the full-time staff all
the tasks Francesca used to take care of.

While Van wanted to keep us all out of the office by meeting downstairs, he was kidding himself. I could swear we were
all thinking about the big empty room upstairs, with the crazy
impression now and again that Francesca would suddenly
come down the stairs.

There was a question that was nagging Van. It took a while
before he dared to tell me. It was haunting me as well, all of us,
who hadn't seen Francesca after the accident. And we did not
dare ask, any more than Van did.

"I really do have to know," Van said eventually, not exactly to
me but in front of me (we were going through the Luxembourg
Gardens). "I keep struggling with the *images*. What state was
she in, when they picked her up?"

I suggested we ask Heffner. I told him that it would help
me, too.

Heffner had not been involved in the investigation after the
accident—the case was cut and dried, he said—but he agreed
to ask his colleagues.

I apologized: "You might think it's only of secondary
importance."

Heffner corrected me: "No, it's fundamental, how it happened. When someone dies a violent death, family and friends
need to know how it happened."

He got back with his answer very quickly. No wounds, no
blood, he said—he had grasped that that was the real issue.
The side of her skull had been crushed. The fractures had not
opened.

No one in the inner circle of The Good Novel had asked,
but when I shared these details, everyone told me they were
relieved. Unbearable visions faded. It became possible to

imagine Francesca lying on the ground, pale, her eyes closed, but beautiful.

I often thought back on how Heffner had phrased it: "No, it's fundamental . . . When someone dies a violent death, family and friends need to know how it happened." Because he had not told us everything he knew. While what he did tell us was true, he had kept some things to himself.

Francesca had died of fractures to her skull, with no other wounds, and no blood. All the same, she was unrecognizable. The left-hand side of her head, including her temple, forehead, and cheekbone, had been smashed in, and the symmetry of her face had been destroyed.

I read the coroner's report. When he saw that I was writing the history of The Good Novel, Van showed it to me. I had taken Heffner's words at face value, but Van had suspected there were things he had left out. He had gone to the coroner for the report.

He did not want to change anything in the office he had shared with Francesca, he did not even want to put her papers away. For a month he did not let anyone into the room. I would knock, and open the door, and go no further.

With Ivan's consent, Heffner continued his investigation in his spare time. (He was progressing very slowly, as they had landed him with a major case.)

"Sooner or later," he warned, "you will have to open Francesca's desk, and sort her papers."

"Do you mean, read them?" asked Van.

"Read her papers."

I was there at the time of this conversation, and I noticed that Heffner, who had never said Francesca's name out loud while she was alive, now no longer talked about her in any other way.

Van did not answer yes or no. And later, he did nothing, said nothing that Heffner might have understood as a go-ahead.

I asked him if he preferred to put her papers away himself. "I certainly don't," he said. I offered to help Heffner sort through them, and he accepted.

He was leaving the office just as Heffner and I went in.

Francesca's things were filed according to a very clear principle. On the right-hand side of her desk, on the desktop as well as in her drawers, was everything that had to do with the novel and with literature: books, of course, articles, and notes. On the left-hand side there were the documents and papers regarding the administration of the bookstore. Heffner went through them one by one—I don't understand any of that. He showed them to The Good Novel's accountants. Aubert confirmed his impression: the bookkeeping was riddled with glaring irregularities. Francesca had kept a lot of the bills to herself, and paid them herself—the biggest ones, to be honest, loan repayments.

We might have guessed that these loans were considerable, particularly when Francesca decided to sell her chalet in Méribel. But we were stupid. We did not even suspect she had taken out any loans, we were so persuaded that a large fortune means a fortune without limits. We had no idea, for example, what an advertising campaign might cost, of the size of the one she had devised for the bookstore's launch.

In one of the desk drawers, on the left, at the bottom, were Francesca's personal things. The drawer was not locked. We found photographs of Violette, private correspondence, and a little notebook with a blue-gray cover, where a few pages were filled with Francesca's large handwriting.

I was the one who happened upon the notebook, otherwise I would never have heard speak of it, I suppose. They would have kept it from me.

I read it right away, standing up, blind to anything else. It took all of five minutes. There were seven handwritten pages.

No doubt Heffner saw me reading, and he saw that these few pages were affecting me deeply. No sooner had I finished than I closed the notebook and handed it to him. He read it in turn. When he had finished, he handed it back to me. But I didn't want it: "Those are letters, and they're addressed to Van."

"Not exactly letters," said Heffner. "I would swear that Francesca never intended to send them."

"Her drawer wasn't locked."

"Precisely. You keep your notebook close at hand, you know that you will never send it—at the most, perhaps someday the person it is intended for will read it—and that is why you write it. That's all you want."

56

There is nothing in this notebook about The Good Novel at its beginnings, nothing about the initial conversations in January, 2004 in Méribel, nothing about the months of preparation in Paris, or the bookstore opening at the end of August, 2004, nothing about the assaults or attacks against the committee members. The entire notebook is written by someone called "I" and is addressed to someone as "you," and it is clear from the numerous details that this "you" can only be Ivan. Every entry has a date, from July 2, 2004 until the long explanation on January 20, 2006.

A year and a half, seven pages: it is like reading an essential journal.

In the beginning, from July, 2004, to May, 2005, it is like a portrait, with a few light brushstrokes.

July 20, 2004.
You are looking. You are listening. You reply more often than you take the initiative to speak. I know no one who is less centered upon himself than you are.

November 4, 2004.
When you laugh, your eyes light up. Their blue becomes pale and shining.

These are just examples. There are four pages of this portrait.

At the end of 2004, the tone changes. The "I" goes on stage, becomes active. It joins the "you."

December 25, 2004.
The forest at Marly. It has been snowing. Cold, sun. It is hard for me to resist taking you by the arm and walking close to you.

On February 19, 2005, Francesca writes down a dream—I already referred to it.

We are in a room where there are a great many people . . . I can't look straight at you . . . With one foot, you step on my toes . . . You are standing next to me. You are pressing your body against mine and at the same time, you take hold of my wrist behind my back . . . Everyone saw what you did.

With the entry dated April 15, 2005, there is a change of direction. It's no longer about waiting and observation. Something has happened. There has been a confession, and then an immediate retreat, withdrawal. (That, in any case, is how Ivan remembers it; he remembers clearly explaining that his heart was taken. He remembers the conversation almost word for word.)

April 15, 2005.
The moment had come to talk to you.
Everything has been said. You love someone else.
I say: that's perfect. I wasn't asking for anything. I am expecting nothing from you.
I must look like a child who is lying.

Nothing more. But on the next day, the sixteenth, she goes back over that moment. She is not pleased with herself. It's not entirely her fault—Van would not let her speak—but she was ambiguous:

April 16, 2005.

I let my attraction overstep its bounds. And yet I had sworn I would say nothing. Why did I talk to you about it, when I had resolved not to make the least little gesture toward you, and I'm still resolved, and will remain so? What is done is done. But I said too much, and too little.

You must have thought I was stepping aside when I learned that you loved someone else. You were not mistaken. That's not all, however. Some day I will have to tell you why, how and why I am not free. This is not easy for me. It's so hard for me to think about it, to start with. And I must be sincere: I have little desire to dot my i's.

Anyway, I said the most important thing. I am expecting nothing from you. I told you so.

But how did you understand? And did you really understand? I had just suggested the contrary.

But I'm giving myself too much importance. Why should you care about what's deep in my heart? You have shown me your own, and the face that you see there. I'm glad you did. It is what you had to say. It simplifies everything, both for you and for me. How I am tied, or how I am free, matters little: you are not free.

After these lines on April 15 and 16, and right to the end, the notebook entries state the facts. It is a diary of self-effacement.

April 19, 2005.

For you, in any case, there is no more doubt. Things are simple. You have shown me a message from the young woman, that you don't understand. I translated for you. Give me time, she is saying. Keep talking to me.

June 11, 2005.

Little Anis is working at The Good Novel. It's impossible not to like her, that's the problem. It would have been easier for me if she had annoyed me, or been unpleasant with me.

June 15, 2005.
Every day. Every day I see that radiant young woman.

June 18, 2005.
Orta. I used the pretext that I have work to do on the house. Alone, alone. I could sell the bookstore, never set foot in Paris. Without going that far, the easiest would be if I withdraw from The Good Novel. You could run it very well without me. But I don't even have the strength to make that simple decision.

August 20, 2005.
Méribel, for the last time, no doubt. As my beloved old grandfather used to say, quoting a Jesuit friend of his who was dying: one must arrive naked.

The last page of the notebook is dated January 20, 2006. It is the longest of the texts. These words for an introduction: *After our lunch at La Grille.*

This time, it's finished, I've lost you. Talking about Henri, you said, as if it were perfectly obvious: You love him, and I did not correct you.

I would not be so blind as to think everything has been said. I said so little, over my full plate where a tear fell with a little plop. But no doubt for you everything has been heard.

I do not want to lose you. But nor did I want to go on lying, or being insincere. You probably did not understand my reasons: I was so confused, once again. I am going to try, in writing, to be a bit clearer. Maybe some day you will read this page.

My grandfather had been dead for three months, and I had no close family left, when I met Henri. I could hardly stand. He held out his hand. I didn't know where to go, and what he showed me was dazzling.

He wasn't what he is now. He was an extremely intelligent senior executive, enterprising and creative. And then he was stricken with the two viruses of money and power, and he became cynical. But that dazzling love when we first met—that is something I remain faithful to. I no longer force myself: I am not free from it. It is not a principle, still less an effort of will.

In those days I conceived of our love as something written in eternity. I do not conceive of it as anything else today, the love we had then. What came later did not soil that period of our love. Time has had no hold on it, nor has death, since in a way, that love is truly dead.

And while that love may be, for me, a kind of steady beacon, it does not mean that I live with it serenely. I love you and I am tied by a love elsewhere, in the past, something both dead and alive, and wrenching.

That is why, even though I am so happy to see you, I could only let you know this in the vaguest of ways, the one time I opened myself to you, in an unfinished sentence, before telling you firmly that I expected nothing from you. That was so much simpler to say, that I was expecting nothing, and moreover it was true. I had nothing to offer you and I wanted nothing from you, or above all with you.

It so happened that at that time, you were in love with a young woman, and I immediately thought that she was expecting everything from you. The situation was simple, was it not?

But if I am to be sincere, I don't want to hide from you the fact that every day, in your presence, I have experienced what people call somewhat excessively the sufferings of death and passion.

You must have wondered why I disappeared, sometimes, why from time to time I wouldn't answer. Here is why: no matter how much one tries to expect nothing, to want nothing, it is not

*easy to see a young woman playing the role one would have liked
to have in another life, and to see her happy and, what is even
harder, to see her making someone else happy.*

*Everything is fine. There is nothing for me to find fault with,
nothing at all. I hold no grudges, either with you or with her, of
course, or even with myself. But what may happen, simply, is
that the ordeal will get to be too much for me, and I may feel
obliged to take my leave, out of weakness, or in a surge of energy,
so that at last I can catch my breath.*

Van and I spoke about those few pages for hours. I had difficulty believing they had been written by that great lady—I
could still see her poise, her assurance, how boldly she stood
up to each blow, her admirable eyes and her singular beauty.

She was contradictory but simple, explained Ivan. As a woman she was faithful to a first love, yet when she was in love, she
did not know which way to turn when she saw that her rival was
winning. Intrepid and weary, serene and suffering. Both the
indomitable woman who faced up to things, with a smile on her
face, and a broken woman who, in the end, collapsed.

Ivan and I began to use her expression, "to take her leave."
To talk about Francesca's death we would say, She has taken
her leave. The day she took her leave. Since Francesca took her
leave.

57

At The Good Novel, sales continued to decline. And yet things seemed normal at the bookstore. There were fewer curious onlookers, and the regulars remained faithful. Discussion continued on the Web site. *Los Detectives Salvajes*, Bolaño's great novel, published in Spanish in 1998, had at last been translated into French. It caused quite a stir, with its fury, its flights of fancy, its Gaudiesque frenzy over nearly nine hundred pages. One book, at the opposite end of the spectrum, that was unanimously praised was the short *B-17 G* by Bergounioux, which had gone out of print and was now re-issued by Argol press with an afterword by Pierre Michon.

But the figures did not lie, sales continued to decrease. Oscar roused Van out of his apathy. They launched an appeal on the Web. They didn't want to act alarmed, they just wanted to understand why sales were going down, and to do something about it. The appeal was published in the newsletter. It was entitled, *What's Going On?* There was an eloquent chart with a declining curve, like a dune gently collapsing. Both Van and Oscar thought it was pointless to blame, in their appeal, the three parasitical bookstores.

Reactions of solidarity and commitment were numerous. *We hear you, hang in there, all business ventures have their ups and downs.* And still business did not pick up. Those who had shown their support must have been the same ones who came to the bookstore to buy their books.

The decline continued. Only Internet sales remained stable. So, thought Ivan, it's not the long-distance customers who are dropping out.

But online sales had reached a ceiling. They were still much higher than average for France, but markedly insufficient to make up for the drop in brick-and-mortar purchases.

"It's perfectly possible," suggested Oscar, "that some of our supporters are buying fewer books."

Ivan would not throw in the towel.

"Perhaps it's cyclical," he said. "It's great to have a huge number of books, but you have to find time to read them. I can easily imagine that the friends of The Good Novel have bought a lot over these last months, in the enthusiasm of discovery, the joy of commitment, and maybe now it's not so easy to climb through all the piles to get to their bed, and so they're taking a break just to reassure their spouses."

They talked about it as little as possible, but they could not forget the three bookstores that polluted the air and the mood around The Good Novel. Heffner had sworn he would find out who they belonged to, and who had wanted to open them there.

Bills for modest amounts arrived at the bookstore—water, gas, electricity. Ivan went to fetch the ones which, in the past, Francesca had paid without saying anything, that they had found in her desk. He noticed that all the bills had been been sent to her address at rue de Condé. He had a vision of the letter box overflowing with unopened envelopes.

He was doubly mistaken. There was no letterbox at 30, rue de Condé, but an old-fashioned concierge who delivered the mail. And the letters had been opened. Proof of this was given one day at the end of April when Ivan got a call from Francesca's notary. Maître Marin-Gaurond asked to see him. Van made an appointment for the next day, at the notary's offices on the rue Dalayrac.

Marin-Gaurond was an affable man. He asked Ivan to sit down and said, "Monsieur Doultremont has asked to me to inform you of his intention to dissolve The Good Novel, Simplified Joint Stock Company as quickly as possible, and to see with you how to go about closing down the bookstore."

Doultremont saw no reason to try to keep a business going when it was losing money, particularly as it had never even managed to break even.

"I believe I own 1 percent of the capital," said Ivan.

"Indeed—1 percent of a business that is in debt and in deficits. It will be calculated down to the last cent."

Van did not understand whether that meant to his credit or his debit, but at that point he didn't care.

"I am almost certain that Madame Aldo-Valbelli had made provisions to guarantee my situation," he said.

"And indeed she did," said Marin-Gaurond, "as long as you were CEO of the joint stock company. What Madame Doultremont did not allow for was the liquidation of the joint stock company and the closing of the bookstore. Let me explain . . ."

"There is no need, I see," interrupted Van.

Something told him he would have to be quick.

"Would you be so kind as to ask Monsieur Doultremont if he would agree to sell The Good Novel to me? Not the property, obviously, but the business."

"Naturally. It is not something we had envisaged, but it is worth looking into."

Van got his answer two days later. Doultremont agreed to deal with Van. The business was worth €500,000.

"Even with the difficulty that we had breaking even?" asked Van.

"In light of the business's financial situation," confirmed the notary.

Van launched a subscription drive over the Internet. Delvaux had a friend, a lawyer, look into the possibility of a cooperative. Bylaws were drawn up. They were posted on The Good Novel's Web site.

The appeal was widely distributed. It showed up on a majority of cultural Web sites, and on the blogs of writers, actors, and politicians. Support was immediate, a great deal of money was pledged. The mail began to arrive in sackfuls at The Good Novel. More than eight thousand checks came in. After six weeks had gone by, they had raised €102,000, in other words, a good fifth of the €500,000 they needed.

Ivan posted the two figures on the Web site and thanked everybody. The cooperative was formed. Donations would continue. In the meantime, they would borrow.

Armel Le Gall stopped in at the bookstore one day. He had just arrived at the Gare Montparnasse. Ivan and he had lunch together in a crêperie on the rue du Départ. Le Gall couldn't get over it, he had "emptied his fuel tanks" in January. He was in the habit of beginning the year with what was basically a purge. But sooner or later he would be set afloat again. He had started writing again, after three months of writer's block, a new subject. He could breathe. Never mind about the abandoned project. He had just spoken with his publisher. They were going to make a film of his *Sea Horses.* He pulled an envelope from his pocket.

"You can fill in the bearer," he said.

With Le Gall's check they had reached half of the value of The Good Novel. In the meantime, Oscar had gone to great lengths. He had gotten advice from the booksellers' union, made a study of possible locations, and found premises where the rent was reasonable. Given the budget that they could count on, there were three addresses that seemed feasible: one in Besançon, one in Caen, and the third in Paris at the rue d'Hauteville.

"Where is that?" asked Ivan. "I can't see us leaving Paris."

"In the 10th. A very lively neighborhood," said Oscar, "near the *grands boulevards*."

The previous tenant had been a wine merchant.

"He had nothing but *grands crus* there," said Oscar. "Wine is not easy these days. It's a fairly big space. I think we could really make something of the place."

58

And we did make something of the place. It took us less than a month to settle in. It didn't require a lot of renovation work. The day we put up the words THE GOOD NOVEL on the pediment of the little display window, I don't know which was strongest—pride, worry, or disappointment at how small these letters were compared with the ones we'd had on the rue Dupuytren.

We were afraid that Doultremont might open an ordinary bookstore in the superb premises we had left behind at the Odéon. But we've just learned that they are going to open some sort of high-end electronics supermarket, and Doultremont has left France to go live in Brussels.

The Good Novel is off to a new start on the rue d'Hauteville. The clientele is no longer quite the same. It's strange, in the same town, with the same books.

We've kept the same opening times. The evening hours are still just as gratifying: every day there are half a dozen devotees who read, standing there silently, until closing time.

One thing that is holding up well, and can only get better, is online sales. As soon as we have the means, we will do everything to promote it. The future of the bookstore is there, and we have a bit of a head start.

Armel Le Gall makes regular contributions to The Good Novel. Van converts them into co-op shares. "You'll see who I name in my will," grumbles Armel. In the meantime it helps us to keep the bankers quiet.

Oscar has put his redundancy pay to good use. He is finishing his novel. "It's good to have some time," he says. I'm eager to read it. According to what he has said about his work, I can already guess it's something powerful, like Conrad. He hopes he'll make a little bit of money from it.

He'll need it, if he's to see his plan through, to open a bookstore like The Good Novel in Tananarive.

"Madagascar is changing," he says. "People are investing. They're building the first luxury hotel. There's no reason to think the country won't develop. When things start getting better, I'd like to be there, too, and for books to be a part of it.

"And besides, in the century of the Internet, geographical location isn't so very important. I think we should share the world. It's happened before. For me, Africa and Asia ought to be enough start with, I'll leave you the rest."

"He reminds me of someone," says Ivan. "Do you remember? The desert will bloom: that's also my conviction."

A few days ago, Folco came in with a newspaper from Argentina. Apparently a Good Novel clone is going to open in Buenos Aires. Ivan remembered that in the spring of 2005, at the height of all the controversy in the press, requests for information about the bookstore came from several places around the world, Berlin, Milan, a few others, Buenos Aires, in any case, that's for sure. He no longer cares about keeping an eye on everything. "What more can I hope for, that the idea of The Good Novel will spread as much as possible," he says.

We haven't had any news from Ruth for a while. I called Houston. Things are going well, there, for The Good Novel. Word has got around in academic circles, and with the help of the Internet, they don't want to go anywhere else. The foundation is studying the idea of opening another bookstore. Ruth was extremely interested to hear what is going on in Buenos Aires: while The Good Novel goes to bat in Houston for English-language novels, she had been thinking of setting up some sort of

Buena Novela in a Spanish-speaking country. Perhaps her foundation will be able to assist the Argentine Project.

We see a lot of Yassin. He lives only a few streets away from The Good Novel, on the rue Jarry. He wanted to go on doing the cleaning at the bookstore, for free. We refused. Maybe that was a bit unbending of us, maybe we were wrong. At least that's what Yassin says.

Sometimes he buys books from us. And he's doing us a big favor. He reviews what's being translated from Arabic, particularly where Iraq is concerned. It's a small sphere, he said the other day to Van in my presence. A good title for a novel, commented Van, who is convinced that Yassin is writing, too.

Paul is doing okay. His treatment is coming to an end. He came by the bookstore twice. He's going to have to find a roof. A doctor from the clinic has a stepbrother in real estate, and Paul asked him to hunt down the cheapest rent in the West. That, in fact, is how he had ended up in Les Crêts. In those days, he was looking for something in Savoie. This time he's looking at the opposite end of the country, in Ille-et-Vilaine, or the Deux-Sèvres. Van thinks it's a change for the better, that he has agreed to leave Chambéry and what was keeping him there.

The committee is working well. Obviously it has become impossible to add more titles to our stock, unless we deduct the same number. We're short on space. It's hard to cut back. But we have no choice.

Marie Noir gave us an idea. We put together a file with all the titles we don't have and that we dream of ordering for The Good Novel. If one of our customers is particularly enthusiastic about an author, or a part of the world, or a century, he or she can consult a long list of titles, as if it were an annex of the bookstore. Like a traditional card catalogue, with index cards, our paper file is housed in a big wooden box. On top there is a little sign, "Order from us. We'll have your books in a few days." And of course this additional file is on the Web site. For those who buy online, the time difference is not very great, whether they order a book that is already in the shop or one that is in the virtual stock.

Heffner is continuing his investigation, in secret. Without an official mandate, it's more difficult. It takes him twice as much stubbornness, and time, and luck. There is one thing he is absolutely certain about now. It's important. He is convinced that, during Francesca's lifetime, Doultremont did not try anything against The Good Novel.

Perhaps someday we'll call him by his first name. He's a friend, now. But he remains very discreet. We don't know anything about his private life.

As for me, I am glad to have more time for myself again. I've needed it to put together this history of The Good Novel, I mean the first part of the history.

I got Van to talk for entire evenings. He has a very accurate memory, particularly about conversations. And he had kept a lot of documents, articles, notes, all the letters that came into The Good Novel, the venomous ones and all the others. Not to mention the electronic files, hundreds of e-mails, copies of forums: he saved an incredible amount of stuff. The chronology is fairly easy to establish. After all, it hasn't even been three years.

For the rest, I don't need a lot, and Van even less—so it really isn't a lot—but rents are expensive in Paris, and I'm looking for work. We don't both need to be at The Good Novel. There is only one thing I will not do, and that is work in a bookstore.

Last night, Van said, "I've done my accounts, I'm penniless. Makes me feel younger."

I said gaily, "I think so, too."

We were toasting bread, in our little kitchen. I love toast. I spun around, put my arms around Van's neck, placed my cheek against his chest and said, "It seems to me the time has come to ask you something I've been thinking about for a long time. Would you consent to give me your hand?"

"Too late," he said softly.

"What's that supposed to mean, too late?"

"I'm nothing more than a bundle of fatigue, Anis. There was something exceptional about Francesca—she gave *means* to anyone who came near her. She may not have managed to give her daughter the means to live, but she gave other people the means for their ambition. Not everybody wanted to use them, or knew how to use them. As for me, nowadays I get the impression that I was only able to make use of them with her, associated with her: I was driven by her, and her hopefulness, and the strength of conviction which may have been nothing more than the energy of her despair."

Van had not put his arms around me, and it hurt. I drew back, and looked him straight in the eyes, and shook my head. I even think I was smiling.

I could see Francesca's smile. I had learned from her that there is not a great deal of difference between strength and weakness.

And then, now I know how you try to woo someone who no longer believes in himself, how you must be patient, and trusting despite appearances, and it can take a long time.

I've had a new idea. I talked about it with Armand Delvaux, and no one else. He thinks it's a good idea, and he's decided to look into it. There is no doubt that the concept inaugurated by The Good Novel is vital. It has to be used elsewhere, if not by private individuals, then by public authorities. After all, there is the radio station France-Culture, Arte on television, and there are over a thousand art-house cinemas in France. Every one lives better for it, and no one complains that public funds could be put to better use.

Sooner or later, The Good Novel will be looked on as a laboratory. No one will say that the experience was in vain. Francesca and Van wanted to do something good. And they did, that's the least you can say.

Join the ongoing discussion at:
www.thegoodnovel.com

Laurence Cossé worked as a journalist before devoting herself entirely to fiction. She is the author of *Bitter Almonds* and *An Accident in August*, both published by Europa Editions. *A Novel Bookstore* is her ninth novel. She lives in France.